...iously on two wheels, career... ...reet.

...age rapped, "Driver! What is wrong?"

Sheer terror was mirrored in those Oriental orbs.

"Go 'way!" he moaned. "Go 'way, Quon!"

Doc looked over his shoulder and out the back window.

The thing that followed them was whipping and flapping like an angry greenish flag.

It was a clutching *arm*, hideously yellow of finger, and trailing a chattering rag of emerald silk that threatened to slip off the gaunt hand with every whirl and gyration the pursuing phantasm underwent.

The taxi could not have been traveling less than fifty miles an hour—yet the furious green limb followed madly.

Its talon-like fingers with their curving nails bore down less than three yards behind the weaving taxi . . .

The New Adventures of Doc Savage
Ask your bookseller for the books you have missed.

ESCAPE FROM LOKI by Philip Jose Farmer
PYTHON ISLE
WHITE EYES
THE FRIGHTENED FISH
THE JADE OGRE

(*Don't miss another original Doc Savage adventure*, FLIGHT INTO FEAR
coming in February 1993)

THE JADE OGRE

Kenneth Robeson

BANTAM BOOKS

NEW YORK · TORONTO · LONDON · SYDNEY · AUCKLAND

THE JADE OGRE

A Bantam Falcon Book / October 1992

ISBN 0-553-29553-5

Published simultaneously in the United States and Canada

PRINTED IN THE UNITED STATES OF AMERICA

OPM   0 9 8 7 6 5 4 3 2 1

DOC

Doc Savage—born Clark Savage, Jr.—was raised from the cradle for his task in life—his job of flitting about the globe righting wrongs, helping the oppressed, smashing the guilty. He is a physician and surgeon—and a mighty good one, the tops in his line. He has the best and most modern equipment at his command, for he has limitless wealth. His main headquarters are in New York, but he has his Fortress of Solitude at a place unknown to anyone, where he goes at periodic intervals to increase his knowledge and concentrate. He's foiled countless crooks, and changed many of them into honest, useful citizens. The world would be a great place if there were more Doc Savages. But there's only one.

HAM

You'd never think a gentleman named Brigadier General Theodore Marley Brooks would be called Ham—would you? But Monk, Ham's pal, had a reason for giving him the nickname. He thought it would irritate the dapper Brigadier General Brooks—and that alone was regarded as a good reason by Monk. Ham is a knockout dresser and a knockout fighter, too. There's very little of the law that he doesn't know down to about six decimal places. But in a fight, the main law that he thinks about is the law of self-preservation, although most of his battles have been in the interest of folks too weak to fight for themselves. His slender black swordcane is something to avoid.

MONK

When you look at this picture, you can understand very well why the subject is called Monk. Hardly any other nickname would fit him as well. He's a tough hombre. His arms are six inches longer than his legs, and with this gorilla build he seldom stacks up against any opponent who's more than a brief workout for him. No one ever calls him by his real name of Andrew Blodgett Mayfair. And maybe they'd better not! There's a ring to it that Monk might not like! Yet Monk has a keen brain as well as a strong body, and is reputed to be one of the world's greatest chemists. His combination of body and brain makes him a big asset to Doc Savage's intrepid little band of crusaders.

RENNY

If you know him well, you can call him Renny. If you want to
be formal, it's Colonel John Renwick. He's a giant of a man.
A six-footer would have to look up at him. He weighs well
over two hundred, and while he doesn't throw his weight
around, he knows how to use it in a fight.

His fists—and they are very big and bony—are very bad
on faces. They can actually shatter the solid panel of a heavy
door. Renny is an engineer, and tops in his line.

LONG TOM

Major Thomas J. Roberts—Long Tom to his friends—is the
electrical wizard of Doc Savage's little group of adventurers.
In spite of his nickname, he is not so tall. Doesn't weigh so
much, either, and the appearance of his skin gives the impression that he might not be in the best of health.

That skin, however, has been misleading to anybody
who ever picked on Long Tom for a set-up. Try taking a
cougar's cubs away, but don't ever shove around Long Tom.
He's as fast as light, and a terrific socker.

JOHNNY

Few persons would take Johnny—whose real name is William Harper Littlejohn—for a scrapper. He's quite studious. He's an archæologist of worldwide reputation.

Anybody who picked up Johnny, however, would be making quite a big mistake. He can fight like a wounded panther when he's aroused. Like a great many gaunt men, he has an inexhaustible reservoir of strength. He's an important member of Doc Savage's little group.

PAT

Pat Savage is a cousin to the man of bronze. She has Doc's metallic coloring—bronze skin, flake-gold eyes—and is extremely attractive. Pat operates one of New York's most exclusive beauty salons, and constantly yearns for excitement. Though highly capable, her participation in the adventures of Doc and his aids is usually against Doc's wishes, for he believes the work of his group too dangerous for a girl.

Contents

I	THE WAYLAYING	1
II	THE METAL MAN	16
III	DEATH'S GHOSTLY TOUCH	27
IV	THE ARM FROM NOWHERE	34
V	"MANDARIN" MYSTERY	47
VI	THE ELUSIVE MANCHU	57
VII	CRYPTIC MESSAGE	64
VIII	THE SECOND PEANUT MUNCHER	74
IX	TARZANA	84
X	THING WITHOUT ARMS	93
XI	TIGHT LIPS	102
XII	TALE OF THE OGRE	109
XIII	A BOLT OF BRONZE	120
XIV	DISCOVERIES	129
XV	PLOT FANTASTIC	139
XVI	QUON WARNS	150
XVII	THE MISSING	158
XVIII	THE UNEXPECTED DEAD	168
XIX	TERROR'S JAWS	177
XX	THE WEIRD BOX	189
XXI	AIR DRAGON	197
XXII	CHINESE SKIES	209
XXIII	STOWAWAY	219
XXIV	THE AWFUL DARK	228
XXV	THE MYSTIC METROPOLIS	236

XXVI	QUON, THE PHANTOM	243
XXVII	LIKELY STORY	252
XXVIII	GREEN BREATH OF DEATH	260
XXIX	CUPID'S SKELETON	266
XXX	CONTAGION	274
XXXI	THRONE ROOM FIGHT	284
XXXII	ELECTRIC HELL	293
XXXIII	LEGERDEMAIN	300
XXXIV	EXTORTION	306
XXXV	COLLAPSE	314
XXXVI	THE DISEMBODIED	326

I

THE WAYLAYING

San Francisco is a city of fogs.

From the first sultry breeze of Spring to the dwindling days of the Fall season, the cottony stuff pours in through the Golden Gate like ghostly combers, to wash over San Francisco Bay and envelop the peninsula on which the metropolis reposes.

Unlike those of London, another famous fog-bound city, the fogs of San Francisco are not stagnant masses of moisture having the consistency of pea soup. On certain days they do lumber in like a damp, prowling animal to deposit a clammy residue on all they touch. Meteorologists refer to these mists as wet fogs. There is also a species of stratus—another word for fog—known as a dry fog. In contrast to the wet variety, the dry fog is as smooth as tobacco smoke and as sinuous as spider silk. It is not as unpleasant to wander through, though it is every bit as impenetrable to sight.

On this day, the fog that enwrapped the hills of San Francisco was of the dry variety. It had formed close off-shore and prowled inland without opportunity to collect ocean moisture—thus its dry quality.

It lacked but an hour to sunset, so the fog was not unpleasantly dreary. In fact, it was rather bright. A poet—and San Francisco had no shortage of these—might have dubbed it "white murk." It had settled low upon the city so that only San Francisco's many precipitous hills poked up to receive the sun, giving the metropolis a fantastical aspect, like an archipelago in a sea of haze.

A man shoved through this vaporous atmosphere. He was a squat, powerful individual, possessing a belligerent strut somewhat remindful of a bulldog. An expensive gabardine

1

coat strained to contain his rolling shoulders, the collar pulled up to his ears to fend off a late Spring chill. The brim of a tasteful soft hat was yanked down lower than good taste would ordinarily permit.

As he walked, the man clutched a cloth hand bag, which he held close to his body—close so that it was not obvious that the bag was manacled to his wrist with steel handcuffs that had been deliberately soiled so they would not catch the light.

The fog was thick. It was impossible to see more than a half dozen feet beyond one's nose. Yet the man strode along as if the opalescent atmosphere was as transparent as glass. The spectral stuff seemed to swallow the sound of his heavy shoes as they tramped along the worn cobbles.

The din of the city—clangings of streetcars and the ceaseless foghorns and ferry blasts from out on the bay—might have explained the seeming silence of the man's progress.

Often, the man paused, cocking his head to one side, as if listening. He evidently detected no sounds other than the normal clamor of civilization, for each time he proceeded as before.

The man seemed to have a specific destination in mind. He deviated from his path only once. And that was when his nostrils wrinkled up at the spicy tang emanating from a part of the city where neon lights threw vermillion and emerald glare into the low-hanging puddle of fog.

The man stopped, hesitated, and muttered a single word to himself.

"Chinatown."

Under the yanked-down hat brim, his dark eyes narrowed.

Abruptly, he barreled across a busy street, dodging a whining taxi cab, went south three blocks, then east two.

He paused often, listening. And hearing nothing he deemed out of the ordinary, continued on.

At the foot of steep California Street, the bundled-up bulldog of a man paused outside a drug store, before which a streetcar was being turned. Some trick of atmospheric turbulence created a zone of clear air around the bulky car.

Evidently intrigued, the wanderer stood watching as the streetcar—which had just disgorged its allotments of passengers—was turned about on a circular track. Several men did this by pushing and shoving the car by hand—a knot of them pushing the front one way and the back the other—until the flat nose of the car was pointing back up the hill. They had to put their backs into it.

The conductor jangled the bell, adding to the ceaseless din. Passengers—among them a number of those who had assisted the strenuous turnabout maneuver—climbed aboard.

But the loitering bulldog of a man had by that time lost interest in the proceedings. His eyes scanned the surrounding white blanket of vapor which was slowly reclaiming the zone of clarity. He fingered an ear forward.

Then he slipped into the drug store, whose sign proclaimed it to be the Wise Owl Drug Store. The owl seemed to blink its eyes every so many seconds—an illusion accomplished by the simple action of two light bulbs timed to wink on and off at intervals.

At a pay phone, the man made a terse telephone call.

"Hello? Connect me with San Francisco Municipal Airport."

After a pause, he asked, "Is the *Solar Speedster* still due in at nine o'clock? You say it will be a half hour late? Thank you."

He dropped another nickel into the slot and requested the steamship pier.

This time, he spoke in low tones, such as would thwart an eavesdropper, should any be lurking near by. Evidently, the other party had difficulty understanding his speech. He was forced to repeat himself.

"I asked if my luggage had been put aboard," he said, testily. "The *Mandarin*. She sails in the morning."

Upon being assured that all was well, the man in gabardine left the booth with his face—what could be seen of it—screwed up into an unhappy knot, and silently purchased a package of gum at the counter.

He paused under the bright winking eyes of the electric

owl, peeling the tinfoil off a stick of gum with a practiced one-handed maneuver. He shoved it into his mouth and began masticating it thoughtfully, his eyes and ears alert. He sniffed the air surreptitiously.

Satisfied that he was not being shadowed, the man in the gabardine coat resumed his eastward progress.

"Blast this fog," he muttered.

The man had not ventured seven blocks when he passed an alley that was like a fallen cracker box stuffed with smoke. As if scenting an unpleasant odor, his nose wrinkled up as he passed it. Bulldoglike, he bared his teeth in a grimace. The man quickened his pace.

At the next corner, he side-stepped onto the cross street, set his broad back to a brick wall, and spit out his gum. His free hand—it was his right—fumbled the buttons of his gabardine coat open, snaked in, and withdrew a single cigarette, which oddly enough, he crushed and placed in his mouth.

He began chewing furiously.

The hand went back into his garment and came out again filled with a big revolver.

It was a .45, the barrel bulldogged off until it was less than an inch in length. The thing was capable of blowing a young posthole through a man's innards.

The man set himself. His jaws ceased their animated chewing. Oddly, he sniffed the air like a hound, as if not trusting his other senses, which in the muffling fog, might have been wise.

As if stepping from another plane of existence, a figure emerged from the bulwark of fog.

He was a Chinese. The way his slanted orbs narrowed made that clear. Otherwise, he was dressed as any other inhabitant of San Francisco. The days of the pigtail and the colorful brocaded silk jacket were long past.

The Celestial possessed a wizened body surmounted by a face that was as yellow and wrinkled as a dried tangerine. In one shriveled claw, he clutched a red rubber sponge. From the other dangled a loop of scarlet cord, apparently of silk.

"Strangler, eh?" growled the man in gabardine.

At that, the wizened individual jumped as if snake-bit. His narrowed eyes flew wide as he whirled toward the unexpected sound.

And received in his eyes a squirt of saliva mixed with tobacco juice.

The fellow made a squeaking sound, sprang backward. The fog immediately swallowed him up.

In a blind attempt to brain the wizened one, the man in the gabardine coat swung his hand bag into the fog. The bag connected. It brought a high-pitched yelp of pain.

"What's the matter, Chinaman? Can't take it?"

The Celestial lunged from the fog. He had lost his sponge, but the red silken cord now stretched taut between two lemon-colored claws.

"I no stlangle you," he snarled. It was an absurd denial under the circumstances. The Oriental blinked and squinted as the painful tobacco juice seared his slant eyes.

"No?" said the other. "Then you won't be needing *this*!"

The bulldogged revolver barrel swept up, the gun sight hooking that taut silken noose. The latter snarled as it parted, leaving two ragged ends hanging useless from too-tight fists.

Suddenly bereft of his tool of murder, the Celestial closed in, holding one smarting orb open with bony fingers. He kicked out.

The waylayer in gabardine grabbed the foot before it could connect. He used his left hand. The heavy hand bag swung free from his manacled wrist, making a heavy clicking sound like the action of the tumblers of a combination safe.

The kick had been a bit of Oriental trickery. The Chinaman flipped his free hand out and accomplished his purpose—settled one fragment of the noose of red silk about the other's thick neck. The silk had been unusually long.

The man in gabardine turtled his head down inside his burly shoulders. Throat muscles like ropes tightened against the garrote cord. Still holding the Chinese by the ankle, he struggled to point the stubby revolver in a useful direction, but the Celestial cannily slipped around behind him.

The noose tightened further, causing a grunt of pain to well up from the man's throat.

He reacted to this by levering with the hand that clamped the Celestial's ankle. The Oriental squawled in agony, producing a sound such as a grass blade makes when it is blown between the hands.

There was not much flesh over the Celestial's ankle bones and the pop as they broke produced a distinct report.

The Chinaman made more squawling noises. He flung his spindly weight on the garrote cord. It cut through the resistance of the struggling man's neck muscles, plugging his straining windpipe.

Convulsively, the man who was struggling to avoid strangulation lifted his revolver straight up and fired twice. The sound was loud. But it seemed to become lost in the incessant tooting of foghorns and squeal of passing streetcars.

The Oriental was fighting like a crippled rat. His opponent swung a foot and kicked the yellow man's remaining leg from under him, but the jerk as the fellow fell only set the garrote cord deeper into flesh.

The victim's face was reddening. Sweat streamed down his nose. He lost his hat, exposing rough, muscular features and sweat-plastered blondish hair.

Grunting and scraping his feet, the man finally succeeded in dragging his would-be throttler to the grimy face of the corner brick wall. The strangler, intent upon his strenuous work, was pulled along in spite of himself.

When he heard the click of his sawed-off gun muzzle against brick, the man in gabardine gave a mighty grunt and swung his thick body around—sending the Chinaman hopping into the wall.

The Celestial bleated in pain. His grip loosened a moment. A moment was all that was necessary. Inhaling a sobbing gulp of air, the man in gabardine threw himself into the energetic task of slamming his muscular body into the wall repeatedly.

The unfortunate Chinese, caught between the human wall and the one of brick, was pummeled into submission in this fashion. His fingers let go of the red silken strangling cord. Left with only one good leg for support, he sat down hard.

"Who sent you?" grated the man in gabardine, towering over the other.

"I lefuse to say," the beaten Oriental singsonged stubbornly.

"Wan Sop?"

The waylayer's bloodied lips thinned.

"Quon?"

"I know not that name," the waylayer who had been waylaid mumbled evasively. His eyes were squeezed tight, squinting against the sting of tobacco juice.

"Liar," said the man in gabardine, who promptly knocked the Chinese unconscious with the stubby muzzle of his weapon—but only after breaking open the cylinder and removing the bullets with the same practiced one-hand manipulation that told he was used to operating with his left hand manacled to the cloth hand bag.

The Chinese made no sound. He simply went slack where he sat. His ratlike chin came to rest in his coat front and his breathing became noisy.

Pocketing his revolver, the man in gabardine got down on his hands and knees and felt around the pavement for the dropped garrote. He cursed the low-lying fog, which swallowed his groping hands to the wrists as if they had disappeared into another realm of existence.

He soon found both torn ends, along with the red rubber sponge. Ripping the cords in twain, he bound the insensate Celestial's wrists and ankles with expert skill. Lifting the man's head by his coarse black hair, he popped the sponge into the gaping mouth whose teeth were red-black with the staining that comes from a life of chewing betel nuts.

Finally, he tied the sponge in place with the shortest remaining length of silk. He stood up.

"Give my regards to Wan Sop when you wake up, Chinaman," spat the man in gabardine just before he melted into the smoky silk of the afternoon fog, rubbing his chafed, raw throat.

A witness—and there were none—might have noted that the man in gabardine retraced his path, returning the way he had come. His progress was as before—except that he took pains to give Chinatown a wider berth on the return walk.

A little less than twenty minutes later, the same man was inserting a key into an aperture below a frosted-glass door panel on which the following legend was inscribed with tasteful black enamel:

GOLD COAST LAPIDARY
J. Baird, Prop.

The key grated the lock mechanism into submission, and the man shoved in, using one thick shoulder for that purpose. He kicked the door shut with the heel of his shoe, his free hand simultaneously sweeping upward toward a wall light switch. The door banged shut.

In the darkness, he froze, his nose wrinkling with evident distaste, his hand hovering at the light switch.

"Damn," he muttered. Then, more loudly, he said, "I know some one is in here."

"You must have eyes like cat," a singsong voice intoned.

"No, but I recognize the stink of joss house incense when it tickles my nose," the man grunted. "And this room reeks of it."

"Since surprise has been lost to us all, you need not delay turning on light."

The man hit the switch. Light flooded the reception area of a mid-sized office suite, disclosing a gaggle of lemon-skinned individuals.

They wore the raiment of modern civilization, but their placid, almond-eyed countenances bespoke the Orient. There were five of them, and as the man in gabardine took them in with hard, unflinching eyes, his gaze went to one in particular, who stood out from the rest by virtue of the saffron quality of his complexion. The others ran more to brown.

"*Hao jui mei jian,*" hissed the voice that had spoken from the darkness.

"Speak English, dammit!"

"I said, 'Long time no see,'" stated the calm voice. "Jason Baild."

"It's Baird, you damned rice-eating footpad," spat the one addressed as Jason Baird. "And I happen to know you speak English as well as any one."

"I prefer to be addressed by my honorable name," said the Celestial, his dark eyes glittering with menace. He was slender, emaciated, with a gnarled yellow rope for a neck and a head that was like an old skull that had been stuccoed with lemon peel. His teeth were big; the lips were so thin the shape of his teeth showed through. His eyes were remindful of dirty clay marbles in his fleshless skull, and his pate was perfectly hairless.

"There's nothing honorable about it," snarled the man who was evidently Jason Baird, proprietor of Gold Coast Lapidary. "*Wan Sop.*"

"And there is nothing wise in your attempts to thwart the will of Quon," retorted Wan Sop. "In fact, it is very foolish of you to do so. You see, we know that you have enlisted aid in your cause."

"Then you know what you are up against," Baird countered.

Wan Sop shrugged unconcernedly. "We do not fear a mere mortal, no matter how formidable his reputation, for we serve one whose power is beyond challenge, and whose jade breath is as inescapable as fate."

Jason Baird's lips writhed in a humorless grin. "Bunk."

"You will come to fear the searing touch of our illustrious master," asserted skull-headed Wan Sop. He cackled something in an unintelligible lingo.

Wan Sop's satellites started forward.

Jason Baird lifted his right hand toward his open coat front.

"*Hul soung!*" Wan Sop shrilled. "Watch out! He has gun!"

The bulldogged revolver never emerged, however.

A brown-skinned Asiatic made an up-and-under motion like a man pitching a horseshoe. It could be seen that the sleeve of the man's modern business coat was cut wide in the

Oriental fashion. Something flashed from within. The space between his suddenly outflung fingers and Jason Baird whizzed like a typewriter carriage returning.

Something struck Baird in the precise center of his forehead. With an explosive grunt, he fell forward—a dragon-hilted dagger clattering on the bare floor by his crumpling figure. It had emerged from one of the ridiculously wide sleeves—no longer quite so ridiculous now that its true purpose was revealed.

"*Ho ho,*" said Wan Sop, eying the sprawled figure that was Jason Baird. "Very Good. You are a true servant of the Armless One, Sing Fat."

"*Dor ja,*" said the one addressed as Sing Fat, in the manner of a person acknowledging a flowery compliment. "I strive for worthiness before the inscrutable jade visage of He Who Will Breathe Death Upon the Universe."

Wan Sop advanced on the sprawled figure, who gave out a groan when kicked.

"Such a foolish one," he clucked. "Strip him, Oh limbs of the Jade Ogre."

The satellites of Wan Sop fell to their knees and rolled insensate Jason Baird onto his back. They began picking apart his clothing, insinuating spidery fingers into pockets and turning them inside out. Contents were examined. A fat billfold was offered to Wan Sop, who, after a careful examination of its contents, pocketed it.

"Nothing, *Sin Song,*" said a man respectfully. *Sin Song* was evidently some form of address akin to "master."

"Remove his shoes," directed Wan Sop.

At that, Jason Baird began kicking furiously. An Asiatic picked up the dragon-hilted dagger and laid the wavy edge of it against Jason Baird's throat. The burly bulldog of a jeweler subsided.

His shoes were swiftly unlaced and his stockings removed.

Wan Sop leaned down to examine the bare soles of Jason Baird's feet. The jeweler began kicking anew. Yellow and brown hands were laid across his ankles, pinioning them.

"A thousand pardons," said Wan Sop, and then dug two

curved finger nails into the leather hide that was the sole of Jason Baird's left foot.

The nails seemed to penetrate the flesh. Sharp points actually disappeared from view. Strangely, no blood seeped.

With a vicious yank that brought a yelp from Baird's lips, Wan Sop reclaimed his finger nails. A ripping sound accompanied this grisly procedure. Jason Baird threshed and howled, as if in excruciating pain. The Orientals displayed fierce grins, clearly enjoying the torture being inflicted upon the jeweler.

Grinning, Wan Sop held up a curling swatch of what seemed to be raw flesh. He allowed this to twirl in the light, showing it to be merely flesh-colored adhesive tape, to which was affixed a folded square of paper.

The bare sole of Jason Baird evinced no injury.

Delicately, Wan Sop pulled the paper free, discarding the flesh-colored tape into a nearby wastebasket. The paper unfolded under his careful fingers. A small silvery key fell out. Nimble yellow fingers flashed out, cupping it before it fell to the floor.

"Your ways are known to us, Jason Baird," intoned Wan Sop. "This item is meant for others, should an unfortunate fate overtake your worthy personage."

"You go to hell, heathen," spat Jason Baird.

Wan Sop pointedly declined to answer this invitation. His gray almond-shaped eyes were on the paper. They narrowed as they absorbed the words scrawled thereon.

"Perhaps you are more clever than we supposed," enunciated Wan Sop slowly.

"Just catching on to that, are you?" Jason Baird retorted hotly.

Just then, a shadow appeared at the frosted panel of the office door.

Wide-mouthed jacket sleeves shivered as ornate daggers were shook from places of concealment and into waiting hands. Lean bodies tensed expectantly.

"Wait," hissed Wan Sop. "It is Seed."

A hand reached for the doorknob, yanked it open.

In the sudden wash of light, a man was framed. He

was a white man, but his furtive air proclaimed him to be a confederate of the group of Celestials that had gathered in the office suite for the purpose of waylaying its owner, Jason Baird. He was short, spindly, and as dried-up as his namesake.

"Enter—quickly," ordered Wan Sop.

The man addressed as Seed scurried in. The door closed. He glanced down at the prostrate form of Jason Baird.

"I see you glommed him," he muttered.

"No thanks due to your illustrious person," said Wan Sop, his tone tinged with irony.

"I pulled my weight," Seed said defensively. "It was that damned Fung."

Wan Sop frowned like an evil moon. "What of Fung?"

"I found him in an alley all trussed up like a Christmas turkey," explained the one called Seed. "He was supposed to grab this bird Baird at a certain corner. I was to distract him by caging a cigarette, while Fung got him from behind. But neither showed. So I went huntin'. Fung's still in that alley, colder than a mackerel."

Low voice mutter raced around the room. A foot reared back as if to kick helpless Jason Baird in the ribs. The blow never landed. A warning hiss from skull-visaged Wan Sop put a stop to that.

"No. He must be made to talk first."

"Do your worst, heathen," spat Jason Baird. "I've nothing to say to you or your yellow cutthroats."

"I wish very little from you," purred Wan Sop. "Merely the time and place of your rendezvous with the bronze man, Doc Savage."

At the enunciation of the name Doc Savage, a hush fell over the office suite. The satellites of Wan Sop seemed to lose all animation, to become standing Buddhas bereft of all menace and confidence. Their crafty eyes became catlike slits. Here and there, a pale tongue emerged to worry thin, bitter lips.

Only the one called Seed displayed any outward emotion.

"Hell's bells!" he said bitterly. "Is Savage involved in this?"

"Not as yet," said Wan Sop, his soiled eyes going to the face of the man called Seed. He passed the note excavated from the sole of Jason Baird.

Seed read it, paled.

"Does this portent bother you?" inquired Wan Sop.

"Bother me?" Seed snorted. "I'll tell a man! Savage is the original trouble-buster. Birds who cross his path always come to grief."

"And those who challenge the might of the Jade Ogre," asserted Wan Sop, "spend the afterlife being pursued by phantom talons whose touch means terrible agony. This Doc Savage will be no different. You will see."

Seed twisted unwashed fingers nervously. "Maybe," he said. "But if it's all the same to you, when Savage mixes into this little affair of yours, I'll just hie myself to parts south. Like Mexico."

"Fool!" barked Wan Sop. "You cannot quit the Jade Ogre. You have been chosen to serve him, and serve him you shall."

"Well, I don't like it. I don't like it one damn little bit!"

"That is of no moment. We have a task before us." Wan Sop cast his narrow eyes down at the unfortunate face of Jason Baird. "You will not reveal what you know?"

"Never," the other gritted.

"Then you shall be made to do so at a place where resistance to the Jade Ogre is impossible. After that"—Wan Sop shrugged unconcernedly—"your destiny is unavoidable."

From a voluminous sleeve, skull-faced Wan Sop produced a hypodermic whose needle was tipped by a protective bit of cork. He pulled this free, thumbed the plunger until a thin stream of bilious liquid drooled forth, and knelt down to empty the contents into the wrist of Jason Baird at a point near the manacle circlet.

It took all six men to hold the husky jeweler down while this was accomplished. They retained their grips until long moments after the jeweler had ceased to twitch and strain. His breathing became shallow. Then, relaxation seized his muscular limbs.

"It is done," pronounced a sibilant, singsong voice.

"It is the will of He Whose Breath Is Death," said Wan Sop solemnly.

"I still don't like this," muttered Seed uneasily. "Savage is poison."

Ignoring the complaint, skull-faced Wan Sop employed the key which had been cunningly affixed to the sole of Jason Baird's naked foot to click open the handcuffs manacling the black hand bag to the jeweler's wrist.

The Celestial shook the bag experimentally. It was heavy for its small size. The contents shook and rattled like children's play marbles.

"What do you suppose is in it?" wondered Seed, licking his thin lips. "Jewels?"

"I do not know," said Wan Sop slowly. "And there was but one key upon Baird's person."

Seed shrugged. "Tough."

Wan Sop regarded the locked bag for several moments fixedly. His crafty eyes went to the handcuff key. On an impulse, he inserted it into the hand bag lock. It turned. The metal mouth of the bag popped open like toothless jaws.

"He is very clever, this man Baird," murmured Wan Sop, taking the open bag to the nearby desk and scattering the contents on the well-used blotter.

A scintilla of illumination seemed to catch the overhead light and shout back brilliance.

A collective gasp came from the lips of the assembled ruffians—with the sole exception of the contemplative Wan Sop.

"Diamonds!" Seed breathed. "Worth a small fortune, I'll bet."

Wan Sop emitted a tittering laugh. "A mere drop in bucket compared to the wealth that lies before us."

Seed shuddered involuntarily. "This business is no good," he grumbled. "I can't stand thinkin' about it. All them people gonna die."

"Think of your share, Seed," remonstrated Wan Sop. "Fix it in your mind and your conscience will trouble your days no more, and your slumber not at all."

"That don't mean I gotta like it," Seed returned, shuffling uneasily. "It's different for you China boys. I may be bad, but

I'm still white. It's my kinda people who are gonna die when this thing picks up steam."

Wan Sop looked away from the scatter of diamond stones. His eyes were thin slits that might have been made by the action of a knife blade across puffy closed eyelids.

"The imagination is no friend to the industrious," he said pointedly.

"I don't follow that," Seed mumbled, his eyes shifting to the cluster of Celestials, who regarded him in impassive silence.

"I believe in your tongue this item of wisdom could be rendered as 'Idle hands are the devil's friend,'" explained Wan Sop.

"Eh?"

"You will go and obtain a fitting vehicle for the removal of this troublesome one," added Wan Sop without answering. "There is much to be done now that this obstacle to the great plan of the Jade Ogre is about to be removed."

"Have it your way," Seed mumbled, shuffling out the door.

After he had departed, Wan Sop carefully scooped up the diamonds and returned them to the black bag. His satellites watched this operation with sullen inscrutability. It was plain that their chief had no thought of dividing the spoils among his henchmen.

Outside a bank of windows, the foghorns mourned the passing of day. Ferries hooted like frightened owls. And the fog pressed against the window glass in a way that made it seem as if the office buildings were packed in cotton.

When the last cold brilliant had dropped into its receptacle, Wan Sop said, "The tool known as Seed is as a sword whose edge has been dulled and chipped by many battles. Such a one can only bring misfortune. He will have to be eliminated."

"It is the will of the Jade Ogre," several Orientals singsonged.

II

THE METAL MAN

Air travel is fast becoming a commonplace in the modern age.

Where only scant years before, flying was the province of the daring birdman, to-day ordinary folk traverse great distances for business and pleasure. Airlines are doing much to promote the sky lanes as a reasonable and safe alternative to rail or boat travel.

Nonetheless, even in this air-minded time, the general public has not quite become accustomed to the seemingly miraculous fact that for the price of a ticket one can span the continental United States in comfort and safety by transport plane.

The passengers on the Union Airlines New York City-to-San Francisco run—designated Trip No. 28—were unnaturally quiet as the great tri-motored duralumin bird, the *Solar Speedster,* droned through the last leg of a voyage that not many years before would have made a celebrity of the aviator who accomplished it.

The passengers—there were less than twenty of them seated in comfortable wicker seats—fidgeted as travelers will after long, stultifying hours in transit. At the cabin's back end, a few played bridge on a folding table set up in the aisle. The throaty snarl of the big radial engines penetrated the partially soundproofed cabin. Their thunder was not a sound conducive to slumber, so none of the passengers slept in their seats, as they might have had they been—for example—traveling by rail.

Instead of resting, the passengers cast frequent glances toward the front of the plane. The pilot was visible through the open windows of the partition separating the control compartment from the rest of the aircraft. He could be seen jockey-

16

ing the control wheel with expert skill. Yet the curious eyes of the passengers were not directed toward the pilot.

The object of their rapt attention—the cause of their quiet, in fact—occupied the seat directly behind the pilot, on the port side of the aisle, where the seats were strung in a single row.

Even seen from behind, this individual was impressive. He wore a quiet brown suit that seemed molded to his broad shoulders. What could be seen of his skin—the back of his cabled neck and occasional glimpses of his lean, corded cheek when he turned his head—showed it to be of a deep bronze hue. Not quite so dark as the strange individual's hair, however, which lay smooth as a metallic skullcap.

The entire effect was that of a man sculpted from metal. Only when the bronze man moved was this illusion dispelled. As soon as he lapsed once more into repose, it resumed. Uncanny, this phenomenon.

Through the long hours of flight, the passengers had watched, fascinated, this unusual personage. Only the stewardess had conversed with this remarkable man of metal, and then only to have him decline the typical fruit juice and cellophane-wrapped cheese sandwich that passed for airplane fare. It was not that the bronze man radiated a do-not-bother-me aura. Far from it. His handsome, regular face suggested calmness. His countenance held no discernible expression—suggesting neither aloofness nor approachability.

Perhaps it was the size of the bronze man that made the curious hesitate. He dwarfed the seat in which he sat. His smooth bronze hair came near to grazing the parachute basket above his head. He was a veritable giant. Many people find such large men intimidating.

And so the bronze man had been left to reading a magazine.

Near the end of the flight, the assistant pilot emerged from the forward compartment to stroll the aisle, answering questions and conveying to the passengers—some of whom were first-time-uppers—the utter unremarkability of commercial flight. It was good public relations—not to mention something for him to do. During the long voyage, only one man needed to be at the control at any given time, thanks to a modern robot-pilot mechanism.

The copilot paused to nod in the direction of the bronze man seated behind the pilot's compartment. The bronze man returned the nod and resumed reading his magazine. On closer inspection, it seemed to be a scientific journal.

The assistant pilot made his way down the aisle, stopping often to speak with passengers. They represented a typical sampling of traveling humanity. There were prosperous businessmen and talkative drummers in seersucker suits. A buttery-looking Chinese gentleman lounged near the rear. A white-haired man of middle age, whose manner and black valise suggested a member of the medical profession, was gazing intently out a window with an expression of thin-lipped concentration.

"Is it true?" a young woman whose golden curls peeped out from under a chic cloche hat asked in a hushed voice.

"Is what true?" asked the assistant pilot in a friendly manner.

The blonde pointed in the direction of the bronze man, trying not to be obvious about it.

"Is it true that that man is Doc Savage?" she wondered in an awed tone.

The copilot smiled. "Yes, it is, miss."

A gloved hand flew to her mouth. "My goodness. I've read about him, but I never imagined I'd actually see him in person."

The blonde was a cute number and the copilot unmarried. He warmed up to the subject of the bronze man called Doc Savage.

"A great many people would pay good money for the privilege of meeting the Man of Bronze," he related.

"I can see why they call him that," noted the blond girl. "But why is he flying as a passenger? I understand that Doc Savage is an accomplished pilot himself, and owns a fleet of ultramodern airplanes. It's even rumored he recently purchased an airline."

The pilot's grin widened. "That's right, miss. Doc Savage owns *this* airline. Mr. Savage is with us to-day because he thought he should see firsthand the type of service we provide.

I imagine after this trip is over with, he will be inaugurating a change or two." The pilot's voice was tinged with pride.

"Imagine that," the blond girl said. "The owner going to all that trouble to improve service."

"Oh, I suppose Mr. Savage has business in Frisco, as well," the copilot added in a genial tone. "But I don't know what that might be."

"I read in a magazine that he's as rich as old King Midas himself," the girl went on, her eyes transfixed on the nearly immobile bronze man.

The copilot laughed heartily. "I read that too."

"But he takes no pay for the work that he does," said the blond girl. Her pretty eyebrows knit together in perplexity. "How did he ever get to be so wealthy?"

The copilot, seeing the focus of the conversation stuck on the subject of Doc Savage, swallowed his cheerful grin.

"Beats me," he admitted, and reluctantly excused himself to converse with his remaining passengers.

If the pilot was expecting to discourse on the subject of his airline and the wonders of flight, he was very much mistaken.

Many questions were put to him. All concerned the remarkable Doc Savage.

The assistant pilot did a good job of answering these inquiries, even when he found himself fielding the same one several times.

Yes, Doc Savage was a very famous person, he agreed. It was said that he was put into the hands of the world's greatest scientists for the sole purpose of preparing him for the work that he now pursued—the dangerous task of righting wrongs, aiding the oppressed, and punishing evildoers where he found them.

The result, the copilot cheerfully related to a curious drummer, was that Clark Savage Jr.—to call Doc Savage by his given name—had developed into a kind of super being. He was a combination of muscular marvel and mental genius. No field of science had he failed to master. Yet his greatest skill lay in medicine. It was said that Doc Savage was the greatest surgeon in the entire world.

Doc Savage, the copilot told another passenger, was

not alone in his work. Five assistants accompanied him on his perilous adventures. Each was a specialist in his respective line—one aid being a chemist, another a lawyer, and the remaining three a geologist, electrician, and engineer. They were reputed to be the best in their chosen fields, save one— Doc exceeded them all.

Doc Savage, the tiring pilot told a matron with a babe in arms, maintained a headquarters in the tallest skyscraper in the world, back in New York City. It was a famous place reputed to contain the most complete laboratory in existence. Few had visited the place. It was to there that people went to Doc Savage in their hour of need. He seldom turned any away, and then only because their needs were better met by others, to whom the bronze man referred them.

By the time he had reached the rear of the air giant, the assistant pilot was hoarse and exhausted. But he had answered every question put to him. It was his job.

As he flopped into the rearmost row, beside the stewardess, the young man reflected that he had never earned his pay more than just now.

He took out a handkerchief, doffed his uniform cap, mopped his sweating brow, and began to make time with the stewardess.

It proved not to be an easy undertaking. It was not that the stewardess was not receptive to his attempts at sweet talk. It was the crunching sounds coming from the seat directly in front of them that hindered conversation.

There, occupying one of two seats—the other was empty—the Chinese passenger the color of butter was industriously consuming a bag of peanuts.

This was in no wise unusual. Chinese were not infrequent passengers to San Francisco, the chief port of embarkation for the mysterious East. But this one seemed not to join in the camaraderie of long-distance air travel. He had been eating peanuts for the past half hour—the same interval of time the copilot had taken to work his way along the complement of passengers.

The Chinaman had been picking the nuts, one at a time, from one brown paper bag, shelling them with plump fingers, and, after harvesting the fruit inside, disposing of the broken hulls in an identical bag set in the empty seat beside him.

Frowning, the copilot hoped that the first bag was not full. The relentless dry crackling of the shells was getting on his nerves, which were already rubbed raw by his ordeal in the aisle. It reminded him, in miniature, of the sound a small plane makes when it crashes. The assistant pilot had witnessed a good friend of his perish that way, and the awful racket had never completely left him.

With an effort, he forced the sound to the back of his awareness and went to work on the stewardess, who had very pretty blue eyes.

Time passed. The tri-motor thundered westward, chasing the setting sun.

The *Solar Speedster,* of course, lost that race.

Darkness clamped down on the air giant. In the control compartment, the pilot flipped a switch, illuminating cabin lights. A warm glow suffused the cabin.

And here and there, drowsiness finally overtook certain passengers. The fact that the harried copilot had satisfied their curiosity regarding Doc Savage might have had something to do with it. Although the reflex that causes people to nod off when night falls probably did more to explain the phenomenon.

Tragedy befell the *Solar Speedster* as the plane began to descend.

The copilot was regaling the blue-eyed stewardess with pilot yarns and corny jokes, one eye on the control compartment, when he felt the tri-motor lose altitude. This was a signal that the aircraft was nearing its destination. Soon, the copilot would be needed at the controls. If he was going to succeed in sweet-talking the stewardess into dinner, he would have to talk very fast.

The copilot did not see all of it. Or if he did, he did not see the thing that happened clearly.

He was first aware of the passenger he assumed to be a doctor getting up from his seat to visit the wash room, which was situated in the tail of the passenger bus. The man looked prosperous, and affected a black Van Dyke beard, which created the impression in the copilot's mind that he was a member of the medical profession.

The copilot noticed the supposed medico cast a bilious glance in the direction of the plumply placid Chinese passenger, who was still working his way through his bag of peanuts. It could be assumed by the doctor's stern expression that he found the noisy shelling sounds distracting.

The doctor disappeared into the wash room. The copilot glanced up the aisle, through the open windows of the control compartment, in the expectation of being summoned to duty.

The pilot sat tall in his bucket, his uniform-capped head swiveling as he surveyed the lights on the ground unrolling before him. The air grew bumpy.

At that moment, the bronze man known as Doc Savage suddenly flinched, as if a pesky fly had buzzed his cheek.

A tendon-wrapped bronze hand lifted to his corded cheek.

And in the control bucket, the pilot slumped over the controls like a puppet whose strings had been cut by invisible scissors.

The robot pilot had obviously been disengaged in preparation for landing, because immediately the air giant corkscrewed into a violent tail spin. The weight of the inert pilot pushing the control wheel forward caused this.

The dark carpet of lights below reeled. Baggage was flung about the cabin. People, too.

Passengers screamed. A woman fainted. The doctor poked his head out from the wash room, his face at once annoyed and alarmed.

Wide-eyed, the assistant pilot leaped for the aisle.

He could have saved himself the trouble.

For up from his seat exploded Doc Savage.

The bronze man moved like chained lightning unleashed.

The partition door was flung open with a crash. Doc lunged into the control compartment, flinging himself into the copilot bucket. Strong metallic hands seized the controls.

The bronze man had no sooner laid hands on the control wheel than the air giant, motors a-bawl, strained its nose heavenward, righting itself once more.

It was as if the tri-motor were a great winged creature responding to the reassuring touch of its master.

The silvery wings of the tri-motor wobbled and strained at their brace wires as they came level with the black, light-sprinkled terrain below.

The craft was back on an even keel before the frantic copilot had worked his way to the control compartment.

"What happened?" he demanded hoarsely.

"That remains to be seen," came the steady, unperturbed voice of Doc Savage.

It was a remarkable voice. Controlled and powerful, it might have been a human counterpart to the throaty roar of the plane's motors. It had the instant effect of soothing the assistant pilot's frazzled nerves.

The copilot turned his attention to the chief pilot. The man was slumped over his control wheel, which moved in sympathy with its counterpart in the bronze man's hands. The copilot had an inkling of Doc Savage's formidable strength from the ease with which he handled the wheel.

Doc hauled the pilot from the wheel. The man fell back into his bucket. His face was a peculiar aquamarine color, like blue and green inks mixing. He did not look at all natural.

"I think there's a doctor on board," the copilot gulped. Then, his ears reddened. "Oh, I forgot! You're a doctor, aren't you, Mr. Savage?"

"It would be best if I attended to the task of flying," the bronze man told him without emotion. His eyes—they were an unusual flake-gold coloring—were intent upon the funnels of ghostly light that the tri-motor's floodlamps were burrowing in the night.

"Yes, sir," said the copilot, moving back into the cabin with haste.

He found himself trying to push through a knot of passengers. Once the plane had been righted, they had jumped out of their seats to press anxiously toward the control compartment.

"Let me through," the copilot said sharply, no longer the polite airline employee. "I need the doctor to come forward."

A man demanded, "Is everything all right?"

"Are we going to crash?" asked another.

"No." The copilot cupped his hands around his mouth, megaphone fashion. "Will the doctor who is on board come forward, please?"

"Let me through," a deep, professional voice called back. "I am a physician."

It took some doing, but between the stewardess and the copilot, they convinced most of the passengers to resume their seats. A few stragglers insisted upon impeding the doctor's forward progress, however.

"It's all right," the copilot said in exasperation, waving his arms. "Doc Savage is flying the plane."

That seemed to do the trick. The aisle was swiftly cleared, although the passengers craned their necks to see into the control compartment, like gawkers along a parade route.

The medico bustled up to the flustered copilot. "I am Dr. Mawson Harper," he announced in a precise, authoritative tone.

Dr. Mawson Harper had a mature face. His hair was crisp and white, marred—if that was the term—by a streak of virile black that crawled back from his hairline to the point where his natural part disappeared. It made the copilot think of a skunk pelt in reverse. His chin was decorated by a neatly clipped Van Dyke beard that, by some weird quirk, was a dab of black streaked with white. His bushy eyebrows matched the ebony streak in his hair, as if painted by the same unkempt brush.

"The pilot fainted or something," the worried copilot explained.

"Let me see," said Dr. Mawson Harper, pushing forward. He walked with careful, mincing steps, and toted his black leather valise.

They squeezed into the control compartment. It was not exactly commodious. Fortunately, Dr. Harper was a small-boned bird of a man.

"I think you will discover that the pilot is dead," Doc Savage said in a calm voice pitched not to carry back into the cabin.

"I have heard of you, Savage," Dr. Mawson Harper said firmly. "Your reputation is impressive. Still, I would prefer to reach my own conclusions, if you do not mind."

The bronze man nodded. He kept his attention on his flying.

Steadying himself against a bulkhead, diminutive Dr. Mawson Harper took a simple square mirror from his valise, which he had carefully laid open on the floor. He brought this to the pilot's gaping mouth, and registering no cloudiness that would denote respiration, pulled back the man's eyelids one at a time. The pilot's orbs were rolled up into his head so far their color could not be determined.

"Dead," pronounced Dr. Harper. He turned to the copilot, who was suddenly ashen, and said, "Help me carry him back into the cabin."

"The passengers will be upset if they see him like this," the copilot protested.

"This man is doing no good here," Dr. Mawson Harper retorted stiffly. "And the passengers can see that fact quite plainly."

"We bring him back, and they'll know that he—he's—" The copilot stopped. He was having trouble with his words.

"They need not be told the truth," Doc Savage inserted quietly.

Such was the calm reassurance of the bronze man's simple statement that a disagreement was averted.

Dr. Mawson Harper and the white-faced copilot gingerly eased the limp body of the pilot from his control bucket and back into the cabin. They deposited him into the wicker seat previously occupied by Doc Savage, first because it was the most convenient receptacle for the deceased man, and second because it would thwart close examination by the passengers. It was for the latter reason that Doc Savage had originally reserved that seat.

Dr. Mawson Harper took out his stethoscope and other tools of his profession and began what was, under the circumstances, as close an examination of the dead man as was possible.

"I will not need you any longer," Dr. Harper told the distraught copilot in a crisp tone.

"Y-you sure he's—gone?" the copilot gulped.

"I am sorry," Dr. Harper said absently.

The assistant pilot swallowed audibly. He had been a good friend of the late pilot; they had completed many grueling transcontinental hops together.

He glanced back into the cabin, his morose eyes running over the strained faces of the passengers.

"It's all right," he called weakly, summoning his voice. There was a frog in it. A tiny one. He hoped the passengers would not notice. "Everything is—fine."

Because he needed to feel useful, the assistant pilot claimed the late chief pilot's seat.

Doc Savage was talking to the "goat head" at San Francisco Municipal Airport, obtaining a weather report.

"San Francisco is socked in," the bronze man reported. "Fog. No ceiling."

The copilot—technically he was in command now— nodded wordlessly. His eyes took in the mist the great tri-motor was thundering through. The floodlamps made it as luminous as ectoplasm. The wing tips were lost in the stuff, with only the roseate-and-lime radiance of the navigation lights visible. They were like fairy creatures keeping pace with the ship, and not part of it.

The copilot asked tightly, "What—what do you suppose happened?"

Doc Savage said nothing in reply. The copilot started to repeat the question, but he remembered that the strange bronze man was, in his capacity as the new airline owner, his superior. He did not know that this was a peculiar quirk of the bronze man's—pretending not to hear a question he preferred, for reasons of his own, not to answer.

But the copilot noticed that the bronze man's metallic lineaments reflected in the windscreen, and that his odd eyes, like pools of golden flakes constantly stirred by tiny winds, were animated.

A few moments later, Dr. Mawson Harper entered the control compartment. The copilot removed his earphones in order to catch what the medico had to say.

"It was a heart attack," Dr. Harper pronounced gravely.

"You are certain?" asked Doc Savage without emotion.

Dr. Harper nodded. "There is no doubt. His coloration is

the telltale blue of heart failure. It is a tragedy. He appears to have been a young man."

"He turned twenty-eight last month," said the copilot woodenly. He swallowed again. It was plain that he was taking the death of his fellow birdman hard. Only his sense of professional responsibility kept him from tears. Those would come later.

The copilot returned his earphones to his aural organs.

He listened to the long interlocking A and N of the radio beam that indicated the tri-motor had returned to its true course.

"Are you up to landing?" Doc Savage asked.

"I—I think so. Sure."

"Ride the beam," the bronze man instructed. "You should do fine."

"Thanks," said the copilot, strangely buoyed by the bronze man's confident manner.

The bronze man heaved out of his seat. He had been looking into the mirror that enabled the pilot to monitor the well-being of his passengers. The way he moved purposely for the back of the cabin told that something had caught his attention.

No sooner had the bronze man entered the cabin than the stewardess emitted a piercing scream.

III

DEATH'S GHOSTLY TOUCH

Doc Savage was a student of human psychology. He had studied the subject intensely, just as he had mastered many disciplines.

He knew that the stewardess's scream would bring the passengers out of their seats with aisle-blocking results.

He got a break. The stewardess had fainted. The passengers began lifting out of their seats, the better to see. But there was nothing to see. The stewardess had fallen behind a seat, and that kept them seated a moment longer.

The bronze man sprinted the entire length of the cabin while the passengers were still swiveling their startled faces in the direction of the ear-jarring sound.

Doc flashed to the next-to-last row of seats. On the starboard side of the cabin, the butter-hued Chinese gentleman who had earlier been dining on peanuts lay asprawl both seats, as if lost in slumber.

Dr. Mawson Harper, catching up, took in the strange greenish-blue tint of the Celestial's face and exploded, "My word! Not another one!"

The Celestial's almond eyes were open in a glassy stare that told he was dead. His lips were slack, and a thread of spittle crawled from one corner.

Doc Savage moved on to the stewardess, saw that she still breathed, and lifted her into a solitary seat. He reached into his coat and brought forth a phial, which he uncorked and passed under the stewardess's nose. She jerked and recoiled from the repellent odor of smelling salts, blue eyes fluttering open.

She blurted out, "I—I—Did I faint?"

"It is all right," the bronze man told her in a steadying tone. "Breathe deeply, please."

The stewardess pointed across the aisle, jerked out halting words. "I-I think—that—man—is—"

"I know." The bronze man straightened. Turning to bird-boned Dr. Mawson Harper, he gestured toward the medico's black valise, saying, "May I?"

"By all means," returned the doctor, offering his medical bag.

As the passengers watched in growing bewilderment, the bronze man undertook a cursory examination of the blue-faced Chinese. He felt of the man's plump wrist, checking the eyes for life with a darting pen light, and noting the man's temperature by feeling his finger tips.

Dr. Harper did not have to perform his own examination to come to the same conclusion as the bronze man.

"Dead," he said, fingering his neat black Van Dyke.

Doc nodded. His weirdly active flake-gold eyes were taking in the placid-faced Chinese's odd coloration.

"No doubt a heart attack victim," added Dr. Harper, with just a trace of sadness in his tone. "He is just as blue in the face as the poor pilot."

"It would be an unusual event for two persons to succumb to identical ailments at virtually the same time," the bronze man pointed out, slipping a paper sack out from under the dead Celestial's crumpled arm.

"But not entirely unheard of," Dr. Harper said quickly. "When the pilot lost control of the ship, this man was undoubtedly seized by panic. If he had a weak heart, fright could easily have brought on sudden death."

Doc Savage said nothing. He was looking into the paper sack.

"What have you found?" Dr. Harper asked, mustache points quirking like curious cat's whiskers.

"Peanuts," Doc Savage replied, emptying a tiny amount into one metallic palm.

Dr. Harper nodded. "Yes, I recall now. This man had been eating peanuts, and making a commotion doing so, I might add. It brought me out of a sound sleep twice."

Noticing that the peanuts in the bag were whole, the bronze man began hunting among the seat cushions, carefully moving the body about. Although the Chinese gentleman was no flyweight, Doc repositioned him with evident ease.

Soon, he dislodged another paper sack—this one containing the broken shells that had been carefully deposited there.

Doc Savage held this up to the light so that Dr. Mawson Harper could peer inside.

"I hope," Dr. Harper said solemnly, "that when it is my time to go, my last meal is more sumptuous."

Doc Savage plunged a metallic hand into the bag and brought it out full of cracked and broken peanut hulls. He did this several times, letting the shells sift through his impressive fingers. No outward expression registered on his sculpted features.

"Sometimes a man will swallow something wrong," Dr. Harper said thoughtfully, "and begin to choke. The resulting panic could induce a heart stoppage—although I cannot recall reading of such a case induced by a mere peanut."

Doc let the last of the peanut hulls rattle back into the bag and gathered up both bags. He started forward. The bronze giant had to duck slightly to negotiate the aisle—and the tri-motor was designed for the comfort and convenience of its passengers. Gazes followed his big body as he moved with a catlike and soundless grace. The occasional passenger dawdling in the aisle melted back into his seat like snow pushed aside by a plow.

Carrying his black leather valise, Dr. Mawson Harper trailed him, impressed in spite of himself by the bronze man's great size. "There is nothing to be alarmed about," he assured the passengers in a loud voice. "A passenger suffered a heart attack, that is all."

The fact that Doc Savage did not contradict this un-equivocal assertion did more to quiet the nervous passengers than the assertion itself.

"I trust this unfortunate occurrence will not impede our timely arrival," Dr. Harper said as he followed the bronze man. He was looking worriedly at an old-fashioned pocket watch of the turnip variety. "I must catch the liner *Mandarin* before it sails in the morning, for I have important business in Hongkong."

"We should be no more than an hour delayed in arriving," the bronze man told him.

"I would be interested in your opinion of the pilot's—er—state, Savage. It is unusual that a man of his youth would succumb to heart failure. These airline pilots must pass a rigorous medical examination before they are certified to fly."

Doc Savage did not reply to that. Instead, he said, "We should be landing shortly. I will be needed at the controls."

Dr. Mawson Harper took the hint. He resumed his seat, whereupon he was immediately beset by curious passengers.

His intensely black eyebrows jumped and squirmed in annoyance as he dealt with the plaintive questions of his fel-low passengers.

The stewardess—recovered now—also worked the passengers, putting out a delectable lower lip as she mustered a brave front.

This busy attentiveness kept their minds off the dead man in the rear of the *Solar Speedster* and the equally dead pilot seated forward—although the passengers had not yet grasped the pilot's true condition.

Doc Savage eased his towering frame into the pilot's seat.

"I radioed ahead for an ambulance," the copilot said thickly. "Guess I should have asked for two, huh?"

"An ambulance is a mere formality now," the bronze man told him, setting the paper sacks on the floorboard. His flake-gold eyes caught a glint of something on the grooved flooring. He plucked it up between forefinger and thumb.

The copilot stole a glance. He thought he discerned a tiny shard of glass in the bronze man's cupped palm. He could not imagine where it might have come from. It disappeared into the bronze man's coat.

Doc Savage seized the control, which was wobbling slightly.

"I can spell you, if you would like," he said gently.

The copilot let out a gusty sigh of relief. "Thanks," he said gratefully. "I don't mind telling you that I'm shaking like a leaf."

"Any man would, under the circumstances," Doc told him.

The copilot folded his arms tightly. Only then did they stop trembling quite so much.

The *Solar Speedster* was volleying toward its destination on the California coast. Tendrils of fog swirled about her metal wings as she sliced earthward. Her radial motors thundered in unison, creating platters of shimmering metal that ingested big gulps of fog and threw them back as ragged streamers.

Soon, the tri-motor was in the thick of the vaporous atmosphere. Visibility was zero. Not even the wing lights could be made out, now.

"You're a better aviator than I am if you can set her

down in this pea soup," the copilot said nervously. "I can't see the ground at all."

"We should be coming up on the beacon at any minute," Doc told him without a trace of concern in his voice.

No sooner had the last syllable been enunciated than a whirling beam of light showed like a ghostly finger through the wall of fog.

"There it is!" the copilot ejaculated, relief shaking his voice.

The beacon had been set on a shore promontory by a large oil concern as an aid to air and sea navigation, but also by way of advertising. It was powerful. Over a million candlepower.

The copilot offered, "The airport is due north."

"I know," the bronze man said, booting the tri-motor around in a way that showed he was familiar with the San Francisco approach.

It was the smoothest landing the copilot had ever been privileged to witness. In his retirement years, he would later describe it to his children and grandchildren, exaggerating only slightly.

Using only the radio navigation beacon and the lighthouselike beacon to guide him, Doc Savage slanted the big thundering tri-motor down onto the tarmac.

Neither the copilot nor the passengers had any inkling when the air wheels had touched ground. The fog was too thick to permit that. But somehow they kissed the tarmac so gently that only a slight jarring of the tail wheel told of contact with the ground.

The bronze man cut the engines and threw the ship around. The radials coughed and sputtered, propellers clicking to a halt, one by one.

The copilot turned his face to the bronze man and mumbled a single heartfelt word, "Thanks."

Doc Savage nodded. He flung himself from the seat and went to the deceased pilot. The man had fallen forward, out of sight of the passengers. The bronze man noted that the pilot's hands and visible features were still a mixture of green and blue. Oddly, they seemed less blue now. But corpses, Doc knew, often underwent changes in hue, the result of chemical changes in blood gases, among other things.

Beyond the deceased man, out the porthole, the bronze man noticed a short stair being rushed into place, permitting egress from the air giant.

It also permitted ingress for the throng who awaited the *Solar Speedster*'s arrival, Doc Savage saw to his deep chagrin.

The throng proved to be composed largely of newspaper photographers. Here and there, a newsreel cameraman lugged his bulky equipment. There were a few uniformed police, who made half-hearted efforts to fend off the crowd, but gave it up in the face of overwhelming numbers and allowed themselves to be jostled toward the tri-motor.

Obviously, the copilot's request for an ambulance had included the knowledge that the famous Doc Savage was aboard.

Doc rushed down—down because at rest the tri-motor slanted at a steep angle—to the exit door and flung it open.

When the magnesium flashbulbs began popping in his bronze countenance, Doc Savage hastily shut the door. He was no lover of publicity. It was a hindrance to his work, not to mention a profound nuisance, at times.

The bronze man threw himself behind the controls once again, engaged the ignition, and the starters ground to life. The radials, still warm, responded like race horses, snorting exhaust and frightened crimson sparks.

Doc sent the tri-motor rolling and bouncing into the lee of a massive hangar, the shouting throng in hot pursuit.

Engaging the brakes, Doc advised the copilot, "I would prefer not to become entangled in any publicity."

The copilot grinned. "You got it, Mr. Savage."

"If the authorities would like to question me, inform them that I have gone to meet a Jason Baird, who owns a jeweler's concern on Montgomery Street."

"I'll tell them," the copilot promised.

Doc floated to the door, knocked it open, and dropped to the tarmac, his muscular thews cushioning the impact of the short drop.

There was a door on this side of the hangar. He passed through it.

A few moments later, the bronze man reemerged, wearing a grease-stained mechanic's coverall, the bill of a cap pulled low over his bronzed features.

He slouched as he walked, and so melted into the dense fog of the San Francisco Municipal Airport.

The pelting throng swiftly surrounded the idling trimotor, shouting demands for Doc Savage to emerge. A few attempted to wrench open the passenger door, but to no avail. They lost a good fifteen minutes waiting for the door to be unlocked, and as they finally piled in through the opening, the grinning copilot apprised them of the bronze man's clever departure.

Their disappointment vanished when they were shown the two blue corpses. Flashbulbs popped. Newshawks demanded answers. A woman indicated Dr. Mawson Harper, who was attempting to squeeze through the knot of reporters to the exit door.

"That man is a doctor."

The press descended upon a sputtering, red-faced Dr. Harper, who showed little patience as he parried the seemingly unending questions put to him.

IV

THE ARM FROM NOWHERE

The first immigrants from China arrived in San Francisco aboard a brig. There were only three—two men and a woman. That was back in the halcyon days of the Gold Rush, during which the seaside city began to acquire its wild, boomtown reputation.

Evidently, that initial trio of Oriental pioneers fell into the habit of writing letters home, for in the decade following, proud clipper ships brought in excess of twenty-five thousand peasants and coolies to do the menial work of Gold Rush days, and to build the railroads that fed the boom.

The promise of fortune brought many of these. Famine impelled others to make the daunting Pacific crossing.

Less than a hundred years after the first Chinese disembarked from their ship, their numbers had risen and fallen several times, owing to various exclusionary laws enacted against their immigration, ruinous tong wars, and other social difficulties.

Currently, the Chinese community of San Francisco numbers perhaps sixteen thousand Sons and Daughters of Heaven.

So it was no surprise that among the taxi cabs lined up in the fog near the San Francisco Municipal Airport operations building, there should be one rattletrap flivver piloted by a young Chinese individual.

This worthy was reading a newspaper printed in Chinese which he had propped up on the steering wheel when a voice instructed him from the rear seat, saying, "Montgomery Street, please."

The Chinese cabby started. He craned his long neck around fearfully.

The man seated in the rear was big, imposing. His face was in shadow, but the cabby caught a glimpse of compelling golden eyes set in a face that made him think of a brazen idol.

"Montgomely Stleet. Velly good," he said, throwing the cab into gear. With a grinding of gears, the hack whirled into the fog.

The Chinese cabby blinked the surprise out of his face as he chased his own headlights into the jagged terraces of the city. He had not heard his rear door open, or close. The bronze apparition had entered the hack like a ghost.

So shaken was he by this, that the cabby eschewed all conversation during the ride. The fare did not seem to mind. He offered no comment himself.

Passing streetlights illuminated the silent fare's face at intervals and reinforced the impression given of a brazen idol—but with an Occidental face.

When the driver finally turned his cab onto Montgomery Street, in the business sector known as the Wall Street of the West, he inquired, "Which addless, please?"

The fare stated a street number.

After the cabby had pulled up before a modernistic edifice—all of San Francisco's buildings were relatively new, inasmuch as the city had to be completely rebuilt in the aftermath of the great earthquake of three decades gone by—he turned around to ask, "You want me wait fo' you? Take you elsewhele?"

"If you do not mind," stated the bronze-skinned fare.

"Slow night. Not mind at all."

Doc Savage stepped out into the fog. He passed into the marble lobby, and after consulting a directory of occupants, rode the elevator to the fourteenth floor, seemingly oblivious to the stares of the uniformed elevator boy.

At the darkened glass panel that bore the name "Jason Baird," he paused to knock twice.

No sound came from beyond the frosted glass.

Doc Savage reached into his coat, to a special vest he wore that was lined with numerous pockets. These contained articles and equipment, most of the bronze man's own invention, which came in handy during the course of his exploits. It was from this that Doc had produced the smelling salts that had revived the fainting stewardess aboard the *Solar Speedster*.

This time, Doc brought forth a simple steel probe. He inserted this into the lock. The mechanism surrendered with barely a protest.

Doc entered.

At once, the faint tang of incense smote his sensitive nostrils. Briefly, a strange sound saturated the dark office suite. It was a low, mellow trilling. Possessing a throaty, exotic quality, it ran up and down the musical scale, but without adhering to a definite tune. It might have been the product of a wayward wind coursing through the rigging of a ship, or between the spires of the San Francisco skyline.

But the eerie, melodious strain was neither of these. It was a sound Doc Savage made in moments of mental excitement, when he was surprised or puzzled, or otherwise in the throes of some strong emotion. Often, he was unconscious of its origin.

This time, the trilling sound denoted puzzlement. It trailed off.

His acute hearing telling him that the suite was unoccupied, Doc snapped on the light switch.

The room sprang into view. It was an outer foyer to an office suite. The appointments were modern, businesslike but tasteful.

Doc's golden eyes roved the reception area, seeking any unusual signs.

He first spotted a discarded pair of handcuffs. They lay on the floor. He stooped, picked them up. Both circlets were unlocked.

Reaching into his equipment vest, the bronze man brought out a pencil-thin flashlight. It operated by a spring-wound generator instead of batteries. Doc gave the crank a wind and thumbed on a beam of light that looked strong enough to penetrate the fog pressing against the bank of windows on one side of the suite.

Doc raced this along the floor. The silver-dollar-sized circle of brilliance came to rest on a damp spot on the bare floor. The bronze man went to this. He knelt again, touching the liquid, then bringing a moistened finger up to his nostrils.

Since the time the bronze man's father had placed him in the hands of the scientists and other experts for training, Doc had practiced a rigorous series of exercises for two hours each day. A portion of these exercises were put aside for the development of his senses.

The sharpening of Doc Savage's olfactory senses were accomplished in a number of ways, but chief among them was the employment of a variety of phials, each containing different scents. Upon blindfolding himself, Doc would pass these bottles—the contents of which were changed often—under his nose and he would attempt to identify each by scent alone.

Years of this routine had refined the bronze man's ability to recognize an amazing variety of odors at a sniff.

Doc's sensitive olfactory organs told him that the scent

was a powerful narcotic, commonly administered by syringe.

Prowling the room, Doc went next to the reception desk. The drawer contents were unremarkable. But on the floor, hidden behind a stout leg where it had evidently rolled, was a sizable gemstone.

Doc's knowledge of geology enabled him to identify it as a diamond. He weighed it in one practiced hand, judging it to be thirty carats by jeweler's measurement.

The diamond was worth more than a thousand dollars.

Doc Savage's keen deductive abilities swiftly gave him a fairly accurate picture of what had befallen Jason Baird, the man he was to have met only an hour before.

Doc knew that it was the habit of jewelers carrying valuable gems to handcuff the carrying bags to their wrists. This was a sometimes risky practice. Determined jewel thieves have been known to saw off the hands of their victims, after first knocking them unconscious, naturally.

Obviously, Jason Baird had been victimized in his own office—the handcuffs removed, and the jeweler himself doped. The absence of blood or a scuffle indicated no serious injury had been inflicted during the theft.

Doc deduced that the fallen diamond had dropped from the jeweler's carrying bag when the thieves—the telltale odor of joss incense indicated that they were Chinese or some other species of Oriental—had spread their ill-gotten swag on the desk for examination.

Doc went next to the door leading to the inner office.

The door proved to be unlocked. It came open easily. The area beyond was intensely dark.

On the verge of stepping across the threshold, Doc Savage froze. His weird trilling came anew, was quickly throttled.

Unexpectedly, an arm lunged out of the darkness!

It was predominantly green. The fingers were outstretched claws with long, curved nails. They glowed yellow and pale.

Doc, recognizing only the unexpectedness of the apparition, faded to one side, letting the arm shoot silently past.

It seemed to waver and hesitate, as if intent on following the bronze man. But Doc had moved far to one side. The glowing yellow arm continued on, trailing a ragged tail of green silk like a fluttering comet.

For the arm was attached to no visible body!

With an utter soundlessness that smacked of the supernatural, the phantom arm arrowed for the frosted glass door bearing the name of Jason Baird.

Its grasping claws had barely touched the glass when there came a yellowish flare of light.

In that moment, Doc shielded his golden eyes with a great bronze beam of an arm.

It was perhaps fortunate that he did so.

The flash was followed by a powerful blast of heated air. Glass jangled. An acrid tang blew through the room.

When Doc lowered his arm, all that remained of the frosted glass door were geometric shards scattered on either side of it. The wood casement was splintered and scorched.

Pausing only to ascertain that no other menace lurked within the inner room, Doc went to the corridor door. His flashlight roamed the floor. He stepped out into the corridor, but all he discovered were the bits of glass litter.

Of the ghostly yellow arm and the silken sleeve which covered it, there was no sign. It was as if it had never existed.

Doc's trilling briefly filled the room. It trailed off on an incredulous note.

Reversing his course, the bronze giant ventured into the inner office. According to papers he discovered on the desk, this was the private sanctum of Jason Baird.

It had been searched, but not in an obvious manner. Papers out of order and careless positioning of a jeweler's loupe so that it teetered on the verge of falling off the desk, told Doc that much. No self-respecting jeweler would allow such an important tool of his trade to be treated so cavalierly.

While Doc Savage was considering the scene, the desk telephone jangled.

Doc scooped it up. Instead of answering, he paused.

"Hello? Hello?" a gruff, impatient voice said. "This is the chief of police of San Francisco speaking. I want to speak with Jason Baird or Doc Savage."

"This is Doc Savage speaking," the bronze man said instantly.

"Mr. Savage," said the chief of police in a distinctly more respectful tone. "The airport gave me this number. I understand you were aboard the *Solar Speedster* when the pilot and another man died mysteriously."

"I was," Doc admitted.

"A passenger named Dr. Mawson Harper has certified that both individuals were victims of heart attacks. Have you anything to add to that?"

"Dr. Harper is known for his charity work in China and the Orient," Doc told the official. "If he has stated heart failure as the cause of death in both instances, professional courtesy requires that I not contradict his judgment without clear evidence to the contrary."

"Well, it's damn strange," muttered the police official. "I myself have never heard of such a thing happening. The bodies have been taken to the morgue. But I would have preferred to have heard your version of events."

"I had urgent business with the jeweler, Jason Baird," Doc explained.

The official cleared his throat uncomfortably. "I understand. As far as I am concerned, the honorary commission you hold with the New York Police means that you have the same courtesy extended to you during your stay in San Francisco."

"Then perhaps you might assist me," Doc suggested.

"Just say the word."

"I am at Jason Baird's office at this moment," Doc related. "He was not here to meet me, as we had arranged. Since our business was urgent, there is reason to suspect that foul play may have befallen him."

"Want us to put out a dragnet for him?"

"That would be a start," Doc said. "I will go next to Baird's home. Perhaps something is to be learned there. You may contact me at the Hotel Raleigh."

"The Raleigh. Got it." The police commissioner terminated the conversation.

Outside the building, Doc Savage entered the rattletrap taxi, rapped out the address of Jason Baird, which was in the fashionable Nob Hill section of town, overlooking Golden Gate.

The fog was still a thing of dry, silky, clutching tendrils and frequent billows that ghosted up side streets and across the main throughfares like rolling monsters from some ectoplasmic netherworld.

The Chinese cabby drove through these billows as if they were not there. This might be attributed more to recklessness than skill. More than once, he narrowly avoided running over stray pedestrians abroad in the night.

He also had the distressing habit of driving to the top of the steep hills and, after releasing the gas and brake pedals both, letting the cab career under its own power to the foot of each slope.

This was evidently the driver's way of economizing on gasoline.

The looseness of the steering mechanism made this a risky practice.

This unsafe behavior prompted Doc Savage to ask, "Driver, what is your name?"

"Sneeze," replied the driver.

"Is that your Chinese name?"

"No. 'Melican name."

"Then what is your Chinese name?"

"Ah Choo," said the driver, giving his knee a slap and rocking from side to side. He tittered like a girl. Evidently, he thought himself quite the humorist.

When his bronze-skinned passenger did not join in the mirth, the cabby said, "So solly. True name Ho."

"Please drive with more care, Ho," Doc instructed.

The humorous cab driver subsided.

Mist-shrouded row houses built in the gothic style with swelling bay windows flashed by. Where the city reared up on one of its many hills, these snaked in upward sympathy with the rolling street.

Eventually, the cab coasted to a rest before a well-appointed home at the foot of Nob Hill.

"Wait here," Doc Savage directed, stepping from the tonneau. The Spanish-style edifice had been built on a slope, and was shaded by shivering eucalyptus trees. Steep steps were necessary to reach the front door. Doc went up these with catlike grace.

No one answered the bell, so the bronze man slipped around the back where he was less likely to be seen.

The back door, too, was locked. With, of all things, an unpickable combination padlock. From his vest the bronze man removed a metal tube. He unscrewed the cap and, taking care not to spill a drop, emptied the liquid contents of the tube onto the juncture where the eye-and-hasp were secured by the padlock loop.

A hissing puff of smoke crawled out of the collapsing tangle of metal. The padlock simply dropped free.

When the acrid vapor had thinned, the bronze man put his shoulder to the ornate panel. It gave easily, the hasp dripping semiliquid metal.

The tube had contained a corrosive acid perfectly suited to gutting stubborn locks.

Racing his generator flashlight before him, Doc Savage reconnoitered the house.

It proved to be unoccupied. It had also been searched. The searchers had been less careless about their work than they'd been in Jason Baird's office. Perhaps because the house was so big and their time to conduct the ransacking—for that was what it amounted to—had been so short.

The bronze man found little of interest. On a mantel, two framed portraits were set. One showed a rather blondish man with the fierce face of a bulldog. The other was a girl, very blond and quite attractive in a prim, studious way.

Doc returned to the taxi, feeling that he had accomplished nothing.

"Hotel Raleigh," he told the driver.

After the cab had entered traffic, the Chinese hackman, Ho, perhaps sensing his passenger's unhappy mood, attempted another bit of levity.

"Did you hear about the Celestial who like Lindy so much he name his number one son after same?"

When the bronze man did not reply, Ho went ahead anyway.

"He call him One Long Hop!" The nervous tittering resumed. The cabby threw himself into it, with the result that his rattletrap machine began to swerve dangerously.

Before Doc Savage could admonish the driver, the latter emitted a lamblike bleat of terror and threw the wheel sharply to the left. The cab, wobbling precariously on two wheels, careened down a side street.

Doc rapped, "Driver! What is wrong?"

Whether the Celestial cabby actually heard the question or not remained unknown. He threw the wheel about once more, clipping a shuttered news kiosk and losing a front fender in the encounter. It banged away.

His slanted eyes went to the rear-vision mirror. Sheer terror was mirrored in those Oriental orbs.

"Go 'way!" Ho moaned.

Doc looked over his shoulder and out the back window.

The thing that was following them was whipping and flapping like an angry greenish flag.

It was a clutching arm, hideously yellow of finger, and trailing a chattering rag of emerald silk that threatened to slip off the gaunt wrist with every whirl and gyration the pursuing phantasm arm underwent.

The taxi could not have been traveling less than fifty miles an hour. Yet the furious green limb followed madly. Its talonlike fingers with their curving nails bore down, less than three yards behind the weaving taxi.

It was visible through the milky fog, thanks to the way the skin of the clutching hand glowed.

"Go 'way!" Ho shrieked. "Go 'way, Quon!"

Impelled by a hard turn of the wheel, the taxi jounced over a corner curb and scooted down a dark side street.

"Driver!" Doc urged. "Whatever you do, do not stop."

"Alla same to you," the cabby screeched, "I no stop ever!" He sounded beside himself with fear.

Doc watched the phenomenon of the pursuing disembodied arm with boiling flake-gold eyes.

The nature of the phenomenon defied easy explanation. Somehow, the pursuing talon of a hand was determined to overhaul the fleeing taxi. When the wildly careening machine turned left, the arm followed, with only the most fleeting hesitation.

Once, as the taxi driver trod the brake pedal to negotiate a sharp corner, the arm zoomed perilously close to the rear window, but the hack pulled away just in time.

Seeing that the mad, chattering comet of bone and fabric could not be shaken, the bronze man reached into his equipment vest.

"Hold the wheel steady," Doc rapped.

"Steady as she blows!" the driver shrieked, mixing his aphorisms.

Doc had out a padded metal phial in which tiny spheres somewhat resembling silver cherries reposed. These were miniature grenades of the bronze man's own devising.

He fingered one from the phial, and threw open a door. He got out on the running board, keeping one arm hooked around the window post for safety's sake.

The arm was a wild, grasping thing. It gyrated as if possessing invisible wings, beating insanely. Fog streamers ripped back from its bony fingers. The manner in which it knifed through the dry haze was uncanny.

Doc flicked a tiny lever on the grenade and pitched it.

The toss was good. It almost struck its target. Or perhaps it went through it. In the fog, it was impossible to tell.

The grenade let go with a *whoom,* and a fire plug geysered water upward.

Doc reached into the seat and obtained another grenade. This time, he tried an underhand toss.

The result was spectacular.

A blast of hot air, eye-hurting yellow light, and bitter smoke blew a hole in the fog.

It was eerie. One moment the fog was thick enough to stuff pillows with. The next, it sprouted a yellow ball of light. It faded, leaving a void that was nearly a sphere.

The cab turned a corner as Doc watched the fog hesi-

tate, regather, and slowly fill the vacuum where the disembodied hand had formerly existed.

It was as if even the fog was fearful of touching the spot
where the unearthly thing had been.

Doc climbed back into the tonneau, clapping the door
shut.

"It is all right, driver," the bronze man said. "The thing
is gone."

"I make tlacks good?" Ho asked anxiously.

"Yes."

"Huh. You likee my tlacks, I makee more."

The hackman bore down on the gas, and the cab surged
ahead, showing astonishingly more life under the hood than
had been demonstrated so far.

The agitation with which the cabby drove told the
bronze man that any attempt to persuade him to backtrack to
the spot where the pursuing arm had been obliterated would
be to no avail.

Pocketing his grenades, Doc Savage settled into the
cushions, strange lights playing in the depths of his whirling
flake-gold eyes.

"Driver," Doc said. "You mentioned a name back
there."

The driver blinked. "Name? What name that?"

"Quon."

"Oh, Quon," breathed Ho. "Honolable ancestor, is
Quon. I play to him. He obviously hear plea. We safe. Quon
vely good."

Doc Savage seemed to accept that explanation. He settled back into the rear cushions as the twisting byways of the
fog-bound metropolis flicked past.

When the taxi pulled up before the Hotel Raleigh, the
Celestial turned around in his seat and extended a sheet of
paper with a serious face.

Doc accepted the sheet. To his surprise, it was a laun-
dry ticket.

"Bill for taxi lide," Ho told him. "One come. Two
goes. At fifty cents a went—four dollar, including tip." The
Celestial beamed, his odd sense of humor restored.

The bronze man paid the man—including the exorbitant tip—and entered the lobby.

Once Doc had registered, the desk clerk informed him that there was a message.

The message was a request to call the chief of police of San Francisco.

Doc used a lobby telephone.

The chief got directly to the point.

"We have been unable to locate Jason Baird," he said.

"Keep trying," the bronze man said.

"There is one thing," the chief added hastily. "According to the steamship pier, Jason Baird has reserved a cabin on the liner *Mandarin,* which leaves at ten o'clock to-morrow morning. Shall I station men at the docks to hold him?"

"That will not be necessary," Doc told him. "I intend to be aboard the *Mandarin* when she leaves port."

Doc terminated the conversation and went to claim his room.

There, he put in a call to the San Francisco morgue.

Upon identifying himself, he asked, "Have you conducted autopsies on the two blue bodies?"

"You mean the green bodies," the medical examiner corrected.

"You say they are green?" Doc said.

"These two stiffs," the medical examiner vowed, "are as green as limes. Whoever pronounced them heart attack victims on account of their color must have the queerest kind of color blindness I ever heard about."

"Have you started the autopsy procedure as yet?" the bronze man asked.

"No."

"Any objection to my observing it?"

"None whatsoever."

"Expect me directly," Doc Savage imparted.

V

"MANDARIN" MYSTERY

Day begins early along the Embarcadero—the two-hundred-foot stretch of concrete wharves and shedded piers which constitutes San Francisco's teeming water front.

Tractorlike jitneys, dragging flat trucks loaded with goods, moved in and out of the yawning pier doors. Stevedores in hickory shirts hustled oversized bales with cargo hooks. Electric winches rattled and whizzed, depositing boxes of freight into waiting holds.

The air was redolent of the odors of sea commerce—oakum and copra, coffee beans and raw sugar. And of course there was the ineffable aroma of rotted fish, wet pilings, and salt air.

At eight o'clock, the Ferry Building siren gave a warning screech, and the transpacific liner *Mandarin,* bound for Hongkong, China, prepared to receive passengers.

The gangplank gate was opened. The first mate, clad in a starched white uniform and jaunty cap, stood by to greet the early arrivals. He squared his immaculate shoulders proudly.

For despite her exotic destination, the *Mandarin* was no roving tramp of the sea. Of Canadian registry, her keel had been laid in Glasgow, Scotland. She was over eighty feet wide and somewhat less than seven hundred feet would catch her length. Her ebony hull was decorated by a smart emerald stripe running the length of her water line. Her superstructure might have been carved from polished ivory, and the black five-pointed star emblazoned on her green-and-white funnels proclaimed her to belong to the Black Star Line.

To seasoned ocean travelers, that meant the *Mandarin* was a luxury vessel of the highest class. Indeed, she boasted appointments as lavish as a gymnasium, a swimming pool, a bank, two dining salons, a spacious sea garage, and a theater that showed only first-run talkies. Those who could afford to book first-class passage on the seagoing leviathan would lack for no comfort during the long Pacific crossing.

The individuals climbing the gangplank were a mixture of first-class, cabin, and so-called "Asiatic steerage" ticket holders. Most of the latter were Chinese, returning to their homeland to visit relatives or maintain business contacts.

One early boarder, upon presenting his ticket to the first mate, went immediately to an upper deck, where he could watch the file of humanity coming up the gangplank.

His almond eyes and sallow features told that he was a denizen of San Francisco's bustling Chinatown. Although he affected ordinary attire, he wore a black Mandarin's cap that failed to conceal the fact that his yellow moon of a skull was utterly hairless.

Evidently, this individual soon became bored with his solitary watch, for he plucked from an inner pocket of his very American suit jacket two small paper sacks. He set these on the polished mahogany rail, and proceeded to fish peanuts from one of them. He shelled these by crushing the peanuts in a yellow fist and depositing the ruined, inedible hulls in the companion bag.

His slitted eyes were unreadable as he worked his way through the filled sack. The expression on his round face might have reflected boredom, or just the placidness of countenance so common throughout the Far East.

At one point, his eyes relaxed sufficiently that their color became apparent. They were a soiled gray, like marbles that had lain long in the dirt.

The procession of passengers mounted the gangway for the better part of two hours. The *Mandarin* was not scheduled to steam from port until ten o'clock sharp, so the early arrivals were desultory.

One passenger, obviously in his cups from a late night on the town, had to be helped up the gangway by three fellow Celestials. He wore a Chinese-style silk jacket and billowy pants, which brought a rare frown to the visage of the Celestial on the upper deck. Chinese were not known to be imbibers of the grape.

Another seemingly sick passenger came aboard not long

after. He was a white man, although his face, from the moment he gained the deck, tended toward green around the jaw line. He held one hand before his mouth as he offered his ticket, in the manner of a person who is stricken with seasickness.

After the man had hastened below, a deck hand told a steward, "That one is in for a rough trip if he's already sea-sick."

"You said it."

As events later showed, this chance comment proved prophetic.

Later, a swashbuckling individual ascended the gangway. He cut a large figure, did this personage. For he wore a riotous costume of silk and worn leather and sheepskin boots that would be appropriate attire in the wild mountains of the Asian interior. His straight nose and pinched eyes bespoke of Manchu blood. Manchus tend to be taller than most Orientals, but this particular specimen topped seven feet in height.

He surrendered his ticket with a low grunt, and passed on. Other passengers—white and otherwise—gave him a wide berth.

One deck hand could be heard to remark, "All that guy needs is a sword through his belt and bandoliers crossed over his chest to fit my idea of a Chinese bandit chief."

Nervous laughter greeted this observation. Soon, the giant Manchu was forgotten amid the gayety and bustle of departure.

At quarter to ten, the ship's horn gave a warning blast, signaling the imminent departure hour.

A taxi cab deposited two arrivals about that time.

One was a rather spry-looking man who walked with a cane. His face was decorated with a rather long tail of beard, whose snowy whiteness matched his hair.

Gallantly, he held the door open for his companion.

The woman who emerged from the taxi was a vision. This was obvious despite the fact that her face was artfully concealed by a black veil that prevented close examination of her features.

Her age was difficult to ascertain. As she stepped from the cab, she radiated youth and vigor. Her carriage was almost regal. A spray of expensive orchids encumbered her dress front, only partially crushed by a mink stole. Her smart frock clung to her exquisitely molded form in a way that was most pleasing to the eye.

Appreciative gazes turned in her direction as she mounted the gangplank. Perhaps it was the aura of mystery about her that drew every eye. For a chic turban swallowed her hair, further masking her identity.

For all anyone knew, she could have been as homely as a horned toad and as bald as a hard-boiled egg. She might have been American, European, or a Fiji Islander. It was impossible to tell as she and her companion walked briskly through the covered Black Star pier.

At the top of the gangplank, the white-bearded old man presented two first-class tickets smartly.

"Here you are, my good man," he said self-importantly. "Please direct Miss Vine and myself to our cabins."

First Mate Bill Scott gestured to a steward, who hastened to comply.

After the odd-looking pair had been led away, another steward sidled up to the first mate.

"Who," he asked wonderingly, "was that?"

"I don't know, but they must be important," the first mate undertoned. "The ritzy dame took the Royal Suite."

The steward whistled. The Royal Suite was reserved for personages of utmost importance. Mere money could not secure it. One had to have status, or pull with the steamship company.

"I think she's in pictures," the steward muttered.

First Mate Scott lifted an eyebrow, "What makes you say that?"

"The way she dressed," the other explained. "She has Hollywood written all over her."

The first mate thought that was a reasonable enough explanation. He put the mystery out of his mind; the liner was due to depart soon.

The final patrons climbed aboard, out of breath and sweating from exertion, as is the way with stragglers. There are always a good number of these, it seems.

Dr. Mawson Harper was one of the stragglers. He piled

out of a cab, flung money back at the driver, and hectored a stevedore into taking his luggage, which was considerable.

Striding up the gangway, he chanced to be struck on the nose by a falling object. He swatted at his goateed face, thinking the annoyance a bothersome fly. Seeing a broken fragment of peanut shell click off one white spat, he looked up angrily.

Hastily, the loitering Chinese withdrew from sight.

Muttering under his breath, Dr. Harper finished the strenuous climb.

He complained to the first mate in a loud voice, and received profuse apologies in return. Since it was so close to the departure hour, and the *Mandarin* crew were deep in the task of preparing to put out to sea, no one bothered to act on Dr. Harper's complaint.

At two minutes to departure, a touring car screeched to a stop at the Black Star pier. Both rear doors flew open and three men emerged.

They walked in a tight knot down the pier, heads swiveling nervously. And in the center walked a man in a gabardine coat, a tasteful fedora pulled low over his features.

The knot of men—the curious first mate saw that they were a grim group—paused at the foot of the gangplank.

The man in the center touched the top of his fedora. This was evidently a signal, for one of the men started up the gangplank.

The man in gabardine followed after. The remaining individual fell in behind.

It was clear that the two men functioned as bodyguards to the man in the gabardine coat. Their faces were tight with concern and their hands fumbled at coat buttons or fluttered in such a way that weapons could be yanked from concealment at the first hint of danger.

Halfway up the gangplank, the man in gabardine abruptly clapped both hands to his face.

He made no outcry. He simply covered his visage reflexively, teetered on his feet briefly, and pitched forward on his face.

The canvas sides of the gangway prevented the man

from rolling off and into the lapping water. One outflung arm got tangled up in canvas stays, and the man came to a rest with his face exposed to the bright morning sun.

Hoarse shouts emerged from the throats of his would-be protectors.

"What happened to him?" one rasped worriedly.

"I dunno," said the other. "But look at his face."

The fallen man's face was a distinct aquamarine, not unlike a tropical sea.

The loitering peanut-eating Celestial on the upper deck took one look at the azure hue of the fallen man's face and plucked up his paper sacks. He disappeared from sight.

One of the bodyguards, after putting an ear to the fallen man's chest, went sick-eyed and called up to the first mate, who was clambering concernedly down the gangway, "Fetch a doctor, will you?"

First Mate Scott hastily reversed direction.

Every passenger liner comes equipped with a ship's doctor. The *Mandarin* was no exception. But finding one individual on a liner of the *Mandarin*'s size was a daunting task. She boasted a crew of five hundred, and accommodations for over a thousand passengers. The first mate worked the big liner's annunciator boards. When that failed to produce results, he got on the ship's efficient telephone system—every first-class cabin was equipped with modernistic telephones—and spread the word for the physician to come on deck.

By the time the ship's doctor had been mustered out of the ship's bar, the stricken passenger had been carried into the captain's private quarters amidships.

The man's necktie had been loosened and his jacket and shirt unbuttoned. A serious-faced man with a black streak in his white hair and a white streak in his black Van Dyke was seated on the berth on which the stricken one reposed. He was touching the useful end of a stethoscope to various points of the man's exposed, unmoving chest, and frowning.

The two bodyguards shifted their feet in the cramped quarters, wearing sheepish expressions. Their faces fell further when Dr. Mawson Harper popped the stethoscope earpieces from his ears and said, "I regret to say that this man is dead."

At that moment, the ship's doctor barged in, followed by the first mate.

"And who might you be?" the medico roared. He had been taken to task by the first mate and was determined to re-assert his authority on board.

"I am Dr. Mawson Harper, a passenger on this liner," Dr. Harper said gravely, stowing his stethoscope into his black valise.

"And I just happen to be the ship's physician," the other shot back angrily. "Which means that man is my patient."

He rushed over to the man on the berth and yanked open his own black bag.

"It was a heart attack," Dr. Harper inserted stolidly, as he gave the man room to work. "That much is obvious."

"If you do not mind," the ship's doctor snapped back, "I'll make my own determination."

At which point the captain put in an appearance. Behind him hovered a hulk of a colored gentleman in cook's whites. The big Negro had his chef's hat in his hands and was knead-ing it nervously. His eyes were very wide, showing a great deal of startled white.

It was evident that the cook had summoned the cap-tain. No one had thought to do this until now.

"If no one minds," the captain bellowed, "I would like to know what in Davy Jones's name is going on here!"

The captain was a rather substantial wart of a man, with a face like a rubbed-raw corn. He looked wider than taller, al-though only by the measure of a child's thumb. His voice rasped, as if cured in brine. There was a great deal of volume to it, though.

"This man suffered a heart attack while boarding the ship," explained Dr. Mawson Harper, his bushy black eye-brows low over his intensely black orbs.

"Is that so?" the captain said slowly.

"Yes," Dr. Harper replied. "I heard the commotion and thought I would offer my assistance." He glanced at the red-faced ship's doctor. "I did not realize I was poaching on an-other man's territory."

"I sign the death certificates on this vessel," the ship's doctor put in angrily.

"Is that man dead?" the captain demanded, his face acquiring the coloration of a stewed beet.

The ship's doctor hesitated. Finally, he grumbled, "I am afraid it's true."

"Heart attack?" demanded the captain.

The medico nodded wordlessly. Evidently pride and professional rivalry disinclined him for agreeing with his fellow practitioner, but he had no choice in the matter.

The captain shoved through the knot of spectators, and said, "Let's see who he is."

"That's Jason Baird," rasped a man—one of the erstwhile bodyguards. The man licked his lips worriedly. "He hired us to protect him—guess we're out of a job now."

The captain sat his square body down on the berth beside the dead man and began investigating his pockets. He extracted a wallet, and examined papers he found therein.

"Says here he's Jason Baird, all right," the captain muttered. "President of Gold Coast Lapidary."

"We never met him before today," the bodyguard admitted.

"Yeah," the other added thickly. "Our boss ain't gonna like it when he hears his client dropped dead on us. We're out a pile of dough."

"Maybe not," the captain said suddenly, reading through a sheet of paper he had found in a secret pocket of the dead man's wallet. "According to this, your client experienced a premonition of danger, or something of the sort. This is a notarized request that in the event of his untimely demise, his body is to be shipped to Hongkong and the custodians—I guess that means you two—are to be reimbursed by the receiving party."

The bodyguards exchanged weak glances. They shrugged.

"I guess we're off the hook then," the first one said.

"All right," growled the captain, getting to his feet. "We'd better contact the Harbor Police about this if we're to be getting on our way. See to it, mate."

The first mate began shooing gawkers from the cabin. He

lavished special attention on the big Negro cook, whom he could not recall having seen aboard before.

"You!" he snapped. "Back to the galley!"

"Yassuh," said the big black cook in a sheepish tone, drawing his chef's hat over his woolly pate. He hastily betook himself away.

Descending a deserted companionway, he took a cross-ship passageway that brought him to D Deck, portside. The galley was nowhere near D Deck, portside.

In fact, the hulking dusky-skinned cook paused before Cabin No. 67 and ducked inside. He did not emerge again.

The Harbor Police had a small station not far from the pier where the *Mandarin* lay berthed. Ordinarily, their responsibilities were limited to policing harbor traffic and monitoring incidents of cargo poaching.

Technically, the death of a passenger aboard a berthed liner fell under their jurisdiction.

The police listened to the corn-faced *Mandarin* commander—he introduced himself as Captain Gooch—as he explained the circumstances of the death of the body identified by personal papers as Jason Baird, and consulted among themselves briefly.

When they were through, they asked only to see the body, the death certificate, and the dead man's final instructions.

They were escorted to the ship's morgue—the *Mandarin* actually had a full one, owing to the Chinese tradition of shipping their dead back to their homeland for burial—where the body lay.

"You gonna perform an autopsy?" one of the officers asked the ship's doctor in a tone that suggested he would prefer a negative reply.

The ship's doctor cast a questioning eye in the direction of Captain Gooch, who shook his head in the negative.

"No," said the medico promptly.

"Good. Because we'd have to keep you here until it was done," the officer explained. "Better you put it down as a heart attack—which it obviously was, anyway—and we can all get on with our lives."

That done, the police debarked the liner. So too did the erstwhile bodyguards to the dead man, after consulting with the private agency which employed them. The agency evidently trusted in being reimbursed by the deceased's next of kin without the formality of its two men crossing the Pacific unnecessarily.

Captain Gooch turned to his first mate and growled, "Let's cast off before an iceberg sidles up to our hull."

The final all-ashore call was given, and the bunting-festooned gangway hastily raised. The shore filled with waving well-wishers.

The great steamer gave a harsh blast and lines were cast off.

Tugs butted and nudged the big black liner away from the concrete finger of a pier and assisted it in rounding the peninsula, through the constantly dredged channels, toward San Francisco Bay and the open sea.

A fog was rolling in through the Golden Gate. It was very wet and clammy, somehow being remindful of a dead man's final breath. There was a fog dome over Alcatraz Island as they passed it, a spectral sight.

The two imposing steel towers of the new Golden Gate Bridge reared up on either side of the bay, their tops lost in the fog. Below, work barges toiled under the suspension bridge, which, when completed, was promised to be eight miles across, the largest such span in the world.

At this moment, she represented a jaw-dropping spectacle for the passengers lining each rail and a headache for the busy *Mandarin* crew.

Swearing harshly, Captain Gooch ordered the *Mandarin*'s powerful deck fog dispersers to be brought into play. These shot streams of electrified water into the air to absorb moisture droplets. They barely made a dent in the vaporous mist.

When the *Mandarin* had safely picked her way past the last harbor buoy, and the tugs left off, Captain Gooch turned to the quartermaster at the wheel, saying, "Your course is two hundred and fifty-six degrees. Change over to the metal mike as soon as she's ready."

"Aye, cap'n."

The great steam turbine engines began to pulsate. There was none of the horrific deck vibration so common in passenger liners a few years back. Two of the liner's great funnels began belching dirty white smoke. Although the *Mandarin* was a "three-stacker," one—the last—was a dummy.

From the navigation bridge, the Pacific fog was approaching like a marauding monster of white and gray tendrils. It slathered across the sea greyhound's bow, depositing a film of moisture that made the skin crawl and itch. Nothing could be seen past the *Mandarin*'s forecastle and stem.

"Going to be a damn long voyage," Captain Gooch said feelingly, squaring his belligerent shoulders. "Damn long."

VI

THE ELUSIVE MANCHU

Thirteen miles out of San Francisco, the fog was still rolling ponderously toward shore. It seemed without end as it cascaded over the liner *Mandarin*. The ship's hungry flower-mouthed ventilators sucked in great quantities of the stuff, distributing it into the engine room and cabins far below, making miserable those who dwelt there.

When the *Mandarin* had set sail, her passengers had lined the rails and filled the promenade deck, making merry.

But the relentless clammy fog had cast a pall of discouragement over them, and they had retreated to staterooms and smoking lounges. Only stewards and deck hands, going about their nautical duties, prowled the liner's slippery superstructure.

As the fog-haunted *Mandarin* steamed past the Farallones, some twenty-five miles out, the door to Cabin No. 67 opened, and a man emerged.

He bore no resemblance to the Negro cook who had

earlier taken refuge in Cabin No. 67, except perhaps in his general outlines. This apparition appeared less tall, although this might have been open to debate, since he was much rounder of girth than had been the cook.

Instead of cook's whites, he wore a flamboyant costume of gaudy silks and worn leather. The deck crew would have recognized him as the flamboyantly garbed Manchu who had created such a fuss by the mere act of boarding the liner. His broad features were fierce, even in repose. One eye drooped sleepily—the result of some past altercation involving a knife.

Outside the door, he paused to touch the scraggly mustache that adorned his upper lip. Orientals usually lack facial hair, and this gesture might have been an example of Manchu vanity.

The big Manchu made his way through the private portion of the ship, where only crewmen were allowed.

He moved with surprising stealth for one of his size. Handmade sheepskin boots might explain that. Several times, he hesitated before coming around passage turns, retreated in advance of approaching crewmen, and managed to find niches and other places of concealment where he could linger undetected.

Moving in this way, he found himself outside the ship's morgue, in the lowermost deck of the ship, near the steerage section.

It was refrigerated, the bulkhead door dogged shut to keep heat from the pulsating engines from hastening decomposition and releasing unpleasant odors from the cadavers housed within.

The big, silent Manchu was in the act of undogging the ponderous morgue door when a deck hand happened around the corner.

The deck hand practically skidded to a halt in surprise.

"Hey, you!" he barked. "What are you—"

The Manchu left off his furtive labors. He retreated around the next twist in the passage.

The deck hand followed, fists balled angrily.

No sooner had the deck hand reached the turn in the passage than two monstrous saffron hands lunged out and grasped the wary sailor by the neck.

Fingers clamped down, choking off any outcry.

The deck hand lifted frantic fingers, but the hands at his

throat might have been cast of tempered steel. Try as he might, their grip could not be budged or repealed.

The sleepy-eyed Manchu's fingers worked their way to a certain spot on the flailing deck hand's neck, at the base of the spine. Remorseless fingers kneaded and manipulated.

The deck hand went as rigid as a board. Eyes open wide in horror, he found himself carried bodily to a storage room and laid out on the floor.

He had visions of a quick, silent knife stroke across his unprotected throat, but such a thing never came to pass.

Instead, the silent Manchu quitted the storage room, leaving the deck hand to his private terror.

Outside the ship's morgue, the hulking Manchu resumed undogging the door. It leafed open. He disappeared within.

The ship's morgue was not much different from morgues in large metropolitan cities everywhere—except that it was much smaller, of course.

The bodies were kept in refrigerated drawers. Three walls were checkerboarded with the wooden panels, equipped with handles.

In this case, the body identified as that of Jason Baird lay under a sheet on the porcelain autopsy table. The *Mandarin* was nothing if not prepared for any eventuality which could possibly befall its patrons—including untimely death.

The big Manchu moved toward this. Breath steam dribbled from his parted mouth. His fingers reached for the covering sheet.

A sound stopped him.

"Joe!" a shrill voice said in shock. "What happened to you!"

The incredulous voice came from outside the morgue.

Hands dropping to his sides, the big Manchu went to the door. He put an ear to the bulkhead wall. It was thick, but sounds were coming through with fair audibility. That was because they were so loud.

A boatswain's whistle blew shrilly, summoning aid.

Evidently the paralyzed deck hand had been discovered. Help was being summoned.

"Speak to me, Joe," the discoverer pleaded. "Say something!" The whistle shrilled again.

If this caused the mysterious Manchu any concern, it was not reflected in his impassive features. Steam eased from his flaring nostrils. He listened intently for some moments.

Feet drummed along the passage.

"What the hell is going on here?" an authoritarian voice demanded. It was the ship's physician.

"Search us," another voice rattled back. "We found Joe in the storeroom. He's having some kind of spell. His eyes are open, but he can't move. Never seen anything like it."

"Let me see," ordered the medico. "Come on, shove aside. I need room, dammit!"

More crewmen were filling the corridor. Evidently, every one wanted to see the seaman called Joe and the weird condition that had overtaken him.

When this had gone on for several minutes, and the passageway outside the morgue continued to fill with seamen, the eavesdropping Manchu hesitated, as if contemplating the wisdom of making a break for it.

It was conceivable that he could have remained in the morgue indefinitely; no one ventures into a morgue when they do not have to.

Then the medico's voice lifted over the din.

"Some of you," he shouted. "Help me lug this man into the dead room."

That was all the Manchu needed to hear. He had no choice now. He popped out of the morgue less than three yards behind a huddle of *Mandarin* crewmen.

One happened to have pulled away from the group to light a cigarette.

The match flame disclosed the Manchu, half in, half out of the door.

"Hey!" the seaman sputtered, dropping fag and match in surprise.

Every one who could turn his head in the narrow passage, did.

The Manchu broke and ran, trailing a pack of determined seamen.

Several of the latter clutched belaying pins and wore the expressions of men who intended to put them to good use.

* * *

The Manchu put on speed. He ascended a companionway, cut across a deck, and banged down another companionway, emerging on the port side of the liner.

Howling, the crewmen surged after him, jostling one another like logs bumping along a flume.

The Manchu was wily. He seemed to have a good grasp of the bowels of a modern express liner. He knew exactly which passages led to dead ends. In one case, he seemed to sense where a trap had been laid for him.

A waiting group of seamen saw him flit past their position, adjacent to the noisy main galley. They pitched after him.

"There he is!" one yelled.

The seaman indicated the startled Manchu, who was crouched outside a stateroom door. He seemed to be picking up something that he had dropped.

At the sight of the pursuing throng, he left off whatever he was doing and plunged up a companionway.

His pursuers reached the bottom of the companion. That was as far as they got. A few managed to place shoe leather on the lowermost companion steps.

Abruptly, they all lay down and began sleeping.

It happened without any preamble. The seamen were shouting lusty threats one moment; then they were a snoring pile of navy blue.

Most of them happened to collect on the exact spot where the Manchu had been spotted, seemingly attempting to pick up a fallen object.

The Manchu was next seen lurking in the dark sea garage, just aft of the forward cargo holds. He was caught in the act of attempting to secrete himself within a lashed-down sedan.

A warning shout was directed toward him and he left off that activity, plunging into the cavernous spaces.

Although many tried, no one seemed able to locate the Oriental apparition. They fished lights into closed autos, checked under chassis, opened trunks and rumble seats.

"Where is he?" one sailor shouted in exasperation.

No one knew, although few let that inhibit them from venturing opinions.

Eventually, they went topside, where the fog still held ghostly sway.

A voice—later no one could identify to whom it belonged—called out from the fog, "There he goes. Heading for the fo'c's'le!"

There was a general rush in the direction of the forecastle. Owing to the fog-slicked decks, quite a few pursuers upset and had to be helped back to their feet.

This only added to their fierce determination to locate the marauding Manchu.

Determination proved not to be sufficient, however.

The crew found themselves standing amid clammy wreaths of fog on the forecastle, cursing the soupy conditions vociferously.

Eventually, some one got organized enough to summon the first mate by annunciator.

First Mate Bill Scott hove into view with fire in his eye and a chip on one gold-braided epaulet.

"Somebody," he growled, "had better tell me a story that makes sense."

"He was eight feet tall!" a seaman insisted, drawing up on tiptoe in an attempt to simulate what he had seen.

"Moved like a ghost!" said a steward.

"Chinese he was," added another.

The first mate cut them all off with a sharp gesture.

"Describe this lubber," he demanded hotly.

It took some doing, but eventually the first mate received a coherent description of the big Manchu. It tickled a gray cell. First Mate Scott had remembered taking the man's ticket. He was a cabin passenger. Definitely not steerage.

Since most Asiatic passengers aboard the liner were in steerage, this rather narrowed down the search.

Narrowed it to one individual, the first mate found upon checking the ship's register, which was stored in the purser's office.

"The devil's name is Sat Sung," he gritted, slapping the book closed. He turned to a knot of waiting seamen.

"Let's palaver with the worthy Oriental gentleman," he added gratingly. "Cabin No. 67."

They broke into Cabin No. 67 after failing to obtain a response. They were fairly confident the cabin was unoccupied. Five minutes of pounding with belaying pins on the door led to this conclusion.

Inside, they found little luggage—surprisingly little for a transpacific passenger. They also found an immaculately white cook's uniform.

The first mate took up the uniform. It looked big enough to swim in.

"That nosy black cook!" he snapped, another gray cell coming to life.

A visit to the ship's galley produced no black cook large enough to fill out the oversized uniform.

"Anyone knows who belongs to this?" First Mate Scott called in exasperation, waving the offending garment.

No one did. As it developed, the entire galley crew was present to listen to the first mate's apoplectic tirade. There was no missing cook. A least, not one whose name appeared on the Black Star Steamship Company payroll.

This was considered very mysterious by all. Very mysterious indeed.

"I guess we take this to the skipper," said the first mate, evincing no enthusiasm for the task whatsoever.

Captain Gooch was regarding the impenetrable fog bank with one squinting optic and the gyro-compass repeater with the other when First Mate Bill Scott strode up onto the glass-enclosed bridge and executed a snappy salute.

He told his story in clipped, no-nonsense sentences.

"The interloper is still at large, cap'n," he finished, bracing himself for the wrathy reply.

"Keep searching, blast it!" the captain bit out. "Once we steam out of this infernal fog, the passengers will want to be swarming all over deck. We can't have a damn phantom Chinaman terrorizing the vessel."

"I agree," said a resonant voice, speaking impeccable English.

The captain and first mate whirled at the sound of the strange voice. Their jaws dropped a half second apart.

For there, standing in the shadow of the Fathometer, stood the giant Manchu listed on the passenger register as Sat Sung!

VII

CRYPTIC MESSAGE

The appearance of the swashbuckling Asiatic, Sat Sung, on the bridge of the *Mandarin* defied immediate comprehension.

The bridge was not unguarded. Yet the odd figure stood well within the bridge confines, as if he had been projected there by some contra-natural means.

It dawned on some of the apprentice officers that such an intrusion was not to be taken lightly. The Manchu was promptly surrounded.

By this time, Captain Gooch had found his tongue.

"Who," he growled, "in blue blazes are you?"

"Doc Savage," the Manchu said quietly, his voice vibrating with controlled power.

First Mate Bill Scott stood with his jaw distended. The point of his chin was practically resting on his uniform front, so it could not distend any farther. He closed his mouth with the dull click of meeting teeth.

"I know that voice," he snapped. "You tricked us into lighting out for the fo'c's'le."

"Ventriloquism," the other explained.

"I don't believe it," the first mate scoffed.

The Manchu who claimed to be Doc Savage lifted huge hands. The bridge complement tensed. A revolver was produced. The quartermaster leveled it at the Manchu's deep chest.

"May I," the Manchu asked politely, "prove my claim?"

Captain Gooch hesitated. "Just do it slowly," he allowed.

"Thank you." The hands drifted up to the broad Oriental features. They came away clamping yellowish lengths of adhesive tape.

64

Where they had come loose—over the outer corner of each eye—two short rectangles of metallic bronze showed against the surrounding saffron skin.

The bridge crew barely registered that much. They were looking at the big Manchu's black eyes—now no longer slanted.

It was evident that the saffron tape had been used to pull the corners of the impostor's orbs into almond shapes.

Next, obsidian-hued glass shells were removed from these eyes, revealing whirling pools of golden flakes. A collodion scar was lifted. The sleepy aspect of one eye vanished. The straggly mustache came loose. It had been affixed with common spirit gum.

"If some one will allow me," Doc Savage offered, "I will be happy to remove the chemical dye on my face and hands."

"Not necessary," grumbled Captain Gooch. "You're Doc Savage, all right. But what are you doing skulking about my ship?"

The captain's tone was surly, but there was a note of respect in it. It was plain he was not certain how to react to this unorthodox behavior on the part of the renowned Doc Savage.

"I am afraid I have gone about this in the wrong way," said Doc Savage. "If we could speak alone, captain, I would be happy to explain my actions."

Captain Gooch hesitated. His rubbed-raw corn of a face worked as he considered.

"We'll go to my cabin," he said at last.

"The ship's morgue would be preferable," Doc stated.

"That's where he was discovered," the first mate put in suspiciously.

"My unorthodox behavior will be easier to explain in the morgue," Doc added.

That decided the commander of the *Mandarin*.

"Take over, mate," Captain Gooch told the first mate. He strode up to the bronze man, the ship's officers making way.

"I'm going to be very interested in whatever yarn you're about to spin, Savage," Captain Gooch said as he led the bronze man from the bridge.

* * *

Down in the ship's morgue, the *Mandarin*'s physician was enwrapped in an examination of the deck hand who had been left in a weird, staring paralysis.

"This beats everything!" the doctor was muttering to himself. "I've never seen anything of its like. If only you could talk," he added for the benefit of the unfortunate patient, whose eyes were jerking about in their sockets like frightened animals.

When Captain Gooch pushed open the bulkhead door, the medico looked up and launched into a long-winded complaint.

"Captain, this thing makes of sorcery," he sputtered. "It's not a disease—I don't think."

Captain Gooch cut him off abruptly.

"Belay that bilge," he growled.

Then Doc Savage stepped into the room. He had to duck to avoid hitting his bronze hair—he had removed a coarse black wig and scrubbed his face clean of citrine dye—on the door frame.

"My word! You're Doc Savage!" the physician gasped.

Doc Savage strode over to the wide-eyed deck hand. He lay on the porcelain autopsy table, side by side with the sheeted corpse, there being no other suitable place for him. It was not a position conducive to peace of mind. The man's face was crawling with perspiration.

"You are familiar with the principal nerve centers of the human body?" Doc Savage asked the astonished doctor, his eyes going to the man on the slab.

"Of course. But I don't see what—"

The bronze man grasped the unfortunate seaman's neck, manipulated a spot near the spine, and suddenly the man let out a scream of pure terror. His upper body jerked up, animated once more.

"I—I—I—" he blurted. "What happened to me? My muscles were all locked up."

"You will be fine, sailor," the bronze man told him. "You were suffering from a temporary paralysis induced by the manipulation of a sensitive spinal nerve center."

The man pushed off the table. When his feet touched the

floor, his expression indicated surprise and relief that his legs functioned.

"Permission to go, cap'n," the man asked, his eyes on the bronze man in gaudy Chinese raiment. He remembered that his attacker had been so attired—even if Doc Savage no longer bore any resemblance to the phantom Manchu, Sat Sung.

"Hop to it, then," Captain Gooch growled, waving him off.

The sailor hastened from the morgue.

Captain Gooch turned to Doc Savage. "What about the members of my crew found sleeping at the bottom of a companionway?" he demanded.

"They happened to step on a number of glass globules, which I set in their path," the bronze man explained without emotion. "When crushed by trampling feet, these globules release a highly volatile anæsthetic gas that produces sudden unconsciousness. They will come around shortly."

"That leaves only the tiny matter of what you were doing prowling my morgue,"' Captain Gooch said, not quite certain whether to be mollified or not.

"My interest," Doc Savage told him, indicating the sheeted cadaver on the table, "is in this man."

"Baird!" the medico exploded.

"The heart attack victim?" Captain Gooch chorused, his red face reddening further.

"This man did not die of a heart attack," Doc Savage stated. "He was murdered."

"Nonsense!" the ship's physician burst out. "I myself examined him." He whipped the sheet off the prostrate corpse. "Just look at that face—blue as the sky."

"Look again," Doc suggested.

Every one looked. The ship's doctor let out a gasp. For the body on the table was no longer the hue of a tropic sea. His skin was now a very definite green.

The medico gulped, blinked, and seemed to have trouble with his tongue.

"You have yet to perform an autopsy, have you not?" the bronze man inquired.

The medico swallowed. "Well, I—no. Not yet. We've only just sailed. But all the signs point to a massive coronary."

Growing impatient with the difference of medical opinion, Captain Gooch cut in, tight-voiced.

"Savage, just what is your interest in this man, Baird?"

Doc Savage fixed the *Mandarin* skipper with his eerie golden eyes. They were calm, steady. Yet the optical trick of the light that imparted the illusion of constant whirling seemed to exert a quelling effect on testy Captain Gooch.

The skipper's blunt head had been hunkered down into his bulging shoulders. Now it seemed to rise up on his thick neck, as tension was released. His beet-red fists lost their tightness, fingers loosening.

"Jason Baird," the bronze man explained, "requested that I accompany him on this voyage to Hongkong. He claimed that his life was in danger. I agreed, securing a cabin on this vessel under the assumed name of Sat Sung in order to complete the crossing without attracting undue attention. It was my hope to draw out those who sought his life."

This seemed to mollify Captain Gooch further. He was used to having celebrity passengers traveling incognito.

"This Baird," he said, indicating the form tented under the sheet with his pugnacious jaw, "must be a good friend of yours, for you to go to all this trouble."

"On the contrary," Doc countered. "I have never met the gentleman."

Captain Gooch seemed to regain his belligerence at this point.

"Then why in the name of all that's salty did you book passage to Hongkong on the strength of a man you say you don't even know?" he roared.

"Jason Baird is a friend of my cousin, Patricia Savage," Doc stated, seemingly unruffled by the captain's testy manner. "It was at her behest I agreed to confer with Jason Baird. But when I reached San Francisco, he was not at our agreed-upon meeting place. I discovered clues that led me to believe that Baird had been abducted by Chinese kidnapers. Because of certain things Baird had intimated to my cousin, there was reason to suspect the man might be taken aboard the *Mandarin* by his abductors."

The captain snorted. "Well, you were wrong. This man came on board under his own steam. In fact, he had two bodyguards with him. They were no more Chinese than I am. They stayed behind in San Francisco."

"It is possible Baird had escaped his captors during the night," Doc said.

Captain Gooch nodded. "We found a note in Baird's pocket, asking that his remains be transported to Hongkong in the event that something happened to him." He rubbed his blocky jaw thoughtfully. "I never put much stock in premonitions, but if ever a man had one, it was this man."

"I would like to examine the body now," Doc asked.

The captain and the doctor exchanged glances. Neither seemed to think of an objection, so Captain Gooch said, "Be my guest."

Doc Savage stripped the sheet all the way off the body on the autopsy table.

The ship's physician gasped audibly.

Doc Savage and Captain Gooch looked at him curiously.

"Where—where are his clothes?" the medico blustered.

Doc eyed him sharply. "You did not disrobe him?"

"No!"

The dead man was, in fact, as nude as he had been, presumably, when he had come into the world. The livid green coloration of his face carried down to the tips of his toes, which resembled deformed peppers.

The man looked sunken, emaciated to a marked degree. Bodies often get that way after several hours, so this was not deemed unusual.

After only the briefest of glances at the cadaver's features, Doc Savage went to the man's wrists, turning them as much as rigor mortis would permit. Next, he scrutinized the cold bottoms of the feet carefully.

The soles were not quite as green as the rest of him, but they were green enough.

Thus, the parallel stripes of sticky white adhesive showed quite plainly against the queer discoloration.

"What the hell?" the medico grunted.

"Jason Baird informed my cousin Pat that in the event he

fell victim to his enemies, instructions were to be found taped to the bottom of his left foot," Doc related thoughtfully. "Evidently, whoever removed this man's clothes, also took possession of the tape."

Captain Gooch turned to face the unhappy ship's physician.

"Who the hell could have gotten in here to rifle this man's body?" he thundered, his crimson face working with fury.

"No one—any one," the medico said, flustered. "I've never heard of such a thing happening—not on any ship on which I've served."

"I hope that isn't an aspersion on my captaincy," the *Mandarin* skipper glowered.

The ship's doctor could see that he was only digging himself a deeper hole. He swallowed his words.

"Well, I intend to get to the bottom of this," Captain Gooch said forcefully. "Make no mistake about it."

"An examination of the dead man's cabin might be in order," Doc Savage remarked. "I assume it is free."

"It is," Captain Gooch said. "Along with a flock of others. Passenger bookings still haven't recovered from that fool maritime strike last year."

They went to Jason Baird's cabin, which was amidships, on A Deck. It was Cabin No. 12, an outside stateroom, which means that it opened on the deck and afforded a nice view from its portholes.

The captain prepared to unlock it, but Doc Savage intervened. He nudged the door with his still-yellowish fingers.

The portal fell open at his touch.

"I'll be holystoned!" Captain Gooch muttered, eyes squinting angrily.

Doc beat him into the stateroom.

The decor was unmistakably Asiatic, in keeping with the *Mandarin*'s overall theme. There was altogether too much bamboo and shimmering silks in the appointments. The aim was for a kind of exotic opulence, but the end result made one think of an overly ostentatious chop suey palace.

A cursory examination showed that the stateroom had been rifled. Luggage was strewn about. There were three big steamer trunks set on the Oriental rug. These had been pried open, irrespective of their sturdy locks. Clothing was everywhere.

They spent some moments picking through the confusion of clothing and toiletries. Captain Gooch fumed in silence. For his part, the medico looked bewildered.

If there was an expression on Doc Savage's metallic countenance, it was not readable.

Captain Gooch finally straightened up from his examination of the stateroom, squaring his shoulders like a bull confronted by a red flag.

"I'm going to see about this!" he spat. "Burglary—on my ship!"

"Mind if I continue my search?" Doc asked.

"Be my guest," said Captain Gooch, charging off. The ship's physician looked momentarily at sea. Mumbling excuses, he followed in the captain's wake.

This left Doc Savage to pick up the folded square of adhesive tape.

He had spotted one corner of the thing peeping out from under a rifled steamer trunk, earlier.

Doc shoved the trunk aside, retrieved the tape fragment.

It proved to be a rather soiled piece of tape, such as might have been plucked from the bare sole of a man. There was a folded square of once-white paper clinging to the tape. Doc separated the two.

The bronze man scrutinized the paper once he unfolded it. Both sides were blank. He held the sheet up before a porthole, through which was coming only wan light, owing to the persistent fog outside.

The weak radiance was enough to disclose the sharp edges created by the impression of a small key against the paper fibres.

Doc Savage's scarlet-and-gold Chinese silk tunic was fastened with wooden dowellike buttons that passed through cord loops. He undid two of these, and drew out a simple stick of a kitchen match.

He rasped the sulphur head into life with a flick of a

thumb nail. Yellow flame wavered, tracing shadows across the bronze giant's impassive features.

Holding up the square of paper, Doc applied match flame.

The paper was evidently fire-resistant. It caught, browned along the lower edge, but did not truly burn.

The invisible writing which had been inscribed on the paper in simple lemon juice—Doc had detected the telltale odor—showed in whitish letters:

UNDER THE HOTEL GOURMAND—

The last word was an unreadable smear. Conceivably, perspiration had obliterated it. The shod foot was subject to perspiring freely.

If Doc Savage was disappointed by the unfinished nature of the secret message, he gave no sign.

Lowering the sheet of paper, his strange flake-gold eyes began to roam the stateroom.

They came to rest on one of the big steamer trunks. It was not the one under which he had found the paper originally, but another one, which stood on its side, its two halves separated on its hinges and spilling articles of apparel.

The bronze man had given this trunk a seemingly cursory examination, as he had every square inch of the stateroom.

Yet Doc went immediately to one side of the trunk, which was plastered—in the fashion of luggage that travels often—with gummed stickers bespeaking the owner's global sojourns.

Part of Doc's training included mental exercises. As a result, he possessed what was sometimes called a photographic memory. He had only to take in a thing once and it was indelibly imprinted on his keen brain.

Without hesitation, Doc Savage's questing fingers went to a colorful sticker advertising that the owner had once stayed in the Hotel Gourmand, in Paris.

The sticker was warped and wrinkled with age. It seemed to bulge up in the center, as if the gummed back was coming loose.

Doc touched this experimentally. The bulge did not give as it should. He dug his fingers into the edge, tearing the sticker free.

A quick bronze hand caught the falling ivory square before it fell to the Oriental rug.

The bronze giant unfolded this into an ordinary sheet of stationery. The letterhead was printed with the crest of Gold Coast Lapidary—Jason Baird's concern.

The message was typewritten:

> DOC SAVAGE:
> IF YOU ARE READING THIS, THAT MEANS SOMETHING UNTOWARD HAS HAPPENED TO ME. POSSIBLY I AM DEAD. IF THE LATTER IS TRUE, YOU SHOULD KNOW THAT A CHINESE DEVIL NAMED WAN SOP—OR ONE OF HIS CUTTHROATS—IS RESPONSIBLE. WAN SOP IS A THIEF. HE STOLE A LARGE SHIPMENT OF DIAMONDS FROM ME. IT WAS FOR THIS REASON I ASKED YOUR COUSIN, PATRICIA, TO REQUEST YOUR ASSISTANCE ON MY BEHALF.
> SAVAGE, I KNOW YOU DO NOT ACCEPT PAY FOR HELPING PEOPLE LIKE ME. SO I HAVE MADE ARRANGEMENTS WITH THE REGINA BANK OF HONGKONG FOR THE ESTABLISHMENT OF A TRUST FUND IN THE AMOUNT OF TWENTY THOUSAND DOLLARS. THIS WILL BE TURNED OVER TO THE PERSON WHO RECOVERS THE STOLEN JEWELS AND RETURNS THEM TO THE BANK. YOU MAY DO WITH IT AS YOU SEE FIT, BUT FROM WHAT YOUR COUSIN TELLS ME, I IMAGINE YOU'LL TURN THE TWENTY THOUSAND OVER TO CHARITY.
> GOOD LUCK.

The note was signed: "Jason Baird—to be read in the event of his demise."

Grimly, Doc Savage refolded the paper and stowed it in the folds of his gaudy tunic. He fastened the odd wood buttons, and quitted the stateroom like a ghost composed of scarlet silk ribbons.

VIII

THE SECOND PEANUT MUNCHER

On her maiden voyage, the *Mandarin* had broken the existing records for an across-the-Pacific passage. She was capable of twenty-three knots on the open sea.

She was only doing about nineteen now, due to the seemingly endless fog. Her whistle gave out intermittent blasts, sending harsh echoes rolling and tumbling along the wave caps like scrappy canines. The rushing of water past her ebony hull was like a distant Niagara.

Captain Gooch had been industriously attempting to maneuver around the fog bank all afternoon, but the soupy stuff seemed to be crawling over the entire Pacific in a manner that brought to mind a sullen herd of driven ghosts. He paced the flying bridge like a caged beast, cursing saltily and often.

At day's end, the solar orb sank into the sea, seeming to take the stubborn stratus with it.

Darkness clamped down on the leviathan liner as she ran, a bone of foam in her mouth, through the black Pacific swells.

Lights strung along her superstructure blazed into life, creating shimmering pools in the surrounding water. Overhead, the lesser lights of the tropic stars peeped down.

The stewards spread the word through the lounges and smoking rooms that the decks were no longer fog-bound. Passengers surged up companionway steps. The dinner hour had come and gone and viands had been consumed. The *Mandarin* patrons were in a mood for revelry.

The orchestra hastily assembled on the spacious promenade deck.

As the warbling of a hi-de-ho singer wafted across the high seas, the rails began collecting loungers. Deck chairs and tables were quickly claimed by those indifferent to the eerie display of phosphorescence that trailed the liner's wake like a blue-green comet of the deep.

One of those who displayed no interest in the luminous phenomenon of the sea was a scrawny, lemon-faced Chinese with curious gray eyes. He carried two small paper sacks to the promenade deck and settled himself onto the comfortable cushions of a deck chair. One, he balanced on his stomach. The other was placed within easy reach on the deck floor.

Busy crunching sounds soon came from the lounging Celestial. He had the look of a steerage passenger, so most of those who prowled the *Mandarin*'s decks paid him little heed.

The noises with which he went about his eating prompted the deck chairs on either side of the Asiatic to go unclaimed. Most passengers were interested in rest or romance. The noises the Celestial created were conducive to neither pursuit.

Had anyone bothered to take the empty chairs, a casual glance would have revealed the source of the noisy munching.

The Celestial was methodically digging handfuls of peanuts from the sack perched on his lean stomach, shelling them with a firm squeeze of his yellow fist, and popping the fruit of the nut into his mouth. The empty shells were deposited, a group at a time, into the waiting sack at his elbow.

The Celestial seemed to be pointedly minding his own business. Leaning back in a reclining position, he seemed to give casual passers-by no more than fleeting glances. His eyes rested most often on the twinkling, cold stars above, as if the Asiatic were communing with his illustrious ancestors.

On occasion, his soiled gray eyes flicked furtively toward a passing stroller, as if in an effort to recognize one in particular. They never lingered long.

Few returned the Celestial's gaze. One exception was Dr. Mawson Harper, who glared back as he passed by. The physician had evidently recognized the moon-faced lounger as the same individual who had dropped a peanut shell upon him as he had boarded the liner.

Suppressing a guilty look, the Celestial averted his eyes. Dr. Harper passed on.

One passer-by did hold the placid peanut muncher's attention longer than most.

Perhaps it was the man's flashy attire. He wore a suit that was too loud. His shoes were an unlovely yellow hue. The hat that surmounted his rather large head boasted a brim wide enough to possibly tempt a wheeling sea gull into alighting. It was of the variety designed to conceal the visage of the wearer.

The hat was not yanked down to conceal the man's features, however. In fact, he seemed entirely unashamed of them, which was remarkable, given the man's physiognomy.

The man's face seemed to be composed largely of out-thrust jaw. It was very blue, as if he were not in the habit of shaving. His hair was inclined toward the shaggy, and disordered strands of it hung low over alert sheep-dog eyes.

A few paces behind the hirsute man, a similarly dressed individual followed warily.

This man was shorter than the first by almost two heads, and walked with the light step of a dancer. He looked like a habitué of race tracks; possibly a washed-up jockey who had become a tout.

In contrast to the casual manner in which the first man strolled the deck, the latter walked gingerly, his gimlet eyes darting about. They passed over the peanut-munching Chinaman without a flicker of interest.

They were not typical vacationers, these two, so it was only natural that they attracted more than their share of curious glances.

One who took especial interest in the flashily dressed pair was a rather colorless young man who called himself Rex Pinks.

Pinks was no vacationer, either. He claimed to be the society reporter for the San Francisco *Comet*. His presence on the *Mandarin,* he explained to any who would listen, was a combination of business and discretion.

Pinks had written an unflattering piece on a wealthy San Francisco dowager—a woman whose husband was a big wheel in local politics—and the husband had raised hell with Pinks's editor, demanding that the reporter be fired.

The society desk decided that Rex Pinks should take advantage of the next departing liner. The Black Star Steamship Company had been only too happy to oblige with a complimentary cabin. The liner business was in a slump, and publicity was considered the best remedy.

Rex Pinks had been haunting the lounge and cabarets the better part of the day. The passengers had included the usual bored upper-crust specimens, none of whom Pinks, who was prone to seasickness, felt worth the trouble of a Pacific crossing.

Or so he had thought until he went topside and his eye alighted on a mysterious creature who kept her face obscured by a black veil. This vision of femininity kept company with a spry old duffer tricked out in a commodore's uniform whose sharp face was decorated with an Uncle Sam beard.

Intrigued, wan-looking Rex Pinks straightened his rather disreputable tie and sauntered up to the table where the pair seemed to be pointedly scrutinizing patrons as they passed by. This made Rex Pinks think of spies. He had always been an imaginative sort, and had expectations of writing a novel some day.

"Excuse me, miss," Rex Pinks said by way of introduction. "My card."

The spry old gent intercepted the proffered press card. He gave it a glance, grimaced, and said querulously, "Miss Vine does not desire press attention at this time, my good man."

"See here, grandpa," Pinks protested.

He wasn't quite certain what actually happened next. He had endeavored to step around the older man when something tangled his legs up. He fell. It was quite a spill. The air around him turned blue with profanity and the deck became quiet. The orchestra hastily launched into another tune. Dancing resumed.

"On your way, sonny," invited the old man.

Rex Pinks ashamedly picked himself off the deck. The reporter had had ideas of asking the mysterious vision to dance.

"I happen to be with the *Comet*," Pinks said, mustering all the indignation his wounded pride would allow.

"And I happen to be Miss Vine's press agent," returned

the old man, examining his dark cane critically. "If she should decide to grant interviews, you will be summoned to her presence."

The way the white-haired man said it indicated that this was about as likely as the *Mandarin* sprouting bat wings and flapping its harridan way to the moon.

Rex Pinks knew an awkward situation when he was embroiled in one, and gave the mysterious Miss Vine a tip of an entirely imaginary hat as he backed away from the table.

"My apologies," he said sincerely.

"Don't go too far," the mysterious Miss Vine said in a voice that made Rex Pinks's toes curl alarmingly. "You might walk past a scoop."

"And you might not," added the press agent darkly.

The young newspaperman was so intent upon not turning his back on the veiled woman that he backed into the flashily dressed man and his like-attired companion.

"Hey, what's the idea, mug!" the latter growled.

Rex Pinks had not always been on the society desk. He had come up the hard way. From the police beat.

The moment he heard the tough voice, his blood ran cold. He recognized that gravelly growl.

He managed to get his nerve under control as he turned around to look into the blue-jawed face of the man he had jostled.

"Good grief," he said apologetically. "I-I'm s-sorry."

"Get outta my way or you're gonna be sorrier," the blue-jawed man's diminutive companion said threateningly.

"Nix, Kitten," the blue-jawed one put in. "The guy wasn't lookin' where he was goin'. That's all. Ain't that right, guy?"

"Y-yes, s-sir," Rex Pinks stammered. "I'm s-so s-sorry, Mr. Wool."

"I wouldn't go speakin' people's name too loud, guy," the blue-jawed one growled, low-voiced.

"Got it," said Rex Pinks, backing away in the opposite direction.

* * *

This naturally brought him back into the vicinity of the mysterious veiled woman, Miss Vine, and her graybeard of a press agent.

"You know who that was?" he blurted, the earlier altercation all but forgotten. "Delbert J. Wool."

"I fail to recognize that name," commented the white-bearded one in a supercilious tone of voice.

"Fuzzy Wool!" Rex Pinks breathed. "He's quite the tough guy."

"A gangster?" asked the woman, interest in her vibrant voice.

"Well, no, not exactly," Pinks told her. "More like an adventurer. He used to guard rum runners during Prohibition days. The little guy with him, believe it or not, is his bodyguard, 'Kitten' Borzoi. Wonder what they're doing aboard this floating Chinese tea shop."

"Probably looking for excitement," said the mysterious Miss Vine. "I know I am." She sounded very bored.

Rex Pinks stole a sidewise glance at her hidden profile.

The veiled woman seemed to be looking in the direction of the Chinese gentleman who was busily consuming peanuts. Or perhaps her hidden gaze was focused on the short, self-important-looking bantam of a man strolling in their direction. He was a rather striking individual, owning to the black streak running through his crisp white hair and the white one bisecting his natty Van Dyke.

The *Comet* scribe recognized the latter as Dr. Mawson Harper, whose charity work in the Far East had garnered him no little ink.

He was about to inquire of the girl if she knew Dr. Harper, when a commotion drew his eyes in the direction of the starboard rail.

Some one screamed. A woman. Another voice joined in. The sound was choked, inarticulate.

That person sobbed out, "That man! He fainted!"

Which made Rex Pinks wonder what all the fuss was about. People do not ordinarily react with horror at the sight of a fainting man. He bolted for the starboard rail, the mysterious Miss Vine and her press agent only a step behind.

For a graybeard, the press agent was making good time. He was actually keeping pace with the reporter, sprinting with his cane held high. It was the cane that had earlier tangled up his legs, Pinks realized.

Miss Vine was no slouch, either. Rex Pinks found himself rapidly overhauled. If nothing else, the girl was an athlete.

She also knew her mind.

A knot of passengers had gathered around the stricken passenger. Miss Vine waded into them with a will, shoving where she had to, until she reached the fainting man's side.

"Who is it?" Rex Pinks demanded, struggling to gain the stricken man's side. The latter lay supine on the still-slippery deck. He had fallen face-downward. A wormlet of blood crawled out from his nose where it had flatted against the deck, the weight of the man's head having compressed it.

Rex Pinks swallowed his question. He did not need an answer. The fallen one's flashy attire told him all he needed to know of the fainted man's identity.

"Fuzzy Wool!" Pinks gasped in surprise.

Bending over the fallen one was the adventurer's bodyguard, Kitten Borzoi. The man was frantic. He was trying to shake his employer back into consciousness.

"Boss! Boss!" he moaned. "What eats ya? Don't be like this!"

He looked up, his features twisted with emotion.

"Somebody call a sawbones, pronto!"

Remembering Dr. Mawson Harper, Pinks craned his neck in an effort to locate the physician.

"That's queer," he muttered. "He was just here a minute ago."

"Who?" Miss Vine wanted to know, expectation transforming her languid attitude.

"Dr. Harper," Pinks supplied. "He's a charity doctor."

"Oh," said Miss Vine, interest departing her voice.

"Wasn't that who you were staring at a moment ago?" Pinks asked pointedly.

"Not really."

The aloof Miss Vine was looking down the deck. Pinks saw the influx of passengers, drawn by the excitement.

* * *

There was one exception: the Chinese lounger, seated not far distant. He was attempting to polish off his bag of peanuts.

His impassive gaze was directed toward the starboard rail, but he displayed no outward desire to investigate further.

"That who you were watching?" Pinks asked on a hunch.

"You're a nosy sort, aren't you?" the girl asked.

Rex Pinks grinned. "I'm a reporter, remember? Nosy is my middle name."

"Watch it doesn't get chopped off," warned Miss Vine, folding her arms. "Your nose, that is." It was quite cool on the *Mandarin*'s starboard side and she wore a light spring coat to ward off the chill. She thrust her hands into the garment's front pockets. Although her veiled eyes were indiscernible, Rex Pinks was certain that they were trained on the nearby Celestial.

Abruptly, the Chinese lounger gathered up his paper sacks and moved down in the direction of the commotion. It was as if he sensed the scrutiny he was under.

Miss Vine looked away, Pinks noticed. He followed suit.

Still hovering over the body, frantic Kitten Borzoi was in the process of turning his employer over onto his back, which disclosed the odd bluish tint that his sheep-dog face had acquired.

This brought audible gasps all around.

"He's blue as an iceberg," Miss Vine blurted out.

"Where's that doctor?" Kitten yelled in horror.

Pinks, puzzled by the absence of Dr. Harper, detached himself from the crowd. There was no sign of the goateed physician. Throwing his head back to examine the upper deck, Pinks noticed the Chinaman had taken up a position where he could see the excitement without having to rub elbows with the growing crowd. He had set his paper sacks on the gleaming rail and was again working through his stash of peanuts. His oddly-gray eyes looked no more alert than those of a somnambulant cat's.

Pinks raked the upper deck with his gaze. Except for the loitering Oriental, it was virtually deserted on this side. He decided to check for Dr. Harper below deck, and started for a companionway.

As a result, he missed what happened next.

But he heard it—or the aftermath, rather.

A man said hoarsely, "Get back! It's happening again!"

Pinks doubled back. The crowd was still gathering, so he had his work cut out for him. By the time he had wormed through the throng, the spry press agent was down on one knee, endeavoring to roll the limp form of Kitten Borzoi off that of Fuzzy Wool.

Kitten Borzoi's face was only slightly bluer than that of his erstwhile boss, whose coloring shaded more to aquamarine.

"What happened?" Pinks demanded of no one in particular.

"The little guy was trying to help the other one," a man ventured. "Then he grabbed at his face all of a sudden and plopped across the first guy."

"Huh?" grunted the wan-faced society reporter, looking around for the mysterious Miss Vine. He spotted her moving purposely back toward amidships.

Catching up, he said, "Looking for anyone in particular?"

"None of your business, thank you,'" she snapped.

Pinks shrugged, but kept pace. He noticed that the girl seemed to pay particular attention to the deck chairs as she passed them.

"If you're looking for a certain peanut-munching Oriental," Pinks offered, "I'm the lad to ask."

Miss Vine stopped abruptly. She whirled. "Then spill it, buster," she said sharply.

Pinks stepped out of her range of vision so she was looking past and in the direction where Fuzzy Wool and Kitten Borzoi had, evidently, fainted.

He indicated the upper deck with a jerk of his thumb.

"There," he said smugly.

The mysterious Miss Vine tilted her head back. Pinks tried to peer past her veil, but the mesh was too dense.

"Ah-hah!" said Miss Vine, charging for the handiest companionway. "Wait here while I toss him down to you."

"Nothing doing," said Rex Pinks. "Where you go, I go."

He had cause to regret his bold statement a moment later.

There was a companion amidships. Miss Vine was making for it, her eyes on the lounging Chinaman. The Chinaman happened to look in her direction—their direction, actually.

He brought his hand up to his mouth, presumably to swallow another handful of shelled peanuts. He held his hand before his mouth even after he started chewing. He might have been seasick.

"I don't like the way he's looking at me," Miss Vine muttered, ducking into the dark maw of the companion.

They had taken no more than three steps when the mysterious Miss Vine abruptly gasped, faltered, and, with a frantic flurry of limbs, shucked off her coat, frock, turban, and veil as she reversed direction.

They made a disordered trail to the starboard rail, where Miss Vine lost no time in plunging into the wrinkled waters of the Pacific with a great splash.

The society reporter caught a fleeting glimpse of a trailing object following close behind. It was very long and very green and flapped a ragged tail behind it like a serpentine comet.

Whatever this object was, it executed a sharp dive just seconds behind its apparent quarry. A single splash came over the rush of passing water.

Rex Pinks had been a reporter long enough to have lost most of his illusions—but not, as yet, his chivalry. He started for the rail, working his tie loose. Determination was written on his pale, dissolute features.

This resolute expression turned to startlement when something big and bronze flashed out—seemingly from nowhere—and bowled him over.

Rex Pinks yelled "Hey!" and sat down hard.

As he was picking himself up, he heard another splash—larger than the one that had accompanied Miss Vine's plunge into the drink.

He jumped to the rail, peered down.

There was a moon, so there was enough glitter of

moonglade on the dimpled, inky sea to show several floating objects.

Among them was a train of blond hair. It floated, disembodied, tendrils of hair spreading in all directions like a yellow jellyfish.

There was no sign of the body that should have been attached to the hair—no sign of any life at all.

IX

TARZANA

Doc Savage had grabbed a life preserver before vaulting the *Mandarin's* rail. He let it slip from his strong fingers as he went into his dive, and it struck the water a split second before his mighty form.

The bronze man hit the cold Pacific on a dive so shallow his remarkable hair barely got wet. When his head bobbed up, it began shedding moisture like the proverbial duck's back. It was a peculiar quality of Doc's metallic skin and hair, this.

Doc treaded water, his flake-gold eyes roving the surrounding sea. The life preserver floated at hand.

The *Mandarin,* as tall as a ten-story house, plowed on past. But the bronze man seemed unconcerned about that.

A voice cried. "Man—I mean woman—overboard!" It was Rex Pinks's voice, already sounding distant. The liner's horn gave a hard blast. Her thrumming engines slowed. Still, momentum carried her deep into the night. The steaming leviathan would continue more than a mile before she could safely come about.

Doc Savage spotted the blond hair bobbing near by. He set out for it, grabbed the thing, and lifted it clear of the water.

The underside of the scalp was netting. A wig. There was even a maker's label: "Patricia, Inc."

Doc flung the waterlogged thing away, his eyes stark.

There was no sign of the body that had been attached to the hairpiece. The bronze man jackknifed into the water.

He spotted the faint yellow glow first. It was dwindling. Something intercepted it, and he lost sight of it. Then it reappeared, like a yellow bone in moonlight.

Doc redoubled his efforts. Feet kicking, his mighty hands strained before him.

He discerned the girl's ankles only when they were a few feet in front of him. It was that dark under the water.

The bronze man grasped one ankle. It kicked back at him. He retained his grip, arresting the downward course of the diving girl. Pulling, he got hold of a trim wrist, and levered the swimmer around.

There was a brief, underwater struggle. Very brief. Doc played the beam of his flash on his own grimly metallic features, and the other became quiescent.

Neither one of them had much air in their lungs, and the Pacific is very deep. The girl was forced to kick toward the surface.

Doc followed. Once, he cast a hasty glance downward. The ghostly arm was only a dim shape now. It seemed to fold and collapse, as if the corrosive action of salt water robbed it of life.

It did not follow them back.

When Doc's head broke the surface, he found himself face-to-face with a rather attractive young girl whose hair, burnished by moonlight, was just as bronze as his own. Her eyes, of unusual golden tint, narrowed at him.

"I was wondering when you'd stick your oar in," she said tartly.

"Miss Vine?" Doc said dryly.

"As in Hollywood and Vine. But you may call me Tarzana," she added. "It's a moniker Ham hung on me."

"Ham is the one of the white beard, I take it," said Doc Savage, bringing the life preserver between them for support.

"The very same." The bronze-haired girl blew brine off her delectable lips. "Say, Doc, where have you been? I've had my eye peeled for you ever since we left port. I was beginning to think you'd been left behind."

"Later," Doc said, casting an eye in the direction of the *Mandarin,* whose engines were coming to a dead stop.

Some one went to work on a lifeboat davit. All liners on the Pacific run are equipped with quadrant gravity davits which enable a single person to accomplish the tricky task of lowering a lifeboat into the water.

Three seamen were attempting it, and for some reason they were having their difficulties. It might be suspected that each had visions of heroism he was unwilling to share.

"Care to swim for it?" Doc suggested.

"Sure," Pat said, teeth chattering.

"It will be warm aboard the ship," Doc said, as they fell into a brisk dog paddle.

"That's not why my teeth are chattering," said Pat, who was actually Patricia Savage, Doc's cousin and only living relative. "Did you see that spook of a—*thing*—that was chasing me?"

"It was identical to a pair of apparitions I encountered in San Francisco."

Between breaths, Doc Savage related his experience in Jason Baird's office and the incident in which his taxi had been pursued through the fog-bound streets of San Francisco by a tenacious glowing arm without attached body. He used few words, but the picture they painted was so unnerving that Patricia Savage shuddered noticeably.

"Was it real?" Pat wondered at one point.

"Our breath might be better saved for the swim," Doc told her.

A boat got down into the water at last. It wasn't the one the seamen were struggling over. They were still at that.

This boat had a single occupant. He let the lines run out and fell to tugging the pullcord of the motor. It came to life on the third pull and the lifeboat began puttering in their direction.

Doc helped by bringing out his tiny generator flashlight once again. It was waterproof in addition to being generator-powered. He thumbed it on. The beam made a fair lighthouse in miniature.

When the motor boat came alongside, they recognized

the man at the tiller. The dark cane balanced across his knees gave his identity away.

"Ham!" cried Pat Savage. "Brother, am I glad to see you!"

"Are you all right?" Ham asked anxiously. He still wore his long white beard, and when he bent over to assist Pat into the launch, it dipped in the water, began to grow heavy with brine. The elastic holding it in place bowed downward with the strain.

Pat laughed. It was a laugh of relief. "Watch the whiskers, Santa!"

Ham yanked the false whiskers free, revealing his sharp-featured but intelligent face and wide, mobile, orator's mouth, and helped Pat over the gunwales in the accepted precautionary manner. The launch did not capsize, although it tipped precariously.

Doc clambered aboard next. He still wore his outlandish Manchu garb, although not the facial disguise.

Ham, who was in reality Brigadier General Theodore Marley Brooks, a member of Doc Savage's band of assistants and by reputation one of the finest lawyers Harvard had ever matriculated, was resplendent in his white commodore's uniform.

For her part, Pat Savage wore a water-soaked garment that left little enough to the imagination and seemed to have once kept a live tiger warm.

"My," Pat remarked ruefully, glancing about the boat. "Aren't we the merry band?" She laughed again, musically this time.

"I assume there is a purpose to that getup, young lady?" Doc asked in a disapproving tone.

"Sure is! I happen to be Miss Tarzana Vine, of Hollywood. On my way to the Philippines, there to shoot my latest picture, *Tiger Girl of the Jungle*."

"We figured if we couldn't spot you ourselves, Doc," Ham put in, "Pat was going to appear in that rather fetching garment, as a kind of publicity gag."

"Assuming the stunt would draw me out, eh?" Doc said.

"Something like that," Pat admitted cheerfully. "And it

was a good thing I had it on, or I'd be in an embarrassing way right about now."

Doc Savage fixed his beautiful young cousin with his intent flake-gold eyes. "I thought I told you to stay out of this, young lady."

"What else is new?" Pat said, unconcerned. "And don't get so snooty about it, Doc. If it weren't for my passing along Jason Baird's request for help, there wouldn't be any excitement for me to horn in on. So there."

A searchlight sprang to life along the *Mandarin*'s bridge rail. It raced along the wrinkled black back of the ocean and fixed them with a radiance so bright that all three lifeboat passengers had to shield their eyes.

It was at that point that Pat thought to ask a question. "So where is Jason Baird, anyway? Ham and I couldn't hunt up hide nor hair of him, and believe me, we prowled that ark looking."

"Jason Baird," Doc Savage explained, "appears to be in the ship's morgue."

"Oh," said Patricia Savage, the enthusiasm leaking from her voice. It was a very small voice now and she had no more questions until after they had been hauled back aboard the *Mandarin*.

Captain Gooch met them on the deck. Seamen put a major effort into keeping the passengers at bay, among them a very vocal Rex Pinks.

"This," growled Captain Gooch, "no doubt has an explanation attached to it."

"My cousin, Patricia Savage," Doc said by way of introduction. "And this is my associate, Ham Brooks."

Captain Gooch talked above their polite greetings, saying, "We have two more passengers in the morgue. Or at least they will be in the morgue once the crew gets done stowing them below. They are doing an excellent imitation of the Pacific Ocean."

"I do not catch your drift," Ham said, clutching his cane.

"The two of them," Captain Gooch said, "are very blue

and very, very calm. Which is more than I can say for the rest of my passengers."

"There is an explanation for what has happened," Doc Savage started to say.

Pat jumped in. "I'll say there is! Captain, if you want to nab the killer of those men, just look for a Chinese with the smell of peanuts on his breath!"

This brought a doubtful look from the captain.

"It's not as crazy as it sounds," Pat insisted. "I'm not sure how he was doing it, but somehow he was using all that peanut munching to hide what he was really up to."

Doc said, "He was blowing tiny glass capsules of some poison through a small tube concealed in his fist. The poison seems to vaporize shortly after being absorbed through the pores of the victims. It was the same method of murder which claimed the life of the man identified as Jason Baird."

Captain Gooch started incredulously. He rocked back on his heels. The way one side of his blunt jaw was working, he was masticating the inside of his cheek—a habit some persons lapse into when subject to strain.

Captain Gooch was plainly under strain now.

"And how do you come by this information all of a sudden?" the skipper asked, tight-voiced.

"Before Pat went overboard, I was down in the morgue examining the body identified as Jason Baird," Doc explained patiently. "I found clear traces of poison on his face. I have yet to identify it, but it seems to arrest heart action."

"Well, for your information, my ship's doctor and that Dr. Harper both agree the two fresh corpses got that way from heart attacks," Captain Gooch said levelly.

Doc shook his head. "Induced by poison. I witnessed a similar murder on the plane from New York. In that case, the capsule was meant for me. But the killer's aim was poor. He felled the pilot instead. By the time I caught on to the truth, the killer was dead—a victim of his own poison, which produces a bluish cast that lends credence to heart attack diagnoses. Probably, he committed suicide."

"Some one is trying to keep you out of Jason Baird's troubles," Pat said excitedly. She seemed actually delighted at the prospect. Pat liked trouble.

"Think he swallowed one of his own capsules by accident?" Ham wondered, his dark eyes aglow.

Doc did not answer. Instead, he said, "Captain Gooch, I suggest the ship be searched for the Oriental Pat saw."

"I got a good look at him, too," Pat said energetically. She reached under the short skirt of her tiger-skin garment and pulled out a single-action six-shooter such as might have sent Jesse James to his just reward. She pulled back the hammer—the trigger of the antique weapon had been filed off—and it made a warning sound like a walnut that had been stepped on. "So I know exactly who to aim this cannon at."

"There will be no shooting on my vessel," Captain Gooch said angrily. He moved out his jaw and added, "And you might explain what you were doing overboard, Miss Savage."

At that moment, the first mate came striding up.

"Cap'n, there are three tough guys demanding to know about the dead passengers," he said. "Claim they're friends of Wool and Borzoi."

"Let's get their story, then," Captain Gooch growled. He turned smartly on his heel and marched for the morgue, adding, "Next, some one will inform me we have pirates in the bilge."

"Ranty, isn't he?" Pat murmured as she, Doc, and Ham followed in the captain's wake.

"It might be better not to antagonize him," Doc cautioned. "We will need his cooperation if we are to get to the bottom of this mystery."

"You're one to talk," Pat scoffed. "I noticed you didn't volunteer anything about that spooky hand that tried to chase me clear down to Davy Jones's locker."

"As I recall," Doc put in, "you were chasing *it* when I caught up with you."

"I guess I shook it off when we hit the drink," Pat said thoughtfully. "I don't quite have it all clear in my mind, but when I found myself under water, it was still following me. It reminded me of a yellow shark. I guess I discouraged it somehow, because it decided to head for the ocean floor. Whatever it was, spook or not, it doesn't corner very well."

"I, for one," said Ham Brooks, "would like to see this phantom arm you claim to have seen."

"Claim, my sweet aunt," Pat snorted. "It chased me clear over the rail."

Down in the morgue, the ship's physician was having a hard time explaining the sudden deaths of Fuzzy Wool and Kitten Borzoi, notorious hard-boiled adventurers.

"I tell you, they suffered heart attacks," the medico was protesting.

"Heart attacks, nothing," a reedy voice retorted hotly. "They were never sick a day in their lives—both of 'em. They were bumped off, I'm tellin' you."

"See here now!" Captain Gooch called out, striding down the corridor. "What is the meaning of this?"

The men—there were three of them—had the ship's physician surrounded just outside the closed morgue door. The doctor was very pale. The trio towered over him, their faces hard and antagonistic.

When they turned, they hastily backed away from the flustered medico. Perhaps it was the sight of the captain, bedecked in his gold braid and brass buttons.

The imposing specter of the bronze figure that was Doc Savage might possibly have been a motivating influence as well. The trio showed immediate symptoms of nervousness.

"We're friends of Fuzzy and Kitten," the one with the reedy voice said. "I'm Alva Nally." He jerked a thumb in the direction of the other two. "This here's Joe Knopf and Shad O'Shea."

Joe Knopf was the shortest of the trio. His lean head jerked about nervously, suggesting a worried ferret. Shad O'Shea ran more to muscle and bulk. He possessed a long, cadaverous face that brought to mind a gloomy dray horse that had lost its master, which conceivably the big man had.

"And this quarter of the *Mandarin* is out of bounds to passengers," Captain Gooch shot back.

Doc Savage stepped forward. "What do you fellows know about a passenger named Jason Baird?"

The men froze at the sound of that name. Shad O'Shea's rough features grew longer. The others fidgeted.

"Nothin'," Joe Knopf said thickly. "Never heard of the guy."

"These men are lying," Ham said instantly.

"Maybe they need a little old-fashioned persuasion," said Pat, spinning the cylinder of her six-shooter. It made a clicking like a rattlesnake stirring.

A long-legged stork of a man came gliding down the passage, then. He was brought up short by the sight of Doc Savage and the others. Even to the most undiscerning eye, it could be seen that he bore the same hard stamp as the trio headed by Alva Nally.

Furtively, the human stork caught the eye of Joe Knopf, made a sign with a long-fingered hand, and withdrew.

Knopf hissed to his friends. "Chick wants us."

"I think we'd better be on our way," Alva Nally said hastily.

"Not so fast!" Captain Gooch thundered.

"Let them go," Doc Savage suggested.

"Yeah," quipped Alva Nally. "It's still a free country, ain't it?"

Reluctantly, Captain Gooch stepped aside as the hard-bitten trio joined up with the fourth man and they made quick time to the companionway leading to the upper decks.

"Those scuts bear watching," Captain Gooch said thoughtfully, after they had gone. The skipper began turning around to confront the bronze man. "Now, Savage—" he began to say. His mouth went slack. For the mighty Man of Bronze had vanished.

Ham Brooks and Patricia Savage added their gasps of surprise. The bronze man had been hovering behind them until just a moment ago.

"Now where did *he* go?" Captain Gooch thundered.

"I would say," Ham Brooks drawled, "Doc has decided to follow your advice."

"And what advice is that?" Captain Gooch roared.

"He merely has gone to watch the scuts."

X

THING WITHOUT ARMS

The liner *Mandarin* was finally under way once more, and her innards throbbed to the sounds of her mighty engines.

This constant sound helped Doc Savage trail his quarry unsuspected. The quartet consisting of Alva Nally, Joe Knopf, Shad O'Shea and their unidentified stork-legged confederate had hastily fled down a cross-ship passage.

The bronze man had divined their path. The passage was the handiest egress from the area of the morgue. Doc had left the others by a different direction, whipped up a companion, and, through a series of rapid shortcuts, gained the passage.

There was no sign of his quarry. The bronze man had not expected the four to linger long.

Doc was negotiating this cross-ship passage when he became aware that he was being followed.

The person doing the skulking was employing stealth. He hung back carefully. When the shadower stepped, he took care with the placement of his feet, walking neither on tiptoe nor the balls of his feet, but pressing his shoe soles down squarely.

It was very effective. Doc Savage did not catch on immediately. He had traversed nearly half of the *Mandarin*'s capacious width before his supersensitive hearing apprised him of the measured footfalls following close behind.

There was another sound mixed in with this. An odd one. It was a soft, whispery sound, a rustling. It sounded like nothing the bronze man had ever heard before.

Doc pretended ignorance of this. He continued walking as before. One fine-textured bronze hand drifted up to the wooden buttons of his scarlet Manchu tunic. Under the garment he wore his multipocketed vest. In addition to containing a host of useful items, it was lined with a chain mail of the bronze man's invention, which combined the useful properties of being light in weight and flexible. It was proof against anything short of military-caliber bullets.

Doc Savage carried any number of gadgets in his trick vest. They ranged from the simple to the complicated. The contents of his vest changed from time to time, depending on the situations the bronze man expected to encounter.

One item which Doc habitually carried was a collapsible optical device which, by changing lenses, could be converted from a tiny but powerful telescope to a microscope or periscope.

Doc brought this out, and with one hand, fiddled with it until he had a tiny, round mirror attached to the thin black telescoping tube.

Pretending to notice that one of his buskin laces had become undone, Doc paused, and stooped to attend to this.

The footfalls halted. And with it the whispery rustling.

On one knee, Doc maneuvered the tricky optical mirror until it reflected the passage behind him.

The passage was not well lit. The wall lamps were shaded bamboo paper, for atmosphere. They shed little direct light, and what did leak out left zones of darkness between the well-spaced lamps.

A figure had come to a stop in one of those crepuscular zones. It stood immobile, a weird, shadowy thing.

There were several things wrong with the figure, Doc discerned through the reflecting mirror.

It was rather short, almost stunted, the shoulders shriveled. The main part of it was a kind of cone. There were no legs to be seen. The head was too large, grotesquely so. And it seemed to taper upward, as if the shadowy thing was being poured down from above, the way sand filters down through the narrow neck of an hourglass. The exact point where it left off and darkness began was impossible to glean, even by Doc Savage's practiced orbs.

Most strange was the manner in which the nebulous figure's arms hung at its side. They seemed thin, shriveled, unreal.

When circulating air pushed out by the ventilation system touched them, they swayed in a manner that was lifeless and unnatural.

Doc Savage straightened, having observed as much as good sense would permit. He continued on.

The whispery rustling resumed, soft footfalls trailing him like careful mice.

The bronze man quickened his pace to put as much distance between himself and the pursuing entity.

There was a companionway at the end of the tunnel.

Doc floated up the companionway stairs. This brought him to B Deck, portside.

There, he paused. The whispery rustling continued. His pursuer was mounting the stairs with methodical deliberateness.

Somewhere, the ship's bell rang eight bells. Eight bells. The end of first watch. Midnight.

The deck was dark. The moon was on the other side of the rakishly slanted funnels. Shadows pooled and clotted everywhere, like crouching spiders of the night.

Stateroom doors lined the inner wall. All closed. Many, if not most, passengers had turned in for the night. One porthole hung open, inviting sea breezes.

Doc Savage hastened along the rail, found a wooden box which was locked with the padlock-and-hasp arrangement. It was a fire hose compartment—sizable enough to conceal a human form.

There was no time to pick the padlock. Doc grasped the hasp, twisted. Tendons like hawsers rolled and bulged along his powerful arms. The rivets holding the hasp to the wooden lid splintered, tore free.

Doc flung up the lid, scooped out the rubber-and-cotton hose, and deposited it in the shadow of the box, where it would not be readily discerned.

Stepping in, Doc pulled the lid closed after him. He waited, his sensitive ears alert.

Doc Savage lived a dangerous life. Peril seemed to dog his existence. It was a life he had accepted and a life which he pursued with vigor.

But he had not survived the perils of his calling by

being unnecessarily reckless. From the moment Doc became aware that he was being shadowed to the clever gleaning of the shadowy nature of the entity, the bronze man had exercised caution.

His secreting himself in the fire hose box might have seemed timid, even cowardly, to some. But the bronze man knew that some one—some thing—entirely out of the ordinary had taken an interest in him.

He did not know what it could be, but the memory of those grasping, sickly, yellow phantom arms clawing for him was very vivid.

Doc listened intently as the soft footfalls came on deck, the silken, whispery rustle sounds a menacing accompaniment.

When he judged the creature to have just passed the hose box, Doc Savage prepared to spring out to ambush the thing.

Came a clatter of feet and a puzzled shout.

"What the hell!" a voice called.

Doc sprang erect, the force of his powerful lunge breaking one hinge of the box lid, which fell away with a clatter.

Great bronze hands reached out, took hold of a figure in the shadows.

"Hey!" shouted the figure. "Let me go, you!"

Doc had the figure by his upper arms. He pinioned them to the captive's side, to prevent the employment of weapons.

Still holding the captive, Doc frog-marched him into a shaft of moonlight peeping past a black funnel.

The leprous light delineated the features of a man. His pale, frightened eyes met Doc's flake-gold orbs, widened with recognition.

"I know you," he breathed. "You're Doc Savage!"

"What is more to the point," Doc said levelly, "is your identity."

"I'm Rex Pinks. With the *Comet*. I was with your cousin just before she went overboard. That *was* Patricia Savage pretending to be a Hollywood actress, wasn't it?"

"It was," Doc admitted, scrutinizing the captive. "Now you might explain what you are doing sneaking about this deck?"

"Not that it's any of your business," wan-faced Rex Pinks said defensively, "but I was following the weird Oriental."

"Weird?" Doc inquired.

"Let me go and I'll tell you," Rex Pinks said, squirming uncomfortably. "My arms are going numb."

"No tricks," Doc warned, releasing the man.

"Not from me," Rex Pinks promised.

Doc released the reporter.

"Look," Rex Pinks vouchsafed, "I may have been the only one who saw it clearly except for you and your cousin, but I *did* see that ghost arm."

"And?"

"Don't kid me, Savage. There's a swell story back of this, and I'm hunting it."

"How does that hook up with this so-called weird Oriental you claim to have seen?" Doc prompted.

"I'm coming to that." Pinks licked his lips, his eyes squinting up and down the deck. "After you and Captain Gooch went below, I got to hunting for that peanut-munching Chinese."

"I imagine half the crew is about that particular duty," Doc interposed.

"Yeah, but they're down in steerage, rousting a lot of innocents. I figured that would be the last place he'd be hiding. So I've been cruising the upper decks." Rex Pinks hesitated. "This is going to sound screwy, Savage."

"I am listening."

"I was mousing around and I turned a corner and saw this—this thing," Pinks breathed. "It was weird—a man. Or kinda like a man. He was dressed in some sort of ornate Oriental costume of gold-and-green silks. He walked like an old ghost, hunched and soundless. I caught a glimpse of his face and—"

"Go on."

"Savage, his face was made out of *jade*!" Rex Pinks said breathlessly.

"Jade? Are you certain?"

"I'm a society reporter," Rex Pinks breathed. "Believe me, I know jade when I see it. And this creature's face was jade. Its expression was blank, inhuman. On his head was some kind of a crown, but like nothing you ever saw. It came to a point, and midway up the spire were other jade faces, just like the main one. They were set in a ring so each one faced a different direction. But that's not all."

Rex Pinks hesitated, as if summoning his courage.

"Go on," Doc said.

"This jade-faced thing had no arms!"

Doc Savage said nothing. The description the San Francisco reporter had given matched—with additional details—the weird, shadowy pursuer Doc Savage had been attempting to ambush.

"No arms—get it?" Pinks went on excitedly. "Remember that hideous yellow arm that we all saw? It was covered by a sleeve of green silk—exactly the same green color the thing I followed up here was wearing."

"If you followed it up to this deck," Doc asked in a level voice, "where is it now?"

Rex Pinks looked around. "Beats me. I kept my distance so as not to tip it off. When I got to the top of the companionway steps back there, I waited until I thought it was safe to come out. When I did, there was nothing. I was so shocked, I cried out. That's when you jumped me. Were you following it, too?"

"More like the reverse," Doc stated. The bronze man was studying the reporter's face for traces of deceit. He said, "I jumped out of the fire hose box when I judged the armless figure had passed only a little distance. But only you were on deck."

Rex Pinks frowned. "What're you saying?"

"Merely that the personage who followed me had no time to find a suitable place of concealment on this deck," Doc said.

Rex Pinks swallowed several times. "You don't mean—you can't think—"

"You are the only one here," Doc Savage pointed out in an unemotional voice. "And you were the only one with my cousin Pat when the detached arm attacked her."

"I had nothing to do with that!" Rex Pinks protested. "I was only after a story!"

"Then how do you explain the absence of an emerald-garbed Oriental with a jade face and no arms on this deck?"

"Maybe—maybe he jumped overboard," Rex Pinks suggested uncertainly.

"I would have heard a splash. As would you."

"That's right." Pinks looked about wildly, snapped his fingers. "He must have ducked into one of these staterooms, then. That's it! He's probably inside one right now."

The dissolute society reporter pulled away and began rattling doorknobs and banging on the superstructure walls. This brought a number of sleepy-eyed passengers to their doors.

None of them had jade faces.

There ensued some argument, which the sight of the Man of Bronze soon quelled.

After Doc had reassured the passengers and they had withdrawn, he pointed out an obvious fact.

"Did you notice how the doors all squeaked when they were opened just now?" the bronze man asked. "Salt-water action on the hinges. Had a door opened or closed, one of us would have heard it plainly."

"Maybe," Rex Pinks said vaguely. He was raking the superstructure for clues. "Too high to climb," he muttered. "There wouldn't have been enough time to do that, anyway."

His baffled eyes alighted on the solitary open porthole. It was not many yards distant from where Doc Savage had secreted himself.

"He wriggled through that porthole!" Pinks shouted exultantly, moving toward it.

When Doc caught up with the reporter, Pinks was endeavoring to poke his head into the open port. He craned his head around, trying to examine the stateroom interior. This activity did not go unnoticed by the stateroom occupant.

"What is the meaning of this!" a truculent voice shouted.

"Come out of there, you!" Pinks demanded. "The jig's up!"

This brought a prompt response. The stateroom door opened, squeaking audibly, and the glowering visage of diminutive, bird-boned Dr. Mawson Harper was thrust out. His virile black eyebrows were jumping angrily and his matching Van Dyke was quilled like a porcupine—evidently the doctor had been awoken from a sound sleep.

He took one look at Doc Savage standing there and lost his glower.

"Savage!" he said in surprise. Tying a bathrobe more tightly about himself, he stepped out, adding, "Whatever are you doing aboard this ship?"

"Never mind that," snapped Rex Pinks. "Who else is in there with you?" he demanded.

Harper looked confused. "Why, no one. And what business is it of yours, may I ask?"

"I'm a reporter," Pinks shot back. "Everything is my business."

"We trailed a marauder up to this deck," Doc Savage inserted, simplifying facts somewhat. "He apparently vanished without a trace in the vicinity of your stateroom."

Dr. Mawson Harper took this in with the expression of a man who had been stung on the nose by a bee.

"I am alone. If you doubt me," he said promptly, "just have a look."

Rex Pinks burst into the stateroom almost before the invitation had been vocalized.

He lost his eager expression once he was inside. The stateroom was a parlor-bedroom-bath suite. This was the parlor. It was no more opulent than a harem room.

There was a soft divan directly under the open porthole—the *Mandarin* boasted many soft sofas and chairs among its sumptuous accommodations—and it was unoccupied.

Rex Pinks raced through the remaining rooms. He came up with nothing tangible.

When he had rejoined Doc Savage and Dr. Mawson Harper in the parlor, he leveled an accusing finger at the porthole. "I tell you, he had to climb in through that porthole!"

"Nonsense!" Dr. Harper said flatly. "Such a thing is impossible."

"Yeah? Why is that?"

"Liner portholes are designed to be too small to admit the human body," Doc Savage pointed out. "This way no one is likely to fall overboard in rough seas."

Rex Pinks grunted and climbed up to the porthole to test this statement out for himself. He stuck his head out through the circular aperture. It went through easily enough—but his shoulders proved too broad to allow egress, and he was not a particularly broad-shouldered individual. In fact, he was rather skinny.

Sheepishly, Pinks climbed back down.

"I don't get this," he muttered uncertainly.

"I think we will learn no more here," Doc Savage said, stating the obvious. "Thank you for your time, Dr. Harper."

As they quitted the stateroom, Dr. Mawson Harper remarked to Doc Savage, "You know, I am beginning to question my belief that those men who died on that plane trip were, in fact, victims of heart attacks."

Doc paused. "What leads you to say that?"

"Why, the simple fact that there have been three more such victims on this ship," Harper imparted. "I have been puzzling it over, wondering if this were some new epidemic at work. Tropical diseases are my specialty. But now that I know you are aboard the *Mandarin,* another theory has occurred to me."

"And what is that?" the bronze man wanted to know.

Dr. Mawson Harper blinked. "Why, isn't it obvious? Some villain is trying to kill you by fiendish means."

"The possibility had crossed my mind," Doc said dryly.

"Indeed. Have you any idea what could be back of this?"

"That," Doc Savage told him, "remains to be determined."

XI

TIGHT LIPS

"I don't trust that bird!" Rex Pinks said gratingly as he and Doc Savage descended into a lower deck. "Did you notice his feet? He was wearing sandals, like a damn coolie."

"Dr. Harper is known for his charity work in the East," Doc offered. "It is not unreasonable for him to wear Oriental footgear. They are quite comfortable, actually."

Pinks noticed that the bronze man's progress was leading them deeper into the *Mandarin*'s metallic entrails.

"Where are you going?" he asked, puzzled.

"Purser's office."

"Mind if I tag along?"

"It would make keeping an eye on you that much more convenient," the bronze man told him without inflection.

"If you think I'm going to be the goat in whatever is going on," Pinks said tightly, "get that idea out of your head once and for all."

Doc Savage made no reply to that vehement assertion, merely striding on purposely. He cut a bizarre, gigantic swath in his Manchu costume, like a fixture out of the era of Genghis Khan, the great Asiatic conquerer.

The purser's office was situated on B Deck.

The lone purser idled in back of the wire cage, behind which was the ship's safe, where cash and other valuables were typically stored for the duration of the voyage.

It was also where the ship's registry of passengers was held for safekeeping.

Doc strode up to the cage and asked to see the *Mandarin*'s register.

The purser blinked, gulped, and mumbled apologies while he contacted Captain Gooch through an ordinary telephone of the European type, with the transmitter and receiver of a single piece.

The conversation was brief. After he had hung up, the purser retrieved the register from the big safe and pushed it through the slot in the wire cage, saying, "The skipper said it was okay, Mr. Savage, but he didn't sound none too happy with the idea."

Doc accepted the book—it was ponderous, bound in black leather—and paged through it until he had found what he was looking for. His golden eyes seemed to rest only a moment on the page.

The book clapped shut, stirring pale Rex Pinks's somewhat disordered hair. He frowned, having failed to catch a glimpse of the page to which the bronze man had turned.

Returning the book, Doc thanked the purser and asked, "Has a passenger named Chick Alfred stored any valuables in the safe—particularly gems of any kind?"

The purser consulted a ledger. He looked up. "No valuables at all," he said. Then he added, "But that particular passenger was here earlier, asking after another passenger. I had to break the news to him."

Doc Savage's flake-gold eyes showed a flicker of interest.

"News?"

"He wanted to know which cabin belonged to Jason Baird," the purser explained. "I guess he didn't know the man was dead."

Doc Savage thanked the purser and turned away. Rex Pinks followed briskly.

"I didn't know there was a dead passenger—other than Fuzzy Wool and Kitten Borzoi," he ejaculated. "What happened to this Baird?"

"Collapsed as he was boarding," Doc Savage explained. "You did not know?"

"I went to my cabin first thing," Pinks said glumly. "I get seasick easy. I find if I lay down a while, I get used to the rocking of the boat."

They walked along. Pinks looked behind him from time to time, as if concerned about skulkers.

"Who are we going to visit?" he inquired suddenly.

"The passenger, Chick Alfred."

"That name rings a bell." Rex Pinks started. "Say, wasn't he palsy with Fuzzy Wool?"

"They were associates."

Doc turned a passage corner, began mounting a companion.

"This is one of the things I hate about these tubs," Rex Pinks complained. "All this damn stair climbing."

Eventually, they came to A Deck. Doc Savage worked his way along the starboard side. The seas were running high, but there was surprisingly little rocking or heaving on the part of the *Mandarin*. She displaced nearly forty thousand tons, so her ebony prow knifed through the choppy water with little resistance.

Along the superstructure, only one porthole bled any illumination.

"What am I bet," Rex Pinks undertoned, "that our intended hosts have left a light on for us?"

"Too bad you have no one to take you up on that wager," Doc told him.

"What does Chick Alfred have to do with anything?" Rex asked. "Think he bumped off Fuzzy and Kitten?"

Doc Savage stopped before the stateroom door, knocked firmly.

The stateroom porthole—the one spilling yellowish light—popped out and disgorged an arm. At the end of the arm was clutched a big Army automatic. Its dark gullet was pointed in Doc Savage's approximate direction.

A harsh voice warned, "I can't aim so good from where I stand, but at this range, it won't much matter."

Doc Savage raised his mighty arms carefully. Rex Pinks followed suit, his sickly features going slack.

"I didn't bargain for this," he muttered uneasily.

The stateroom door popped open, and a storklike man showed his sallow face. His eyes went narrow at the sight of the Man of Bronze and the dissolute reporter.

"I assume you are Chick Alfred," Doc said.

"I ain't sayin'," the other growled. "What are you doing here?"

"I have some questions for you," Doc stated.

"What makes you think we got any answers?" asked the man, who was obviously Chick Alfred.

"It might be," the bronze man rejoined, "that between us we can get to the bottom of what is transpiring aboard this vessel."

Chick Alfred frowned. A cigarette hung slack off his lips, dripping ash.

"O.K.," he said. "C'mon in. But be snappy about it. We don't want what happened to Fuzzy to happen to us. Get me?"

"Amen, brother," said Rex Pinks fervently, as he followed the bronze man into the stateroom. The door clicked shut behind them.

The stateroom parlor was crammed with nervous individuals. There were four in all, including Chick Alfred and the man at the porthole, who was climbing down off the divan on which he had been standing.

"Say," Rex Pinks burst out. "I recognize these lads. Alva Nally. Shad O'Shea. And that's Joe Knopf, pulling his arm from the porthole. Where have you lads been that I hadn't noticed you aboard before?"

"And who the hell are you?" Chick Alfred wanted to know.

The society reporter drew himself up proudly. "Rex Pinks, with the *Comet*. I used to pound the police beat."

This seemed to impress no one except Rex Pinks, who lost a little of his cocksure manner.

Doc Savage said, "Let's start with your connection to Jason Baird."

"Nothin' doin'," Chick Alfred said. "That's our business."

"Tough guys," Rex Pinks snorted.

"They come tougher," ferretlike Joe Knopf allowed. "But not many."

Doc Savage pressed on.

"How is it you did not know Baird was dead until now?" he asked. "Surely, the news of the stricken passenger reached your ears."

"Sure, it did," Shad O'Shea put in. "But we didn't know

that was Baird. Hell, there's gotta be a couple thousand people on this oversized wash tub."

"That does not explain your interest in him," Doc pointed out.

Rex Pinks snorted. "Knowing their types, they probably had notions of lifting his wallet and dumping the body overboard."

"That ain't our style, guy," Alva Nally protested in his reedy voice.

"Yeggs who are sensitive about their reputations," Pinks laughed. "Haw. Now I've seen everything!"

At that, Shad O'Shea stepped up to the society reporter, blocked out his jaw, and lifted a case-hardened paw.

Rex Pinks threw up two bony fists in the manner of John L. Sullivan. His sickly features registered fright.

"I'm not afraid of you!" he insisted.

At which Shad O'Shea hooked a foot around the inside of the reporter's right knee and upset him onto the Oriental rug.

This brought a ripple of tension-relieving laughter from the others, which Doc Savage dispelled with a direct question.

"The deaths of Fuzzy Wool and Kitten Borzoi—who is back of them?"

The laughter trailed off like a garden hose that had been trod upon. Feet shifted. Fingers scratched at hair, throats, and behind ears.

"Earlier this evening," Doc continued, eying the uneasy quartet, "you were all interested in the bodies in the morgue."

"What of it?" grumbled Joe Knopf.

"I can arrange a viewing."

"They don't have the stomach for it," Rex Pinks inserted, picking himself off the rug. "Strictly drug-store cowboys, these boys."

That decided the quartet of hard cases. They expressed acquiescence in a variety of surly voices. A few choice words were vented in the society reporter's direction, but no violence seemed imminent.

*　*　*

That settled, Doc Savage escorted them down to the ship's hospital, which was now under guard.

The two guards conferred among themselves briefly after Doc Savage had stated the purpose of his visit. The sum of their exchange seemed to have mostly to do with the wisdom of disturbing Captain Gooch, who had evidently retired for the evening.

They decided that the skipper would be more upset by the intrusion into his slumber than by the invasion of the ship's morgue. Or at least, they believed, his wrath would be staved off until morning if they allowed the bronze man and the others into the morgue.

"It's fine by us if you want to see the stiffs," was the inelegant way one of the pair put it.

Doc Savage entered first.

The porcelain autopsy table was bare now. Doc Savage showed no astonishment at this.

His steady flake-gold eyes roved along the wooden morgue drawers. There were paper squares slipped into tiny metal frames just above the brass drawer handles.

The bronze man stopped when he came to one marked "D. J. Wool" in ink. Beside it was a drawer labeled "K. Borzoi."

Doc Savage hauled these out, exposing the covered upper bodies.

As the others crowded around, steam coming out of their open mouths, he peeled away the covering sheets.

The revealed faces of Fuzzy Wool and Kitten Borzoi were a particularly livid green—like jade busts.

"What done that to 'em?" Chick Alfred blurted out, his cigarette teetering off his loose lips. It struck the tiled floor like a tiny meteor sputtering to earth.

"Poison," Doc Savage stated quietly. "A species of poison which creates symptoms close enough to those of a heart attack that only a careful examination would disclose the truth. The blue coloring seems to progress to this shade of green as rigor mortis sets in."

"Then they was murdered!" Alva Nally grunted.

Doc nodded grimly. "The question is, by whom?"

No one offered any reply to that.

Doc Savage slammed the drawers shut and went to another. He yanked this out, to the squeaking of steel rollers. A bronze hand plucked off a draping sheet. He held it over the cadaver so that its face remained in shadow.

"Is this the man you know as Jason Baird?" he demanded.

"Yeah, yeah," Chick Alfred said quickly. "That's the guy."

"Interesting," Doc said, pulling the sheet higher. "Inasmuch as the label clearly indicates that this dead man was named Chen."

Rex Pinks pushed forward. His eyes went wide at the sight of the unmistakably Asiatic face Doc had exposed to the light.

"Huh!" he grunted. "That's no white guy!"

Doc pushed the drawer closed and went to another. This time, he exposed the true face of Jason Baird to the light. His face was as green as those of the others—if not more so.

"You have never seen the face of Jason Baird, have you?" Doc accused.

The four gunmen—for want of a better term, that was what they were—looked away sheepishly. Their attitudes were confused, tentative.

"Whoever killed Jason Baird also did for Fuzzy and Kitten!" Rex Pinks said wonderingly.

"Yeah," Shad O'Shea snapped. He prodded his barrel chest with a big thumb. "And whoever that bird was, he's gonna answer to us for what happened."

"What is the connection between Baird and your friends, Fuzzy and Kitten?" Doc asked.

"When we find out," Chick Alfred said meaningly, "we'll let you know. Thanks for the tour, bronze guy. It was swell."

With that, the four gunmen filed out of the morgue.

Rex Pinks gawked at the bronze man.

"You're just going to let them go!" he blurted.

Doc said, "It is clear that they are hiding something."

"Say it again, brother!" Pinks ejaculated. "But what are you going to do about it?"

"Nothing," Doc told him, starting off.

Rex Pinks exploded at that calm admission. "Nothing!" he howled. "I always heard you were quite the fire eater, Savage. What about figuring out who that armless spook was? He—or it—could be prowling the ship while we're standing here jawing." The society reporter was gesticulating as they walked along. He noticed that Doc Savage seemed to be bound toward a specific destination. "Where are we going, by the way?"

"I," the bronze man told him, pausing to look the flustered society reporter straight in the eye, "intend to retire for the evening. I suggest you do the same."

The bronze man continued on, leaving Rex Pinks standing slack-jawed in amazement.

XII

TALE OF THE OGRE

The solar orb, an angry ball that might have been kicked out of the crinkling aquamarine and cobalt that was the Pacific Ocean by an impatient Father Neptune, heralded the start of the second day of the *Mandarin*'s voyage to distant Hongkong, China.

Captain Gooch had arisen with the sun. He was now watching the spectacular colors of daybreak from the flying bridge in silence. The *Mandarin* skipper was partial to starting his day in the solitary cubicle that was the flying bridge.

Presently, First Mate Bill Scott ascended the narrow iron stairs and knocked on the partition door. His knock was timid. He knew how much the captain cherished his morning commune with nature.

"Permission to enter, cap'n," the First Mate called through the flimsy door.

"Enter, blast it," Captain Gooch said gruffly.

Upon entering, First Mate Scott offered a snappy salute

that touched the bill of his white dress uniform cap without disturbing its jaunty angle.

"No sign of that Chinese," he reported crisply. "It's like a haystack down in steerage. With none of the hay savvying anything—especially the whereabouts of our needle."

Captain Gooch scowled like a dried apple.

"Keep looking," he bit out. "We have three dead passengers to explain to the Hongkong office. I won't have the name of my good ship plastered all over the newspapers as a jinx."

"Yes, sir," the first mate said briskly, leaving the liner captain to his thoughts.

The search for the Chinese passenger who seemed addicted to peanuts had been intensified during the night, when prowling deck hands would not unduly alarm the passengers. But it had borne no fruit. With the coming of day, obvious searching would have to be curtailed.

Privately, First Mate Scott doubted that the Chinese would be brought to light before breakfast, so he made arrangements to calm the passengers' nerves.

Most oceangoing liners issue their own daily newspaper while on the high seas. The *Mandarin*'s was no mimeographed sheet, but a four-pager printed on a small printing press, filled with the latest news gleaned from around the world via ship-to-shore shortwave radio.

Going to the radio room, the first mate conferred with the radio operator whose responsibility it was to condense radio reports into copy for the ship's sheet.

"Sparks, I want something on page one saying that it was heart attacks that got all three of them," he instructed.

"Got it," said Sparks, who immediately got busy.

Within an hour, folded newspapers featuring this soothing item began appearing outside stateroom doors, on sterling-silver breakfast trays borne by snappy-looking stewards, and in the *Mandarin*'s two big dining salons.

One of the first editions to roll off the press was conveyed to the Royal Suite by a steward who was noticeable for two reasons.

One, he was very large. He looked like he belonged

down in the boiler room, bare to the waist and perspiring freely.

The second reason was the way he carried his tray—high and close to his face. He took great care to walk with the exposed side of his face close to the walls. The tray concealed the other side. That way, although his striking physique drew stares, his features went unrecognized.

Shifting the uplifted tray to the other hand—thereby concealing his face from the other side—the Herculean steward paused to knock on the door of the Royal Suite.

"Breakfast," he called.

"But I don't remember ordering—" a feminine voice started to say. The door fell open and Pat Savage peered out, looking annoyed. Her annoyance evaporated at the unexpected sight of her famous cousin.

"Doc! Where have you been? Quick, come in!"

The bronze man slipped into the stateroom, setting down the tray on an elaborate lacquered table.

"Swell digs, huh?" Pat said exuberantly. "It set me back a few shekels, but believe me, it will be worth it once things start to pop!"

"You might recall," Doc interposed, "that last time you mixed in an adventure, you nearly had your throat cut."*

"In my dictionary," Pat said tartly, "nearly is on the same page as never."

Pat Savage was a young woman who loved adventure. Whatever was in the Savage family blood that fostered a yearning for excitement and danger, she had a strong dose of it. Too much for the bronze man's liking. He had in the past gone to great lengths to steer his vivacious cousin out of the path of peril. Too often Pat stubbornly found her way clear to horn in on one of Doc Savage's adventures—as she seemingly had now.

"What do you know about Jason Baird's difficulties?" Doc inquired.

Pat lost a little of her enthusiasm at the sound of the deceased man's name.

"Not a whole lot, I freely admit," she said, suddenly

*Spook Hole

subdued. "I knew him through his sister, Maurine, who was a client at my beauty shop."

Pat Savage owned a combination beauty parlor and gymnasium on Park Avenue catering to an exclusive clientele that had made the bronze-haired young woman quite well-to-do in the year or so it had been open.

The bronze man looked interested. "Would that be the Maurine Baird known for her work on germ cultures?"

"That's her. She took off for China a few months back. What of it?"

Doc did not reply to that. Instead, he asked, "Baird said nothing of the nature of his troubles?"

Pat shook her head. "Only that he needed your help right away. He was very mysterious about it. Say, I just remembered! He said if anything happened to him to check the sole of his left foot for instructions. Did you find anything?"

"What makes you think I looked?"

Pat Savage put her hands on her shapely hips and cocked one eye at her bronze cousin.

"Don't kid me, Doc. I know you don't miss a trick. I would have barged into that ice chest of a morgue myself, but I was sopping wet, and wasn't about to catch my death. So fork it over."

With a sign of resignation, the bronze man produced the sheet of paper he had taken off the sole of the corpse identified as Jason Baird.

Pat accepted it and gave the lemon-juice-inscribed message a scan.

Her expression had lost of bit of its intensity of interest by the time she was done.

"Diamonds," she murmured, plainly disappointed. "Not a very big pot of gold at the end of this unhappy rainbow, is it? Did you find the sparklers?"

"Not as yet," Doc admitted.

"How about that sneaky peanut muncher?"

"He has not turned up as yet—although the ship's crew are still searching."

Pat Savage's attractive face acquired a peculiar expression.

"Any clue as to that claw of a thing that chased me off this barge?"

Doc avoided the question by saying, "There have been no further indications of that type."

"Well, what have you been doing all night, then?" Pat said in exasperation. "Sleeping?"

"As a matter of fact, yes."

The answer so floored Pat Savage that she took an involuntary step backward.

"Good grief! Please do not tell me that three blue-faced dead men and some missing diamonds aren't enough to stir your blood any more?" she explained. "I might just up and have a heart attack myself."

"We have at least one assassin on board this ship," Doc pointed out. "And there are near to two thousand persons aboard the *Mandarin,* counting passengers and crew. Finding one man will be task enough. Accomplishing this without falling victim to this insidious poison-capsule artifice will be a feat."

Pat jumped to her cabin telephone, scooped it up.

"I'll ring Ham in on this."

"Monk too, if he is on board."

Monk was Monk Mayfair, another of Doc Savage's group of five assistants.

"He is not," Pat said. Then: "Ham. Pat. Come a-running. Doc's here and he wants us to help him stir the stew."

Ham Brooks evidently occupied an adjoining cabin, because he came through the door almost before the phone receiver had been set back on its cradle.

The wasp-waisted lawyer was resplendent in fresh commodore's uniform. Since it was presumably now resting on the Pacific floor, his white beard no longer adorned his hawklike visage.

"Don't let cranky old Captain Gooch see you dressed like that," Pat clucked good-naturedly. "He'll think you're fixing to take over his command."

Ham looked injured.

"I suppose I have you to thank for Pat's presence on this ship," Doc said dryly.

Ham Brooks looked sheepish. "I can explain, Doc. Pat fibbed to me."

"I did not!" Pat flared.

"Well, she did not tell quite the complete truth," Ham amended."I was told that you needed your speed plane in San Francisco. I agreed to fly Pat out there."

"Well, you *might* have needed it," Pat rejoined.

"When we landed," Ham continued, "Pat had me search high and low for this Jason Baird. The local constabulary informed us that he was missing, and that you intended to book passage on the *Mandarin* regardless. So, we cooked up this Hollywood-actress-and-press-agent imposture, finagling the Royal Suite for Pat."

"Just to keep an eye on matters, Doc," Pat interjected.

The bronze man regarded the dapper lawyer with his weirdly compelling golden eyes.

"I distinctly told Pat that she was to stay clear of this matter," he pointed out.

"News to me," said Ham, unjointing his handsome cane, revealing it to be a sword cane. The blade work was excellent—Damascus steel.

"Where is Monk?" Doc asked. "He would hardly be left out of an affair such as this if he could help it."

Ham proceeded to fidget. "Ah, as a matter of fact, Pat did call him. I believe he had the exact time of our rendezvous wrong, for he failed to show up at our warehouse hangar at the appointed hour. We were forced to take off without him."

"I told Monk seven o'clock sharp," Pat insisted.

"That ape never could tell time properly," Ham said airily. He twirled his cane elaborately, which had the opposite effect than the one the dapper lawyer had intended. He looked as guilty as sin.

"You fake!" Pat snapped. "You called him back and changed times, didn't you?"

Ham colored, gulped. "I—"

Pat cast a jaundiced eye in the dapper lawyer's direction. "I *thought* you were in a bigger rush than usual to leave," she added, her tone tart.

"I imagine Monk will have some choice words for the two of you when this affair is over," Doc Savage said pointedly.

The bronze man changed the subject.

"It will be difficult for me to have free rein aboard this ship," he explained. "Especially in the heavily traveled passenger areas. Care to undertake some legwork?"

"Action. Swell!" Pat said, snatching up her tiger-skin costume. "Tarzana Vine at your service."

"One moment," Doc said, reaching for the scanty garment. The bronze man plucked an object from the orange-and-black striped pelt, held it up to plain view.

The others leaned in to make it out.

"That's queer!" Pat said, mouth pouting prettily.

Ham sputtered, "Is that—?"

"Yes," said Doc. "It appears to be a tiger's claw."

"How about that," said Pat. "I bought this rag at a costume shop, back in Frisco. Suppose it belonged to the original tiger? The one who donated the skin, I mean."

"It is," Doc said, "impossible to determine. Pat, exactly what happened when you encountered the disembodied arm that chased you into the sea?"

Pat frowned. "I started up a companionway, itching to get my hands on that peanut muncher. For some reason, there was no light. I remember brushing some one in passing."

"Rex Pinks," Ham suggested fiercely.

Pat shook her bronze head. "I think he was behind me," she said slowly. "I'm not certain. At any rate, that was when I saw the bony arm coming for me. It glowed in the dark. It was so frightsome, I lit out for the rail. But what does the tiger's toenail have to do with what happened?"

Pocketing the claw, the bronze man said, "Perhaps nothing."

Ham Brooks asked, "What do you want us to do, Doc?"

"Determine if there was a passenger who had to be helped up the gangway back in San Francisco," Doc related.

Pat brightened. "A cinch. But who is he, Doc?"

"I do not know if there is any such person," the bronze man admitted.

Pat drew her brows into a curvacious line. "Then why—"

Doc went to the door. "Also, as you travel about the ship, watch yourselves carefully. If you hear a whispery rustle of a sound, flee to safety. Do not attempt to fight the thing that is the source of it."

"What thing?" Ham wondered.

His question came too late. The bronze man had closed the door after him.

Pat Savage said ruefully, "Looks like we do our reconnoitering in the dark, figuratively speaking."

Although the liner *Mandarin* boasted two sumptuous dining salons abaft of the bridge, they were by no means equal to the task of seating the entire passenger list at one time.

Thus, there were two seatings for each salon. The first and second—called cabin—class passengers were permitted to breakfast at the first seating, which began promptly at eight o'clock.

It was nearly that hour now, and when Doc Savage emerged from the Royal Suite and his meeting with Ham Brooks and his cousin, Pat, he encountered great difficulty avoiding the influx of passengers toward the dining area.

There were a small number of elevators strategically placed throughout the liner. Although they were spacious, they were not practical for moving large numbers of persons between decks. Consequently, their use was discouraged except in the case of elderly or invalid passengers.

Doc Savage sought one of these out now. It was the most private method of reaching C Deck, and his own cabin, where he intended to change into less conspicuous garb.

Doc turned a corner and discovered bantam-sized Dr. Mawson Harper leaning on the elevator call button impatiently.

Instead of retreating, the bronze man pushed forward.

Dr. Harper started when he became aware of the bronze man's presence. So silently did Doc move that only his rather large shadow, intercepting light from the corridor door, betrayed his presence.

"Savage!" Dr. Mawson exclaimed, turning. "I did not hear you approach." He stroked his white-striped ebony Van Dyke thoughtfully. "Are you by chance taking first seating for breakfast?"

"No," Doc told him.

"Unfortunate, for I have something I would like to share with you."

"Yes?"

"I got to thinking about it last night. After that incident when your rather attractive cousin went overboard. I saw that frightful limb—although I did not see it very clearly, due to the darkness."

"The point, please," Doc prompted.

Dr. Harper gave the call button another impatient push. "As you know, my specialty is tropical diseases. I often do my research in the Orient. I have traveled extensively there."

The lift arrived. The doors parted and they stepped aboard.

The elevator was of the self-service type. There was no control lever; the passenger simply depressed the button which corresponded to the deck number. Dr. Harper pressed D Deck. Whining, the cage sank.

"I have been all over Asia," Dr. Harper continued. "China. Siam. Cambodia. Burma. It was in the latter country that I heard a rather fanciful tale that makes me think of that hideous floating arm of an apparition."

The elevator was slow. It creaked as it descended.

"Go on," Doc suggested.

Dr. Harper's voice sank an octave. "Have you ever heard of the Jade Ogre?"

"Eh?"

"The Jade Ogre," Dr. Harper repeated. "His Chinese name is *Yook Kweitzu,* which means the same thing."

"I have not."

"He is a being the coolies and rice farmers of Cambodia hold in superstitious awe. It is said that this Jade Ogre was a warlord of feudal days. A very wicked man. He had many enemies, and one in particular, the fabled Leper King of old Cambodia. This warlord sought to eradicate the Leper King, but his assassins were unequal to the task. The Leper King continually evaded the traps and snares set to claim his life.

"One day, this warlord who was to become the Jade Ogre in frustration beseeched the diety Siva—Hinduism reached Cambodia, as you may know—for the power to smite his enemy dead.

"And the diety Siva answered, saying to the warlord that if he cut off his arm, and threw it into a brazier as a sacrifice, he would receive in return the power to reach any point on earth and destroy his enemies.

"Being a wicked man, this warlord did this, offered his left arm to a headman, who lopped it off with a swift chop of his sword."

Dr. Harper kneaded one shoulder absently, as if in sympathy with the act of maiming he had described. He resumed speaking.

"When the arm was cast into the fire, and the stump of his shoulder healed, the warlord had a dream. He dreamed that the spirit of his amputated arm had flown out into the night to take the Leper King by the throat and had throttled him to death.

"When he awakened the next morning, or so the legend goes, word was brought to him that the Leper King was dead—strangled in his sleep."

"A rather fanciful tale, as you say," Doc commented.

"There is more," Harper said quickly. "With the Leper King out of the way, this warlord was free to take possession of his throne in a Cambodian city whose name is handed down as Bankor." The white-haired doctor paused. "You have knowledge of archaeological antiquities, Savage. Have you ever heard of Bankor?"

"That name," Doc admitted, "is unknown to me."

The elevator finally grumbled to a stop and Doc Savage permitted Dr. Mawson Harper to step off. The bronze man followed.

Dr. Harper paused to continue his tale, evidently relishing the telling of it.

"Natives I have spoken to swear it exists, deep in the rain forest. Whatever, this warlord grew in power and evil. Whenever anyone challenged his wicked reign, he had only to go into a trance and he would experience a vision of his enemy falling before his disembodied arm. Always, upon coming out of this trance, the enemy would be reported dead—throttled."

Dr. Harper paused. "This warlord was so taken by this hideous faculty, and made so many enemies as a result of his many cruelties, that he had his right arm cut off and consigned into the flames. Thus, he acquired double the power to slay his opponents.

"It was said that one day he whispered his secret to a dancing girl, unaware that she was a spy. This girl told others, and when it was made known that the warlord emperor could not send out his arms while awake, he was set upon in his very throne room. Lacking arms, he was helpless to defend himself, and he was carried bodily to a blazing brazier and cast into the flames.

"But the diety Siva, favoring this man, saw to it that he was not consumed. His face was destroyed, however. Thereafter, he wore a jade mask, fashioned to resemble that of Siva, and fixed in place by rivets of silver. Exiled, shriveled, and helpless, he repaired to his former temple stronghold, there to brood and in his sleep send out his unstoppable arms to deal with his enemies. Thereafter, he was known as the Jade Ogre, an armless thing with a face of imperial jade."

"A long time ago—if it ever happened," Doc pointed out.

"That is my point," Dr. Harper rejoined. "According to the legends, the Jade Ogre was given the gift of immortality by Siva, in return for the promise that he would project his mighty arms out into the world, slaying at will." Dr. Harper paused. His expression assumed an abashed look. "Of course, I am a man of science. I only pass this story along for its possible historical value. But you can see how what happened yesterday made me think of it. And for the life of me, I cannot explain that detached arm I saw. Can you?"

"Not as yet," Doc Savage told the medical man.

"Then you have an idea, I take it?" Dr. Harper asked, his Van Dyke seeming to bristle with interest.

They had been walking along a passage toward the main dining salon. It was rapidly filling with humanity—families, businessmen, and a smattering of society bloods—pouring down various companionways, intent upon partaking of the *Mandarin*'s breakfast fare. Rich smells of cooking eggs, bacon, and ham wafted out and caressed their nostrils.

Doc Savage came to a full stop. His head lifted; his attitude was one of intense alertness. Queer lights came into his strange flake-gold eyes.

The bronze man quickly excused himself and plunged into the tidal wave of passengers, leaving Dr. Mawson Harper to squint after him.

His optical efforts came to naught, however. The bronze man that was Doc Savage quickly melted into the crowd. His metallic head was visible briefly, but somehow—despite the fact that Doc towered over the tallest man in the crowd—it too was soon lost to sight.

XIII

A BOLT OF BRONZE

Patricia Savage was nothing if not a straightforward example of the gentle sex.

As soon as she had her cousin's blessing to mix into the mystery aboard the *Mandarin,* she checked the action of her big six-shooter and shoved it into a hand bag, which was altogether too large to be the ultra of fashion this year, but was commodious enough to swallow the well-worn revolver right down to its ivory grips.

"Now, Pat," dapper Ham Brooks cautioned, "let's not get carried away. We merely desire to ascertain a few facts on Doc's behalf."

"Facts, my foot," Pat said eagerly. "I aim to hunt me up the man, ghost, or devil behind this mystery. And when we meet, I intend to trade hot lead."

The dapper lawyer paled visibly. He knew Doc Savage's feisty cousin—knew also that the bronze man would hold him responsible if she sailed into harm. He thought fast.

"Aren't you forgetting something?" he inquired coolly.

Pat examined herself in a full-length mirror. She wore a

breezy summer dress that clung to her figure in such a way as
would cause a grizzled old salt to pile up on a reef if he had
the good fortune to cross her wake.

Pat looked up, her rather exquisite eyebrows puzzled.

"Your mystery-woman veil," Ham reminded.

"It doesn't exactly go with this frock, you know," Pat
pointed out.

"Hmmm. Perhaps you might resort to dark glasses,"
Ham suggested.

"You're not," Pat asked suddenly, "trying to stall me, are
you?"

"Jove, no," protested Ham. "It's just that if it became
widely known about the ship that the lovely cousin of the famous Doc Savage were aboard, it could lead to complica-
tions."

"I'll buy that," Pat allowed, skipping into the bedroom.
Rummaging sounds could be heard from that adjoining room.

Ham Brooks made a dive for Pat's hand bag, which
had been left on the arm of a divan. Holding his sword cane
under one arm, he dug out the six-shooter, broke the action,
and shook the cartridges into the vent pocket of his white
jacket.

Replacing the revolver, he whirled as Pat flounced back
into the room, stylish smoked glasses obscuring her eyes.
The sudden motion brought an audible clicking.

With alacrity, Ham shoved one hand into the pocket to
keep the heavy cartridges from knocking together and be-
traying his subterfuge.

"You resemble," Pat said suspiciously, eying Ham's
awkward pose, "Napoleon with a bad case of fleas."

"Shall we go?" Ham invited, tapping his commodore's
cap with the head of his cane.

Snatching up her hand bag, Patricia Savage preceded the
dapper lawyer out of the Royal Suite.

If she noticed that her bag was lighter by six shells, the
bronze-haired beauty gave no sign of it.

They collared First Mate Bill Scott amid the funnels
and ventilators and coilings of hose and rope that festooned the
sun deck. It was all but deserted at this early hour. Evidently,

that was the reason the first mate was conducting his search here.

"I say," Ham Brooks hailed the officer, "we would like a word with you, my good man."

First Mate Scott scowled when he saw them. He had self-control enough to mask the grimace after a moment, but his distrust for anyone associated with Doc Savage—the man who had given him such a runaround the day before—was impossible to completely conceal.

"I know who you two are—now," he said flatly.

"Watch me vamp this sourpuss," Pat undertoned as they drew near.

Pat Savage strode up to the man, bestowed upon him her most dazzling smile—the one that was ivory framed in rich bronze.

"We'll only take a moment of your time, captain—"

"Actually, I'm first mate," the other inserted.

"Was there a man brought aboard in San Francisco under difficult circumstances?" Pat asked pleasantly. "Either in a wheelchair or some other way that would indicate he was ill?"

The first mate did not have to think about that one for very long.

"There was," he offered reluctantly. "A Chinese gentleman. Three other Chinese helped him aboard. Why do you ask?"

"I wish I knew," Pat offered truthfully.

"Doc Savage asked us to look into this possibility," Ham Brooks explained. Then, shifting the subject, he asked, "Have you had any luck running down that cat-eyed peanut muncher?"

"That's what I'm doing up here," First Mate Scott said glumly. "Captain's orders are to search without getting the passengers all jumpy. So here I am."

"Where do we find this queasy Celestial?" Pat wanted to know, returning to the matter of the Chinese passenger who had to be helped aboard the *Mandarin*.

"I don't recall his name, but the chief steward should be able to tell you to which cabin he was taken."

"Thanks," Pat said brightly, turning on her heel.

Ham Brooks hastened after her, one hand still thrust into his pocket.

Finding the chief steward proved to be an undertaking.

He was not to be found in either of the dining salons, which were jammed to the ornate walls with breakfasters. Some one in the galley thought he might be found in his cabin. He was not in his cabin, but a passing steward thought they should look in the crew lounge.

The crew lounge proved to be utterly bare of occupants.

"What say we split up?" Pat said, turning to face the frustrated lawyer. All their tramping around had caused his outfit to acquire wrinkles. Ham fancied himself a modern-day Beau Brummell, and reacted to wrinkles with a horror usually reserved for flesh wounds.

"I think Doc would prefer that I keep an eye on you," Ham said paternally.

"Squirrel fodder!" Pat snapped back. "We can search twice as fast if we take opposite ends of this overdone hooker."

"Need I remind you that some one has already made an attempt on your life?" Ham pointed out sternly.

Pat yanked her six-gun out of her gaping hand bag and waved it about the air. "And need *I* remind you, Mr. Fancy Pants, that I can round off a fox's ears with this cannon?"

Ham Brooks paled. He opened his mouth to protest, but Pat beat him to his words.

"You take the stern," she said, "I've got the bow. And brother, do I intend to scour the scuppers."

With that vehement promise trailing behind her, Pat Savage quitted the crew lounge.

Ham Brooks spent a moment composing himself. He removed his cap and ran a natty white handkerchief across his perspiring brow. The dapper lawyer decided that his most prudent course of action was to tail the pretty trouble-seeker.

That proved difficult, inasmuch as Ham was dressed entirely in white—a color not exactly designed for skulking about in.

Almost as soon as he entered into the cross-ship passage outside the lounge, he was confronted with a dilemma.

"Starboard or port?" he muttered to himself, his head swiveling back and forth as he tried to see in two directions simultaneously.

He decided to go left—to the port side of the liner.

He had catfooted all the way to the companionway at the passage's port terminums when a storage room door clicked open and Pat Savage stuck her pretty bronze-haired head out.

Ascertaining that the passage was now clear, she glided out and moved toward a companionway that would take her into the *Mandarin*'s very bowels.

Grinning fiercely, she murmured, "Never trust a lawyer."

The matched pair of officers guarding the ship's morgue were only too eager to allow Miss Tarzana Vine to enter the morgue. They were not the same two as had given Doc Savage the same privilege the night before. That duo had required convincing. Pat had only to smile invitingly and sign one autograph for each of them to get her way.

If they harbored any resistance to the notion, Pat allayed that impulse with a bald-faced fabrication.

"The captain said it would be all right," she told the pair, putting a disarming lilt into her speech.

Once the autographing chore was completed, one of the seamen undogged the door. Pat stepped in. Immediately, her teeth began chattering.

"Brrr," she said, watching her breath expel in a fluffy little puff of steam.

She circled the room, reading the hand-inked drawer labels, until one tapered finger touched a slip of paper marked "J. Baird."

Slinging her hand bag over her shoulder, Pat took hold of the drawer handle and began walking backward. The drawer squeaked and rumbled on its rollers with each step she took, gradually revealing a sheeted form like a mummy in a cocoon.

When she had exposed the upper body, Pat stepped around and carefully folded back the sheet until the corpse's head shone like a dull emerald under the overhead light.

Perhaps it was the weird jade green of the dead man's face—or possibly it was the ugliness of expression that death had stamped upon his dried-up features—but at first glimpse of the visage under the sheet, Pat Savage brought a tight bronze fist to her mouth. Her eyes went wide. She stepped backward, recoiling.

"Oh!" she exclaimed. "Oh!"

Exhibiting great agitation, the bronze-haired girl gave the morgue drawer a shove and charged out of the door, practically bowling over the two guardian seamen who had heard her exclamation of horror—or so they assumed it to have been.

"Are you O.K., Miss Vine?" one asked solicitously.

"Hardly!" said the supposed actress, sweeping past them like a blustery bronze wind.

"How do you like that?" one seaman said to the other. "She gets her way and now she can't give us the time of day!"

The second seaman replied sourly, "You know those actress types—all teeth and no heart. Give me a stay-at-home gal any day."

Her chiseled features tight with some contained emotion, Patricia Savage roamed the liner *Mandarin,* searching.

"Doc will want to know about this!" she muttered, her voice strained.

Pat prowled the outer decks on both sides of the vessel. She barged her way into both dining salons, rubbernecked for several fruitless minutes, and went topside once more.

"That cousin of mine could be disguised as a ventilator for all I know," she complained when no one was within hearing. Unnoticed by Pat, an eavesdropper did lurk in the vicinity. A pock-featured Chinese man was padding along several yards behind the young woman. He wore a black mandarin's cap over his very round head, which made him look rather benign.

Pat stopped, snapped her fingers, and cried, "The skipper! I'll bet that shriveled old salt knows where Doc's hiding."

Abruptly, Pat reversed herself, just missing the Celestial,

who ducked behind a hornlike ventilator. He lay in wait, his dirty gray eyes knife slits in his skull-like face.

Pat Savage seemed unaware of the lurking Oriental as she cruised past the open mouth of the ventilator.

Soft cat feet slipped up behind her, and two yellow claws stretched a red silk cord over her head. The cord descended.

Possibly Pat would have sensed the attacker had she not been so intent upon her quest. It is a truism that the more one concentrates upon the contents of one's mind, the less sensitive the five senses are to external stimuli. Pat possessed excellent hearing. It was just that she was not listening to the slight sounds her eardrums were receiving.

The cord whipped across her smooth bronze throat, digging in. Pat emitted a squeak of surprise. It was barely even that. A mouse would have raised more of an outcry.

She saw stars. Bright, varicolored ones.

"You know too much, missy!" a rattly voice hissed in her ear.

Pat found herself yanked backward. A sandaled foot kicked in a cabin door. It was not locked. She was flung inside, the cord around her neck serving as an effective fulcrum.

The cord released; Pat went sprawling.

She did not wait to see who her assailant was. Even as the bronze-haired girl went tumbling and skidding along the Oriental rug, accumulating painful friction burns on elbows and knees, she snaked a hand into her capacious hand bag.

The cabin door slammed close and the rattly voice cackled, "Now you cannot get out."

"Fine with me, buster," Pat said, showing the Celestial the business end of her six-shooter. "As they say out West, grab a fistful of sky."

The Chinese stood rooted. His face, rather than showing consternation or some other appropriate expression, went as placid as an amber pond with two dirty lilypads for eyes.

"I could say it twice," Pat warned, picking herself up, "or I could just drill you here and there for effect."

The Celestial hissed, "It would seem that I have no choice." His dangling hands shook, as if with agitation.

Then, with deliberate slowness, he brought his hands up to his shoulders.

"Hold that pose," Pat warned, stepping forward. Her silken hose showed rents here and there, but she could navigate.

"You're the lad with the peanut habit," Pat stated.

"I am known as Wan Sop, chief limb of the Jade Ogre."

"Never heard of you—or it," Pat shot back.

She was looking about the room out of the corners of her eyes, in case there was another assailant lurking in the cabin.

A shadow crossed the porthole facing the starboard rail. Pat's bright eyes flicked to it, the muzzle of her six-shooter following.

And in that instant, the Oriental, Wan Sop, lifted one claw to his mouth. Pat shifted her six-shooter back. She brought the side of her free hand spanking down on the hammer, to which was welded a spur, and began fanning the thing, wild-West style.

For all her speed, Pat was rewarded with a series of ineffectual clickings.

Her pretty features registered shock, horror, amazement, fear by turns. She took an involuntary step backward, stricken momentarily speechless.

"You die!" hissed Wan Sop.

And then the cabin door exploded inward and a bolt of bronze struck Wan Sop with no less force than forked lightning. Wan Sop was yanked half around. A metallic fist came up, connected with a dry, crunching sound and the Oriental's pocked moon of a head rocked back like a pineapple jerked on its stem.

He collapsed to the rug, one hand outflung, the other under him. The black mandarin's cap fell off, disclosing an utterly hairless yellow face which, as his lips drew back in a grimace, took on the aspect of a death's hand.

He did not get up again.

Doc Savage reached Pat's side, demanding, "Are you all right?"

"No!" Pat bit out furiously, breaking the action of her pistol. "But when I get my hands on that Ham, I'm going to feel a whole lot better, let me tell you. Look at this! That sneak snuck all the shells out of my gun. I could have been killed!"

Pat's eyes suddenly went to the prostrate form of Wan Sop.

"Doc!" she breathed. "Look!"

Doc turned, his golden eyes alert.

Wan Sop had fallen on his face, the force of Doc Savage's powerful uppercut having corkscrewed him around before he went down. After falling, he must have contorted and twisted somewhat, because now his unlovely orb of a visage was half turned to the porthole light.

The face of Wan Sop no longer looked like that of a benign skull that had been sheathed with the skin of a lemon.

It still retained the pock-marked aspect that was remindful of old lemon peel. But now the color of his features was a deep blue, like a ripening plum. It made his staring eyes look like pebbles, and his mouth resembled that part of a plum that had been burst under squeezing fingers. His betelnut-stained teeth had something of the aspect of a line of plum pits.

"Ugh," said Pat, turning away.

Doc Savage went to the body. Carefully, he turned it over.

One bluish fist was clenched tight. Doc pried the fingers loose, disclosing a simple object. He brought it up to the light.

Pat blinked at it.

"Macaroni," she said, regarding the slim, cream-colored tube.

"Long enough to function as a blowgun," Doc explained, "which could then be chewed and swallowed, thereby consuming the evidence."

"And would sound like he was eating peanuts!" Pat gasped. She went a little green around the line of her jaw. "I heard a crunching noise before he went down. I guess he swallowed the capsule meant for me."

"It would seem so," Doc said.

Pat found her composure and said, "I call that the nick of time."

Doc explained, "I have been trailing this Wan Sop—if that is his true name—since I spotted him in the breakfast crowd, earlier. I had hoped he would lead me to any confederates he might have placed aboard ship. Instead, he picked up your trail."

"How long ago?"

Doc stood up. "Since before you visited the ship's morgue. He lingered near by until you reemerged, and followed you topside."

"The morgue!" Pat exclaimed suddenly. "Doc, do you know that that man who was killed while climbing the gangway isn't Jason Baird, after all?"

"I was," the bronze man stated, "practically sure of it."

XIV

DISCOVERIES

"You mean you knew it all along!" Pat exploded.

Doc Savage had fallen to searching the cabin.

"All along, no," he rapped. "I did not personally witness the man thought to have been Jason Baird succumb to the poison gas capsule—otherwise I would have interrogated the pair of bodyguards who escorted him aboard before they left the ship. But I did contact the San Francisco authorities by radio-land-line telephone and learned that their questioning of the duo showed that they were detectives in the employ of an agency known for its good reputation. They had never met Jason Baird before sailing. The impostor had made arrangements by telephone for the operatives to travel with him and merely showed up at the agency office the morning the *Mandarin* sailed."

Pat's pretty brows puckered. "I don't get it."

Doc Savage was going through dresser drawers examining such items as he found therein.

"I myself had never met Baird, so I could not identify the man," he continued. "The only others on the ship who could were you and, according to their friends, Fuzzy Wool and Kitten Borzoi."

"That's why they were murdered!" Pat shouted.

Doc nodded. "And that is why there was an attempt on your life, Pat. To prevent anyone from discovering that the man in the morgue was not the true Jason Baird."

"So who *is* the dead one?" Pat wondered.

Doc left off his search of the drawers. He moved about the cabin, his golden eyes active.

"At a guess," he ventured, "a dupe—possibly a confederate of this Wan Sop and whoever else may be mixed up in this mystery."

"That's pretty cold-blooded," Pat stated. "Murdering one of their own to cover their tracks."

Doc said, "No doubt they had their reasons for disposing of him. Do not forget that the dead man is a white man, and so far all the others have been Asiatic, including the one who attempted to murder me on the San Francisco plane."

Pat shivered prettily. "Don't remind me."

Doc straighted from his searching.

"Anything interesting?" Pat asked, curious.

"All indications are that this cabin belongs to a Chinese named Wan Sop," Doc said.

"The question remains, is Wan Sop this man's name?"

Doc went to the body, knelt. He began going through the dead Celestial's pockets. They were in strange places about the native costume the man wore.

"Be careful, Doc," Pat pleaded, her eyes on the cadaver's blue-and-turning-aquamarine visage.

"The poison has no doubt lost its potency by now," Doc stated calmly. "It seems to evaporate rather quickly."

He pulled out a simple billfold from a hip pocket and stood up.

Identity papers indicated the dead man was indeed named Wan Sop. Among the papers was a receipt for a valise deposited in the ship's safe.

"A visit to the purser is in order," Doc said.

"Anything that puts distance between me and this blue-faced cadaver," Pat said fervently, "has my vote."

They encountered Ham Brooks on the way to the purser.

"Doc!" he called, pounding down a companionway, his natty cane held high. "I located the stateroom where the sick passenger was taken!"

"I forgot to tell you," Pat injected. "There really was a sick passenger who got on at San Francisco. How'd you know that, anyway?"

"Conjecture," the bronze man said.

Ham puffed up and fell in cadence with them. He jingled when he walked, which reminded Pat Savage of another thing that had slipped her mind.

"All that loose change," Pat told Ham Brooks archly, "is going to ruin the swanky hang of your coat."

Ham colored. His face actually turned scarlet, which when contrasted to his snowy hair and equally white attire, made him resemble a mortified snowman.

"Deuced nuisance, change," Ham said, flustered.

"You don't say?" Pat said, abruptly snatching at the dapper lawyer's sword cane.

"Why—!" Ham began, reaching out. Pat switched the cane between her hands, frustrating the dapper lawyer.

"This," returned Pat fiercely, "is my property until I say otherwise."

Ham looked as if a leg had been amputated. He was seldom without his cane. "I protest!" he complained.

"I came near to being killed because I was shooting dead air at a Chinaman," Pat explained.

Ham subsided.

Doc Savage filled in Ham regarding the events of the morning.

Ham said, "I investigated the cabin where the sick man was taken, Doc. He wasn't actually sick, according to the chief steward, just well into his cups."

"And?"

"There is a Chinaman, a rather well-dressed one, ensconced on a steamer chair outside the cabin. He is happily eating his way through a bag of peanuts."

"A guard," Doc said.

Pat shuddered. "Another peanut muncher!"

They came at last to the purser's office. Doc presented the receipt and requested a look at the valise.

This time Captain Gooch had to come down in person.

His response, upon hearing of a fourth blue-faced corpse on his ship, was to threaten to put them all in irons and lock them in the ship's brig.

"Do liners have brigs?" Pat asked, puzzled.

"They do not," Ham put in. "This man is merely trying to buffalo us." Ham drew himself up before the *Mandarin* skipper. He towered over the man. "Captain Gooch," the dapper lawyer said pointedly, "I must warn you: These heavy-handed tactics do not impress us."

In a voice so calm that every one immediately lost their ire, Doc Savage said, "It might be a good thing if we all had a look inside that valise." Then he added, looking at Captain Gooch, "Starting, of course, with you."

Captain Gooch saw the logic in that, not that it particularly appealed to him. Tersely, he ordered the valise brought out.

After it was shoved through the cage slot, they saw it was a simple black valise.

"Locked," Captain Gooch muttered, tugging at the clasp.

The bronze man produced a silver key, saying, "Try this."

While Captain Gooch frowningly did as he was bade, Pat asked, "Where did that come from?"

"Wan Sop's wallet," Doc explained.

"Oh."

The valise clicked open and every one went very quiet. Captain Gooch's chafed features visibly paled as he peered inside. Every one else crowded closer.

"Diamonds!" Ham exploded.

"The missing jewels," Pat added.

Doc said, "That key matches the outline I discovered on the message from Jason Baird's stateroom."

Captain Gooch looked up. "Message? What message?"

"I neglected to bring you up to date on the most recent results of my progress," Doc told him.

"Do tell," Captain Gooch said thinly.

"After you had left," Doc continued, "I discovered a message, signed "Jason Baird,' concealed in a steamer trunk. It told of a theft of diamonds such as these by a thief identified as Wan Sop. Pressed into the paper was an outline of a key identical to the one you hold."

"You still have that message?" Gooch demanded.

Doc produced the thing. Captain Gooch read it over, then removed the key from the valise lock and pressed it against the impression. No one present doubted but that it was a perfect fit.

"This seems to prove that those diamonds belong to Jason Baird," Doc pointed out.

"Now, all we have to do is find him," Pat put in.

Captain Gooch looked prepared to chew nails.

"Unless the dead have learned to walk," he sputtered, "he's down in the morgue—isn't he?"

No one seemed inclined to answer that, so Captain Gooch roared the question a second time.

"Well, isn't he?"

"He is not," Doc related, and then explained the complicated series of discoveries that had led them to the inescapable conclusion that the man in the morgue was not, in truth, Jason Baird.

"Let me see if I have this straight," Captain Gooch ground out through too-tight teeth. "This Wan Sop steals these diamonds from Jason Baird, who is a jeweler by trade. He brings them aboard, and poisons everyone who can recognize that the man who he framed as being Baird, isn't really him?"

"That is the rough shape of it so far," Doc allowed.

"I think," Captain Gooch said, clapping the valise shut and thrusting it back to the purser, "that I had better contact the steamship company."

He charged off.

* * *

Ham Brooks looked at Doc Savage.

"I guess that leaves us clear to investigate the supposed sick passenger."

"It does," Doc said, starting for the nearest companion-way.

The others followed.

Ham spoke to Pat out of the side of his mouth as they hurried along.

"Looks like we're going to have some excitement," he offered.

"I already had my share for the day, thank you," Pat said frostily. "I have been chased by a floating arm, disarmed behind my back, nearly poisoned by a Chinaman—and I've been at sea less than twenty-four hours."

Ham smiled. "This isn't getting your pretty goat, is it, Pat?"

"You leave my goat out of this," Pat snapped. Then, "I don't know," she admitted in a more subdued tone. "As far as enjoying nearly being murdered twice in a row, I think I have a glass jaw, or something."

Which coming from the action-loving Pat, was quite an admission, indeed.

Ham took advantage of this momentary lack of nerve to make an offer.

"Trade you six perfectly dry six-gun shells for a sword cane," he said.

Pat asked suspiciously, "You didn't unscrew the tops and pour out the powder, by any chance?"

"You have my word of honor," Ham said gallantly.

"Considering your profession," she retorted, "that's not the kind of guarantee I would take to the bank. But right now I'm feeling desperate. It's a bargain."

They swapped items before they reached B Deck, starboard, where the cabin Ham had found lay.

From this point on, their attitudes were ones of stealth. They crept along the deck, ducking when they passed portholes, so as not to be seen.

Pausing behind a handy ventilator, Doc and Ham were peering along the starboard rail to where the Chinaman was contentedly munching peanuts, while Pat hastily stuffed shells into her six-shooter. She clicked the action together and said, "Now that I'm loaded for bear, wolf, or skunk, nobody had better give me any guff!"

"The cabin is supposedly registered to a Mr. Lee," Ham inserted. "Probably a fictitious name chosen not to sound necessarily Oriental."

Doc undertoned, "Wait here."

The big bronze man withdrew, and set his throat muscles. The others could see that they were pulsing strangely.

From some indefinite point near by, a singsong voice seemed to call out, "*Hing Dai!*"

At the sound of that voice, Pat Savage felt her blood run cold.

Ham, seeing her expression, formed a question mark with a crooked finger.

"Wan Sop!" Pat breathed, one hand going to her throat.

"*Hing Dai!*" the voice that sounded like the dead Wan Sop came again. "*Gou Meng! Gou Meng!*"

The Celestial on the steamer chair came bolt upright. His narrow eyes switched back and forth anxiously, like those of a cornered animal.

Again came the disembodied voice. "*Gou Meng!*"

This time, the formerly seated Celestial came running in their direction, crying, "*Ching gow!*"

Pat pulled back the hammer of her six-shooter, ready to let it fall with explosive results.

There was no need for gunfire, as things turned out.

The Celestial hove into view and Doc Savage snagged him by the neck. The Oriental was for some reason still clutching his sack of peanuts. This fell from nerveless fingers, precipitating nuts about the deck.

"*Aeii!*" he shrieked.

The Oriental's sandaled feet made running motions. These availed him nothing, despite their frantic quality, for Doc Savage was holding the man's feet off the deck. The Asiatic was attempting to run on thin air. He presented a comical picture.

Doc squeezed. The Celestial gave a sigh and went limp.

The bronze man laid him out on the deck, behind the ventilator.

He waved for the others to follow.

"That was you!" Pat hissed suddenly.

"Ventriloquism," Doc said. "I had only heard Wan Sop speak once, and then only briefly, but I imagine my voice imitation was sufficient. I merely called for help and the lookout responded."

Ham, who knew enough Chinese to know that the language was difficult enough to learn to speak, never mind imitate and throw simultaneously, said, "Whew! It worked!"

They eased up on the unguarded stateroom door. Doc employed his tiny periscope device to peer into the porthole. He angled this about some.

"Spot anything, Doc?" Ham wanted to know.

Doc Savage shook his head, collapsed the device. Next, he reached into his gadget vest and removed a tiny whitish button which he inserted into the lock aperture.

Ham, recognizing what the bronze man was about to do, unlimbered an amazingly compact machine pistol from a padded holster under one armpit. It resembled an oversized automatic fitted with a tiny drum magazine. This was a super-machine pistol, another product of Doc Savage's inventive mind. It fired so-called "mercy" bullets, which were filled with a quick-acting anæsthetic. Doc did not believe in killing, if it could be avoided.

The dapper lawyer set himself as Doc applied another button to the aperture and faded back a safe distance.

Almost at once, the lock began spilling a bright sparkle and a sizzling sound like bacon frying.

Hot metal dropped and ran.

When the terrific heat of the Thermit—for that was the compound the bronze man had brought to bear—finally subsided, Doc moved swiftly.

He reared back and kicked at the door. It slammed in. He jumped through the aperture.

The others piled in, Pat coming last.

* * *

The parlor was empty. Doc motioned for them to hang back as he moved to the bedroom.

The door was ajar. He flashed to it, using one bronze hand to ease it open, ready to jump back and fling a glassy object he had plucked from his vest—one of Doc's tiny, thin-walled anæsthetic grenades—if the need arose.

The door fell open all the way. The bronze man's eyes were molten.

No sound came from the next room. Doc plunged in.

Ham Brooks and Pat followed.

"Jove!" Ham exploded.

Doc was bent over a bamboo chair, to which was lashed the pale-faced society reporter, Rex Pinks.

Ham unsheathed his sword cane and employed it to sever the red silk gag that had been tied around the news-hawk's mouth. It fell loosely. Pinks opened his mouth to speak, but only a muffled sound emerged. They all saw that the inside of his mouth was a scarlet wound, as if his tongue had been cut off at the root.

"Good grief!" Ham said.

"Horrible," added Pat.

Doc tore the lashings free by main strength. The bonds snapped with dry twangs.

Rex Pinks reached up with his hands and dug them into his raw-looking mouth. It took some squirming, but in the end he got the wet, red sponge out past his teeth.

"*Pah!*" he spat. "The damned thing soaked up saliva, and swelled up three times its size. I thought it would pop my jaw out of hinge for sure."

"These bonds are rather loose," Doc pointed out, as the reporter found his feet.

"I had almost worked free," he explained.

Ham, ever suspicious, demanded, "What are you doing here, Pinks?"

"I was searching for that peanut muncher," Rex Pinks shot back. "I trailed him to this cabin. But there was a guard posted near by. He jumped me. I got dragged in here, and tied up for my pains."

"Was the man you trailed the same one who was lurking

about when my cousin, Pat, went over the rail last night?" Doc asked.

"The very same. He had a pocked death's head face and no more hair than a cue ball."

"Well, he's joined the ranks of the blue-featured departed," Pat put in without sympathy.

"What about the guard outside?" Pinks wanted to know. "They set one outside to guard the cabin."

"He has been taken care of," Doc told him. "We are searching for another individual whom we believe may be held in this cabin."

"You must mean the man under the bed," Rex Pinks said to the astonishment of those present.

They all fell to looking under the bed—all except Ham, who kept his intricate supermachine gun trained on Rex Pinks.

"Not very trusting, are you?" Pinks put in sourly.

"Your turning up here is rather surprising," pointed out Ham, one eye on Doc and Pat as they hauled a trussed form from under the cabin bed.

The form was swathed in canvas, which had been tied with stout cord at various useful places, such as the waist, upper arms, knees, and ankles. Thus was the captive completely immobilized. There was a yellow silk hood over his head, but no holes for sight.

Doc removed this, exposing short blond hair surmounting a muscular face remindful of a pugnacious bulldog.

Pat gasped involuntarily.

"Jason Baird!" she exclaimed.

XV

PLOT FANTASTIC

The silence which followed Pat Savage's surprise exclamation was not long, perhaps less than thirty seconds. When it ended, it popped like a cork from a bottle.

"What do you mean—this man is Jason Baird?" Rex Pinks burst out. "Baird's extinct!"

Doc Savage removed the red silk gag from the human bulldog's mouth. He plucked out a red sponge identical to the one that had tortured Rex Pinks, and tossed it aside.

"Savage," Jason Baird said thickly. "You found me!"

"I helped, don't forget," Pat chimed in.

Ham Brooks employed his sword cane to saw through Jason Baird's bonds, taking care to avoid puncturing the canvas with the tip, which was coated with a sticky brown substance—an anæsthetic compound.

Once freed, Jason Baird tried to climb out of the canvas. He managed to sit up, but only briefly. He wore native Oriental garb, which fit him loosely.

"My arms and legs feel dead," he said weakly.

"Loss of circulation," the bronze man told him.

Doc went to work, flexing the man's right arm and kneading muscles to stimulate blood flow.

As he did this, he rapped out quick orders. "Ham, station yourself outside the cabin door. It will be some minutes before we can move out. We do not want interference."

"Righto," said Ham, skipping away.

"Pat, watch Pinks."

Acquiring a blood-thirsty expression, Pat Savage directed her six-shooter in Rex Pinks's direction.

"Do I get a trial by jury or are you just going to do me in on general suspicion?" the reporter asked in an injured voice.

"We'll let you know," Pat retorted.

Doc indicated Rex Pinks. "Do you know this man?" he asked Jason Baird.

"Yeah," the jeweler said without enthusiasm. "I've seen him around. He's a pencil pusher with the *Comet*. Has a moocher reputation, as I hear it."

"I resent that!" said Rex Pinks, who otherwise offered no defense of his character.

"While we're stuck here," Doc said, "let's have your story, Baird. Beginning with why you asked for my assistance."

"We already know that—don't we?" Pat asked. "It's over the stolen diamonds."

"No," said Jason Baird, feeling returning to his right arm. Doc switched to the left. He worked briskly, as if time were of the essence.

"Maybe Pat has told you about my sister, Maurine," Jason Baird said.

"She is well known for her experiments in germ cultures," Doc said.

Baird nodded. "Maurine went to China about three months ago. She was on the trail of a species of tropical plant that she thought would be a boon to the world. At first, her letters came every week or two. Then they stopped. Without explanation. I made inquiries of the Chinese authorities, and they reported that she had seemingly vanished. Since she was working deep in the south of China, far from civilization, I was not unduly alarmed at first."

Jason Baird's left arm began showing life, starting with the fingers, which wiggled like pale worms slowly suffusing with pink.

"Then, a Shanghai jewel importer, an acquaintance of mine, brought me word that Maurine was no longer in China, but in Cambodia. Deep in the interior. He learned this from natives. They claimed that she was insane and a prisoner of a weird individual called Quon."

Doc said, "Quon?"

"That is the name they gave. I could learn nothing further, except that this Quon, whoever he is, holds forth in a ruin in the heart of Cambodia—which is also, for some reason, known as Quon."

Rex Pinks tittered mirth at that. "A loony yarn if ever I heard one!"

He was ignored.

Scowling, Jason Baird went on. "I made inquiries with the government of Cambodia. They were evasive at first. When I pressed them, they cut off all communication with me."

Doc left off the arm and went to work on Jason Baird's legs. The jeweler was able to sit up now. His face was very pale. His words tumbled out like stones down a hillside.

"It was shortly after that that I received a visit from a devil of a Chinese who called himself Wan Sop," Baird continued. "He showed up in my office one day just about two weeks ago, in the company of a pack of half-castes—Cambodians, I think they were—and threatened me."

"What sort of threats?" Doc asked.

"He said that I was to stop searching for my sister. That a terrible fate would befall me if I continued along my lines of inquiry. He said there was nothing I could do for Maurine. He hinted that she was—she was dead. But he didn't come right out and say this."

Jason Baird paused. His bulldog face was perspiring freely as restored circulation brought stinging pain to his extremities.

"This only made me more anxious to do something," he related. "I booked passage on the *Mandarin*, and contacted you through Pat. Somehow, Wan Sop and his cutthroats found out. I think they may have tapped my telephone. I was shadowed everywhere I went. I managed to stay one step ahead of them. But the night before the *Mandarin* was to sail—the night I was to meet you, Savage—there were several attempts to get me. At my home and office. I decided my safest bet was to walk the streets. I was carrying the valise with the diamonds, which I was going to donate to charity on your behalf if you agreed to come to my aid."

"The diamonds have been recovered," Doc inserted.

"They're yours now," Jason Baird said sincerely. Then, going on with his story, "Wan Sop caught up with me," he admitted grudgingly. "He's a devil. He drugged me and got me aboard the Mandarin. This *is* the *Mandarin*, isn't it?"

"It is," Doc confirmed.

Jason Baird made motions indicating that he was prepared to stand up. He couldn't quite make it and had to be helped into a chair.

"I guess the rest you know," he finished weakly.

"Wan Sop has perished," Doc Savage said.

"His own poison got him," Pat interjected.

Baird nodded. "I can't think of a more fitting fate for that skull-faced devil."

Doc asked, "How many other Chinese have you seen about the ship who are in his employ?"

"Only one. There was a white man, called Seed. I overheard them talking about him. Whatever is behind all this, Seed was getting cold feet. Wan Sop decided to get rid of him. I heard him boasting of it to the other one, saying that he would be buried in my place and no one would ever know."

Pat Savage looked away from Rex Pinks long enough to exclaim, "He must be the dead one in the morgue we thought was Jason."

"Have you any idea why Wan Sop wished to keep you alive, Baird?" Doc wondered.

"None whatsoever."

"This tale gets taller and taller," mocked Rex Pinks.

Pat prodded the colorless reporter with the black end of her pistol. "Ixnay, ibscray!" When Pinks looked blank, she added, "That's 'Nix, scribe,' to you!"

Rex Pinks subsided.

"Are you up to travel?" Doc asked Baird.

"I can manage."

Jason Baird found his feet, teetered, almost fell.

The bronze man had to help him limp from the cabin.

Outside, the rail was conveniently scanty in the way of passengers. Breakfast had seen to that.

Ham met them. He had sheathed his sword cane, but his machine pistol waved excitedly in the air.

"Where to now, Doc?" he asked, low-voiced.

"Royal Suite. It is the more remote, and secure."

They moved past the ventilator where they had left the

insensate Chinese sentry, intending to collect the erstwhile lookout.

Empty shadow pooled in the spot where he had been. He was no longer there.

Ham looked as if he was about to explode with rage.

"He's gone!" he wailed.

"Didn't you check him?" Pat demanded hotly.

"No," Ham said in a harried voice. "I was too busy watching the door. He must have been spirited away before I left the cabin."

"Maybe he threw himself overboard," Rex Pinks offered. "To save face over his failure."

"Not likely," Ham said contrarily.

"A fine turn of events," Pat huffed.

"Let's finish the recriminations in private," Doc suggested.

They used an elevator. All of them managed to squeeze aboard. By the time the lift put them off on A Deck, Jason Baird was able to move under his own power. He walked like a man whose feet had been pressed to hot coals.

As they walked along, Ham asked, "Doc, what about that secret message you found in the fake Baird's cabin? The one that claimed this matter was over stolen diamonds."

"A ruse," Doc explained. "To throw us off the trail."

"I heard them laughing about that, too," Baird added. "The idea was to make it easy for you to locate the diamonds on the ship so that you'd think you solved the mystery. They were going to plant the diamonds somewhere where you'd be sure to stumble across them."

"A very expensive ruse, don't you think?" Pat put in archly. "Those rocks are worth a few dollars."

"Not as much as the thing that this Quon is cooking up," Baird rejoined. "Whatever it is, it had Wan Sop seeing dollar signs and frightened that Seed fellow half to death."

"Sounds rather big," Ham mused.

"Sounds ridiculous," Rex Pinks scoffed.

"It is big," Baird said. "Big—and horrible. And somehow my sister Maurine is in the middle of it. Savage, you must help me find her!"

They had come to the Royal Suite. Pat unlocked the door. They slipped in.

Jason Baird was assisted to a comfortable chair and given water. It seemed to refresh him, and he was better able to enunciate his words after he had gulped down half a glassful.

"Baird," Doc inquired, "had you hired detectives to accompany you on the voyage?"

"Not detectives, exactly," Baird told him. "More on the order of adventurers."

"I see." Doc went to the stateroom telephone and got the ship's operator. He asked to be put through to a certain party and then spoke briefly in a low voice.

When he returned, Ham asked, "I suppose you have fetched Captain Gooch?"

"That will come later," Doc said.

"You know," Rex Pinks piped, "none of what this Baird has told us explains that glowing arm of a thing."

Baird glowered. "Arm?"

"On several occasions throughout this affair," Doc told him in a level voice, "there have appeared disembodied, luminous arms, of a distinctly Asiatic character, which have pursued either Pat or myself. The first one I encountered in your San Francisco office. The second pursued me as I left."

"It's true, goofy as it sounds," Pat added. "And mine near to drowned me."

Jason Baird's blocky, pugnacious face assumed an expression of utter disbelief. He examined the faces about the room as if reluctantly concluding he had fallen into the company of lunatics.

He said, "Are we talking about Oriental demons?"

"That has yet to be determined," Ham said, precisely. "But if Doc Savage says such a thing chased Pat, you may safely wager all you own upon the truthfulness of it."

"Rubbish," Jason Baird said harshly.

Rex Pinks shoved his rather dissolute face into Jason Baird's own.

"Interesting that this ghost arm should first appear near

your office, Baird," the reporter said slowly. "About the time you claim you were captured, too."

"Go peddle your papers," Baird spat back.

The knock at the stateroom door interrupted the exchange before it could grow more heated.

Doc crossed to the door, opened it.

Cautiously, their hard eyes sweeping the cabin for signs of danger, four men filed in—Alva Nally, Joe Knopf, Shad O'Shea, and storklike Chick Alfred.

"You called us," growled Chick Alfred, the apparent straw boss of the erstwhile Fuzzy Wool crowd. "We're here."

"Yesterday, you gentlemen showed great interest in the apparent demise of Jason Baird," the bronze man stated.

"What of it?" said Shad O'Shea, looking mournful.

"Yeah," grumbled Alva Nally. "We've been through this third degree before. You don't cut any ice with us, so maybe we'd better blow."

They started back out the door.

Doc Savage stopped them with a command.

"Not so fast," he clipped. The men hesitated. "I would like to introduce you to Jason Baird," added Doc, gesturing with a bronze arm to the real Jason Baird.

"You tryin' to fun us?" Joe Knopf spat. "Baird's dead. They got him set up in his own private ice chest with his name on the front door."

"On the contrary," Doc said.

"That's right," said Baird, coming to his feet. "I'm Jason Baird."

Momentary silence attended this declaration.

"Prove it," snarled Chick Alfred.

Jason Baird held up his left wrist. There were indentations made by his too-frequent wearing of a manacle bracelet.

"If you four are who I think you are, you'll know what this means," he challenged.

They gathered around the real Jason Baird, examining his offered wrist.

Chick Alfred said, "How much did you offer Fuzzy to tag along for this voyage? If you're Baird, you'll know that."

Jason Baird said, "A thousand dollars a man."

"You're Baird, all right," Alfred decided. "But I don't get it. Who's the other bird? The dead mug?"

"A hoodlum named Seed," Doc told them. He addressed Jason Baird. "Am I correct in assuming that Fuzzy Wool and his friends were the bodyguards you actually hired for the voyage?"

Baird nodded. "Yeah. In case you turned me down, I wanted to be ready. Also, I knew I'd need a small army to fight Quon, if I could reach the ruin where he hangs out. You boys are Fuzzy's men?"

"We were," Shad O'Shea said gloomily. "Fuzzy went West, along with our pal, Kitten. And we still have our peepers peeled for the guy what done for him."

"That individual is called Wan Sop," Doc offered. "And I am afraid you are too late on that score."

"What d'ya mean?" Chick Alfred growled.

"He was killed this morning."

"You kill him?" Joe Knopf wanted to know.

"He succumbed to the same poison that was used on your chief," Doc explained.

Chick Alfred grunted. "Can't say I'm not disappointed. I had plans for that damn chink."

"Since it now appears that we are all working toward the same goal," Doc stated, "it might be wise for you to throw in with us."

Chick Alfred looked to Jason Baird. "You're the boss, as far as I'm concerned. What you say, goes. How do you want it?"

"If you will work with Doc Savage," Jason Baird said flatly, "I will pay you the agreed-upon fee for your efforts."

"Sounds jake to me." Alfred turned to his confederates. "What d'ya say, boys? We may still get a chance to pay somebody back for what happened to Fuzzy and Kitten."

The other three—Nally, Knopf, and O'Shea—did not take long in offering to go along.

Alfred turned. "O.K.—what are we up against?"

Doc Savage answered that. "As yet we do not know. There is an individual calling himself Quon who may be holding Baird's sister, Maurine, in the Cambodian interior. Our main task is to rescue her. At the same time, this Quon may have other agents aboard—in fact, may be aboard himself."

"What makes you say that, Savage?" Baird asked suddenly.

"He's probably the spook without any arms," Rex Pinks suggested. "I saw him, even if nobody else did."

The quartet of adventurers seemed to take notice of Rex Pinks for the first time.

"Ain't you that snoop?" wondered reedy-voiced Alva Nally. "The one that attends all those sissified posh parties?"

"I used to be a police reporter," Pinks said in an injured tone.

"Retirement must be swell," Knopf said, emitting a jangling laugh.

Raucous guffaws came from the others.

Doc interrupted. "There is a being aboard ship who appears to lack arms," he said. "He dresses in Asiatic fashion. It would be well for everyone to avoid this entity at all costs. He may be dangerous. There is much we still do not know."

"Any description?" Chick Alfred asked, interested.

"Look for the guy with the jade face," said Rex Pinks sourly. "You can't miss him."

This time it was the society reporter who was the recipient of disbelieving stares.

Jason Baird, his voice strange, croaked, "There is something I forgot to mention."

Doc looked at him. "Yes?"

"Wan Sop had another name for this Quon," Baird said thinly. "I thought at the time it was just Oriental hocus-pocus meant to scare me."

"Spill it," Rex Pinks said impatiently.

"The other name of Quon was the Jade Ogre. They referred to him as the armless one who will breathe death on the universe."

"Rubbish!" snapped Ham Brooks.

"Armless guys; flyin' arms—I don't like this," muttered Shad O'Shea in a morose tone.

Doc said at this point, "We know that one Chinese agent of this Quon is loose on the *Mandarin*. We captured him not an hour ago, but he vanished subsequently. Locating this man, and questioning him, may lead to some answers."

"What's he look like?" demanded Shad.

Doc launched into the description of the missing Chinese, detailing his ratty features and general appearance. He did a fair job—good enough that anyone who paid attention to his words would have been able to pick the worthy out of a police line-up of his close relatives.

"Boys," enthused Chick Alfred. "Let's hunt!"

"Good idea," said Ham.

Doc turned to his cousin, who was reaching into her hand bag for her ivory-handled pistol.

"Pat, you will stay here with Jason Baird," he directed.

"See here, Doc—"

"That is an order, young lady!" Doc said sternly. "You have had two brushes with death already. Isn't that enough?"

"That second time doesn't count!" Pat reminded, eying Ham Brooks. "I was practically toothless."

Leaving the bronze-haired girl to mutter dire things, they vacated the Royal Suite.

Outside, Doc Savage rapped out brisk orders, dividing the party into pairs, and assigning each duo to certain quarters of the ship for search purposes.

"Ham, Pinks, you will come with me," he finished.

The three groups of men set off in three different directions.

"We should talk to that Captain Gooch," Ham suggested, as they slipped down an aft companionway. "He'll want to know what's happened."

"We will," Doc assured him.

They were pushing their way through the hotel-style revolving doors which gave access to the indoor foyer from the promenade deck, when a single gunshot smote their startled ears.

"The bow!" Ham rapped.

Instantly they reversed direction, Ham becoming tangled in the revolving door due to concern for his sword cane. He fought free.

Pounding back toward the bow, they raced around a corner and came upon a sight.

Chick Alfred, Joe Knopf, Alva Nally, and Shad O'Shea were standing in a semicircle about a twitching form.

Doc sank to his knees beside the Chinese man. He lay on his back, his eyes jerking wildly in his head, a spreading pond of gore widening about his back.

Doc lifted the mortally wounded man's head, began rapping out quick questions in perfect Cantonese.

The Oriental seemed to hear, despite his obvious distress. He shrieked, "*Quon! Quon!*"

Then he expired. Every twitching limb settled down at once. The body lost all animation.

Hot lights of anger in his flake-gold eyes, Doc lowered the man's head. He noticed a flat silver automatic lying on the rubber-tiled deck. A twist of gray smoke lifted from the muzzle. It was expensive, the workmanship exquisite. Doc scooped it up in one big bronze hand and came to his feet.

"Which one of you pulled the trigger?" he asked, tone metallic. For the bronze man never condoned killing—even of the wicked. He had a policy of avoiding bloodshed whenever possible.

"Not me," said Joe Knopf.

"Wasn't me," added Alva Nally.

Shad O'Shea gazed skyward, as if anticipating rain.

Doc Savage turned his active orbs on Chick Alfred, who immediately began looking uncomfortable.

"Don't look at me, Savage," protested the gunman. "I only just got here myself." Alfred indicated the now-still Celestial. "He was lying just like that when I found him."

Doc Savage said sternly, "Getting to the bottom of this is more important than exacting revenge for the murder of your friends."

"Maybe it was Quon that done it," said Shad O'Shea, looking down from his aerial examination. He began to whistle a popular tune. His mournful face tried to look innocent. He managed only a species of benign bemusement.

Doc tossed the automatic over the rail, scrutinizing the faces of the quartet as the distant splash came.

None of them betrayed by their expression any pang of loss over the expensive death weapon.

"Now might be the proper time to bring Captain Gooch into this matter,' the bronze man said without inflection.

This brought glum expressions all around—even to Ham Brooks. No one was looking forward to the *Mandarin* skipper's reaction to these latest events.

XVI

QUON WARNS

The revelation that Jason Baird was in fact not to be numbered among the deceased passengers of the liner *Mandarin*, and the further revelation that there were two more candidates for the ship's morgue, was more than harried Captain Gooch could stand.

"You're all under ship's arrest!" he thundered, the glowering first mate hovering at his side.

"I never heard of such a thing transpiring on a passenger liner!" Ham Brooks protested vehemently.

"Once we get to Hongkong," Captain Gooch shot back, "you can look it up in the maritime law books! But for the rest of the voyage, you'll all take your meals in your cabins and like it!"

To everyone's surprise, Doc Savage said calmly, "That will be satisfactory, Captain Gooch."

They were gathered in the captain's quarters. Pat Savage and Jason Baird had been summoned hither. It was quite a crowded scene.

Pat began to protest. "But, Doc—"

"The less we are exposed," Doc stated, "the safer we will be. Our goal now is to reach Hongkong unmolested."

Doc's strangely compliant attitude seemed to take the wind out of wrathy Captain Gooch's sails.

He did, however, order stewards to see that the passengers complied with his commands. Doc Savage, he personally escorted to the cabin the bronze man had secured as the fictitious Manchu, Sat Sung.

"The British authorities in Hongkong will probably arrest you when we berth," Gooch warned. "I don't think the drag you have back in the States is going to amount to much."

"You might," Doc suggested, "alert Scotland Yard to the situation."

"Good grief! Do you *want* to land in a British hoosegow?" Gooch spluttered.

"What I would like," Doc told the captain, "is safe passage to Hongkong for myself and my friends. You might arrange for the Royal Suite, where my cousin Pat is quartered, as well as Jason Baird's cabin, to be guarded twenty-four hours a day. They are the two most likely marked for murder."

This made perfect sense to Captain Gooch.

"I'll see to it," the *Mandarin* skipper promised, stomping off to give the orders. He was shaking his white-capped head as he departed. Never in his years on the high seas had he encountered such turmoil as seemed to swirl around the enigmatic Man of Bronze.

The next several days were relatively uneventful.

Doc Savage maintained contact with the others via the *Mandarin*'s telephonic system.

"I, for one, will be ecstatic when this voyage is concluded," Ham fumed on one occasion.

Pat Savage put it another way:

"Walking the plank looks mighty enticing from where I sit. And I do mean 'sit'!"

"You will survive," Doc said dryly.

"What's keeping me going bughouse is the thought of the excitement I'm going to see in Cambodia!" she added cheerfully.

Doc sighed. "I was hoping you would see the wisdom of remaining in Hongkong, if not returning to the States," he said.

"Nothing doing! I've always wanted to see Cambodia. This may be my only opportunity, the way you keep pouring cold, nasty water on my excitement chasing."

"We will settle this later," Doc promised.

As for Jason Baird's hired adventurers—Chick Alfred, Alva Nally, Joe Knopf, and Shad O'Shea—Alfred succinctly expressed the collective opinion of his hard-bitten crowd.

"We're goin' stir-crazy in these cabins!"

"There is a popular expression you might want to keep in mind," Doc Savage told him.

"Yeah? Which is that?"

"Talking until one is blue in the face. In this instance, not complaining might keep your face from turning blue."

That reminder seemed all the Chick Alfred crowd required. No further complaint emanated from that quarter.

Every one settled down by the third day out of San Francisco. Inasmuch as the *Mandarin* was an express liner, there were no port calls en route. Honolulu was bypassed. The cobalt Pacific stretched wide in all directions about them. No other vessels were sighted along the route they were traversing.

The bronze man did not actually take his own advice about remaining indoors, however.

On several occasions—always in the dark period after first watch—he eased from his cabin to prowl the big black luxury liner.

Each time, he did so in disguise, usually as a Negro cook or steward. Once, he even resorted to assuming the identity of the nonexistent Manchu, Sat Sung, for the purpose of going to the lowermost deck and mingling with the so-called Asiatic steerage passengers.

Steerage is not exactly luxury accommodations. It is more on the order of a military barracks, featuring large compartments crammed with rows of close-packed cots. Rank odor from the nearby bilge lent a certain atmosphere. The proximity to the engine room set the beds to vibrating.

Doc went among these cots, his tiny generator flashlight lense squeezed down until it emitted a beam of intense light seemingly no wider than a strand of brilliant silk.

With this, he examined the features of sleeping passengers, looking for the telltale facial contours that would mark the native Cambodian. Doc was familiar with the peoples of the Orient, knew that the natives of China differed in certain particulars from the inhabitants of bordering Indo-China and Cambodia.

Doc picked out several half-castes whose light-brown skin tones and flattish physiognomy betrayed Cambodian heritage. He memorized their features in turn, and moved on.

A light-sleeping Chinese happened to come awake while Doc was making his rounds, discerned the wayward beam of light, and jumped to a reasonable—under the circumstances—conclusion.

"*Chock lou!*" he shrilled. Then: "*Gong Gwong!*"

In the ill-smelling murk, the sleepy-eyed Chinese could be forgiven for thinking that the compartment was inhabited by several robbers and crooks.

Doc doused the light and moved for the exit door as the sleepers came awake, hollering and reaching for their valuables—most of which were hidden under pillows and mattresses.

Here and there, matches flared and hissed, disclosing goggle-eyed Oriental faces. More cries came. Several languages were represented, but Cantonese and Mandarin Chinese predominated.

Fortunately, Doc happened to be fluent in them all.

The reason this was fortunate was that such fluency enabled him to evade the sharp implements that were being drawn from nightclothes with the intention of ending his life. Voices called out warnings to duck.

Doc Savage did likewise. A Malay creese sizzed past an ear, to clang off a sturdy bulkhead. Feet sought his ankles, attempted to topple him. Men were crawling in his direction, the better to avoid presenting easy targets themselves.

The bronze man shook off the grasping hands, stepping around scuttling ambushers.

He reached the door, felt the weight of a crouching Asiatic inhibiting the portal from opening.

Reaching down, Doc lifted the man bodily. The latter worthy squawled and shrieked maledictions. Hissing figures closed in.

Doc used the shrieking one to bowl over the others. He

got the door open, plunged through, while pursuers tangled up with the thrown individual.

A meaty *thunk* told of hatchet blade imbedding itself into the inner side of the panel. The force of the impact caused the door to slam closed, and the ugly sound evidently persuaded any would-be pursuers to hang back, lest they intercept further aerial blades.

Doc made it out into the passage and up a companionway to the shadow-enwrapped promenade deck without further incident.

He did not tarry in the vicinity, but by a series of devious routes picked his way back to his own cabin, moving with the stealth that he had learned from observing the masters of the art—the great cats of the jungle.

The bronze man reached his cabin and turned in for the evening.

The next day, there were no queries regarding the steerage incident. By this, Doc took it that his intrusion was not reported to the captain. This was expected. Orientals, as a rule, prefer to settle their differences amongst themselves.

After that, the bronze man avoided the steerage deck when he went about in the night.

During his nocturnal forays, Doc Savage also kept up his daily two-hour regimen of exercises. The sun deck was invariably deserted in the post-midwatch hours, and he took them there.

These exercises—lasting a full two hours of breakneck activity—were responsible for the remarkable state of near-perfection that the bronze man had attained in life.

There were sweat-producing physical routines that would have prostrated most men during their most elementary stages. Doc's mighty bronze muscles—he conducted these exercises in a black silk bathing suit—worked against one another until he was covered in a thin film of perspiration.

The bronze man did not neglect the mental part of his regimen, though. He performed prodigious mathematic calculations—multiplying, dividing, extracting square and cube roots of large figures entirely in his head—simultaneously with his physical ritual.

Then Doc moved to the portion of his regimen in which his senses were keened. These exercises involved pitting his aural organs against a device that put out sound waves in frequencies both above and below the range of normal hearing. The glass phials and their varied scents sharpened his sense of smell. His sense of touch was kept honed by use of Braille writing—the series of upraised dots that enable the blind to "read."

Fully two hours transpired during this ordeal, all of it undertaken at a pace that would have laid a lesser man low.

It was while exercising on the fifth day out of San Francisco that Doc Savage received the warning.

It was a moonless night. There was no wind. The sun deck was very still. No ships were visible on the horizon. There was only the constant rushing of water along the sides of the hull and the astringent scent of open ocean. Smoke from the two working funnels passed overhead like boiling rags.

Doc was working up a sweat when the ship's bell rang out three pair and one single bell. Half past three in the morning.

No sooner had the tiny echoes of the single bell faded than another sound intruded. Deep, resonant, foreboding.

Bong—bong—bong!

Doc Savage froze at the unfamiliar clangor.

It was reminiscent of nothing so much as the sound made by a great brass gong as it is struck.

Doc's acute hearing told him it came from amidships. He turned to face the source of the sound—he had been looking out toward the stern—when he saw the hideous arm.

It simply hung, motionless, in the shadow of the rearmost funnel that loomed over the aft section of the sun deck. It glowed with a soft, lambent light. Three bony fingers and a ghostly yellow thumb were curled back so that the forefinger was pointing its elongated length at the bronze man.

For a moment, Doc's melodious trilling roved the scale, tuneless and curious.

Then, came a voice as disembodied as the motionless floating arm of an apparition.

" 'Tis stated in the classic: True gold fears no fire!"

Doc's flake-gold eyes were focused on the spectral arm.

Because of its luminous quality, it was difficult to discern in detail. The tube of green silk that draped the thing from bony wrist to trail in tatters beyond the point where the stump should be, did not glow.

Carefully, Doc shifted to the left.

To his surprise, the thing shifted with him, so that the accusing fingers remained pointing in his general direction.

In the interim, Doc saw enough of the other end of the thing to see that the green-hued silk draped the unseen stump. The arm did not melt into invisibility; neither did it appear attached to any being or form, seen or unseen.

The sourceless voice spoke anew.

"Oh Bronze Man who knows no fear, know fear now! For I am Quon, Lord of Quon, Blessed by Siva, known as the Jade Ogre. Venture not into Cambodia, the domain of the Jade Ogre. For your face is known and the limbs of Quon are everywhere."

The weirdness in which the discorporate thing floated, as if disconnected from all reality, was unnerving.

"Death awaits you, Oh Bronze One," the hollow voice went on. "This is the last warning of Quon, the Jade Ogre."

Doc lunged for the thing then.

Bong—bong—bong!

The suddenness of the phantom gonging caused Doc Savage to veer to the left cautiously. The sound seemed to emanate from the murk beyond a yawning ventilator.

The arm of Quon began to move then. It had been as stationary as if fixed in amber, but now it was issuing toward the stern.

Doc faded farther to the left. He could see a dark wet spot on the pointing finger. It was vaguely greenish. Something about the coloration convinced him to avoid contact with the outstretched digit at all costs.

Doc swept around and behind the thing. It was moving more swiftly now. The bronze man realized why as he glided up from behind it.

The forward progress of the *Mandarin* was leaving the arm behind! It was not moving at all.

Doc lunged for it then. He did not use his hands, but pulled a tiny grapnel and line from his vest. It took a moment to pay out the silken cord, preparatory to employing the device.

A moment was all it took for the arm to be left behind.

It passed silently over the stern rail of the sun deck, continued along, high above the promenade deck below.

From the rail, Doc attempted a toss. The first missed by a mere foot. The second fell short.

By the time he had hauled back the grappling hook for a third toss, the arm was a speck of yellow radiance many yards to the broad stern of the liner. It was over water now.

Doc Savage watched it intently for several moments, his eyes troubled by vague eddies, then turned to investigate the vicinity of the sun deck.

He found only one thing out of the ordinary.

There was a tiger's claw caught in the rim of a small window set in the false funnel. The funnel was used for storage of extra deck chairs and other useful items.

Doc removed this, examined it briefly, and stored it in his equipment vest.

He made a circuit of the funnel, discovered a padlocked door on the other side. He put his ear to it. Detecting no sounds, he completed his circuit.

There was only the single open window. It was too small to admit his giant form—or that of an ordinary man, for that matter—so Doc settled for spearing the ray of his tiny flash within.

The questing fan of light disclosed crates, boxes, and several deck chairs in need of repair.

One object in particular stood out. A chest. Fantastically ornate, it smacked of some Asiatic Pandora's box, for each side boasted a carven face, cold-eyed and grim of mein.

It was too small to conceal any being larger than a small child, however.

Hearing the footfalls of a seaman making his rounds on the deck below, Doc Savage was forced to abandon his investigation of the dummy stack.

Collecting his exercise equipment, he quitted the sun deck, his bronze features inscrutable.

XVII

THE MISSING

The liner *Mandarin* steamed through crowded Sulphur Channel between Stonecutter's Island and Hongkong in the middle of the eleventh day out of San Francisco. It was not a record crossing—but good time was made.

It was not an hour too soon for Doc Savage and his party.

They took the liberty of emerging from their cabins as the tugs came alongside to help guide the oceangoing greyhound through Victoria Harbor.

"That Hongkong?" grumbled horse-faced Shad O'Shea, squinting in the direction of a broad island whose shores were crammed with what looked like statternly derelict ships, mostly water-logged junks. Upon closer inspection, these proved to be inhabited, for ragged natives passed between them.

"It is," Jason Baird remarked. "The name means Fragrant Harbor, even though it doesn't exactly smell that way. They sometimes call it the Pearl of the Orient."

Chick Alfred grinned. "Looks kinda like Frisco to me."

Indeed, the island that was Hongkong bore more than a passing resemblance to the city they had left behind, particularly in its steep hills and close-packed office buildings. Its terrain tended toward verticals more than horizontals. There was no enveloping fog, though.

There was also, they quickly learned, no pier massive enough for the *Mandarin* to berth at. The hard-working tugs were nudging the liner to the port of Kowloon, on the other side of the bumpy island. Kowloon was attached to the Chinese mainland, and was the major transshipping point to the rest of Asia, the nearby Canton River being too narrow for freighter traffic.

The harbor was a choke of junks, sampans, and the curious double-ended ferries that shuttled between Kowloon and Hongkong. Except for the numerous junks and sampans, their brown matting sails like the soiled, broken wings of cast-down butterflies, it was also remindful of San Francisco Bay.

At sight of the big liner entering the harbor, sampans began making for the great ship. They fell in behind its turbulent wake as it was brought up to a long concrete finger of a pier.

Lines were made fast. The immense steam turbines, many decks below, fell silent. A trunk line, designed to allow telephonic communication between ship and shore, was affixed to the *Mandarin*'s connector port.

Pat Savage, watching the approaching sampans, asked a question.

"Do they still have pirates in these waters?"

"They do," Doc told her. His eyes were not on the harbor, but on the passengers milling about. The fact that the Pacific passing had been largely uneventful, once they had been confined to their accommodations, had not lulled the bronze man's concerns one iota.

"Well, prepare to be boarded, me hearties," exclaimed Pat, pointing to the converging sampans.

All eyes fell in the direction the lovely Pat indicated.

The sampans were propelled by conical-hatted coolies employing ironwood poles. Other Asiatics crowded their tire-fendered scuppers, hoisting jointed bamboo poles to which were affixed tiny sacklike nets.

There were lifted to the rails of the lowermost deck. Excited gobblings came from the sampans.

"Any one understand their lingo?" Pat asked, worriedly.

"They are merely begging for coins," put in a smooth voice from behind them.

Pat turned at the sound of the unfamiliar voice. Up minced diminutive Dr. Mawson Harper, striking in his striped white hair and black beard. The physician paused and executed a courtly bow in Pat Savage's direction.

"Dr. Mawson Harper, at your service," he said gallantly.

"I do not believe we have had the pleasure of meeting, Miss Savage."

Pat had abandoned her Tarzana Vine guise, and the brisk ocean breezes were toying with her extraordinary wealth of bronze hair. She had been collecting admiring gazes, and a similar one had alighted on the doctor's Van-Dyke-decorated face.

Pat allowed her hand to be taken. "I am quite fluent in Cantonese," he explained, "being a frequent visitor to these parts. I take it this is your first time in the Orient?"

"I almost didn't get to come at all," Pat said, eying Doc Savage pointedly.

The bronze man said, "Dr. Harper is known for his charity work throughout Asia."

"Tropical diseases are my field," Dr. Harper elaborated. "Of course, I am not the pioneer your famous cousin is," he added modestly.

"Doc's trying to inoculate me against my present malady," Pat remarked airily.

Dr. Harper blinked. "Which is?"

"Excitement chasing. You'd think he'd understand, having caught a dose of it himself. But no soap. He's trying to send me back to the States while he plunges headlong into Cambodia."

"Cambodia is a fascinating place," Dr. Harper said, digging a dollar coin from a pocket and tossing it over the rail. The toss was careless, but a dangling net on the end of a bamboo pole expertly snagged the coin. Other passengers catching on to the idea, began tossing coins in like fashion. The excited volley of Cantonese rose to a swell.

"Looks like I'm going to have to settle for Hongkong," Pat grumbled, adding a coin of her own to the silvery rain.

Miraculously, few coins plunked into the water. Nearly every one plopped into a waving net, which would be hastily hauled down, emptied, and lifted anew.

Pale Rex Pinks sauntered up at this point, peered over the gleaming rail, and pointedly declined to contribute to the proceedings, pronouncing it "cheap blackmail." He and Ham Brooks exchanged bilious looks, after which Ham produced a silver dollar and made a show of tossing it down. He managed to precipitate the coin into the drink.

Preparations to allow passengers to go ashore continued. The gangway was set in place. At the end of the pier, an official-looking vehicle awaited, two British police in khaki shorts and matching blouses standing about, both impatient of demeanor.

"Should we make a dash for it, Doc?" Ham wondered.

"Not necessary," the bronze man said.

The dapper lawyer looked worried, but said nothing. Then Captain Gooch, trailed by his stern first mate, bowled up the promenade deck.

"Savage," he said gruffly. "I am afraid I will have to remand you into the custody of the British authorities."

"Understandable," Doc told him. There was no trace of resentment on his calm, metallic visage.

This seeming compliance seemed to make Captain Gooch uncomfortable. The irritable skipper shuffled his clumsy feet and added, "I've asked them not to go hard on you, and offered to speak on your behalf."

"Thank you," Doc said quietly.

There seemed to be nothing more to say.

The gangway gate was opened and the Hongkong bobbies, at a signal, came pounding up the incline. They were escorted to Captain Gooch's side.

"I am officially turning over Doc Savage and his accomplices to you," Captain Gooch said in an important tone, once the official niceties had been dispensed with.

"Jolly good," one of the bobbies said in crisp British tones. He turned to the bronze man, touched his white sun helmet in salute, and added, "We are to escort you to Government House, Mr. Savage. I am under instructions to afford you and your party every courtesy. If there is anything His Majesty's government may do for you, please be good enough to let us know."

Before Doc Savage could respond to this flowery outpouring of cooperation, Captain Gooch shoved between them. He stuck his jaw out and tried to push his belligerent face into the first bobby's own. He was too short to accomplish that, but his voice volume more than made up for his lack of physical stature.

"Damn you, I collected a morgueful of bodies because of this man!" he roared. "Savage should be in irons! Why are you treating him like the grand poobah?"

"Mr. Savage has rendered certain services to His Majesty's government in the past," the first bobby explained with studied formality.

Captain Gooch's eyes bugged out. He sputtered some moments, then turned on his heel to vent his wrath upon the passively waiting bronze man.

"Is this why you suggested I contact Scotland Yard?" he demanded, his face reddening.

"It was," Doc admitted.

Captain Gooch drew himself up on the toes of his polished boots. He looked like a runty human volcano about to blow its top. Words seemed to failed him, however. His face had crimsoned to its upmost, it seemed; his voice had achieved its maximum register.

Silently, he lowered himself to his flat heels. They clicked. His eyes retreated into their sockets, narrowing.

"First Mate Scott," he said slowly, his words grinding together like flinty stones.

"Cap'n?"

"Get these—these blasted trouble-hounds off my good ship!"

This was done with alacrity. In fact, Doc and his party were allowed to be the first to disembark the liner.

The British authorities had not been prepared for a party quite so large, so Doc, Ham, Pat, and Jason Baird were bundled into the waiting official car, while Chick Alfred and his men, along with Rex Pinks, sought a taxi. An argument immediately broke out. The native cabby insisted his conveyance could accommodate but four individuals, so the colorless society reporter was forced to secure a cab for himself.

The price evidently gave him pause, so he settled for engaging a ricksha. The various parties were whisked away then, the ricksha taking up the rear.

They went only as far as the ferry pier, where they

transferred to a double-ended ferryboat and made the short but colorful passage to Hongkong itself.

A more formal delegation met them on the other side. Official vehicles conveyed them to the Government House, in the shadow of Victoria Peak, the highest prominence on the busy island. This time Rex Pinks did not have to spring for his fare.

There, polite noises were made and promises exchanged, the upshot of which came down to the fact that Doc and his party had their liberty. The past services the bronze man had rendered to John Bull were evidently sufficient to cut through all manner of official red tape entanglement.

The British governor who was in charge of this wound up his speech-making and asked Doc Savage, "How long do you intend to remain in our Victoria City?"

Victoria City was the official name—seldom used—of Hongkong.

"Not long," Doc told him. "We plan to travel on to Cambodia, once we have secured a suitable plane."

"Has this anything to do with the unfortunate deaths aboard the *Mandarin*?" the governor inquired.

"I believe so," Doc stated.

When the bronze man did not volunteer any further information, the governor stood up and began shaking hands all around.

"Very good. Good luck to you, chaps."

And that was that. They were free to go.

Outside Government House, Rex Pinks looked bewildered.

"That's it?" he wondered. "I thought we'd at least spend one night in the local pokey."

"When one travels with Doc Savage," Ham Brooks put in, a trifle superciliously, "one is accustomed to being accorded a certain respect."

"Unless one just happens to be his only living relative," Pat Savage inserted archly.

If this dig had any effect upon the bronze man, he gave no sign. They collected sufficient of the stubby taxis that struggled through the maze that was Hongkong traffic to accommodate the entire party, and wended their way to one of the better British hotels on the island, gaping at the similarity the city bore to San Francisco—at least, to the Chinatown sector. Streetcars, they found, were plentiful, except that they were called, after the British fashion, trams.

After the long confinement, they agreed that they could stand remaining in the city one day before embarking upon the journey to the Cambodian interior.

"A night on the town sounds swell," Pat enthused. She sobered when she noticed the forlorn expression her comment brought to Jason Baird's face. The jeweler's attitude reflected concern over the fate of his missing sister, Maurine.

"Oh, buck up, Jason," Pat said soothingly. "We'll find Maurine. Doc's never failed yet."

"We will meet here in the lobby in two hours," Doc Savage told the assembled group.

"Not me," protested Rex Pinks. "I'm going to see as much of this burg as I can before we shove off."

"What makes you believe you are coming with us, Pinks?" Ham Brooks asked disdainfully.

No one answered that directly, so Doc Savage said, "You are welcome to accompany us."

This remark was greeted with facial expressions ranging from studied indifference to sour annoyance.

"I can see I'm popular with this crowd," Pinks snapped.

At that, the colorless society reporter turned on his heel and stormed out of the hotel lobby into the raucous bustle and din of Hongkong.

"I don't like that guy," muttered Shad O'Shea.

Wearily, they repaired to their rooms.

At the appointed hour, the tiny band began to collect in the hotel's sumptuous lobby. Chick Alfred and his crowd showed up first. They huddled in one corner, near the shoeshine concession, and conferred in low voices. Their manner was furtive, suspicious. It was plain that they did not relish being so far from their usual haunts.

They left off their discussion when dapper Ham Brooks put in an appearance. The eminent lawyer had changed clothes, affecting a natty white linen suit such as is commonly worn in the tropics. It was well past noon and Hongkong was sweltering.

"Where's your chief?" Chick Alfred asked.

"Doc will not be long," Ham imparted.

Joe Knopf grumbled, "Me, I'm for leaving this burg behind—but fast!"

Ham was about to make some comment when Rex Pinks sauntered into the lobby. A sullen silence fell over the group at that juncture. Ham fell to brushing an imaginary speck of dust off his faultless attire.

If Pinks was upset by being ignored so elaborately, he gave no indication of it.

Doc Savage materialized next. The bronze man's strange golden eyes swept the lobby.

"Where is Pat?" he asked Ham.

"I imagine she will be down in a moment," the dapper lawyer offered. "You know how women like to be late."

Momentary concern flickered across the bronze man's regular features. It was a rare display of emotion. Doc had schooled himself never to betray his inmost thoughts by outward expression. He had started for the lobby desk when his missing cousin stepped off the elevator.

"Jove!" Ham exclaimed.

It was not Pat's breathtaking beauty that inspired the startled exclamation, although, truth to tell, Pat was a vision in a canary-yellow gown that would have been the rage of Paris, if only Pat were now in Paris instead of China.

What made Ham Brooks clutch the ornate knob of his cane until his knuckles whitened was the sight of Pat's escort—Dr. Mawson Harper. The bantamlike medico more than ever resembled a strutting midget rooster. He carried his shoulders with inordinate pride.

Spotting the others, Pat disengaged her arm from the doctor's own and, with a word, left him at the elevator. She strode up to Doc Savage, her smile mischievous.

"Guess who I found, Doc," she teased.

"I see you are enjoying yourself, as usual," Doc said without reproval.

"Actually, our goat-chinned friend is a bit of a bore," Pat

admitted cheerfully, "but he's offered to show me the Thieves' Quarter of the city. Can't very well pass that up, now, can I?"

"It would be better if you remained with us."

"O.K.," Pat said instantly.

This quick acquiescence caught the bronze man flat-footed. He was rendered momentarily speechless.

"If I get to go to Cambodia with you fellows," Pat added quickly, her eyes twinkling.

"That," Doc told her, "is impossible."

"Suit yourself," Pat said lightly. "See you in the funny papers." She breezed back to the elevator, where Dr. Harper gathered up her offered arm. With a tip of his hat in the bronze man's direction, he escorted the vivacious Pat out the hotel's rear exit.

Ham sidled up to his bronze chief, said, "I don't like this. That bird is easily twice Pat's age. And look how he's making calf eyes at her."

"We will have to make arrangements to ship Pat back to America," Doc said firmly.

"How?"

"That, we will have to work out later." Doc strode over to Chick Alfred and his entourage.

"I will need two of you to shadow my cousin to see that she encounters no difficulty," Doc stated.

"We work for Baird, not you," Joe Knopf retorted. Gratitude was evidently not in the runty gunman's nature.

"And we are all in this together," the bronze man pointed out. "If you cannot cooperate here, there is no point in traveling on together."

"You got a point there," Chick Alfred said reluctantly. He turned to the others. "Joe—Shad. You got the detail. Hop to it."

"One moment." Doc went to a lobby writing desk, scooped up a sheaf of envelopes deposited there for the convenience of guests. They bore the hostelry's address and ostentatious crest. The bronze man divided these into two equal bunches and passed one to each member of Chick Alfred's crowd.

"Every half hour," he instructed, "give one of these to a

messenger and have him return it to the front desk, along with word of your whereabouts."

"What for?" demanded Shad O'Shea, idly fanning his pack of envelopes with a big paw.

"It is the surest method of ascertaining your safety," Doc explained. "If you fail to report in, we will undertake an exhaustive search for you, using the last-known location as a starting point."

Chick Alfred grinned. "Slick," he said approvingly. "You got brains, Savage."

Clutching their envelopes, Joe Knopf and Shad O'Shea headed out the back exit.

"If that were my cousin," Rex Pinks said pointedly to no one in particular, "I wouldn't let her sail off with that fussy little guy."

"If Pat were related to you," Ham Brooks sniffed, "you would soon come to understand that the young lady has a mind of her own."

"What's keepin' that Baird?" growled reedy-voiced Alva Nally, who had thus far been silent.

Doc went to the front desk and inquired after the absent jewel merchant.

The desk man rang Baird's room. Obtaining no answer after several rings, he reported this to the bronze man.

"He must have gone out, sir," the desk man stated in clipped British tones.

Doc thanked the functionary and got the others together, explaining the situation in brisk, economical sentences.

"We had best investigate this," he finished tightly.

There was a grim push in the direction of the elevators.

XVIII

THE UNEXPECTED DEAD

The door to Jason Baird's hotel room, they discovered upon stepping off the surprisingly up-to-date elevator, gaped ajar. There was no sign of life. A hallway runner was up off its tacks, indicating a recent struggle.

Doc Savage took instant command of the situation.

"There will be no shooting," he admonished, glancing at the assortment of pistols and other weapons Chick Alfred and Alva Nally had produced from their garments.

Alfred rammed a sharp jaw in the direction of Ham Brooks, who stood handy, his sword cane exposed in one hand and one of Doc's compact supermachine pistols in the other.

"What about that?" he growled.

"Mercy bullets," Doc explained. "They do not kill."

The lethal weapons were returned to their places of concealment with ill-disguised reluctance.

Doc laid bronze knuckles on the rich panel, rapped twice, and called Jason Baird's name. He put an ear to the panel and listened some moments.

When it was apparent that there would be no reply, the bronze man grasped the knob and pushed inward. The panel fell out of its jamb.

"I do not like this!" Ham hissed.

Fingers going into his coat front, Doc Savage brought out one of his anæsthetic glass balls which vaporized instantly, producing swift unconsciousness. He pegged one in through the door, drew it shut.

"Retreat," he called.

When the others hesitated, he lifted great bronze arms, sweeping them before him, an irresistible human bulldozer.

"What's the idea, guy?" Alva Nally muttered, after they had turned a corner.

"Gas," Doc explained tersely.

"Fat lotta good that'll do us. How're we gonna check the joint out if it's all gassed up?"

"The mixture renders itself harmless after a few moments' exposure to oxygen," Doc related, glancing at his wrist watch.

When he decided enough time had elapsed to make entry safe, he eased down the corridor and threw the portal open. The others followed him in.

"Hell's bells!" snarled Chick Alfred, once he got a look at the room.

It had been ransacked—or at least furniture had been upset during the course of a terrific struggle.

There was blood on the carpet, a scarlet sprinkling of it. The spatters led back to a closet door, where they stopped abruptly.

"They musta bundled Baird up in something," Alva Nally theorized.

"Yeah," said Chick. "It covered for the fact that they were takin' him away, and he was leakin'."

"Maybe," Rex Pinks mused. "Unless he just stopped bleeding all of a sudden."

Ham started. "Doc, you don't suppose Baird is dead?"

"Unlikely," Doc interposed. "Those minions of the so-called Jade Ogre kept Baird alive during our crossing of the Pacific; they are not apt to dispose of him at this late date."

Doc's eyes scoured the suite. The others were milling about, their expressions grim and frustrated, hands dangling uselessly. The loss of Jason Baird, after all that had happened, was getting them down.

The bronze man spotted the tiny strand of silk that had been anchored to an upended chair leg just before Ham Brooks walked into it.

"Ham!" Doc rapped. "Stop!"

Doc's men were well trained. Ham stood stock still. His dark eyes darted rapidly.

"Do not move," Doc said swiftly. "Any of you."

This brought instant obedience. Doc came up on the immobile barrister, examined the strand of silk. It was very fine. It stretched from the vertical chair leg to the closet doorknob, about which it was looped and fastened by a tiny knot no bigger than a pin head.

"Trip wire," Doc decided. "Back away from it, every one."

Ham blew out a breath of relief only after he had put a good yard between him and the nearly-invisible line.

"Think it's a bomb rig?" gulped Rex Pinks, paling.

"We will have to find out." Taking up a heavy lamp, the bronze man faded back in the direction of the door. The others retreated with him.

"What if there's somebody hiding inside?" Alva Nally wondered.

Doc Savage did not answer the question directly. "Ham, have your supermachine pistol ready."

"Righto, Doc," said Ham, thumbing the safety off the rapid-firer. The compact weapons were equipped with several safety devices. Ham had merely disengaged the last of these. He set himself for come what may.

Surreptitiously, Alva Nally produced a long-barreled revolver.

Doc reared back with the lamp and let fly. It arced true. The lamp struck the cord in its approximate center, crashed to the carpet. The weight of it was not sufficient to tip the chair, but it did cause the closet door to swing open slightly.

There was no explosion. No sound at all. Chick Alfred started forward. Doc stopped him with a blocking arm.

"Could be a timer mechanism engaged," he said, low-voiced.

They waited several minutes. A ticking clock could be heard from inside the room, marking the inexorable march toward eternity.

Evidently, the waiting was more than Alva Nally could bear, because with a muttered oath, he plunged into the room, saying, "I'll bet there's a rat in that closet! And I'm gonna flush it out!"

Doc's voice was a crash. *"Nally—wait!"*

Holding his revolver before him, Alva Nally grasped the closet doorknob and gave it a hard yank. Simultaneously, he fired twice into the gloomy closet interior. Gun thunder crashed.

Since the others still crowded out into the corridor, not all of them got a good look at what next transpired.

Alva Nally let out a shriek. He took a half step backward, recoiling from a sight only he could see.

"Huh-huh-huh!" he sputtered.

Then a gaunt yellow arm lunged for his throat!

It seemed to exist for only a flash moment. A dully glowing talon, it reached out for Alva Nally's bobbing Adam's apple. His efforts to raise his arms to beat it off were too tardy to succeed. Possibly, the gunman had been paralyzed by fear. Then again, the thing that sought his throat moved like a viper uncoiling.

The questing, bony fingers brushed the retreating gunman. That and no more. Then it erupted in a yellow flash that seared its imprint on every eye that beheld the uncanny sight.

The illusion that the arm still hovered in the place where they had last beheld it was brief.

Alva Nally, however, crumpled to the carpet, his final outcry choked off as if by phantom fingers.

"Nally!" It was Chick Alfred's voice—anguished, rattled.

"Wait!" Doc cautioned.

"Wait, hell! That's my pard in there."

Chick Alfred attempted to push the bronze man's restraining arm aside. He received a surprise. Doc had grasped the opposite jamb of the door, creating a blockage that might have been a metal bar for all the head gunman's ability to budge it. Sweat popped up on Alfred's forehead as he tried. He grunted, first with exertion, and finally in defeat.

"O.K., bronze man," the storklike gunman said thickly. "You win."

"Doc knows what he's doing, fellow," Ham Brooks supplied.

Doc entered the room. The others—Ham Brooks, Chick Alfred, and Rex Pinks—hung back, watching intently.

Alva Nally had fallen backward, his head striking the chair leg where the silk strand had been anchored. His pate had struck with such force that it left a smear of crimson, with a little hair and scalp mixed in, on the projecting leg.

As a consequence, Doc Savage could not see anything of Alva Nally's features until he rounded the upset chair.

Then he did so.

For a moment, Doc's weird trilling came. It roved the scale, sounding as exotic as their location.

"What is it, Doc?" Ham asked anxiously.

"Nally is dead," Doc announced. "You might as well see for yourself."

The trio entered.

Rex Pinks gaped. Strain and incredulity made his sickly features drawn and ashen.

"Jove!" Ham exclaimed. "His face is—blue!"

"That damn Jade Ogre!" Chick Alfred gritted. He looked close to tears. Evidently, the two adventurers had been friends of long standing.

"But how could an arm just fly out from a closet like that?" Ham wanted to know.

Doc Savage was investigating just that question. He had the closet door fully open now, and was shining his spring-generator flashlight about the interior.

The closet contained no clothes. Baird's trunks had not yet been sent from the *Mandarin*. There were a few coat hangers of the wooden variety present. The enclosure was otherwise bare.

Ham poked his sharp profile inside.

"Empty!" he pronounced.

Doc was checking the closet walls with the flat of his hand. The surfaces appeared solid. There were no trapdoors or secret panels. The walls were plaster—not a good material with which to contrive such artifices.

Doc came out, and regarded the outer doorknob briefly.

Noticing this, Ham asked, "It's just a brass knob, isn't it?"

Before Doc could reply, Chick Alfred blurted, "Hey! Where'd that silk wire go to? The one fancy pants almost tripped."

Ham got it then: The silk line was gone. There was no

sign of it, either anchored to the brass knob or looped to the chair leg. He fell to one knee to examine the carpet. It was not thick. He felt around the nap. Of the silken trip wire, there was no sign.

"It's like it was never even there!" Rex Pinks blurted.

"Confounding," Ham murmured. He came to his feet just as Doc was digging into the lock. He brought out a shiny white curl of a thing, held it up. The others goggled at it.

"A cat's claw?" Ham ventured.

Doc shook his head. "Tiger."

A bewildered expression crossed the dapper lawyer's features. He said, "It looks like the one that was hooked into Pat's tiger-skin bathing suit. It can't be a coincidence."

Doc Savage extracted from his utility vest two identical claws. The three reposed in his metallic palm for all to see.

Ham's dumfounded expression indicated that the bronze man had neglected to apprise the dapper lawyer of his spectral encounter with the phantom arm of Quon, the so-called Jade Ogre, on the sun deck of the liner *Mandarin*—an encounter which had led to the discovery of the second claw.

Neither did Doc enlighten him now. Instead, he pocketed the claws after a silent examination of all three.

"What d'we do now?" Chick Alfred asked nervously. "The British law ain't gonna be too understanding to us if we present them with another blue stiff."

"We will deal with that soon enough," Doc rapped, quitting the room. "Jason Baird must be located."

On the way down to the lobby, Rex Pinks ventured a comment.

"You know," he said, "just before Brooks nearly bumped into that trap, I was walking through the same area."

"So?" Ham Brooks and Chick Alfred said in unison.

"So—it proves I'm not hooked in with this Jade Ogre creature," Pinks snapped. "I could have fallen victim to that weird arm as easily as Nally."

"The fact that you avoided the trap speaks more to your suspiciousness than not," Ham Brooks sniffed.

Chick Alfred took hold of the reporter's coat front, made a fist, and drew his nose down to that of Rex Pinks.

"Any guy I find out is in cahoots with whatever's making those damn arms chase people," he said fiercely, "had better have a nice pine box picked out for himself. Get me?"

"Y-you d-don't s-scare m-me," Rex Pinks stuttered.

"Stick around," Alfred retorted. "I'm ain't got goin' yet."

The elevator let them out into the lobby. Rex Pinks was the last to emerge. He had to feel his way along the wall, due to the rubbery quality his knees had acquired.

Ham undertoned, "Doc, you don't think Pinks is really responsible for some of the things that have happened, do you?"

Doc did not reply. He went immediately to the front desk and, to every one's surprise, asked for messages.

The desk clerk pushed an envelope across the polished counter. It bore the crest of the hostelry they were standing in.

Doc thanked the man and unsealed the envelope flap. The note was brief.

SAVAGE:
WE TRAILED HARPER AND YOUR COUSIN TO ICE HOUSE LANE. LOOKS LIKE HARPER MET UP WITH A FRIEND. A NATIVE. THEY ALL JUST WENT INTO NO. 44 ICE HOUSE LANE. WE'RE GOING IN AFTER THEM.

It was signed, casually enough: "Shad."

A metallic grimness settled over Doc's normally inexpressive countenance. It was infinitesimal, this change in cast, but Ham Brooks, long associated with the remarkable bronze man, picked up on the subtle alteration immediately.

"Doc! What's wrong?"

"According to this note, Dr. Harper has entered a building on Ice House Lane, with Pat."

"Yeah? What of it?" Chick Alfred demanded.

"Ice House Lane is nowhere near the Thieves' Quarter, where Pat said they were going," Doc supplied.

"Pat wouldn't fib about something like that," Ham said. "Something is up!"

No. 44 Ice House Lane was a ramshackle thing of colorless planking that looked to have been there since pre-Colonial days. Its roof was in the process of falling in. Its sides were weather-beaten and without paint. Whether it was a dwelling or a commercial building of some sort was difficult to determine. There were no signs evident in any language. In fact, they had to determine the address through elimination, for the slovenly place lacked a posted house number.

Ham was all for storming the edifice, but Doc Savage, showing once more the caution that had sustained his existence through many a bloody adventure, forbore doing so.

"We will reconnoiter, first," he advised.

They did so, splitting up. Ham made a special point of keeping the vapid Rex Pinks within eye-and-earshot.

There were no signs of habitation, skulkers, or trouble hovering about the vicinity of No. 44 Ice House Lane, a cautious investigation proved.

Doc got the other three together and collected their reports. When this was done, he said, "The direct approach might be best. Ham, you and Pinks will stand watch. Alfred, you and I will enter together."

Ham started to protest, but Doc silenced him with a glance. The dapper lawyer detested being excluded from pending excitement. And excitement impended now.

"Come on, Pinks," Ham said sourly. They faded to places of concealment.

Crouching in the shadow of the overhanging pagoda-style roof, Doc asked Alfred, "Can you climb?"

The gunman was staring up at the rear wall, which was blank. "Climb what? I don't see no windows."

The bronze man answered this by taking out his tiny collapsible grappling hook and line. The cord was thin, of stout silk. Only one possessed of the bronze man's immense muscular strength could possibly employ it for ascent, so Doc took a few moments to twist loops and handholds at various points along the line. When this was done, he stepped out into the alley and swung the grapple in tight circles, like a boy with a bull-roarer.

Doc let fly. The hook flew high, caught a fluted projection, and stayed there. No sound attended this. The flukes of the grapnel were silenced by rubber tubing.

"You first," Doc suggested.

Chick Alfred was wiry. He went up the line with enthusiasm. Halfway up, he was forced to pause. Then he resumed his climb. Doc started up, then.

On the roof, they hunted about for a hatch. Alfred was surprised to find one—a round hole of a thing covered over with a chicken-wire grille.

Doc had collected his grapple, reeled in his line. He lifted the hatch and, after spiking light down from his generator flash, dug the grapple into the rim of the hole—it was a kind of skylight, they decided.

The line went down. This time the bronze man descended first.

He disappeared down the hatch with the eerie silence of bronze smoke going down a flue.

Licking his lips nervously, Chick Alfred rattled down after him.

When his shoe soles clicked on the floor below, Chick Alfred found himself crouching in the utter and unrelieved darkness.

"Savage," he hissed. "Where are you?"

Doc replied by capping a fist over the lense and winking his flash once in Alfred's direction, creating a faint bronze lantern of skin and bone.

The wiry gunman sidled in the glow's direction. His heels clicked with what were, under the circumstances, unnerving loudness.

Doc seized him by one shoulder and guided him to a wall.

"We are at a door. Are you game?" he asked.

"Game as I'll ever be," Alfred breathed.

The door came open. Doc was a brief shape passing

through the opening gained. Chick Alfred followed, his big revolver out.

There were no noises inside the big barn of a place. There were odors, though. Copra predominated. The place seemed to be some sort of warehouse or storage building. Hongkong was the major warehouse center for the Far East.

There was another odor that came to their nostrils as they moved about the place, Doc employing his flashlight sparingly. He had twisted the lense until the ray put forth was less than the thickness of a pencil, but exceedingly bright.

"I know that stink," Chick Alfred muttered. "And it don't mean nothin' good."

Doc vouchsafed no comment. The light roved, picked out another door. The place was a maze.

Doc paused to listen and, hearing no sound more alarming than a rat scuttling somewhere, passed through.

The light almost immediately fell upon the source of the ugly odor.

It was Joe Knopf. He was kneeling over a big rattan basket that had been set in the center of a bare floor. His hands were tied behind his back. His posture was not unlike that of a man ducking for apples.

Except that instead of floating fruit, the big rattan basket contained Joe Knopf's expertly severed head.

XIX

TERROR'S JAWS

The sight of the beheaded figure of Joe Knopf held storklike Chick Alfred spellbound. He gaped at the raw, round patch of meat that was the terminus of the deceased gunman's neck, as if unable to comprehend the reality of the fate that had befallen his erstwhile cohort.

Chick Alfred was no weak sister. He had seen things in the course of his rough career. And had done a few things, too.

But beheadings were alien to him. He was having trouble with his composure.

Not so Doc Savage.

The mighty bronze man took in the fate of Joe Knopf with but a momentary flicker of his flake-gold eyes and surged to the nearest door.

He plunged through into the adjoining room, each hand clutching an anæsthetic glass ball capable of rendering any foe insensate.

There was grim purpose in the bronze man's movements, and a hint of recklessness, too. He was moving swiftly, going from room to room, seldom pausing. His golden eyes were molten.

A person who knew him might have guessed that fear for his cousin Patricia was motivating the bronze man now, causing him to shed his usual caution.

Only when he came to a section of the house that was substantially different from the rest in regards to decor did he begin exercising care once more.

Here, the walls were lacquered and trimmed in teak, sandalwood, and other fine Oriental woods. Joss sticks smoldered in copper urns resting on low taborets of ebony. The air was sickly sweet.

All four walls were a-crawl with the riotous coils of Chinese dragons. Doc saw that there was in fact but a single dragon. The tail of the lacquered phantasmagoria happened to terminate in the first room he had penetrated. There was no head. The coilings simply looped—scarlet, gold, and jade in hue—about the room.

At a corner facing the point where the dragon's tail twisted, was a simple door. Doc went to this.

He passed through. Beyond was another dragon-enwrapped room, a continuation of the first, as regards to decor. It was empty. There was no head here, either. But there was another door.

Doc Savage passed through several doors and an equal number of reptilian rooms before he found the dragon's head.

It terminated in the far wall of the final, and largest, chamber of all.

This was not empty, as the others had been.

It was in the nature of a throne room, the bronze man saw.

From the point where Doc Savage entered, the coils spread out from either side of the door to join behind an ebony-and-jade throne set against the opposite wall.

The throne itself was no simple thing, but ornate, barbaric, and designed to resemble the open jaws of the dragon's head, which emerged from the walls in such a way that it was remindful of a saurian beast emerging from another dimension.

The manner in which the dragon throne was constructed made a seat of the dragon's lower jaw. A scarlet cushion served as a kind of bloated tongue.

The upper portion, or head proper, formed a kind of canopy, from which wicked ivory fangs hung down. Round black orbs gleamed evilly in the bestial face.

There was a man caught in the jaw of the thing, Doc saw. Not seated. He lay across the scarlet silk cushion, on his stomach, his arms and legs hanging off each end, like a human morsel about to be consumed.

The top portion of the head gave a mechanical shudder, and dropped several inches, lowering the sharp ivory teeth closer to the victim. Hidden mechanism toiled beyond the far wall. Jaws were preparing to fall anew.

Doc Savage pitched forward.

The man in the dragon's head was not bound, but he was as trapped as if he had been trussed like a Christmas goose. The side teeth—blunt but powerful in their massiveness—were pressing down on the man's shoulders and the small of his back.

Escape was impossible.

Doc saw no button or lever or other controlling feature on the dragon-head throne itself.

His eyes scraped the environs, alighted on a row of jade designs that were set in the floor before the throne, at a spot where they would be reachable only if the one seated on the throne bent himself double to depress them.

The buttons were undistinguishable from one another. There was no way to determine which might, if pressed, halt the crushing device, or cause it to fall at once.

From his equipment vest, Doc Savage produced a phial

of smelling salts, uncorking it. He lifted the chin of the trapped man.

The hirsute features of Dr. Mawson Harper came to light. If this was unexpected, the bronze man's hard lineaments betrayed nothing of surprise.

He passed the phial under the man's narrow nostrils.

Dr. Harper came to with a start. He shook his stark-colored head. His eyes quickly came into focus.

"Where—where am I?"

"In a trap," Doc said.

"I remember now. Yes!" Harper bit out, "They forced me into this hideous thing."

"They?"

"Cambodians. There were several of them."

The mechanism seemed to complete a cycle. The upper jaw once more began to lift slowly. Then it sank. Evidently, a gear-and-ratchet arrangement governed the diabolical device.

Doc said, "There is a row of jade designs along the floor. One of them may halt the mechanism."

"One will. They were laughing about it, the devils." Dr. Mawson Harper gasped. Exertion made his features crimson.

"They told me if I pressed the wrong one," he added, "I would die instantly. I—I guess I waited too long to decide. The damned thing knocked the breath out of me. I blacked out, Savage."

"There is not much time," Doc rapped, testing one ivory forefang with a hard hand. The fang only seemed to be ivory, he discovered. It was metallic to the touch. Steel. Painted.

Doc exerted pressure as the toiling mechanism continued its inexorable cycle. Sweat popped up on the bronze man's high forehead. The tooth of a thing began to twist in its socket. In a moment, it turned a complete revolution.

But it remained fixed in place, like a stubborn molar defying the dentist's pliers.

Doc's mind raced. His gadget vest contained a number of devices—acids, chemicals, Thermit. All were too dangerous to employ here. For they would do more harm than good to the man they were intended to free.

The mechanism jerked downward again, producing an audible groan from Dr. Mawson Harper.

"Savage—" he gasped. "Do—something." His arms were flailing now.

Doc Savage stepped around to the front of the thing, the better to scrutinize the row of oddly placed floor devices.

At that moment, Dr. Mawson Harper's flailing hands flopped on the end design in the row. There came a click.

A bang of a sound came next.

Doc Savage felt the floor fall under his feet, and his lightning reflexes came into play. Strong bronze hands reached out, grasped the paired fangs, held.

His feet, dangling over empty air, found the narrow strip of flooring between the large square opening left by the dropping trapdoor and the dragon throne, and came to rest.

"What happened?" Dr. Mawson Harper cried, his head twisting wildly in an effort to see around the dragon head. His tone was frantic, terrified. "Savage, are you all right?"

"Trap," Doc said. No emotion registered in his controlled voice.

"My stars!"

"Time is short, Harper," Doc said grimly. "I must select a button. Have you any ideas?"

"Try the one on the end. The far one."

Doc immediately complied. He stamped on the jade device, which was raised off the floor slightly, button-fashion.

The toiling sounds in the wall beyond seemed to pause, then reverse at a higher pitch. The sound lengthened to a doglike whine.

And rapidly, like a drawbridge lifting, the dragon's upper skull lifted free.

Dr. Mawson Harper eeled off the would-be death machine.

Doc slipped along the strip of floor, careful to avoid the yawning pit below, and joined him.

He extended a hand to help the shaken medico to his feet.

"Good guess," he said flatly.

"It occurred to me," puffed Dr. Harper, gathering air into

his starved lungs, "that the devils would naturally taunt me with a button that was farthest from my reach."

The doctor seemed to be none the worse for wear after his grim experience, Doc saw. He addressed a terse question.

"Harper, where is my cousin, Pat?"

Dr. Harper stroked his neat Van Dyke. "I honestly do not know. We chanced to encounter an acquaintance of mine—a local merchant who promised to show us some bargains in Oriental bric-a-brac. I am quite a fancier of Orientalia. He brought us to this rather slovenly hovel."

He paused to get a grip on his breathing.

"We had no sooner entered than we were set upon by skulkers, and overpowered," Harper continued. "I suspect they were Cambodians. They took Pat—er, Miss Savage—away." Dr. Harper then did a thing that seemed uncharacteristic of him, given his usually unruffled demeanor. He wrung his hands together.

"This is awful," he moaned. "She had just accepted my proposal."

"Proposal?"

"Of marriage," said Dr. Harper. "I-I confess I am quite smitten by your lovely cousin. And I was pleased to find that she reciprocated my affections."

Doc Savage said nothing for a protracted moment in time. His eyes were steady, almost still, as he regarded the distressed doctor.

"We must find her, Savage," Harper continued miserably. "There is no telling what those devils are up to. I am convinced that this entire encounter was a trap of some sort, and those Cambodians are in league with this Quon entity."

"Come on," Doc rapped.

They continued into the labyrinthine dwelling.

Beyond the dragon throne chamber lay rooms shrouded in gloom.

Each cubicle boasted only one door, forcing them to follow a path created for them. After passing through three more rooms, Doc began to understand that he was moving in a circle, possibly through an outer ring of rooms. There were no discernible windows, but traffic sounds came distinctly through the wood.

Doc employed his flashlight, pausing often to give the generator crank a brisk wind. The light seldom dimmed.

Eventually, they found themselves in the room where Joe Knopf still knelt in the position of supplication that had attended his beheading.

Doc's flashlight passed over the grisly sight but a moment. It was long enough to evoke a choked response from Dr. Mawson Harper. "That—that"—he could barely force the words out—"isn't her? I mean, Miss Savage?"

"No," Doc told him. "He is Joe Knopf, one of Chick Alfred's crowd."

"Thank goodness!" Dr. Harper said with evident relief.

Doc led the man along, eventually coming to the first dragon room, where the tail began.

It was devoid of occupants.

Instead of moving on, Doc Savage loitered, his beam racing along the floor and walls like an inquisitive spook.

"Why do we stop?" Dr. Harper wondered. "There is obviously no one here."

Doc let the quarter-sized beam of light come to rest at a point on the floor by one wall.

The floor was of some light wood. Thus, the dark streak that seemed to disappear under the floorboard was quite apparent.

"I do not—" Dr. Harper began.

Doc cut him off with a curt gesture. "We have been making a circuit of what would seem to be the outer rooms," he explained. "Yet there were no windows anywhere."

"So?"

"Windows are apparent on three outer walls of this structure," Doc elaborated.

"Secret panels?" Dr. Harper guessed.

Doc nodded. "Chick Alfred should have caught up with me while I was attempting to free you from the dragon's jaws. He may have fallen victim to hidden skulkers."

Doc went to the far wall. It was covered with fishlike dragon scales. Doc felt of these.

Whether he would have discovered a secret spring or other cunning artifice was never to be known.

For a section of wall simply jumped inward, disgorging yelling brown warriors.

Doc Savage met the first attacker with a bronze fist that brought the man's teeth together with a loud click and his sandals up off the floor.

He fell into a loose-limbed heap, impeding those who sought to exit the secret room.

Others slashed them aside. There were bright blades visible in the thin flashlight wash. Some of them made busy clickings. Doc recognized the sound. Malay parangs—ingenious scissorlike daggers which, when operated, revealed an inner stabbing blade like a vicious tooth. They could gut a man in an instant.

Doc Savage retreated from the onslaught, began pegging gas grenades. They broke with mushy sounds and men ceased their yellings, sighed, and found resting places on the floor. A brown pile soon formed.

The bronze man urged Dr. Harper from the room, slammed the door, and paused, muscles tensing.

"What is it?" Harper panted.

Doc silenced the man with a hard squeeze. He was holding his breath. Harper followed suit.

Moments later, Doc returned to the room. The Cambodians continued their peaceful snoring.

The bronze giant ventured into the murk beyond.

Chick Alfred was there. He squatted on the floor, endeavoring to hop. The fact that his wrists were wired to his ankles made this somewhat difficult. The streak on the flooring Doc had spied in the other room continued into this one. It terminated near Chick Alfred's shoes, and was identical in coloring to the gunman's shoe leather.

Doc removed a red silk gag, and extracted the equally crimson sponge from between Chick Alfred's jaws.

"The heathens ambushed me!" he spat. "I dragged my feet so I'd leave a trail. Slick, huh?"

Doc demanded, "My cousin. Have you seen her?"

"No!"

Doc worked at the wire. It was too stout even for his prodigious finger strength. He went away, harvested a parang from one of the fallen Cambodians, and went to work.

The blades rasped and whined, and the tight wire popped free, a strand at a time.

Chick Alfred stood up, rubbing his wrists and turning the surrounding gloom azure with lavish profanity.

The room was decorated with a single window. It was curtained off in black crepe, producing darkness. Doc Savage swept the crepe aside and pushed the window open. It was of the type that swiveled outward.

The bronze man shoved his head out and saw Ham Brooks. The dapper lawyer's chiseled features had lifted expectantly to the sound of the pane rasping open.

Doc called, "Ham. Any sign of Pat?"

"No!"

"Where is Pinks?"

"Around the other side, watching the rear."

"Bring him inside. And be careful."

"Righto, Doc."

Doc returned to Chick Alfred. Dr. Harper had crept warily into the room, gingerly stepping over the fallen Cambodians.

Doc Savage went among the fallen, selected a likely subject, and hauled him to a wall, where he set the man in a sitting position. The Cambodian—his features made his lineage certain—lolled his head and snored sonorously.

From his vest, Doc produced a counteractant to the anæsthetic gas that had felled the man and injected it into one naked brown arm.

The man at first acted as if a fly were bothering him. He swatted at his nose, making snorting and grunting sounds. Then he started awake.

Doc was holding his flashlight under his chin. He clicked it on, producing weird upward-straining shadows along his metallic countenance.

At the sight of the grim bronze mask of a visage before him, the Cambodian began blubbering in his native tongue, which was not Chinese, but an offshoot tongue. Doc Savage had made a thorough study of languages and could speak the Cambodian's own dialect with serviceable facility.

He began putting questions to the frightened fellow.

"Quon! No! Quon kill!" the man blubbered. He was using English. Evidently it had not quite registered that the big bronze apparition was attempting to converse in the Cambodian's own tongue.

"Why do you fear this Quon?" asked Doc, reverting to English.

"Quon number one devil. Quon come alongside *Yook Fatszu*—Jade Fever."

"Jade Fever?"

The other nodded frantically. "Many die. First turn blue, like heart stop. Then green, like jade."

"Did you hear that, Savage?" Dr. Harper demanded excitedly. "This mysterious affliction is the product of some criminal mind!"

At that moment, Ham Brooks charged into the room, his supermachine pistol sweeping the confines.

"Fat lotta good you done us, Fancy Dan," Chick Alfred growled.

Ham purpled, but said nothing. Rex Pinks stepped in next. He looked about the room, and swallowed whatever tart comment seemed to be on the tip of his tongue.

"We passed a body," Ham explained. "It looked like Knopf."

Doc nodded. "There is no sign of Pat, Jason Baird, or Shad O'Shea. We are endeavoring to locate them now. This fellow may supply some answers."

"Allow me," Ham offered grimly.

The dapper lawyer stepped up to the frightened Cambodian. He returned his supermachine pistol to its padded armpit holster, then gave his dark cane a twist. The sheath came off and he described flamboyant circles in the air with the gleaming blade before letting the tip come to rest before the worthy's button nose.

The man went cross-eyed as his dark orbs took in the sticky brownish substance that dripped sluggishly from the fine point.

"Savvy poison?" Ham taunted.

The Cambodian savvied. He swallowed a loud gulp, and his limbs began to shake.

"Where white girl?" Ham demanded. "Allasame talk or taste poison."

Ham looked his fiercest, but in fact the syrupy substance was merely a chemical concoction incapable of producing lasting harm, never mind death. But the Cambodian did not know this. The threat looked to loosen his tongue.

While he hesitated, Dr. Harper surged up to him.

"Damn you, talk! Where is Pat Savage, and the others?"

Something about the harsh voice seemed to cause the frightened man to snap. Instead of answering, he leaped to his feet, one arm swatting the long sword to one side.

A streak of crimson opened up along his forearm.

Ham Brooks, taken aback, was slow to respond.

The Cambodian had no available exit. Chick Alfred stood before him and the only door. His eyes sought the open window. Wildly, he lunged for it.

The window was small. The brown-skinned native might have effected a clumsly escape had he had time to dash the panel loose from the frame. But he had no time.

The Cambodian stuck his head into the open slot, and screamed once inarticulately. It might have been words or terror that the man bleated. No one ever knew.

Because he took a violent step backward that was the result of his head coming apart in all directions.

The report of the gunshot came a split second later.

"Sniper!" Doc rapped.

They hit the floor—the Cambodian last.

Moments passed. No further shots came. Dr. Harper raised a frantic face.

Doc tossed a parang so that it intercepted light from the window. It was not fired upon, so he crawled along one wall to the window and employed his handy periscope gadget.

After some moments of Doc manipulating this, Ham Brooks hissed, "See anything?"

"No," Doc said, disgust in his tone. "Whoever the sniper was, he evidently fled."

Then came the caterwaul of a police machine and Doc leaped to his feet.

"We had best make our own escape," he said.

"What about these prisoners?" Ham wondered.

"No time. We may be able to grill them through the authorities later."

They picked their way out of the weird dwelling and, by a process of skulking and evasion, quit the vicinity one step ahead of the British authorities.

A few blocks north, Doc Savage paused in a disreputable alley whose odor partook equally of a display of fresh squid in a nearby shop window and buckets of a local delicacy, shark fin, wafting from another.

There was a "newsboy" quietly standing at a forlorn corner. In Hongkong, the newsboys were invariably elderly women who stood mute, holding long scrolls of what passed for headlines in the Orient. There was no loud hawking or frenzied waving of wares.

Leaving the others a moment, Doc approached the woman, offered a silver dollar for a penny paper, and put rapid questions to the aged one in her native tongue.

Upon receiving murmured answers, the bronze man returned to the others.

"The old woman tells me she saw a number of foreign Asiatics pile into a taxi near this spot. With them was a white woman who answers to Pat's description."

"She's alive!" Ham exulted.

"Any word on Shad or Baird?" Chick Alfred wanted to know.

"None," Doc replied. "But the woman overheard the leader direct the cab to a waterfront destination. We will go there at once."

"Savage, I am no fighter," Dr. Mawson Harper said uncomfortably.

"There's a name for that particular malady," Rex Pinks said acidly. "And it ain't yellow fever!"

"I resent that insinuation!" Dr. Harper fumed.

Doc Savage said, "Harper, it would be best if you return to the hotel. Pinks, go with him."

Rex Pinks started to protest. "I'm not afraid to—"

"We intend to wade into considerable violence," Doc clipped grimly. "Numbers will not matter so much as stealth and skill. If you do not hear from us by daybreak, contact the authorities and tell them everything."

Rex Pinks seemed on the verge of offering further protest, but Chick Alfred quelled that impulse with a glare.

"All right, you win," the cowed society reporter muttered. He threw a contemptuous glance in the direction of Dr. Harper, saying, "C'mon, you old goat."

They found taxis, or rather the ricksha conveyances that outnumbered motor cabs on the island. Doc, Ham, and Chick Alfred squeezed into one, Dr. Mawson Harper and Rex Pinks into another.

They departed in opposite directions.

XX

THE WEIRD BOX

Patricia Savage was a young lady of opinions. She had a reputation of being quite free with them, too. Currently, she had a number of choice ones bottled up inside her, which she yearned to uncork.

"Uncork" was an entirely appropriate word under her present circumstances.

The feisty Pat lay under the gunwales of a motor launch. Her wrists were tied behind her back. Her ankles were similarly bound.

The taste of the red sponge in her mouth was unpleasant, but not as unpleasant as being unable to express her opinion of her predicament.

The bronze-haired trouble-seeker had been in this fix since first entering the weird house in Hongkong with her escort, Dr. Mawson Harper. The ambushing had been an expert thing, as executed.

No sooner had they entered the premises than they were

directed to a door. It opened, and they were pushed through. An ingenious partition bisected the door opening, not unlike a cattle run. Pat found herself in a tiny cubicle; Dr. Harper had presumably been forced into a similar cul-de-sac on the other side of the flimsy partition. Pat had heard him shouting as he was seized, but the shouting had been quickly stifled and the struggling sounds had abated.

Pat's seizure contained more violence. A wall pivoted and brown men were all about her. Pat had unlimbered her six-shooter at the first realization of danger, but had a bit of bad luck. The big fanning spur had gotten tangled in an undetected rent in the lining of her hand bag. While Pat was struggling to wrench it free, she was set upon, and subdued with myriad strangling cords.

Consciousness was squeezed from her by various methods. When she woke up, she was in a dark alcove, seated on a chair, bound and gagged expertly.

A single thread of light came in through a hole in the wall. By twisting, she managed to work her stool over to the light's source. It proved to be a peephole, displaying a chamber like a barbaric throne room that was dominated by a throne fashioned to resemble a glaring dragon's head.

Through this aperture, Pat had witnessed Doc Savage's rescue of Dr. Mawson Harper in its entirety. But she had been helpless to make any sound or otherwise indicate her situation—although she did manage a vigorous nasal humming when Dr. Harper had informed Doc Savage of his successful proposal of marriage.

Some time later, Pat found herself being bundled into a taxi cab, which bore her and her captors to the water front and thence to this selfsame motor launch, not much ahead of converging police sirens.

The motor launch was cutting through choppy water now. It had previously been smooth. By this, Pat assumed the motor launch was rounding the island of Hongkong and was heading out to open water. The motor stuttered and hammered, making a considerable racket.

The cackling of her captors constituted another racket entirely. Pat could not understand Chinese, or whatever language they were speaking, but they sounded excited.

The engines were throttled up. The hammering of the prow against the waves grew uncomfortable. Cold spray sheeted up, sloshed malodorously along the open cockpit.

Somewhere toward the stern, a gun whacked. An automatic rifle. Pat recognized the distinctive report even over the pounding of the prow.

Return fire crackled. Pat twisted to see better, but a foot stepped into her field of vision. She doubled up and, using both feet, kicked out at the foot.

Came a profane-sounding gobble and an Asian fell to the deck. He bounced to his feet and reached in, hauled Pat out by her wealth of bronze hair.

It hurt like the dickens, but it produced exactly the result the bronze-haired girl wanted.

Pat could see over the stern now.

The pursuing craft was a speedboat. It boasted nice lines, which the complement of her own cruiser was industriously attempting to shoot to pieces. Glass jumped out of the pursuing windscreen. A rifle barrel poked out through the hole, spat a puff of smoke and some yellow flame, and the man who had Pat by the hair suddenly discovered that his left elbow had the ability to hinge the opposite way from that which nature had designed it to.

He screeched, attempted to call attention to this phenomenon, and a scarlet stain spread out from his elbow like a virulent flower. But his compatriots were too intent upon discouraging the pursuing speedboat to take much notice.

Pat, her hair released from the Asiatic's grip, allowed herself to fall onto her spine. She employed her feet again.

"Try this on!" she muttered.

The Asiatic went over the side. He was not missed.

The gunfire picked up tempo. Splinters walked along the hull as if a great invisible feline were at work.

Finally the pursuing speedboat sheered off, the person at the wheel remaining hunched and out of sight, where lead could not find him.

The Orientals fell to making speed. They seemed oblivious to Pat's new position near a seat, so great was their desire to escape. Fear rode hard on every brown face.

Working carefully, Pat levered herself up on a seat. She had to balance carefully. Without free hands, she knew, she could easily find herself in the bay. Death by drowning would be a certainty, if that mishap befell her.

Up ahead, a seaplane wallowed in the clear blue of Junk Bay, north of Hongkong. Its dual engines kicked up. Stacks began lipping blue flame. Props commenced to revolve.

The motor launch throttled down, came toward the stuttering ship in a sweeping arc.

A hatch popped in the side of the wallowing seaplane. Lines were thrown. Pat blinked. The men who were throwing the lines were Oriental. Their various skin colorations told her that. Most were brown, a few yellow. Some were the white-brown of old ivory. They wore little clothing, in the fashion of certain outlying provinces. Pat had the impression that they were Cambodians.

The motor launch, her engine silent now, was drawn up alongside the big seaplane float and made fast.

Orientals began scrambling aboard.

Pat was lifted off her seat by two of the wiry fellows and hoisted into the open hatch, where she was received by a pair of the half-naked Asiatics.

That accomplished, lines were cast off. The motor launch was cut loose to drift away.

The great seaplane engines began to make impatient noises. The engines were warm now. The big bus was preparing to vault from the wrinkled azure water.

Pat was carried into the middle cabin.

The sound of the hatch closing told her that the seaplane was about to take off.

It was followed by a heart-stopping noise, a sudden pop like that of a rivet gun. It could only mean that a bullet had pierced the hull at some near point.

The Cambodians scrambled to the cabin windows along the starboard side of the plane. Pat caught a glimpse of the source of their excited shrillings.

The unknown pilot of the pursuing speedboat had gotten himself organized. He was bearing down on the seaplane.

A ragged hole appeared near one seat. Another bullet arrived, entering at a slanted angle. It pierced the cabin roof, this time creating a smooth hole. Steel-jacketed lead, Pat imagined.

The Cambodians cackled excitedly among themselves as the seaplane warmed up. Then one gesticulated in Pat's direction. Her heart sank, even though she could not understand their lingo.

Pat found herself being dragged to one of the windows. She fought as best she could, using mostly her feet, but she was in no position to put up sustained resistance.

She found her face jammed up against the glass. They held her there.

Pat closed her eyes, fearful of a bullet. When nothing seemed to happen, she peeked through one very round orb.

The speedboat was still there. But it was running parallel to the seaplane. It looped back around, as if the owner was wary. She could not make out the person's features.

He was hunkered down for protection against return lead.

After a few careful passes, the speedboat dug in her stern, churned foam, and raced back the way she had come.

Only then did they cease to press Pat's face against the glass. She was yanked away and cast into a seat.

Her spirits were low now. Pat had begun to believe that Doc Savage had been in the pursuing speedboat. Suddenly, she was not so sure of that. Doc Savage would not have given up so easily, she felt.

The seaplane began to move. Engines drumming, the big ship began bouncing along the wave tops. This went on for some time.

Pat's pretty brows began to pucker. It was taking entirely too long for the ship to get on step. She wondered if a bullet had crippled an engine or effected some similar disabling problem.

Abruptly, the engines throttled down and Pat's heart gave a little leap of hope. The seaplane was unable to take off!

She put her face to a window.

The bronze-haired girl saw land—a darkened cove. The seaplane was gliding into this with a silence that was eerie.

A sampan, overweighted with dark forms, was being poled close to the giant aircraft.

Pat watched, interested, as a box of some sort was carried out from the matting shelter prominent in the center of the sampan and brought aboard.

It was carried into the cabin where she sat, set down in the center of the floor.

A hatch banged shut. One of the Cambodians put an ear to the box. It was ornate, evidently carved by hand by some industrious artisan. Prominent on each side was a carven face of distinctly Asian cast. The Cambodian listened a moment, then retreated from the box with a scuttling alacrity.

All over the cabin, Cambodians fell to their hands and knees, kowtowing. They pressed their brown foreheads to the cabin floor and kept them there. Their attitudes were rapt, fearful.

They were like votaries before a pagan idol. Except there was no idol. Only a teak box that might have been a taboret, for it showed curved dragon's claw feet at each of its four corners.

A moment passed. Two. Pat Savage, to whom the ways of the Orient were unknown, watched with a growing dread. The Cambodians were entirely too expectant in their worshipfulness.

Then, one of the carven wood faces began to turn like a great flat screw head. It popped off, revealing a dark cavity. It reminded Pat of a snake's den.

As Pat watched, her eyes growing wider by the moment, something began to emerge from the dark hole.

At first, the emerging thing seemed mechanical. A brass drill, perhaps. Except no drill could be so ornate. From a needlelike point, it grew to a bizarre series of circles and fanciful sections. One section was of jade—a quartet of tiny bland faces forming a ring.

The brass base of the thing soon filled the round hole. It seemed endless.

Then, it became apparent that the brass device was being impelled by some power behind it. This emerged next, revealing coarse black hair, such as would cover a boar or other beast of the wild.

Suddenly, the emerging thing tilted upward, causing the brass spire to erect itself like a fantastic Christmas tree.

Pat would have screamed in horror had she possessed the power of speech then; but it was impossible to expel words past the sponge crammed in her gagged mouth.

For the horrible thing with black hair proved to be a head. A head with a face of cut jade!

The face was placid, humanlike, but without expression. The eyes were mere slits. And the conical brass thing surmounting this head proved to be a crown of some exotic type. Midway up the fanciful spire, four tiny jade faces, mirrors of the one that masked the thing's true features, faced the points of the compass.

The head lifted, turtle-fashion, and turned slowly, as if stirring from a long slumber. The eyes behind the slits regarded the prostrate Cambodians, flicked over Pat Savage briefly. Then the head began to extrude itself from the box.

If what had transpired before her eyes thus far was horror, what next occurred constituted raw terror.

Like a turtle emerging from its shell, the jade-faced creature strained from the confines of its box. It made helpless piglike gruntings, inarticulate and unhuman, as it struggled to squeeze forth.

After much straining, deformed shoulders, many times too narrow to be human, oozed from the round hole in the box's side.

The thing was clad in green silken garments trimmed in gold. There were two curled devices decorating the shoulders, like clipped wings, that popped up after the shoulders had emerged.

Slowly, excruciatingly, the silken torso emerged from the teak box.

First one, then another green silk sleeve flopped, wrinkled and empty, to the cabin floor.

For the weird thing possessed no arms—only the flat, empty sleeves of the maimed!

Pat looked away then. And so she missed the twisted creature's final struggles. The legs emerged. Sandal-shod feet, quite small after the Oriental fashion, squirmed and twisted free.

The thing, as if not possessing the power of upright

gait, gathered its legs under it and squatted there, empty sleeves swaying horribly.

A raspy voice intoned words.

"I am Quon, the Jade Ogre!" it proclaimed.

At that juncture, Pat Savage opened her eyes. She saw the misshapen thing in its full awful glory. This time she did not look away. She could not. The weird creature held her gaze like a serpent transfixing a rabbit.

"You have done well, Limbs of Quon. The great plan is nearer to fruition, because of you."

The words were in English. The supplicant Cambodians did not react to them. They kept their foreheads dutifully pressed to the cabin floor. The creature's words might have been for the benefit of Pat Savage alone. His face—it was identical to the faces cut into the box from which Quon had emerged—swiveled in her direction. The quartet of faces set in the brass spire turned in sympathy, as if taking turns examining their surroundings.

"Know, bronze-haired woman, that no power can release you from the thrall of Quon, who was old when your great-great-great-ancestors were but germs of possibility."

The thing paused. Behind the slits of his jade mask—it was a mask, of that Pat was certain—dark eyes gleamed like evil black buttons.

"As long as Quon possesses you, the bronze white man will not interfere with my plans. And as long as you are Quon's vassal, I will add you to my seraglio."

With that, the bent thing that was the Jade Ogre lapsed into the cackling tongue of Cambodia.

Instantly, the brown men shook themselves off the floor and padded from the cabin.

The engines started up. This time they reached their full throaty potential.

In a matter of minutes, the seaplane was thundering across open water. It got smartly on step, and vaulted into the night sky.

Pat Savage moaned inwardly, for there was no doubt in her racing mind where the big bus was bound.

Cambodia—domain of the Jade Ogre!

XXI

AIR DRAGON

It is a peculiarity of human beings the world over that they will adapt to living in any climate or condition that suits them. The human tribe can be found happily eking out an existence amid arctic wastes, in oppressive tropical jungles, or on the most parched of deserts.

Hongkong, by virtue of its lively commerce, has attracted more than its share of peoples. They cram into tenements and mill about the streets until they are nigh to impassable.

Even at this late hour, sometimes called the dead of night, Hongkong's byways were difficult to negotiate.

Doc Savage urged on the driver of the ricksha in which he, Ham Brooks, and storklike Chick Alfred were traveling.

They often had to detour past the steplike cross streets that link the hilly environs of the heart of Victoria City, causing much delay.

By the time they reached the water-front sector to which the Chinese "newsboy" had directed them, they had lost much time.

"This cannot be the place," Ham Brooks grumbled when they were let off.

The entire coastline, as far in both directions as the eye could see, was a jam of high-pooped junks and sampans and other disreputable seagoing craft of the East. They were crammed together as if piled up by a monstrous typhoon until it was possible to step from rail to rail without fear of being precipitated into the ill-smelling water. Many no longer looked seaworthy. Others hung so low in the water they seemed in imminent danger of sinking.

All were decorated with pennants of devil-chasing red,

197

which fluttered and flapped in the wind, the better to ward off evil spirits, for such was their purpose.

It might have been a cove of derelicts, but this was not the case.

Dark forms moved along shadowy decks. A chicken perched on a gunwale, its head jerking this way and that. A tether could be seen leading from one of its splayed feet to a point somewhere on the deck.

Doc Savage explained, "People, even entire families, live on these vessels."

Chick Alfred grunted. "If you call that livin'."

They were working their way along the docks, now. Here and there, modern craft were berthed.

"They do quite well," Doc elaborated. "Small children and animals are often tethered to a substantial stanchion in order to prevent accidental drownings."

Out on the bay, they heard a continuous popping of a boat engine. Doc seemed to detect it first, judging by the alert way he inclined his head out to sea.

"Somebody's comin'," Chick Alfred muttered. "And mighty fast, too."

Ham unlimbered his machine pistol.

There was an empty slip—the only one, it seemed. From the engine sound cannonading across the bay, it seemed that the motor boat was headed for it.

The sound was awakening the inhabitants of the floating village of junks and sampans. A baby let out a bawl. Vituperative lingo ascended. It could only be profanity, from the sound of it. The chicken on the rail clucked and hopped back out of sight.

Doc urged the others to seek shelter.

Engine cut, the boat ran in hard. It bumped the dock. A line snagged a cleat. The occupant jumped out with no particular care. He almost landed in the drink.

Doc Savage let him walk about twenty feet from the boat before he fell upon the man.

The struggle—what there was of it—was brief.

The man attempted to employ jujutsu. He hooked a leg around one of the bronze man's, exerted tripping pressure.

He might as well have been attempting to fell a banyan tree.

Doc applied a counteracting maneuver and the man went up in the air, seemed to hang there momentarily, and came down on the flat of his back. Gusty air blew out of his lungs, accompanied by an *oof*ing sound.

A flashlight beam picked out contorted features. The beam was wielded by Doc Savage.

The others raced up to see what manner of person the bronze man had snared.

Chick Alfred identified the man first.

"Shad!" he ejaculated.
"O'Shea?" Ham Brooks questioned.

It was indeed big Shad O'Shea. The horse-faced gunman was attempting to lever himself from a prone position, while shaking his mournful head as if to coax his dazed brain back to clarity.

Doc Savage helped the big fellow to his feet. Shad's lungs were making noises like bellows. Breath whistled through pain-set teeth.

Hands on hips, Chick Alfred growled a question. "What the hell happened to you?"

"No time," Shad O'Shea puffed. He addressed the bronze man. "They just poured that cousin of yours into a big seaplane. I tried to stop them with rifle fire, but they jammed Pat's face to a port, and I had to give it up."

"You saw Pat?" Ham ejaculated.

"Where is this seaplane now?" Doc demanded.

"It started to take off, then I guess it changed its mind," Shad O'Shea supplied. "It was hammering toward Kowloon, last I saw of it."

"Show us," Doc rapped.

They got into the waiting speedboat. O'Shea took the wheel. Doc gave the engine cord a hard yank. Most such engines are balky by nature. This one fired up on the first pull.

The speedboat backed up, turned, and dug in her busy stern.

As they rounded the looming shadow that was the island

of Hongkong, big Shad O'Shea, his dray-horse visage more long and drawn than usual, bit out a story.

The trend of it was that he and Joe Knopf had entered the mystery house on Ice House Lane after trailing Dr. Mawson Harper and Pat Savage to the place. He explained how they had, upon penetrating the building, stepped through a darkened doorway and been promptly separated by a partition that had not been visible before.

"I saw what was gonna happen to me," O'Shea continued. "I busted the door down, and shot my way clear. I sent you that message and then went and bought a rifle from a native. You can buy anything here if you flash enough lettuce. But I couldn't get back inside for the life of me. I got up on a roof and tried to see into the windows. By that time, you guys had showed up."

"Some one shot a Cambodian to death as he attempted escape," Doc pointed out.

"That was me," Shad admitted casually. "I figured he had to be up to no good. I was fixin' to climb down and join up with you all, then I spotted them spillin' up from a trap in an alley."

"Them?"

"Chinks. A whole flock of them. They had your cousin, Pat, with them, Savage. I knew there wouldn't be time to go get you, so I trailed 'em to this dock. They piled into a fast boat." The big gunman jerked a wide hand as if to encompass the surrounding boat. "I glommed this one. The rest you know."

Shad O'Shea seemed to realize something then.

"Where's Joe?"

The silence was ominous. Gazes were averted.

"I guess I'm better off not knowin' then," Shad said sadly.

"Don't you worry," Chick Alfred grated. "We're going to give the birds that done it what for."

They were doing forty knots toward Junk Bay. Kowloon reared up like a dinosaur slumbering in sepia. Spray lashed their faces. It was cold, salty. It left crusty residue on their exposed skin.

Doc Savage had the wheel now. His hands might have been actual bronze. They held the speedboat dead on course, with none of the slipping and sliding that normally accompanies high-speed water navigation.

"Should be up ahead somewhere," Shad O'Shea muttered, craning his neck.

The big gunman proved to be more right than any of them suspected.

Out of the night came a cannonading of mighty engines.

Over the popping of the speedboat motor, Doc Savage recognized the fast-approaching sound.

Abruptly, he sheered off. Just in time.

The seaplane lunged out of the blackness, running without lights, and vaulted over their ducking heads.

Their startled eyes followed the Brobdingnagian black shape as it hurtled by, shedding cold droplets of brine over them.

Chick Alfred, one eye on Ham Brooks's supermachine pistol, howled, "Why in hell don't you use that thing?"

"Mercy bullets won't penetrate," Ham said dully.

"Hell!" Alfred snarled. "I'll bring it down myself!" He lunged for the rifle Shad O'Shea had left in the boat. He brought this to his shoulder, took aim, and felt his fingers go suddenly numb.

There came a splash off to starboard.

Chick Alfred realized then that something had plucked the rifle from his strong fingers and precipitated it into the dark bay.

"Why the hell'd you do that for?" he roared.

"My cousin, and possibly Jason Baird, are aboard that seaplane," said Doc. "Injuring them will accomplish nothing."

Ham had the wheel. Doc reclaimed it, gunning the engine and setting the prow on course for night-enshadowed Kowloon.

"Now where are you takin' us?" Alfred demanded.

"Airport."

"We don't have a plane."

"I took the liberty of securing one by telephone earlier today," Doc explained quietly.

"Yeah? What kinda plane?" wondered Chick Alfred.

* * *

As it turned out—once they beached the boat and commandeered a night-prowling taxi to the Kowloon airport—a burning one.

As they rolled in through the gate, they were greeted by the sight of fire trucks hosing down an immense hangar at the south end of the field.

"Who wants to bet that's our bus?" Shad O'Shea said gloomily.

A quick exchange with a scurrying mechanic verified the big gunman's pessimistic theory.

"What happened?" Doc asked.

"Dunno, mate," the mechanic huffed in a pronounced cockney accent. "Some bloke poured petrol on a plane and threw a match. H'I don't want to be around when the chap who chartered h'it finds out. Understand 'e 's no less than Doc Savage, 'imself."

It was dark at this end of the field. The mechanic could be forgiven for not realizing the identity of the personage with whom he was conversing.

Doc followed him into the white scald of light that funneled from a floodlamp atop a nearby hangar.

The mechanic caught a glimpse of the distinctive metallic bronze skin of Doc Savage.

"Blimey!" he gulped. "You're 'im! H'in the blinkin' flesh!"

"There a plane I might borrow?" Doc asked. "A fast one?"

The mechanic eyed the surrounding field. A group of men were pushing a stubby racing monoplane from the hangar adjacent to the one that was now a roaring bundle of conflagration. It was painted silver.

He pointed. "That one. She's a sweet job. Do three 'undred h'if you run 'er flat out." He lifted his voice. "Hey, warm that racer h'up!"

Doc turned to the others. "Ham, wait here."

"But, Doc—"

Doc sprinted for the waiting plane, the floodlight painting his shadow across the tarmac like a grotesque jumping jack.

The 425-horsepower radial motor was idling, making the tiny ship with its fat silver fuselage and incredibly stubby wings dance softly in the streamlined pants over the landing wheels.

Doc Savage boosted himself onto one wing, swung a foot into the cockpit, followed it with the other, and eased his Herculean physique straight down. It was a tight fit.

Doc signaled.

The mechanics jumped out of the way. One tossed the bronze man a leather helmet and flying goggles. Doc yanked these on. It was an open-cockpit job, this tiny ship.

Then Doc batted the throttle with his palm. The engine cans swallowed the sudden flood of gas without gagging. Bawling, the beetle of a crate stuck its tail in the air and ripped across the field, twin streamers of dust whipping back from the wheels.

Doc picked it off the tarmac and banked, giving little heed to the possibility of stalling the overpowered bus. He knew airplanes. This one, if maintained properly, would do almost everything but walk straight up.

The tiny plane flung into the wall of sepia outside of the zone of floodlights. It scooted over black ruts that were low buildings, bucking and squawling as it splashed through air bumps.

Doc pointed the baying snout at the moon and slid up into the night sky as if on a greased string. He headed in a general easterly direction—the direction in which the seaplane had been seen traveling, although the bronze man understood that it was unlikely that the seaplane, for all its size and range, was bound on a Pacific crossing.

Out over the ocean, the tiny beetle crate came out from under a cotton bat of a cloud like a trout from beneath a lily pad, and the moonlight turned her underslung wings into double-edged blades of polished silver.

The giant bronze man snaked binoculars from the cockpit pocket, clamped them to his flake-gold eyes, swung them in a circle. They did not reveal the seaplane, nor had he expected them to. The seaplane had a fifteen-minute start, hardly less than the distance of twenty miles.

Doc had reasoned that the seaplane was bound for

Cambodia. Cambodia lay to the southwest, over a thinly populated mountain district of inland China. The mountains were dangerous by day, potential death by night. They held few emergency-landing fields.

The Pacific would be the pilot's best bet. The seaplane was large enough and staunch enough to drop into the open sea, should it be forced down. There would be naught but an occasional ship below to report its course, and these easily avoided.

Doc angled his tiny ship due south. He poured on speed. The tiny ship responded like a race horse. It became a silvery-blue bullet with wings.

The bronze man flew close to the shore. This part of the world was not exactly awash in modern navigational aids. A pilot would ordinarily have to fly by dead reckoning, using the old trick of following the coastline, or roads and railroad tracks.

An hour later, more than a hundred miles south of the China coast, Doc Savage overhauled the seaplane.

He had not caught sight of it earlier because the craft had lost itself in layers of cumulus clouds. But his deduction that it would follow the coast was correct.

Doc drew alongside the thundering seaplane and waggled his wings in the internationally accepted attention-getting fashion.

The pilot stared wildly, then threw an arm across the lower part of his face. With the other hand, he clawed at the switch panel, dousing the cabin light.

Doc secured only a fleeting glimpse of the fellow's features before he concealed them. He banked, swung the tiny ship back at the slow-moving seaplane.

He dropped a bronze beam of an arm over the cockpit rim, stabbed it downward. The other pilot saw, but gave no sign of complying with the signal.

The tiny crate that Doc had commandeered was unarmed. His options were not profuse. Still, the bronze man was not without resources.

Doc Savage drove directly at the seaplane. He brought the stick back into his stomach at the last possible moment.

The beetle crate hopped the spidery framework which supported the empennage of the other ship. It hung by the nose, propellers guzzling air and squirting it back past the tail assembly in a screaming hurricane.

The air blast hit the seaplane, kicked it over. The big craft flopped into a spin.

And as the other ship corkscrewed, a pugnacious face appeared in one window near the tail.

Jason Baird's unmistakable features! They were soon lost to sight. There was no sign of Pat Savage, or any other passenger.

Grimly, Doc dropped his ship on a wing, straightened, and howled back alongside the seaplane. The other pilot was fighting the controls. He got his craft level, only to be sent tumbling into another spin. Doc followed him down.

The other man, if he had a gun, made no effort to use it. He was behaving in a strangely spiritless manner.

There was a system in that—for the seaplane dropped to within a hundred feet of the sea and roared southward. Doc followed, concern tightening his metallic features. For if he slapped the plane with his slipstream, it would plow into the sea. His opinion of the other pilot mounted.

A half hour later, it went up a great deal more. They had veered in toward the rugged Chinese shoreline. The seaplane turned into one of the innumerable inlets along the shaggy coast and abruptly dropped to the surface.

Soon, a second seaplane left the shadow of beetling cliffs and scudded across the inlet. It was a biplane, wings stubby, fuselage plump, a speed cowl making the giant radial motor look like the head on a grasshopper. It drew a sudsy line down the inlet. The line ended abruptly as the ship blasted itself off.

The biplane was smaller even than Doc's borrowed crate. The pontoons were nearly as long as the fuselage.

It came upstairs like a scared spider on a thread. Doc's flake-gold eyes whirled. The seaplane might not be as fast as Doc's bus, but it lacked precious little. He sent his own crate into a sweeping circle, prepared for whatever was about to transpire.

His suspense was short-lived. Two red eyes, set atop the

cowl of the seaplane, sprang into being and seemed to coyly flutter lids at him. Machine guns, synchronized through the propeller! Two more blood-red orbs appeared, each halfway out on the lower wings.

The craft was firing four machine guns!

Doc rocked his helmeted head back, weird eyes lifting. The sky overhead was a cloud of scarlet sparks. They seemed to materialize in front of his golden eyes and climb upward with incredible speed. Tracer bullets.

Doc rolled his little bus, slapping it away from the rain of red death. The seaplane flashed past, the bawl of its motor penetrating over the exhaust din of the beetle crate. The pilot of the other ship twisted, swinging a fifth machine gun mounted on a ring in the cockpit. He let loose with a short burst, then banked and fell off in a slip.

Moonlight glittered off his craft. It was painted in a weird design, the fuselage a yellow-and-green monster with scarlet blood drooling from distended jaws, the pontoons uncannily like huge talons open to pounce, and the wings great, scaly fins. The whole effect was dragonlike—remindful of some slavering, blood-ravenous creature out of an odious nightmare.

The bronze man spotted something else, too. The wings of the plane seemed to be hinged, fitted so they could be folded back in order that the ship might be stored in a small space.

Doc booted the silver beetle crate under the seaplane. Hot lead rattled on the spars and knocked feathers of fabric off the wings, so he booted out again. There was a sixth machine gun mounted in the cockpit of the seaplane so that it could fire through the bottom of the fuselage.

The sky dragon was a flying machine-gun nest!

The seaplane pounced. Doc rolled his shuddering steed and let it pass, and when it had gone he could look right through his right wing fabric at the yellow and green dragon as it tumbled in the sky and came back snorting fire and lead through six bloody nostrils.

There came a ferocious *knock-knock* against the floor-boards—the insistent tattoo of lead trying to get in. It did get in, and splinters flew up into the bronze man's face. The instrument panel fell to pieces and the eddy of air in the cockpit whirled the pieces about like straw in a Kansas whirlwind.

Doc screwed the beetle ship up toward the chill silver dollar of the moon, momentarily astonished that the controls still worked.

Each time the sky above or ahead acquired a flock of bright, new, red stars, he stirred the control stick and booted the rudder.

Below, the wings of the big seaplane reflected moonbeams like convex mirrors as the craft wallowed with the swell in the inlet. The pilot had crawled atop the upper wing and was watching the one-side air fracas.

Doc Savage was a consummate pilot. There was little about the art of aerial combat that he had not mastered. Still, flying skill alone is not sufficient when one is embroiled in an air tangle with a heavily armed opponent.

Death hammered insistently at the welded fuselage of Doc's borrowed crate. The bronze man skidded away. The maneuver cost him speed. The ugly claws painted on the seaplane floats slashed so close to his head that he instinctively ducked. The ship had hurdled him. It was ahead now.

A black worm crawled out of the fuselage of the dragon ship, spread, and grew into a giant funnel. It was smoke from a smudge pot.

Doc nosed down, but not quickly enough. His propeller sucked in a tendril of the stuff and blew it into his face. It was smoke—mixed with gas.

Doc held his breath, trying to empty his lungs of the stuff. Hornets seemed to travel down his nose and throat and swarm in his chest. Despite his goggles, his eyes began to tear. He recognized the symptoms of common tear gas.

Blinded, the mighty Man of Bronze smashed the stick into the mangled wreck of the instrument panel. The beetle crate bayed like an unleashed hound and rushed for the earth below.

Doc Savage tore off goggles and helmet. The typhoon rush of air washed tears out of his eyes, cleared them. He squinted, peering down through a shower of tracer sparks at the earth.

He was a couple of miles north of the inlet where the big seaplane had landed. There was a beach below, a narrow strip of it, probably rough. He slipped the plane sideways. The dragon ship followed, spewing lead.

Doc brought the beetle crate down to the beach fast, fishtailed it violently, and set it down. With the first bounce, he cut the motor and lifted himself out of the cockpit. The plane slowed to forty miles an hour, thirty. At twenty, Doc jumped, flinging himself clear of the tail assembly. He cartwheeled head over heels twice, hit on his feet, and ran.

Lead hammered pocks in the sand about his running feet. He pitched his bulk flat, rolled into the shelter of a seaweed-covered boulder. The seaplane dived and zoomed so swiftly that the motor roar sounded like a single thunder crash.

The beetle wagon was still rolling fast. Doc lifted his head and watched it grimly. The wheels hit a slab of stone. The streamlined pants caved in. The plane roared, stood on its nose; then the tail flopped back to earth. The propeller, the motor crankshaft to which it was affixed snapped by the crash, dropped and rang like a bell on the stone.

The dragon seaplane moaned downward again, the four-machine-gun orchestration giving the craft the sound of a squadron. The beetle ship did a shuddery, lead-spanked dance.

The surface of the hard rock upon which it had stopped seemed to boil with liquid fire. But the gasoline did not ignite.

The clamor of guns ceased. The dragon ship came out of its dive and glanced upward into the night sky. It did not come back. One, two minutes—and the throaty howl of the motor trailed away.

Made faint by distance, another motor roar came into being. The big seaplane, presumably bearing Pat Savage, as well as Jason Baird, scudded into view, lifting off the sea. It banked, followed the other plane to the southwest.

Only then did Doc Savage emerge from the shadow of the boulder. He watched the departing planes, his flake-gold orbs bleak and unusually still.

XXII

CHINESE SKIES

Doc Savage waited until the motor drone had entirely faded before he went over to look at his borrowed crate.

The aircraft, gnashed and mauled by lead, still hung together, but the snapped-off propeller destroyed any hopes of getting it into the air again.

There was no radio. Contacting Hongkong—or any other Chinese city, for that matter—was impossible.

The bronze man looked up and down the beach. One direction seemed as good as the other. He chose north and began walking, looking for any sign of human habitation.

He followed the beach for two hours, finding not even a fishing shack. China is reputed to be a populous nation, but this section of its coastline proved to be a notable exception.

The moonlight, which seemed so brilliant in the air, was tricky stuff. Doc nearly stumbled over innumerable boulders and rock fangs and once, climbing atop a ridge of stone and leaping down on the other side, landed in water that swallowed him up to his corded neck.

Doc paused to shed his water-logged garments, then milked them partially free of water before donning them and resuming his solitary trek.

When another hour had passed, and there was no sign of life to be seen, Doc gave it up and retraced his path.

Approaching dawn tinted the sea with a variegation of heliotrope and cobalt and salmon. Doc shivered freely in his wet garments, knowing that this would help keep his body warm. It was the morning hour, when the chill was most intense.

Along the way, he dipped into his gadget vest, where he

kept a supply of concentrated food, in pill form, which would provide the nutrients that would sustain his body for some time. They were designed to be taken with water, but the only supply Doc encountered along the way happened to be the briny variety, so he was forced to swallow them dry. It was not pleasant, but then the concentrated food was not intended to appeal to the palate.

The bronze man hove into sight of the spot where he had left the tangled wreck of the silver beetle crate. It was still there.

Had there been any observer at hand, he would have been puzzled by Doc Savage's next actions.

The bronze man stationed himself in the lengthening shadow of the crate, on the sandy beach, and launched into a shortened version of his exercises.

Shortened because the bronze man lacked his sense-heightening equipment. He stuck with the physical and mental gymnastics portions of his daily routine. These not only helped ward off the chill of the Chinese night, but assisted him in killing time until the bronze-colored amphibian arrived.

The engines—there were three of them—were so well silenced, the craft so streamlined, that had Doc Savage not possessed unusual keenness of hearing, he would never have detected the craft's passing.

At sound of the unnaturally quiet engines, the bronze man was galvanized into activity. He clambered upon a tumulus of rock, shielded his eyes from the climbing sun, and made out the craft.

It was big, the streamlined fuselage designed for water landings, with air wheels that cranked up into the boatlike hull.

The amphibious job was flying low, and somewhat slowly, as if searching.

Doc pitched back to his damaged plane, unscrewed the gasoline intake, and made a kind of twisted wick of one torn shirt sleeve. He shoved this into the intake, deep enough that it made contact with the reservoir of gasoline within.

Then, rasping into flame a common kitchen match from a waterproof oilskin pack taken from his vest, the bronze man got the sleeve burning.

He hastened for the shelter of a pile of rock many yards distant. He almost did not make it.

Doc Savage was in the act of vaulting the rock pile when the air became a hot fist that propelled sand and shreds of burning fabric and metal against his broad back.

Doc threw himself flat. The concussion hurt his ears. Sand, duralumin, and other debris rained all around him.

By the time the sound and heat had subsided, the beetle of a crate was merrily ablaze. Smoke crawled along the beach like a vaporous black serpent. It made quite a sight.

It also attracted the attention of the pilot of the big bronze amphibian—just as Doc hoped it would.

The amphibian banked inland, made a low pass over the smoking, smoldering wreck of a plane.

Doc Savage stood in plain view, lifted his muscular arms, crossed and uncrossed them several times.

The amphibian continued inland for a quarter mile or so and began to retrace its path.

It hissed over Doc's head and spanked down on the smooth waters of the Pacific.

The landing was good. The pilot was an expert. He cut the throttle, simultaneously angling the ungainly craft so that momentum would carry it to shore.

Doc did not wait for the big bus to beach itself. He plunged into the water, began swimming toward the amphibian with powerful strokes.

A hatch came open. From the nose, an electric winch dropped a sea anchor. The amphibian continued on until the chain came taut, then began to turn on her pontoonlike hull. The anchor had caught a rock or some similar sea-bottom protuberance.

Doc swam to the open hatch, paused, and treaded water. He lifted his voice. "Ham?"

A squeaking, childlike voice emerged from deep within the craft, returning his greeting.

"That shyster won't come out," said the voice in an amiable fashion. "He somehow ripped the seat of his pants and don't have a spare."

"Monk," Doc said.

A face poked from the open hatchway. It was remarkable

in its wide-mouthed homeliness. The eyes were small, like stars twinkling in pits of gristle under a forehead that seemed hardly high enough to conceal a normal-sized brain.

The unlovely visage belonged to a grotesque figure of a man, being no more than five feet five inches tall, and seemingly, that span wide. His furry arms dangled at his sides, giving the distinct impression that the man could lace his shoes without having to stoop much.

He weighed no less than two hundred and fifty pounds, did this anthropoidal fellow, and the hair on his head and arms was the color of rusty finishing nails.

One of these burly arms reached down to assist Doc Savage into the plane. The too-wide mouth grinned with comical pleasure, threatening the man's ears.

Doc allowed himself to be hoisted aboard.

"I see you made good time, Monk," Doc said quietly.

"Sure," said Monk, who was in reality Lieutenant Colonel Andrew Blodgett Mayfair, one of the world's leading industrial chemists and a member of Doc Savage's tiny band. "As soon as I got your radio-land-line telephone call, I piled into this bus and took off. I made fair time, too. When I put down in Kowloon, what do you think greeted my eyes?"

"Tell me," Doc prompted.

"My good pal, Ham Brooks, havin' a fit because you had left him behind. And him without a plane."

"Some one sabotaged the bus I chartered in case we had to move before your arrival," Doc stated.

As they strode into the bronze-colored amphibian, Doc asked, "Are Johnny, Long Tom, and Renny with you?"

"Heck, no. Johnny's in Europe, Long Tom's still tied up with that hydro-electric project down in Argentina, and Renny's helpin' him out with it."

The three individuals mentioned constituted the remainder of Doc Savage's organization. Johnny was the eminent archæologist and geologist, William Harper Littlejohn. Long Tom was better known as Major Thomas J. Roberts, the electrical wizard. Renny was an engineer of renown and went by the more dignified title of Colonel John Renwick.

"Any trouble with the crossing?" Doc inquired.

"Not much," gorillalike Monk said casually. "Some

weather here and there. I set down in Los Angeles and Honolulu to take on extra gas, but I made it."

An insistent pounding came from the rear of the plane. Doc asked, "What is that?"

The answer came in the form of a strident voice demanding to be let out.

Ham Brooks's sharp tones.

"I understood you to say Ham was hiding," Doc remarked dryly.

Monk shrugged his shoulder up around his nubbin of a head.

"You might say I encouraged the notion a little."

Doc went aft to the spacious cabin—the amphibian could accommodate sixteen persons, although not very comfortably—located the source of the pounding as a lazaret door, and wrenched this open.

Ham Brooks, taken by surprise, fell out. Doc assisted him to his feet.

Ham shook an enraged fist—his ever-present sword cane was nowhere to be seen—in the direction of hairy Monk.

"That—that—bug-faced gossoon locked me up!" he raged.

Monk sneered, "Maybe that'll teach you to not to leave a pal behind."

"I told you when we were leaving our warehouse hangar!" Ham protested, mustering his injured dignity.

"And you weren't there when I showed. You lit out on me!"

"More likely you got mixed up, ape."

The commotion brought the others—Chick Alfred and hulking Shad O'Shea.

"Are we gonna just set here and lay eggs or do we have places to go?" grumbled Alfred.

"We do," Doc told him, striding toward the cockpit.

The others trailed him. The last to go were Monk and Ham, who hesitated as if each was unwilling to allow the other to go ahead, for fear of receiving a remonstrating kick in what is commonly known as the slats.

Reluctantly, Ham went first.

"I'll settle with you later, ambulance chaser," Monk gritted.

"Pick the time and place," Ham sniffed, "and I, for one, will be there."

Doc eased behind the controls, saying, "The seaplane carrying Pat and Jason Baird seemed to be heading toward Cambodia. They have a good four-hour start."

Chick Alfred blurted, "Baird was on that bus?"

Doc nodded. "I spied his face through a cabin window."

"A prisoner?"

"Possibly. I could not tell." And the import of Doc's words produced momentary silence.

The huge bronze amphibian, its three motors turning over so slowly that the propellers exerted no pull, twisted at the end of its anchor chain.

Doc opened the throttles. The amphibian stirred sluggishly and came to life. Exhaust stacks whooped, sprewing clouds of red sparks. Doc thumbed a dash button. The anchor began to winch upward, returning to its hawsehole.

Blooping the motors to throw gushes of air against the empennage for taxying control, Doc ruddered the big bus so that its wallowing nose pointed out to sea. The props began clawing air, picking up speed.

The amphibian sailed over a few swells, then began jumping hollows, smashing from ridge to ridge. It passed off the choppy water. Spray geysered upward and made bawling sounds against the propellers.

Doc pulled back on the control wheel and the amphibian sailed up into the morning sky.

Soon, they were on a southerly course, silenced motors hissing. It was quite peaceful in the heated cabin. Soundproofing the engine design had accomplished this. Both were the handiwork of the bronze man.

As they droned along, Doc filled them in on his encounter with the dragon plane.

This caused Monk Mayfair to remark, "This Jade Ogre must be quite a guy to have covered his trail like that. A guy burned your plane and another plane chased you off the trail of his amphibian. Sounds like he has an organization. Wonder what he's really up to."

"Doc, do you think the Jade Ogre himself was on that plane?" Ham asked.

"I could not say."

"Well," Ham offered, "at least we're rid of that pesky Rex Pinks and Dr. Harper."

Doc vouchsafed no opinion on that score, so they settled down to the business of nursing the big amphibian on its southward flight.

The sun rose. They flew close to the Chinese coast. Doc, roving the radio bands, got in contact with such ground stations as this part of the Orient boasted. He picked up occasional reports of the Jade Ogre seaplane. Once, the dragon crate had been spotted. The reports suggested a Cambodian trend.

At one point, Monk retreated to the rear of the amphibian, returned toting a remarkable animal by one saillike ear.

The creature was a runt pig of some species. He possessed long legs that would have befitted a dog, an inquisitive snout, and eyes that held an intelligent gleam.

Monk quietly released a shoat beside the seat where Ham Brooks was poring over a navigation chart, plotting the course of the Jade Ogre planes.

The pig ambled up to the lawyer's leg and found a dangling thread. He took this in his teeth and started walking backward.

Ham, intent upon his chart, at first did not notice this operation. Then he felt a tiny tug. Absently, he swatted at his leg, no doubt mistaking the tugging sensation for a tropical mosquito. The tugging continued. This time, his fingers brushed familiar bristles.

Ham shot bolt upright, whirled.

"That hog!" he howled, sweeping out an angry foot. "He's at it again!"

The ungainly porker dodged the shod foot with the expertise of long practice.

Monk's homely visage acquired an innocent look. "Who, Habeas Corpus?" he asked.

Ham accused, "You trained him to pull on any threads in

my clothing he could find! That's why the back seam of my trousers is splitting!"

"I thought your trousers were splitting because you're too vain to buy them in your right size," Monk said, innocent-voiced.

"A lie!" Ham screamed.

"That," Chick Alfred interjected wearily, "has been going on since we left Kowloon."

"Does it ever stop?" wondered Shad O'Shea.

"Never for very long," Doc told them, a trace of resignation in his remarkable voice. He made no attempt to interfere as Monk and Ham, the pig Habeas Corpus underfoot, began circling one another as if on the threshold of mortal combat.

In truth, although they would have been the last to admit it, Monk and Ham were the best of friends, and each would have willingly laid his life down for the other, if circumstances called for it. The supposed enmity went back to the Great War, during which Ham had taught Monk some choice French phrases, designed—or so he told Monk—to flatter a French general. Monk had landed in the guardhouse. Not long after Monk's release, Ham had been haled up on charges of stealing a ham from the company mess. Although he had been acquitted, Ham long believed that Monk had engineered the frame, but could never prove this.

This latter fact rankled his lawyerly soul perhaps more than the unsavory nickname of Ham, which he had long since given up all hope of shedding.

As if to prove that their combativeness was all an act, the squabbling pair settled down—Ham to his chart and Monk to scratching his pet pig behind an ear. The animal was something the hairy chemist had picked up in the course of an Arabian adventure. Habeas Corpus had not grown an inch since that time and looked never to do so.

Monk piped up, "Say, Doc, this business has me kinda dizzy."

"You were born dizzy," Ham said unkindly.

"How about helpin' me catch up?" Monk continued. "There was this bird Jason Baird who needed help. Is that how this all got started?"

"It was," said Doc, who went into an extended—for him—accounting of everything that happened since he had nearly been assassinated on the New-York-to-San-Francisco *Solar Speedster,* through the quest for Jason Baird, the tumultuous voyage on the liner *Mandarin*, and the fast-moving events in Hongkong, in which they had lost Pat Savage and Jason Baird—apparently—to the Jade Ogre's minions.

"Whatever is back of all this has to do with Baird's missing sister, Maurine," Doc concluded.

"This is a lot of fuss over one dame," remarked Monk, his homely visage screwing up in thought.

"Jason Baird's sister is not a dame," Ham corrected. "She happens to be an internationally famous expert on germs and their properties."

"This Jade Ogre's gone to a lotta trouble to keep folks from chasing into Cambodia after this Maurine," Monk pointed out. "Why do you suppose that is?"

Doc made no reply, which was characteristic of him.

"If they're keeping Baird alive, it's a cinch they're taking him—Savage's cousin, too—to wherever this Quon bird holes up," Chick Alfred said flatly.

"According to the yarn Dr. Harper spun for Doc," Ham Brooks inserted, "this Quon holds forth in a temple also called Quon."

"Funny that he'd name his hideout after himself," Shad O'Shea said superstitiously.

"Maybe it's the other way around," Chick Alfred offered.

"Doc, how are we going to find this place called Quon by air?" Ham wanted to know. "Cambodia is a large place, is it not?"

"Large enough," Doc agreed, but offered no answer more concrete than that.

They settled down into the long flight. The day wore on.

The afternoon sun put a glittering sheen of nickelplate on the wings of the big tri-motored amphibian. It made the screaming propellers resemble scintillating plates of steel. Below, on the Gulf of Tonkin, it turned into specks of jewel fire against a crinkling carpet of ultra-marine. Irridated by the sun, the coastline of French Indo-China was a low mosaic dais of jade and apricot, rugose and forbidding.

They were barreling inland, across the wide bulge of land below China proper. The cool air of the coast gave way to the humid damp of the jungle. Steam rose from the verdancy below, making ghostly shapes as it hung, unmoving, miles below.

Ham looked up from his chart. "We should be about thirty miles from the Cambodia border," he reported.

Monk, who had his fist-flattened nose pressed to a cabin window, muttered, "I don't see many places where we could set down if we had to."

"Let us hope we do not have to," Doc said without feeling.

A little while later, Ham Brooks went off in search of his sword cane, which Monk had secreted somewhere about the cabin, steadfastly refusing to divulge its whereabouts.

There were many compartments throughout the big amphibian—some within and some without. Ham was rooting through the former now.

He found the cane at last, tucked into a long, narrow chart case. It lay next to an unfamiliar object.

Ham's dark eyes alighted on what he at first mistook for a tube such as would hold a rolled-up chart. But this particular tube was too wide, and ornate beyond all reason.

Tucking his cane under one arm, Ham brought this object into the light, frowning. It was of Oriental workmanship, that much was plain. Predominant were serpents which seemed to possess an excess of heads.

The dapper lawyer examined both ends critically, saw that one boasted a cunning hinge, and attempted to work the cap off.

The cap proved stubborn. There was no obvious catch. He fingered various designs in growing frustration, with no result.

It happened that Habeas Corpus ambled into the cabin at that juncture, in anticipation of curling up in a coil of utility rope and napping.

Hearing the happy click of porcine hooves, the dapper lawyer whirled and instinctively shagged the tube at the ungainly shoat.

"Take that, pest!"

The pig managed to evade the tube, which bounced off a bulkhead, whereupon the stubborn cap simply fell off.

Something yellow and glowing began to wriggle out from the open end.

Habeas Corpus, hackles rising, vented a piggish squeal and lit out for the forward portion of the plane.

He managed to reach Monk's side a half second behind Ham Brook's cry of fear and horror.

XXIII

STOWAWAY

A bulkhead separated the pilot's compartment from the cabin of the big tri-motored amphibian. The door between the two compartments happened to have fallen closed.

Still, the arresting scream emanating from the throat of Ham Brooks penetrated. Long hours spent practicing courtroom oratory had imbued the dapper barrister with a voice that possessed the clear, ringing tones of a church bell.

The robot pilot happened to be engaged; the control wheel was moving of its own accord.

Thus, at the first outcry, Doc Savage pitched from his seat without a second thought. He was the first into the cabin. He paused in the bulkhead doorway, his flake-gold eyes animated.

Crowding close, Monk and the others craned to see past his giant form.

"Blazes!" Monk howled. The others appeared to be struck speechless.

Ham Brooks stood poised, his sword cane out. He was holding it in a defensive position. It was pointed at an angle— a downward angle, they all saw.

The tip of the blade was directed toward an ornate cylinder of some lacquered wood that had come open at one end.

Something was attempting to work its way out of the tube. Ham was threatening it with his cane.

Doc's speed plane was streamlined to the ultimate degree of aeronautical perfection. That did not mean that it was not subject to the usual turbulences that buffet aircraft the world over. When it encountered downdrafts or air pockets, it responded accordingly.

The amphibian was rolling now. The motion was slight. The automatic robot pilot compensated for the motion, which caused the ornate cylinder to roll around on the metal floor somewhat.

With each roll, the thing inside seemed to creep outward another inch or so.

It glowed faintly—a pallid yellow sort of a glow, akin to moonlight on old teeth. The tips of the emerging thing were pointed, like an array of dagger blades. As it crept forward, these remained level, even as the tube shook and rolled.

In a moment, they recognized the thing for what it was: one of the evilly glowing arms of Quon, the legendary Jade Ogre!

"Blazes!" Monk gulped again. "What the heck is it?"

"Don't just stand there, you hairy mistake," Ham wailed. "Get something to catch it. You haven't encountered one before. These things are deadly."

Doc Savage started forward.

At that moment, the amphibian encountered a steeper than usual downdraft. The craft dropped sickeningly, throwing the bronze man off his stride. The ornate hollow tube of a thing went skittering along the length of the floor.

That was sufficient, it seemed, for the disembodied Quon arm to liberate itself.

It bobbed out—that was the only word for it—and, trailing the ragged tail of its silken green sleeve, ascended, its extended digits yawing left and right, as if undecided as to its preferred victim.

It seemed to be zeroing in on the worried lawyer.

Doc spoke up. "Ham. Back away from it." His voice was brittle.

Ham Brooks executed an experimental slashing of the air before and around the rising specter of a limb.

The glowing arm actually shook and retreated slightly under the onslaught, as if possessed of dim intelligence.

Monk Mayfair ducked under one of Doc's arms then. The bronze man had been holding on to the bulkhead opening, to keep the others back from the deadly thing.

Roaring inarticulate defiance like a bull ape, the hairy chemist launched himself at the eerie tableau before them.

"Monk!" Doc clipped.

It was clear to all that Monk was intent upon getting between the glowing limb and its apparent target.

Monk's sacrifice was for naught.

For no sooner had the thing floated up to the level of the dapper Ham's chest, than his sword blade licked out.

It seemed a futile gesture in the face of the grisly menace, but in that assumption every one in the cabin compartment received a surprise.

No sooner had the sword blade encountered the grasping nails of the Quon arm than the latter simply—disappeared.

It was not a fading, or a winking out, such as might attend a manifestation of the supernatural. The arm flared up, erupting into an eye-searing blob of yellowish light. A spiteful hiss accompanied this transformation. It left them blinking away the afterimages from their optics.

"*Yee-o-w!*" Monk squawled.

Taken by surprise, the apish chemist skidded on his heels and ended up in a tangle with the dapper lawyer. The sword cane fell, clanging.

"You hairy mistake!" Ham gritted.

"Ambulance chaser," Monk returned.

Furiously, the quarrelsome pair untangled their limbs from one another, fell to examining their persons.

Ham gave out a groan when he saw that his pants seat— the one from which Habeas Corpus had been industriously plucking threads—had completely split, revealing silken shorts.

"My tropical habit is ruined," he complained. He examined fresh linen trousers that were as dazzling a white as that of his erstwhile commodore outfit.

"Serves you right for wearing white," Monk retorted, not entirely sensibly.

Ham Brooks drew himself up, and said, "I happen to be a thorough believer that a man's clothes should match his hair. A black-haired man should wear black. A brown-haired man should affect brown attire, et cetera."

Eying Ham's shock of white hair, Monk wondered, "Suppose a guy is bald?"

Ham purpled. For lack of a better retort, he sputtered, "Oh, go tuck in your shirt tail."

"Can't. Won't stay. It's my work shirt."

Ham looked momentarily blank. "Work shirt?"

"Sure," grinned Monk. "It keeps workin' over the back of my trousers."

The gag wasn't particularly funny, but it had the tension-relieving effect of causing Chick Alfred and Shad O'Shea to lose their strained expressions.

During the argument, Doc Savage had gone over to the wooden tube, which was still rattling about the floor. He picked this up, began examining it.

The others crowded around him.

"What is it?" Ham queried, sheathing his sword cane with a click.

"A simple hollow of wood, carved with the design known as a naga," Doc said.

"Naga?"

"A seven-headed serpent," Doc explained. "It is an East Indian phantasm."

"What's Hinduism got to do with Cambodia?" Monk demanded, blinking owlishly at the horrid design.

Doc said, "Hinduism is common throughout Indo-China, and has penetrated even into China itself. Recall that the legend of the Jade Ogre had much to do with the Hindu deity known as Siva."

"Shouldn't somebody be flying the plane?" Shad O'Shea muttered worriedly. "You know—in case we pile into a mountain or somethin'."

Carrying the ornate hollow, Doc strode back to the control wheel, disengaged the robot pilot. The great amphibious sky wagon shuddered momentarily, then Doc brought it higher, to about two thousand feet. The downdrafts were fierce.

In a moment, they encountered weather. It was the rainy season. Great nodular cumulonimbus clouds, like anvils of sea foam, appeared before the windscreen, which was becoming smeared with tiny rain drops. Patterings like mice walking on a tin roof filled the control cabin.

Pulling the control wheel to his chest, Doc cleared the clouds. The mice sounds faded. Soon, they had passed beyond the rainstorm.

The ground below was bearded with growth. Rivers meandered, brown unsavory tributaries like dead, fallen thunderbolts. Bullock-drawn carts drew faint serpents of dust along open trails.

When they had resumed a normal course, Doc spoke.

"Monk, was there any opportunity for a saboteur to plant that hollow object on the plane?" the bronze man asked.

Monk scratched his bristly bullet head. "Guess so," he said slowly. "In Kowloon, probably. But Doc, what was that witch's claw of a thing? It was dang uncanny."

"Now you know," Ham sniffed in a superior tone.

"It might be advisable to give the entire ship a thorough searching," Doc suggested.

They needed no more prompting than that. The other passengers began to go through the great amphibian, combing lockers, cubby-holes, and compartments. They found Habeas in one of the latter. The ingenious shoat had managed to open it with his teeth and pull it shut again. Monk Mayfair had expended many hours training the porker to perform such useful tricks.

Monk ambled back into the pilot's compartment, the pig happily swinging by one rabbitlike ear.

"She's clean as a river-bottom rock," Monk pronounced.

"Check every cranny?" Doc asked.

"Didn't miss a thing," the hairy chemist said confidently.

Doc nodded, saying, "That leaves only the nose hatch."

Monk lost his proud expression then.

* * *

Forward of the pilot's compartment, in the nose of the plane—it was really more along the line of the bow, given the amphibian's boatlike hull—was a utility compartment. Among other items, there were collapsible boats tucked in the generous space. The only way to reach the compartment was from a topside hatch. It could not be accessed from the cabin interior—and not at all while the amphibian was thundering through the air.

Monk blinked through the rain-smeared windscreen. "You don't think some bird's actually in that thing?" he said doubtfully.

Doc allowed, "It is a possibility."

"What say we find out?" muttered Chick Alfred. He had a heavy wrench in hand, gotten from a locker, the idea apparently being to brain any stowaway encountered. He slid one of the wide windows open, stuck out his storklike upper body.

"Hey, nix!" Monk began.

"Let him be," Doc said quietly.

Chick Alfred wriggled around in the open window, reared back, and gave a toss.

The distance was not great, and the wrench heavy. Otherwise it would never have made headway against the fierce slipstream.

The wrench bounced off the nose with a bang. Chick Alfred pulled back, and joined the others at the windscreen.

Nothing happened for a long moment. Then, just about the time they had decided nothing would, the hatch unexpectedly reared up.

A man shoved up from the space. He wore a parachute pack. Casting a frightened look in the direction of the pilot's compartment and the great triple row of propellers, he prepared to jump.

Doc rapped, "Ham! Your machine pistol. Now!"

Ham Brooks was nearest to the open window. He unlimbered his weapon, and set the thing on single shot.

Aiming carefully, he pulled the trigger. The report—it was hardly more than a tongue click—was lost in the blade scream, but the stowaway suddenly grabbed at his shoulder. His slant eyes went wide. They rolled up in his head.

Like a jack-in-the-box returning to its place, the stowaway folded slowly. The hatch—which his hand had been holding open—fell atop him like an oddly shaped coffin lid slamming shut.

"Fancy shootin'," Chick Alfred told Ham Brooks admiringly.

Casting a supercilious eye in Monk Mayfair's direction, the dapper lawyer blew an eddy of powder smoke from the pistol barrel and returned it to its padded underarm holster. Ham gave every indication of being a man whose injured pride had been restored.

"Wonder who the guy is," Shad O'Shea muttered.

"His name," Doc Savage said to the astonishment of all, "is Ho."

"Blazes!" Monk howled. "How'd you get wise to that, Doc?"

"Because," the bronze man imparted, "he was the taxi driver whose machine was pursued by an arm of Quon back in San Francisco."

"San Francisco? Then what's he doin' way out here?" Monk squawled.

"There will be time enough to interrogate him after we put down."

"Well, at least we know who stashed that hollow gimmick," Chick Alfred said. "Even if we don't know what the thing was that was in it."

The recollection of the ghostly arm of Quon brought a hush to the soundproofed compartment that lasted quite some time.

They were still engrossed in their thoughts and in a close surveying of the leafy terrain when the dragon biplane reappeared.

The ceiling hung at two thousand feet, and the clouds that formed it were thick. They were flying under it in order to examine the terrain. By Ham's calculations, they had crossed into Cambodia—an opinion Monk disputed loudly.

There was no appreciable difference in terrain. Rice fields, tended by stooped natives, were less common, however.

A thousand feet overhead, the tiny dragon plane looked

little larger than some poisonous germ. But it came downward like a hawk.

Thunder suddenly rattled and boomed and crashed in the sky—a thunder of machine-gun fire.

The amphibian bucked like a prodded bull as lead stung it.

Doc booted left rudder. The amphibian whisked out from under the intense storm of lead.

"What the hell's that?" Shad O'Shea yowled, straining to see in all directions—including straight up through the solid cabin roof.

Red tracer sparks fell past the starboard wing, producing an answer that no one questioned.

Chick Alfred called over to Doc Savage. "This chariot armed?"

"No," Doc rapped. He was concentrating on his flying.

"Then we're sitting ducks!" Alfred howled.

"Get wise to yourself," Monk snorted. "This bus is bullet-proof."

"That won't get that—thing off our tail, will it now?"

Monk was shoving open a cabin window, his supermachine pistol out. He changed drums, replacing the one that was charged with effective-but-nonlethal mercy bullets with another one entirely. Ham took up a position on the other side. Their heads strained and swiveled feverishly.

Monk waited until Doc had brought the amphibian level. The dragon plane was sweeping about, her pontoons hanging like blunt talons, intent upon their destruction.

When the dragon plane came howling toward them, Monk stuck his arm out the window. The machine pistol moaned.

The dragon plane opened up with all six components of her armament. Smoking brass cartridges poured from as many points on the weird craft. They sprinkled down like corn being stripped off a cob.

Howling, Monk ducked. Every one else got down on the floor, as well.

Death rapped insistent knuckles along the air surfaces. A spatter of lead came in through the open window, mangling a seat cushion to rags.

"You hairy goon!" Ham yelled, picking himself off the well-tracked cabin floor. "Why didn't you shut the window?" His immaculate white suit was now as mottled as a toad's hide.

"No time!" Monk shouted as the dragon biplane hurtled over their wing, screaming its futile rage.

Scrambling to his feet, Monk surged to the opposite side, and the window there.

This time, he emptied his machine pistol. It shuttled and smoked. The sound brought to mind the deep bass note of a titanic bull fiddle. Brass empties spilled all over the cabin floor, commenced to slipping and rolling.

These sounds were soon swallowed by the great tumult of the dragon plane coming apart.

It was slanting down, one wing dipping slightly from the backwash of the passing amphibian. A few gray threads—tracers from Monk's pistol—arced toward it.

At first, it did not seem that any of Monk's slugs struck their target.

Then the dragon's spidery tail assembly came apart. Rudders and fins flew every which way. There came a brief flurry of sparks, which quickly came and went. That was just the start of it, however.

The emerald fuselage erupted like a string of Fourth of July firecrackers. The wings folded back, hung flapping for a breath, were abruptly snatched away.

The pontoons simply dropped like stones, the crushed and fiery body of the dragon crate—it seemed a true crate now; one that had been run over by a truck—following it earthward.

The flaming tangle dropped through the mist overhanging the jungle below, illuminating it briefly.

That was the last they saw of the harridan bird of prey. If any noise or flash of fire attended its impact with the ground, no echo of either reached their senses.

"Mighty nice shootin'," Chick Alfred said approvingly.

The hairy chemist lifted his still-smoking machine pistol to his wide mouth, pursed gigantic lips, and blew smoke in nearby Ham Brooks's finely chiseled face.

"Demolition slugs," he said over the dapper lawyer's brief coughing spasm.

A battle royal would have broken out then, except that Doc Savage shattered their concentration with a simple yet startling statement.

"We are very near our destination," he said.

XXIV

THE AWFUL DARK

"Since when!"

This from Chick Alfred. A dumfounded expression overspread the long-legged gunman's narrow features.

Doc Savage said, "The pilot of the dragon plane could not have known to expect us. Too, he had several hours' head start. Therefore, he must have been lurking somewhere on the ground, in order to thwart interlopers into the Jade Ogre's domain."

Monk smacked a rust-furred fist into the opposite palm. "Like he did that first time, when he shot you down, huh, Doc?"

"Exactly." The bronze man was studying the ground below, his flake-gold eyes very alert. "It stands to reason that the dragon bus was stationed somewhere near to the Quon stronghold."

They all got busy scanning the terrain. Binoculars passed from hand to hand.

Ham worked over charts and maps. The amphibian was well stocked with these. Doc Savage believed in being prepared for any eventuality. Good maps of Cambodia and environs were at hand.

"According to this Sumner line I plotted," Ham called out, "we're in a sector of Cambodia not very well explored."

Doc asked, "Precisely where?"

"About fifty miles east of the Mekong River and something like seventy-five north of Cochin China."

Doc nodded. He did not ask to look at the chart to which Ham referred. His remarkable memory, coupled with a deep knowledge of geography, had already placed the spot in his mind.

Doc threw the amphibian in wide circles. It was growing dusky now. They had been flying all day. Fortunately, Monk had taken on a full load of fuel at the Kowloon airport. Extra cans were racked in hatches for refueling in out-of-the-way landing spots.

The jungle below was becoming a shapeless expanse of shadows and low-hanging mist. On successive passes, Doc dropped the amphibian lower and lower, dipping one wing or the other, so they could line the cabin compartment windows and employ binoculars.

This produced result in the form of a twitchy cloud that rose up from the furred jungle floor.

Monk spied this first, blinked. The phenomenon resembled black ashes rising from a banked fire—yet each individual "ash" moved in a convulsive manner.

"Bless me!" he squeaked. "Bats!"

They were indeed the flying mammals, a veritable cloud of them. The amphibian's thunder sent them squeaking and scattering in all directions.

"Spy where they rose up from, Monk?" called Doc.

"That hilly bump yonder," said Monk, inclining his nubbin head to port.

The hilly bump happened to be bisected by a river, a sluggish and serpentine thing the color of mud. It seemed to vanish into the hill and come out on the other side, to resume its ophidian course.

"No place to set down," Monk said glumly.

"The river might serve," Doc returned.

"That stream?" Chick Alfred pointed out. "Looks hardly big enough to land a balsa toy on."

"Doc knows his stuff," Monk said proudly. "Right, shyster?"

Ham Brooks, seated on a fold-down seat in the rear, declined to answer. For one thing, he had a darning needle in his mouth. The rent seat of his white trousers lay across his knees. For another, despite his unwavering policy of never agreeing with the apish chemist, the dapper lawer's admiration for his bronze leader effectively inhibited disagreement in this instance.

"Stow any loose stuff, Monk," Doc directed. "This could be bumpy."

They got to work collecting and storing loose items. The map and charts went into compartments. Habeas was roused from his nap, and found himself, sleepy of eye, placed on Monk's lap.

Every one found a seat and hung on to it. Ham drew on his hastily repaired trousers.

Flying low, Doc dragged the river first. There was a stretch where it did not quite meander so much. It looked reasonably deep. No sign of projecting stones—which did not mean there were not submerged ones.

On the second pass, Doc lined up with the straight portion of the river, cracked flaps, and cut the engines.

"No turning back now," Monk said unnecessarily.

The jungle raced under the wing tips. The craft was wider than the river—not a good thing. Fortunately, no trees grew close to the shores. It was unnatural, as if they shunned the ugly tributary.

The amphibian alighted like a graceful bronze swan. It touched, rose, touched again. Rushing, the hull settled. River water sheeted up along the side windows. Monk had left one open. Muddy water came in and doused a sputtering Ham Brooks.

Recriminations had to wait, however. The momentum was carrying the amphibian toward a chocolate-hued bend in the river.

Doc threw a lever, deploying scoops along the hull. These ingested water, creating a braking effect.

"Not enough," Monk muttered worriedly.

Undoubtedly, the most balky of seagoing craft to maneuver is the flying boat. Doc's bus was equipped with a water rudder. It was the most advanced design achievable, which made it only a little better than a canoe paddle insofar as steering on the water was concerned.

"Brace yourselves," Ham called out.

The bend rushed toward them.

Everyone got set for a spectacular crash.

Except Doc Savage. He was busy cranking down the struts that dropped the air wheels from the boatlike hull.

The river bank looked soft, muddy. Still, the bow of the hull glided up it, making a protracted squishing sound that was hideous to the ears.

Shock absorbers rattling, the air wheels climbed the banks. The amphibian rolled up and over the ground several score yards, then slid to a stop. It left a trail of crushed grass like that of a pot-bellied dinosaur.

"We made it!" Ham exulted. Then, by way of celebration, he picked a mud dollop off one bespattered shoulder and dashed it in Monk Mayfair's pleasantly homely visage.

After they had climbed out, Doc Savage examined the hull for damage. He found none, judged that getting the amphibian back onto the river was a matter of releasing the brakes and applying a modicum of elbow grease, and got everyone organized.

Supermachine pistols were checked and pockets filled with extra ammo drums. Chick Alfred and Shad O'Shea made a show of checking their own pistols.

"Let's see to the stowaway," the bronze man suggested.

They surrounded the amphibian bow. When one of Shad O'Shea's heels clicked on stone for the third consecutive step, he swore and said, "This place is sure rocky."

"We are beached on a landing stage of some sort," Doc offered.

Monk, showing monkeylike curiosity, paused and started to scrape mud off the ground under his feet. He exposed great loose-fitting sandstone blocks, much worn by time and exposure.

"I'll be jiggered," he breathed. "No wonder we made it. The mud protected the hull and the stone supported our wheels." The hairy chemist looked up. "Doc, did you spot this from the air?"

"I could not be certain it would be solid enough to bear the amphibian's weight," the bronze man said modestly.

"Now what would a landing stage be doing way out in the middle of nowhere?" Ham pondered softly.

Doc hoisted up the bow hatch, exposing the still-insensate stowaway, curled amid a pocket of collapsible rubber boats. The man sported a rip in one shoulder and a slight amount of crimson—now brown and dry—where Ham's mercy bullet had winged him. The shells were hollow, and broke upon contact with the skin, releasing their liquid anæsthetic contents.

Chick Alfred and Shad O'Shea gathered about the man.

"What say we beat him awake?" Alfred said fiercely.

"That will not be necessary," Doc said after a brief examination. "He will awaken within the hour." Then Doc closed the hatch.

Monk asked, "Why don't we just bring him out of it? I brought my portable chemical laboratory along. We can mix up a batch of counteractant."

"Awake, he will be an impediment to exploration," Doc said. "He can keep."

Craning his long head around, Shad O'Shea wondered, "What's to explore? All I see is creepers and that hill up there."

"We will explore the hill, then," Doc announced.

They set off. Butterflies fanned lazy wings at their approach. Nervous yellow lizards slunk and leaped from their path. They were walking along the river bank. Cracked stones wobbled and clicked under their feet. The stones were smeared with mud, making progress treacherous.

Ham seemed to be having particular trouble, inasmuch as he was still wearing dress shoes.

"Watch out you don't fall into the river and ruin that pretty suit," Monk jeered at one point.

The dapper lawyer scowled darkly, but took the jibe as a warning. He got on the other side of the hairy chemist, so as not to tempt him into a sudden riverward push.

On either side, the forest—it was more forest than jungle, but had attributes of both—was a welter of banyan trees, towering rattan palms, and the bone-boled fromager trees. Creepers laced everything, lending the only true junglelike touch to the place.

The heat was oppressive. Soon, their clothing was soaked. Doc, Monk, and Ham were used to such hardships. But the oppression and near-constant devilment of biting insects brought complaints from Chick Alfred and Shad O'Shea.

"Pipe down!" Monk told them at one point. "Since I'm on board, you aspiring jailbirds are just excess baggage."

Shad O'Shea threw out his chest and poked it with a thumb that was like a horny corncob.

"See here, you ape," he barked. "We hired on to this thing long before you stuck your busted kisser into it. Jason Baird's our boss. Get that?"

"I hope you red-hots got paid in advance," Monk said pointedly.

That reminded the pair of the diamonds promised for the recovery of the missing Maurine Baird.

Chick Alfred caught up with Doc Savage, his stiltlike legs working like busy shears.

"Savage," he puffed. "What happens if we find Baird's sister, but not him?"

"If you are referring to the diamonds," Doc said, "I imagine they will be equally divided, as agreed."

That seemed to satisfy the gun boss. He wiped perspiration off his forehead. A moment later, it was as drenched as before.

"One thing I don't get," he resumed.

Doc's eyes were on the looming hillock. "Yes?"

"What do you get out of all this chasin'? Publicity?"

Monk's guffaw was loud enough to startle a cornflower-blue parakeet into taking wing.

"You lads don't know much about Doc, do you?" he chortled.

"You always throw your weight around like this, ape face?" growled Shad O'Shea.

"There's a lot to throw," the hairy chemist said airily.

"For your information, my good man," Ham Brooks inserted, "we enjoy this sort of thing."

"Fightin'?" Shad asked, genuinely perplexed.

"Excitement," Monk supplied.

"Well," Chick Alfred said unhappily, "so far you got

your share. Me, I just want those sparklers and my feet planted on the other side of the Pacific Ocean, thank you."

The hill was looming closer now. Twilight had fallen. The silence that clamps down upon the jungle at night was all around them suddenly.

Somewhere a lone bat whirred up and beat frantic wings away.

Habeas Corpus, who had been frolicking out of sight, now trotted close to his apish master.

"Wish I'd thought to bring a pith helmet," Shad O'Shea muttered, bringing his hands to the top of his head protectively. "Don't bats like to tangle up in a guy's hair?"

"Not all of 'em," Monk told him.

"No?"

Monk beamed. "Sure. Bats come all kinds. You take the vampire variety. They could care less for hair. They go for the jugular vein, on account that's where all the good drinkin' is."

Shad O'Shea brought his hands quickly down. But only as far as his neck. He looked for all the world like a man groping to strangle himself.

"Hah!" Monk snorted. "Some tough egg you turned out to be. Afraid of bats."

The river ahead made gurgling sounds.

"Sounds like a jugular to me," Monk added. "Sometimes they gurgle just like that."

The source of the liquid sound proved to be the river entering the shadowy hump of the hillock. A net of vines and creepers seemed to hang down the hillock's face. It twisted and waved slightly as it was impelled by the slow-moving stream passing under it.

"I never saw creepers hang down like that," Ham murmured. "They look like a bally curtain."

Doc Savage was still in the lead. He picked up speed.

There was no moon yet, so the others had to strain to trace the bronze man's passage. There was a strange quality he possessed—a combination of graceful movement and utter soundlessness—that made his giant form repel the eye.

All at once, he vanished.

It was more of a melting. The bronze giant had been walking toward the dark flank of the hill; then he was lost to sight. The vines did not appear to shake after he was gone, but in the tricky light, no one could be entirely certain.

"Doc!" Monk squeaked. He loped forward. The others hotfooted it after the simian fellow.

Monk flung into the fall of vineage.

To every one's astonishment, the hairy chemist likewise evaporated.

Chick Alfred skidded to a stop. He slipped on a slick of mud, fell. Shad O'Shea hesitated, sorrowful eyes narrowing fearfully.

Clutching his sword cane, Ham Brooks plunged in. The blade came out. Furiously, Ham began slashing at the curtain of creepers and lianas. They were thick—tough, ropy things.

But the dapper lawyer had made a fetish of keeping the fine blade razor-sharp. It whisked along the hanging vines.

A clump of vines dropped, splashing milk-chocolate water. Beyond was an intensely black void, Stygian and terrible.

Ham poked his head into the gloom. His voice, forlorn and worried, bounced back as if from a cavern.

"Doc! Where are you?"

Out of the blackness boomed unearthly, ghoulish laughter. The horrible hollow sound froze the blood of every one who heard it.

"*Yiii!*" shrieked Shad O'Shea.

Sudden arms reached out from the tangle of creepers, laid bestial hands on the dapper lawyer's shoulders, and dragged him in as if drawing a poor sinner into the pits of Tartarus.

He was gone in an instant. There remained only the sinister gurgling of the river and the ugly sounds of beating bat wings stirring the Cambodian night.

XXV

THE MYSTIC METROPOLIS

Ham Brooks was a practical man. During the Great War, he had commanded a brigade, and his quick thinking had saved entire regiments from extinction. As a member of the bar, he was renowned for his quick grasp of the facts in the courtroom.

He did not believe in demons, devils, imps, ogres, hob-goblins, or other supernatural fiends.

When the two great paws had seized him, he had been caught by surprise. Surprise will sometimes paralyze a man—even a brave one.

The dapper lawyer felt his feet leave the muddy stone river embankment, and attempted to bring his sword cane to play. But the unseen being that had him in its powerful grasp simply spun him about with irresistible strength. The sword left his hand, brought a splash to the unrelieved darkness.

The booming laughter—descending into the lower end of the register—sent pealings of mockery bouncing off unseen stone walls. Then a new voice dispelled the bouncing echoes.

"Monk," it said. "Stop clowning around."

The voice belonged to Doc Savage.

In the blackness, Ham Brooks blinked several times. Comprehension seized him.

"Monk?" he asked, his voice shocked.

"Fooled ya, didn't I?" mocked the hairy chemist's child-like voice.

"You did not," shot back Ham, his voice gathering dignity about it like a cloak. "And furthermore, you are a dish-faced baboon."

"Hah!" said Monk, setting Ham on his feet. "You thought your ambulance-chasing had caught up with you and Old Nick had finally got around to claimin' your soul."

236

"Rubbish!" Ham snapped. He fished out his spring-generator flashlight, thumbed it on.

Light sprang in the cavern. It brought glimmerings from the chocolate stream and made the moist, anthracite-hued walls of the cavern shine evilly.

Ham swept the beam around. It made homely Monk cover his eyes to avoid being blinded. Ham kept it there longer than was necessary, and swept out with the toe of one shoe, connecting with one of Monk's kneecaps.

"*Ye-e-oow!*" the apish chemist squawled, hopping.

"Serves you right, you tree ape," Ham snarled. The light found Doc Savage. The bronze man was examining a rusty chain that was stapled to the worn embankment. Here, the bank was not as obliterated by the thick mud and the excellent fitting of the stones was discernible.

The cavern—it was more unto a tunnel, Ham realized—was composed of like stones. Sandstone, from the look of them. These specimens had been sheltered from the elements and their workmanship had survived more or less intact, except for loose mortar and pressure cracks.

Ignoring the howling chemist, Ham joined Doc Savage.

"Modern chain," Ham remarked.

"Mooring," Doc said, standing up. He had a flash in his hand, but it had been squeezed down to deliver only wan light.

"For what?"

"The dragon seaplane," Doc offered.

Ham washed the narrow confines of the ancient tunnel with his light. "Would it fit?"

"The wings were of the folding type, similar to the kind that are often catapulted from submarine decks," Doc explained.

Ham looked about. "So this is where the beggar lurked. He must have taxied down the river and taken off."

Doc nodded. "The seaplane being smaller than our bus, it would have been possible to build up sufficient take-off speed on that straight stretch where we landed."

Recalling that their own amphibian was much larger than the now-destroyed dragon biplane, Ham wondered, "But, Doc, how are we going to get our crate into the air?"

"Later," said Doc. He pushed deeper into the tunnel. Ham cast a wary eye back toward the tunnel mouth, where hairy Monk had been.

The simian chemist was stealthily sneaking back toward the creeper curtain, evidently with the intent of bedeviling Chick Alfred and Shad O'Shea, who were lurking outside, calling Doc's name in shrill voices.

Ham spotted the head of his sword cane sticking up from the chocolate water, and yanked it free. He found the sheath and made the sword whole with a hard jerk.

Then he crept up behind Monk and inserted the stick between the apish chemist's bandy legs, with the result that Monk fell out past the creepers.

"Haw haw!" Ham laughed. "That should teach you not to pull the same stale stunt more than once." He raised his voice. "It's all right, you two," he called to Chick Alfred and Shad O'Shea. "I skewered the big bad water buffalo—or whatever this unclassifiable beast is."

Monk bounced to his feet, roaring. He clenched his furry arms, as if about to commit murder.

Coolly, Ham stood his ground. Monk subsided, fell to examining his pet pig, who splashed into view.

Alfred and Shad O'Shea plunged in, their faces not amused.

They took one look at Monk, and their expressions grew more unhappy.

"Well, well," Chick Alfred said bitterly. "Look who pulled a funny."

"You'd think one of Doc Savage's men would not be such a clown," Shad O'Shea grunted.

In the act of dusting himself off, Monk grumbled, "Don't tell me you two red-hots weren't scared."

"Maybe," Shad said. "Maybe not."

Ham said. "We'd better hurry if we're to keep up with Doc."

Their argument put aside for the moment, the quartet pounded after the bronze man.

The going was better in the stone-block tunnel. It reminded Ham Brooks a little of the catacombs of Rome, but with a flow of water down the middle. Tiny splashings drew their beams. These proved to be emerald-colored frogs cavorting.

Presently, they overhauled the bronze man.

Doc Savage had come to a section of tunnel wall that lacked a number of bricks on one side.

"Oh-oh," Shad muttered, blinking at the ceiling warily. "I hope this hole ain't fixin' to cave in on our heads."

"Observe the pattern of the missing bricks," Doc said.

The others stared. Nothing came to them. If there was a pattern to the absent bricks, it was not readily apparent.

"I fail to understand, Doc," Ham complained.

Then, by way of demonstration, the bronze man stepped up to the wall, lifted his arms, and inserted metallic fingers into two of the empty spaces, at a point about even with the top of his head, and placed a foot on the lowermost niche.

He began to climb upward.

"A ladder!" Monk yelled. He stood about impatiently, windmilling his mighty arms, until Doc had started to disappear into a hole in the tunnel roof, then scrambled up after the bronze man, Habeas Corpus under one arm.

The others followed, and ever-reluctant Shad O'Shea being last.

When all five men had assembled above, they found themselves in a stone box. There was no light other than that provided by the handy spring-generator flashlights.

These revealed four walls, composed of sandstone blocks but intricately carved. Their state of preservation was good, but age had caused much splitting and cracking of the blocks themselves.

They recognized the seven-headed naga serpent, a pair of three-headed elephants, and other godlets and demons out of the mythology of the Hindus.

"This place gives me the jimjams," Shad O'Shea said gloomily. "Let's go back the way we came."

"Good idea," Chick Alfred muttered uneasily. "Looks like a dead end, anyways."

Doc Savage proved that the much-carved cubicle was not a dead end by employing another set of missing blocks to gain the roof, which, although old, was not by any means ancient.

The roof was composed of tough nipa thatch laid on a bamboo lashing for support. Doc set one muscular shoulder to a sturdy brace, resumed climbing.

The entire roof lifted, as if hinged. Doc gave a mighty heave and the thing was flung away.

They clambered up and dropped to the other side of the north wall, landing in jungle overgrowth from which chameleonlike *sumpah-sumpah* lizards scuttled away on nervous limbs.

Shad O'Shea had the misfortune to alight on a slumbering viper. Its hissing warned him of peril. He cried out, leaped to one side, and, upon sighting the sinuous thing moving through the lianas, brought a big foot down on its wedge-shaped head.

The snake boasted but one head, so it expired without further ado.

At that point, they decided to look around before proceeding further.

From the air, the prominence on which they now stood had resembled an overgrown mound, exactly the kind of tangle of decayed greenage found in jungle areas.

They saw now, thanks to the brilliant beams of their flashlights, that this was no rude hill, but a city of modest size, which the jungle had long ago claimed.

There were houses—small things, to be sure, but as ornate in their external adornments as the largest building, which appeared to be some sort of many-towered palace.

The towers lay in ruins, like blunt fangs that had been broken off in mortal combat. Some of them lay cracked and shattered where they had fallen, untold generations ago.

They moved among the ruins. The pathways of the former city sprouted banyans and other jungle growth. Creepers had worked through walls—there had been, apparently, a surrounding wall at one time, which stood now only in spots—cracking the carvings thereon.

There were carvings everywhere, done in rows. Every workable surface was bedight with sculptures and bas-reliefs, attesting to energetic artisans.

Now, however, it seemed to be a kingdom where only bats ruled. With almost every step, they squirted from hanging places of concealment and writhed away, emitting ratlike squeals.

"Say, wouldn't Johnny go for a place like this," Monk breathed in awe.

Johnny, the archæologist of the group, would no doubt throw fits upon learning of what he had missed. He found the ruins of humankind's past more fetching than a well-turned ankle.

"Reminds me of the place where that Thousand-Headed Man hung out," Ham Brooks said, clutching his sword cane more tightly.*

"The architecture is not quite the same," Doc Savage pointed out. "This is more along the lines of Angkor Wat, discovered in the last century."

"Anchor which?" Shad O'Shea demanded.

"A Cambodian ruin, deserted for centuries," Doc explained, running bronze fingers along a bas-relief. "A French explorer found it more than sixty years ago. It was believed built by a race called the Khmers, who worshiped Hindu deities, and who later abandoned the place."

"Yeah? What happened to them?"

"That is still unknown. This place appears to be of about the same vintage. Evidently, this is the ruin Dr. Mawson Harper referred to as Bankor."

"Hey, Doc?" Monk cried suddenly. "Come a-runnin'!"

The others converged on Monk's position. The hairy chemist was near the entrance to the ruin of many fallen towers. Its outer walls were riotous with sculpture, some having near to three dimensions.

On one wall was a figure wearing a tall, conical item of headgear and a costume that consisted of a tunic and leggings.

Most startling, however, was the fact that this man-figure lacked normal arms. There were only a pair of quarter-moon shapes, like curled epaulets, perched on the stumps of its shoulders. The costume lacked sleeves—no great inconvenience, inasmuch as there were no limbs to fill them.

*The Thousand-Headed Man

The visage that looked out at them was placid and mask-like, the eyes wicked slits.

"Quon!" Ham breathed.

Doc nodded grimly. "The Jade Ogre."

As if summoned by the cabalistic name, a brassy sound reverberated through the darkness-drenched ruin of Bankor.

Bong—bong—bong!

"Sounds like a gong!" Monk yelled.

Doc Savage worked toward the direction of the hollow, sepulchral sound.

Then they saw him—or it.

The gnarled apparition was standing in the doorway of a small temple or similar structure. It wore green silken habiliments, not unlike those on the armless carving beside them.

The conical thing on its head gleamed of polished brass. It jutted up, adding over a foot to the creature's actual height. Because of its stunted stature, the apparition still topped but six feet. But what it lacked in stature, it more than made up for in eeriness.

Midway up the conical "crown," a small jade face stared out. On either side were the profiles of two identical carven faces.

And beneath the trio of green visages glared the true face of Quon. It was cut of a single flawless piece of jade. Their lights picked that fact out. Oddly, the thing did not recoil from their questing rays, although they splashed light directly in its eye slits.

But that was not the fantastic thing—the thing that held them momentarily spellbound.

For the long sleeves of the apparition, depending from those quarter-moon epaulets, hung slack and empty. Then, as they stood rooted, one arm—the right—seemed to swell and rise. From somewhere came a long-drawn-out hissing, as of a viper venting its sibilant wrath.

The effect was like watching a serpent stir to life within its own shed green skin. The empty sleeve lifted to about shoulder level. It pointed its long, drooping maw at them.

Slowly, bony yellow fingers began to emerge. They possessed long nails, which glowed green. They groped forward like the many-headed naga serpent, each fingernail mimicking a narrow serpent head.

Crouching behind Doc Savage, Habeas Corpus raised his hackles and emitted a warning squeal.

"Watch out!" Monk howled, going for his supermachine pistol. "He's growin' one of them dang spook arms!"

At the sound of the hairy chemist's yell, the spectral figure scuttled back into the doorway.

Almost at once, a green-silk-covered arm shot from the blackness—arrowing directly at them!

XXVI

QUON, THE PHANTOM

The bony, disembodied arm of Quon, the Jade Ogre, launched itself like an ethereal arrow. Its swift passing produced no sound. Neither did it hesitate or deviate from its path.

A path which brought it toward the crouching figure of Chick Alfred.

The long-limbed gunman was attempting to duck. Both Monk and Ham had their supermachine pistols out. In unison, they depressed the firing levers. The familiar bull-fiddle moan filled the jungled ruin. In the darkness, two red-hot rods appeared, crossed. The flapping green comet shot past the scarlet letter X of lead, just under the point where they crossed. It whizzed by unscathed.

The drums ran empty.

"Dang it!" Monk groaned.

There was no time for Monk and Ham to reload.

A cyclonic Nemesis, Doc Savage drifted a mighty bronze arm out, grasping fear-frozen Chick Alfred by his collar. Prodigious muscles bunched up.

For all his leanness, Chick Alfred was not light, Yet Doc Savage plucked him from the path of danger as if he were no more than a collection of broomsticks wired together to form a scarecrow.

The phantom arm just missed the man's outflung arm; a flapping comet, it continued on. It happened to enter another doorway—what seemed to be the main entry into the crumbling palace—and was lost to sight.

Nothing happened. Their anxious eyes passed from the doorway into which Quon had retreated to the one opposite where the arm—apparently—had entered.

Doc's voice came then. What he said was unintelligible to Chick Alfred and Shad O'Shea. But Monk and Ham moved with alacrity, in response. They stationed themselves on either side of the palace doorway.

Doc Savage faded back toward the sandstone hovel where Quon, the so-called Jade Ogre, had last been seen.

Doc pressed his broad back against the carven wall. He plucked out one of the thin-walled anæsthetic balls that had so often proved useful. He shagged this in, then waited for the volatile gas to vaporize, mix with the oxygen and nitrogen in the air, and be rendered harmless.

The bronze man rapped out new orders. Monk replied in kind, producing sounds that were more akin to clucks and gobbles than human speech.

"What kinda lingo is that?" demanded Shad O'Shea, hunkered down near Ham Brooks.

"Mayan," Ham replied, sharp eyes switching back and forth in the fantastic gloom.

"Huh?"

"We use it when we don't want to be understood by enemies," the dapper lawyer added distractedly.

"Crafty, I calls it," grunted the horse-faced Shad, who seemed satisfied by the thin explanation.

In fact, Doc and his aids alone in the modern world spoke the queer tongue of the Maya. They had picked it up in the course of a Central American adventure, one in which Doc had acquired the great wealth that financed his unusual work.

It was not generally known to the world, but Doc Savage had at his command one of the most fabulous treasure troves in existence—a vast cavern wherein was stored the wealth of the ancient Mayan nation. This was located in a lost canyon, the Valley of the Vanished, in the remote recesses of the Republic of Hidalgo. Survivors of the lost Mayan civilization, isolated from the world, kept Doc supplied with mule trains of gold whenever his bank accounts required replenishing.

This was a legacy of Doc's father, now deceased, who set the bronze man on the path of adventure, and saw to it that his son would have the wherewithal to carry on the Savage family work of aiding the downtrodden.

Doc, judging it safe to enter, pitched into the dark space that had birthed the discorporate arm.

He drove the beam of his flash ahead of him.

For a moment, the bronze man's eerie trilling came into being. It might have been a sound from the past of Bankor, perhaps the pipings of long-dead palace musicians. A stark note of puzzlement seemed to underlie its tuneless roving of the scale.

The questing light of exceeding brilliance showed only riotous carvings—and a square hole in the center of the floor.

Doc went to this. He was cautious in his approach. He worked around the square hole, which had all the earmarks of a primitive charcoal pit, where coals were burned for warmth or cooking purposes. His light failed to disclose any danger.

To be certain, Doc extracted from his vest an object like a chopped-off candle, got it going, and tossed it into the square hole.

It burned and sputtered yellow-orange light. It was a small flare. Wavering shadows rippled along the processions of carvings, made them momentarily lifelike.

Nothing—neither sound nor danger—emerged from the square pit.

Not that Doc Savage expected anything to do so. The hole was but two feet square—too small to admit the human form. Or at least the adult variety.

By the light of the sputtering flare, Doc examined the inner walls. His flake-gold eyes roved. Finger tips brushed at loose carvings, felt for cracks and joinings, but there were no secret panels or walls that might be hung on pivots so as to revolve at a touch. The floor betrayed no telltale scrapings.

Doc emerged into the courtyard. A cloud passed from the moon's face and the area became effulgent with light.

The bronze man crossed to the palace, taking care not to walk in a direct line with the opposite doorway, into which the spectral arm had fled.

He joined the others.

"Nothin' came out, Doc," Monk muttered, tiny eyes on the far door. "What'd you find?"

"Nothing."

Monk put out a lower lip. "Secret door?"

"No."

Monk blinked. Then Doc said, "Care to venture inside?"

"O.K. by me."

They went in.

There was a kind of antechamber beyond the door, and beyond that a rectangular stone room. There were no furnishings or other detritus of human habitation in evidence.

And no disembodied arm draped in green silk.

But they did find a square hole in the floor of the larger room. It, like the one Doc had found in the other building, was barely a foot and a half wide and long.

"Could that dang arm have ducked down here?" Monk muttered, standing over the long-cold pit.

"If it did," Doc Savage responded, somewhat hollow of voice, "there is no sign of it now."

"Could be it pulled one of those disappearin' acts. I gotta admit, after seeing that arm grow out of an empty sleeve like that, I'm about ready to believe anything."

Monk, frustrated by the lack of any sign of the arm of the phantom Quon, angled the muzzle of his supermachine pistol into the square hole and let the weapon moan and shuttle briefly, without any effect other than to bring Ham Brooks running in, his handsome face a picture of concern.

"Next time *yell* a warning," he panted.

"How about 'Oink-oink'?" Monk suggested amiably.

Ham, who detested all references to pork in any form, set his polished teeth.

Getting down on hands and knees, the hairy chemist tried to peer into the hole. Ham's flash came into play.

"It's just a hole," Monk muttered thickly. "Deep, but a hole."

He found his feet. "I don't get it, Doc."

The bronze man was finishing his reconnoitering of the various walls. The ceiling, too, seemed solid.

It was an imponderable mystery, this evanishment.

A dejected trio, they emerged into the moonlight, where Chick Alfred and Shad O'Shea were nervously standing guard.

When all was explained to them, Chick Alfred grumbled, "This don't make sense."

"Say it again, brother," Monk said fervently.

"I don't believe in ghosts," insisted Ham Brooks earnestly.

"Whistle a new tune," grumbled Shad O'Shea. "Because where spooks are concerned, I just got religion."

"Be your age," Chick Alfred said sourly.

"Be yours. You saw that Quon go in and not come out again."

"Aw, Savage just missed something, that's all. C'mon, I'll show you."

They started for the sandstone hovel, their heels crushing rank weeds striving up from the shattered masonry of the courtyard with mushy sounds. Their hard faces were grim and purposeful.

They had hardly taken a dozen steps when their jaws dropped and their eyes started from their heads.

Out of the gloom of the sandstone arch came a phosphorescent comet of bony yellow digits and green silk.

Chick Alfred threw himself to the ground. It was an act that possibly saved his life.

Shad O'Shea, however, stood as if transfixed. Perhaps it was the chill that superstitious fear laid over his muscles. Other than to goggle, he seemed unable to respond to the danger that confronted him.

Monk and Ham, their mercy pistols up, strove for clean shots, but to no avail. Fear-frozen Shad O'Shea blocked them.

Moving like a bronze beam of moonlight, Doc Savage found a loose block of sandstone and, without seeming to take careful aim, threw it.

The block flew true. It intercepted the severed limb just as it was about to impact with Shad O'Shea's agape face.

Came a sizzling flash, yellow and hideous. This time, they shielded their eyes. All but Shad.

When the flare of ugly light had died away, he was stumbling around in circles, crying, "It got my eyes! I can't see! I can't see!"

Which, as it turned out, was an exaggeration.

"Light blindness," Doc said, guiding the man off to one side, and safety. "Keep blinking your eyes," he instructed the blubbering Shad.

Once they were clear, Monk immediately emptied his machine pistol into the gloomy interior of the hovel. His drum ran empty. The prodigious rate of fire consumed shells with distressing rapidity.

Ham stepped up and repeated the action, emptying his pistol.

Fishing out fresh drums, they clicked these into place. They advanced on the hovel.

Curiously, Doc Savage did not join them. He stationed himself in the center of the courtyard and was slowly turning in place, his eyes scouring the surroundings as if expecting attack from another quarter entirely. He held heavy shards of sandstone in each metallic hand.

Seeing this, Shad and Chick Alfred copied his actions. Shad seemed able to see now, although his optics still blinked furiously.

Then it came!

From the palace door, a green silken sleeve was lifting with an eerie hissing. Fingers strained to emerge from the empty cloth maw.

"Look out!" Shad shouted. "Another one!"

Monk and Ham whirled, dropping into protective crouches.

The palace door seemed to spit another Quon limb. The

twisted figure of the Jade Ogre, dimly visible, withdrew into the gloom with soundless calm.

Doc flung a block then. He aimed carefully this time. The brick struck the arm back of the wrist, where the silken sleeve hung down in the wide-mouthed fashion of the Orient.

The arm, struck, turned in place as if dodging a hair-second too late. Knocked off course, it turned, its phosphorescent yellow fingers seemingly clawing the still air for purchase. It remained a stubborn five feet off the ground through all these gyrations.

Doc released the other block. It struck the thing on its curved fingers, and, as the others averted their eyes, they felt momentary heat on their faces.

When it was safe to look again, there was nothing to see.

Monk ambled up to the spot. "This is startin' to get me down," he muttered.

"Me, too," said Ham, in a rare moment of agreement.

Doc Savage said, "Ham, you guard the smaller building. Monk, the rest of you, follow me."

They followed the bronze man into the palace chamber. Doc picked up a pair of broken blocks—the same ones he had just used to excellent effect—and stepped boldly into the place.

He wasted no time looking for secret panels. By the light of Ham Brooks's flash, he went directly to the square hole of a charcoal pit.

The action nearly cost the bronze man his life.

The hole appeared as before—a flame-blackened aperture in the foot-worn masonry of the floor.

Like a faint firebrand made in the shape of a ghoul's gnarled arm, the limb of Quon shot up from the pit.

Doc's lightning-quick reflexes saved him. He yanked back his head, and the thing ascended to the smoke-discolored ceiling, touched, and gave up its existence in a brief paroxysm of lemony luminance.

Doc did not pause to witness the now-familiar phenomenon, though. He heaved both bricks into the pit, first one and then the other.

The pit gave back hollow sounds of impact, indicating the shaft was a good dozen feet deep.

"He couldn't have escaped down there," Ham said in exasperation, "A child couldn't wriggle down there."

"Maybe—maybe, it ain't a person," Shad muttered, eying a seven-headed serpent carving warily. "Maybe it's part snake."

"Bosh," Ham snorted.

Shad turned on the dapper lawyer, yelling, "You heard it hiss! Like a snake. Explain it, will ya?"

Twisting his sword cane between frustrated hands, Ham Brooks admitted, "I cannot."

None of them could.

Doc said, "Alfred, guard this hole."

"A pleasure," said Chick Alfred, training a revolver at the hole.

The others followed the grim bronze man out into the leprous moonlight.

Monk called over, "Dang quiet, if you ask me."

Doc lifted his eyes and scanned the surrounding buildings.

A few bats were returning to their nocturnal haunts. They fell like black hail, seemed to become part of the tumbled battlements which were their home.

Doc Savage strode past the hairy chemist. He removed from his many-pocketed vest one of the cherry-sized explosive grenades that were so powerful. He set a tiny timer and tossed it into the charcoal pit.

Every one retreated to safety without urging. The look on the bronze man's face was hard.

The sound was long in coming. Monk, thinking the grenade was a rare dud, started to his feet. A huge bronze hand pushed him down again.

The sound, when it finally came, was distant. A mushy boom.

Immediately, dust, grit, and a few chips of flinty sandstone blew out of the doorway.

The sandstone hovel did not exactly collapse. It was quite stout. But the floor had evidently given way, causing the bricks of the supporting walls to bulge outward and crack. A few fell out, clattering and broken.

In a few places near the entrance, puffs of rock dust squirted up from fissures in the courtyard masonry.

When the dust settled, Doc began picking up broken blocks.

"Gather as much as you can carry," he directed the others.

They followed him into the palace, their arms heavily laden.

Doc made a pile like a tiny cairn at one edge of the charcoal pit. They arranged several of these so that if anything attempted to emerge from the aperture, it would cause the makeshift piles to rattle and clatter in warning.

Back out in the courtyard, Doc Savage took up a position. He scanned his surroundings.

The others milled about, as men will do when uncertain of safety. Fingers caressed triggers nervously. The only noises abroad in the night were the leathery flappings and squeakings of bats. Habeas Corpus crowded close to his master's bandy legs.

"Deuced eerie," Ham said under his breath.

The bronze man signaled for silence. His ears were hunting sounds.

No one heard anything—not even Doc Savage. The oppressive air was slowly cooling. The hush of the jungle night was upon them. No birds called. No sounds at all disturbed the ruin of a city—unless it was their own careful breathing.

A black string of bats wound up from the south. Their cries worried the nerves, sent flesh to crawling.

A voice cried out.

"Help! Help me!"

It was strained to the point of breaking, that voice. It came again.

"I can't outrun it! Somebody—anybody—help me!"

"Who the heck is that?" Monk muttered.

But Doc Savage was already plunging in the direction from which the tangled voice was emanating.

The way was difficult. They soon found themselves climbing a shattered wall and picking through a profusion of green bamboo. Monk, directly behind the bronze man, shot out

long arms and separated the green stuff with such force that
the strong, jointed shoots splintered and collapsed. The others
had it easier as a result.

The way led to a kind of terraced area that formed one of
the sides of the hillock—the city, rather, for there was no
hillock as such, except what was created by the destructive action of centuries of unchecked growth in the stonework battlements of ancient Bankor.

Stumbling down the cracked, uncertain steps was a
man—a white man. His arms were out, flapping like the
wings of a pelican trying to gain flight.

Trailing directly behind him, matching his every weaving step, was a tatterdemalion thing of green silk and glowing,
dead flesh. A limb of the Jade Ogre!

The man was running for his life. He turned to look
back once, showing pale features strained by fear and horror.
Their glimpse of his face was brief, but in the moonlight it was
enough for recognition.

Shad O'Shea was the first to give voice to the man's
identity.

"Cripes! Rex Pinks!"

XXVII

LIKELY STORY

At the shrill sound of his own name, pallid society reporter Rex Pinks tucked his elbows into his ribs, threw his
head back, and mustered all the speed of which his gangling
body was capable.

As if toying with the man, the trailing detached limb
scooted after him, matching his pace.

Pinks stumbled then. The arm dipped, lunging like a
shark closing in on wounded prey. Rex Pinks was oblivious
to the nearness of doom. Frantic, he flung out an arm to
grasp the nearest support. It happened to be a stunted rattan
palm.

Hooking one arm around the bole, Pinks let his headlong momentum fling him around the tree.

The arm followed. For the first time, it showed itself to be not unerring in its intelligence.

The disembodied limb of Quon blindly bumped the palm bole and hissed its last.

When the fading flare had gone, there remained only a scorch mark visible on the palm bole as proof the limb had ever existed.

Doc Savage gained Rex Pinks's side. The colorless reporter was sprawled on a cracked terrace step, panting like a fice dog after a hard run.

"What—what happened?" he gulped.

"You nearly lost your life," Doc Savage related. No trace of surprise showed in the bronze man's steady tone.

Pinks's head jerked this way and that. "Where is it?"

"Gone," the bronze man told him.

"Gone?"

Doc Savage turned his attention to the scorch mark. It was fresh. A tracing finger picked up soot. The stuff felt warm to the touch.

Ham Brooks towered over the reporter.

"Just what are you doing here, Pinks?" he demanded, his voice suspicious.

"Give me—a moment to—catch my—breath," Pinks jerked out. His eyes looked like marbles too long in the sun, glassy and dull.

"A moment, hell!" Chick Alfred complained. "Fancy meeting you here," he added sourly. "Just happened to be in the neighborhood?"

"Yeah," Shad put in. "Funny you should show up just when the Jade Ogre took a run-out powder. Funny—except I don't see no one laughin'."

Monk Mayfair made a succession of faces at the winded reporter.

"So that's Rex Pinks, huh? He don't look like much to me."

The simian chemist reached down and drew the reporter to his feet as if he were an alley cat.

"Didn't you get left behind in Hongkong?" he growled.

"I—I can explain!" Pinks wheezed.

Doc Savage said, "Start with Hongkong, Pinks. What happened after you and Dr. Harper left our company?"

"We ordered the cab back the hotel, as you instructed," Pinks gasped out. "We were halfway there when Harper changed his mind. He said he couldn't bear to leave your cousin Pat behind. He felt like a coward. He told the driver to turn around. He spoke Chinese, so I didn't know any different."

The pallid reporter seemed to have his wind back. His words tumbled out in a rush.

"We arrived at a place—I don't know what it was. Some natives met Harper there. They seemed to know him—or of him."

"Continue," Doc prompted.

"No sooner had they led us inside than we were taken prisoner. I was bound and gagged—the usual stuff, red sponges and lengths of silk. Then they clubbed me good."

The reporter felt of his head. He winced painfully. There was no blood visible in his pale hair.

"When I woke up," he continued, "I was on a plane. They had me stuffed in a trunk. I heard voices. One of them belonged to Jason Baird. I started kicking the trunk and got clubbed again. Later, I woke up in a cell. I didn't know where I was. Brown natives seemed to run the place. Once, a horrible face showed through the cell bars. Savage, you gotta believe me: It was the same face I saw that time on the *Mandarin*. The Jade Ogre's face. It looked at me like a serpent with a carved jade head."

Doc asked, "What happened to Dr. Harper?"

"A prisoner, too. He was in the cell beside me."

Doc looked his interest. "How do you know this?"

"He and I were able to communicate through the wall of the cells. They were thick, but very old. Sound carried through cracks. He said they had taken him, too. And get this: Your cousin Pat was there."

Concern flickered in the bronze man's golden eyes. "You saw Pat?"

Rex Pinks shook his head. "No. I only heard her voice. Once. She was putting up a fuss. I think they were dragging her from her cell." He hesitated. "I—I don't know how to tell you this."

"Go on," Doc urged.

Rex Pinks licked colorless lips with a too-pink tongue. "They never brought her back."

Moans greeted this. Ham turned ashen. Monk made and unmade hairy fists and bared fierce teeth.

Doc Savage stood immobile, a statue of too-calm metal. Only his eyes showed life. Tiny, angry gales seemed to kick up in their aureate depths.

Rex Pinks went on. "Harper took it hard. He was sure she was killed. He said I was going to be next. He knew these natives. And sure enough, they came for me. But I wasn't killed. They dumped me in a war canoe of some kind, and we set out for this place—wherever it is. Are we still in China?"

Monk snorted derision.

"Cambodia," Doc supplied.

The expression on Rex Pinks's pale face was resigned. "Figures," he said. "I didn't tell you one thing."

"Just one?" Chick Alfred jeered.

Pinks ignored this. "In the lead canoe was the Jade Ogre. He sat hunched in the prow like an evil Buddha, his empty sleeves hanging down. They brought us to a point near here. Quon went on ahead. After a while, he came back and forced me to accompany him."

Doc asked, "Forced you? How?"

"I can't describe it. He had no arms to push with. But I could not resist. I was blindfolded at that point."

"This tale is gettin' taller," Monk warned.

"I could hear you men talking, and fighting. Quon left me. Then he came back and untied my gag and blindfold."

"Untied?" This from Ham.

"I know how it sounds," Rex Pinks said desperately. "He was behind me all the time. He had no fingers, of course, but the gag fell away, and then the blindfold. I found myself in darkness. Something pushed me—hard. I stumbled forward."

Rex Pinks paused to gulp a deep breath, then continued hoarsely.

"Naturally, I turned to look. That was when I saw—it."

Doc said, "It?"

"The arm," Pinks breathed, queasy of eye. "It was coming straight for me. I turned and ran and kept running. No matter what I did, it seemed to follow me, never quite catching up. But I couldn't shake it, either. Then I remembered hearing your voice. That's when I yelled. The rest—the rest you saw."

Rex Pinks buried his haggard face in his hands. His shoulders slumped and his entire attitude was that of a man shrunken by ordeal.

No one spoke for a protracted moment.

Then Chick Alfred snorted, "A likely story!"

Ham Brooks turned to Doc Savage. "You don't suppose any part of what this wastrel is saying could be true?"

"It's all true," Rex Pinks sobbed.

"I don't believe it," Monk insisted. "Not the part about Pat, anyways. Pat's a canny egg. No two-bit Asiatic spook could get the better of her!"

Not surprisingly, Doc added nothing to the growing controversy. His flake-gold eyes, chill as diamond points, bored the night in all directions around them.

"What now, Doc?" Monk wondered.

"The amphibian. It is time we got back and interrogated the stowaway."

"Stowaway?" Rex Pinks questioned.

"Yeah," said Chick Alfred. "A China boy. Maybe you know him. Or more likely, maybe he knows *you*."

They began their trek back to the amphibian. They circled the ruin of Bankor. Since they were on the western side, they caught a glimpse of the place where the other end of the muddy river emerged from the ruin. It was a grotto of a thing, obscured by hanging vines that wavered like harp strings impelled by the slowly moving river.

"Musta built the place over the river for convenience," Monk ventured.

"If Pinks's story is true," Doc said, "the war canoes slipped up the western portion of the river undetected."

"That means their hideout is somewhere west, too."

Doc turned to Rex Pinks. "How far, would you judge?"

"That's the thing, I couldn't. They stopped every so often. I don't know how to judge jungle distance."

"He's holding out," Chick Alfred grumbled. "I'll bet my share of them diamonds he's in cahoots with this Quon."

Monk, sensing easy money, said, "I'll take that bet."

"Aw, I'm just blowin' off steam," muttered Alfred.

"Piker."

They reached the beached amphibian in good time.

Sounds came from the thing. Movement. Scampering of feet. They sank to places of cover.

Doc, capping a flashlight with one bronze palm, turned it on. He drew back, sent it arcing toward the ship.

The light pinwheeled, seemed to appear in mid-air, bounced off the windscreen, and rolled to dry ground.

Before it hit, chatterings and scamperings filled the night.

"Sounds like scores of 'em," Shad roared.

"Scores of what?" asked a worried Chick Alfred.

Ham Brooks had an answer to that.

"Monkeys!" he exclaimed. "They're just monkeys!"

Doc lifted from behind a boulder, started forward.

From the shadowy hump that was the amphibian, long-tailed monkeys leaped and skittered away. They sought refuge in nearby jati trees, where they crouched and regarded them with wise, winking eyes.

"Too bad," Ham Brooks said when they reached their plane. "If we had a net, we might have been able to catch Monk a wife."

"Very funny, shyster," growled Monk, who toted a frightened Habeas. The pig's reaction to the sight of what he must have mistaken for a cloud of miniature Monks was to tremble like a dog cast adrift in a rowboat.

"Or do monkeys mate for life?" Ham drawled.

Doc wasted no time in excavating the stowaway from the bow hatch of the plane.

The Chinese, Ho, had awakened by this time. He looked thoroughly frightened. Despite this, he cracked a weak smile at the sight of the big bronze man.

"I feel like gleat Chinese sage," he said.

"Eh?"

"Confuse-ious all over."

When no one laughed at the lame crack, Ho sobered.

"Some straight answers might help your position, which is bad," Doc suggested sternly.

"This insignificant one cannot oblige. So solly."

"Try cuttin' out the post-card Chinaman act," Monk said harshly. "Doc told us you drove a hack back in Frisco. So come clean."

Shad O'Shea suddenly grabbed Rex Pinks by the scruff of his neck, thrust him forward. "Start with this guy. He look familiar to you?"

"No. Never saw that man before this," inserted the bewildered Ho, apparently finding his *R*'s.

"Hah! One liar covering for another."

Monk sidled up to Ham Brooks, began whispering. "You were part of this long before I was, shyster. What do you make of all these shenanigans?"

The dapper lawyer was destined never to reply to that question. For something struck the amphibian's windscreen with a muffled pop.

So keyed up were their nerves that the sound was at first mistaken for a bullet striking. The windscreen was bulletproof, so the fact that it did not shatter surprised no one. Too, often the sound of a rifle shot comes a fractional second after the note of impact registers upon the ears.

No such sound came this time.

"Down!" Doc rapped. He yanked Ho off the amphibian and bore him away.

The others, like startled birds, fanned out in all directions, finding shelter.

"What is it, Doc?" Monk asked, tiny eyes concerned.

Doc indicated the windscreen. In the moonlight, a faintly greenish exhalation was rising in the night.

"Poison pellet," he said. "Probably from a blowgun."

Ham hissed, "Any one see who shot it?"

Rex Pinks jumped up from behind a bush. "There!" he screeched. "Quon!"

Immediately, supermachine pistols began stuttering in

the direction of the pallid reporter's pointing finger. Chick Alfred and Shad O'Shea unloosed hot lead from their revolvers.

Leaves were sickled off trees. Foliage was chopped into spinach. Loitering monkeys howled and fled to distant parts.

Monk, emboldened, leaped for the clump of foliage that had been riddled by lead.

He paused, whirled, and threw up ungainly arms.

"Nothin' here."

"He was right there," Pinks insisted, "staring with that cold jade mask of his. There was something sticking out of his mouth, too. Like a reed."

"Blowgun?" Doc inquired, eying the flustered reporter steadily.

"Yeah. Could be. Sure."

"He just piles it on, doesn't he?" Chick Alfred grimaced. "I didn't see nothin'."

As it turned out, none of them saw anything.

"What do you expect?" Monk said after he had ambled back. "That Quon is part spook, ain't he?"

"I don't believe in spooks," Chick Alfred said harshly.

Doc turned to the Chinese humorist, Ho.

"That pellet was meant for you," he said. "Care to enlighten us why?"

Ho seemed to shiver, as if from a fever. "He—He Who Will Breathe Death Upon the Universe fears that I will betray the location of the temple of Quon."

"Haw! What a yarn!"

"Temple?" Doc prompted.

"I have never been there," Ho said meekly. "But I am told it is a magnificent place of jade, fashioned in the form of the head of Quon, with four faces, each looking out toward one of the four compass directions so that Quon can behold all his enemies at once, the better to send out his Limbs of Retribution."

Despite the flowery absurdity of the man's words, he sounded quite sincere.

"Where is this temple of Quon?" Doc asked.

"I do not know."

"Do better than that, guy," Monk warned.

"I do know that it rests in the center of a mystic body of water known as *Yook Hoy*," Ho said reluctantly. "Jade Lake."

"Jade Lake?"

"Jade Lake."

XXVIII

GREEN BREATH OF DEATH

Before they could set out in search of Jade Lake, Doc announced that they would have to get the amphibian into the air.

This had been in back of their minds all along—the problem of lifting off the meandering stream.

Ham took the controls, after Ho and the pig, Habeas, were bundled aboard. Storklike Chick Alfred, being the weakest from the standpoint of sheer physical strength, was given a supermachine pistol and the task of standing watch.

Doc stationed the others—Monk, Rex Pinks, and Shad—at useful points around the big amphibian, saying, "When I give the word, put your backs into it."

Doc took the bow. The others had the wing bracing struts. Doc signaled Ham to release the wheel brakes.

"Push!"

Like Trojans, they gave it their all. Wheels free to turn, the amphibian began backing up. Sloshing, the tail slid onto the water, then the streamlined hull.

When the craft had settled onto the river, it looked like a bronze duck floating in a stream of milk chocolate, a fantastic sight here in the oppressive silence of the Cambodian night.

They waded out to the open hatch on the port side, clambered aboard.

Doc strode to the controls.

The river was sluggish, but there was a current. The manner in which they had shoved off left the flying boat wallowing with its bow pointed toward land. Gradually, the current seized it. The flying boat commended a lazy pirouette.

Doc maneuvered the water rudder, getting the blunt nose pointed downstream. The air rudder proved useful in this maneuvering, too.

Soon, the craft was bumping and sliding down the chocolate-hued river at a desultory pace.

It was not relaxed in the pilot's compartment, however. The waters may have been sluggish, but the threat of piling up on the stone-bound banks was ever-present. Doc struggled with the rudders, narrowly averting trouble at several junctures.

Where bank-growing trees threatened the wings, Monk and Ham, stationed atop each wing tip, used hastily harvested bamboo poles to lever the great ship out of danger.

Once, a quick-thinking Ham Brooks, spotting an unavoidable jati tree rushing toward them, brought it down with a sawlike stream of lead from his machine pistol. The splintery crash as it fell reverberated through the Cambodian night.

At one point, they were rounding a particularly treacherous bend in the river, nearly a mile downstream of forgotten Bankor, and disaster looked imminent.

The amphibian, caught off balance, began sliding sideways toward the bank, where the port air wheel—Doc had left these down as a precaution—was certain to be knocked off by the weed-grown bank. If that happened, they knew, the entire hull could be dashed open.

Doc banged the engines to life. Props clawed air. Booting rudder, Doc fed gas to the starboard can. It screamed in response, but began dragging the ship nose-on with the bank.

Avoiding an unwanted beaching was impossible, the bronze man realized. He sent the craft surging ahead.

The amphibian climbed the bank under its own power, as it had before. Doc cut the engines. The ship jerked to a halt.

Silence returned. So did respiration.

"Here we go again," grumbled Monk, the first to leap out on the bank.

They pushed off. This time was trickier, but soon they were floating downriver once again.

Time passed. It was difficult to gauge how much distance was being traversed, the river vipered so much.

Monk called down from the wing, "That Quon has had time to get back to his hideout by now, I'll betcha."

No one took him up on it. They were all thinking the same thing.

Then, through the windscreen, came into view a particularly long stretch of river. Where before, each bend snaked into view only after they were on top of it, this section ran for a quarter of a mile in plain sight.

It was by no means ruler-straight, but it could be run.

Monk and Ham needed no instruction. They scrambled back into the tri-motor through wing inspection ports.

Doc brought the engines back, full tilt. The amphibian lunged forward, gathering speed. They held on. She got on step. The nose lifted. The wings grabbed passing air under them.

Shad O'Shea covered his eyes with huge paws, exclaimed, "Oh, mother!"

With less than a rod to spare, they cleared a particularly dense thicket of foliage at the next bend. Dripping muddy water, the hull bottom scraped treetops, giving them a memorable scare.

Doc banked the ship, brought her level. They began to work the tightness from their faces after that.

"Guess I missed spotting that straight stretch before," Monk said to no one in particular.

Ham Brooks took this admission as an opportunity to get in a dig.

"Ape! You should have known Doc would never set down like that without figuring a way to get up in the air again."

Monk was too pleased with events to bother returning the insult.

Considering the time they had expended negotiating the sluggish river, the flight back to Bankor was astonishingly brief.

The upsurge of bats told them that they had passed over the forlorn place.

"I won't miss that joint," Monk observed, scratching his pet pig thoughtfully. "Right, Habeas?"

The pig looked up, and actually appeared to say, "Next time leave the ambulance chaser behind to chase the bats."

"Sure thing," said Monk.

Chick Alfred, Shad O'Shea, Rex Pinks, and Ho each bestowed upon the pig a variety of astounded looks.

Ham punctured their incredulity with a single word: "Ventriloquism."

"Prove it," Monk said, good-naturedly. In fact, the gag *was* the product of ventriloquism. Monk had practiced a series of touch and hand signals that prompted the pig to assume a believable attitude whenever the apish chemist threw his squeaky voice.

Jade Lake proved to be three miles west of Bankor and well named.

Even by moonlight, it resembled a mirror of highly polished jade.

The mirror reflected, in gigantic terms, a quartet of faces as green as the lake itself.

When they first saw it, the effect was as if four huge Quon faces peered up from a window to Hades set in the very earth itself. This sight brought gasps from Rex Pinks, Shad O'Shea, and even Ho, who quailed from the window at the sight of the emerald apparition.

"*No! No!*" Ho shrieked. "Quon sees me! He knows I have betrayed him."

"Cut it out," Chick Alfred said unkindly. "You're gonna give every one the willies."

As they flew nearer, they spied the temple, which squatted in the exact center of the lake of green moonlight.

The thing was old, hideously ornate, but each side was dominated by an identical mask made of blocks cut and shaped to create the image of the so-called Jade Ogre. These grim countenances were what were reflected heavenward.

"Now we know why it's called Quon," Ham interposed.

Doc banked, circling the temple—for it seemed to be just

that—and discerned no sign of life. There was a float moored to a stone jetty that projected from the eastern face of the hideous temple. It obviously served as a seaplane mooring, for the seaplane that had carried Jason Baird, Rex Pinks, and—presumably—Pat Savage floated beside it like a dragonfly at rest.

"Musta been where that dragon crate tied up when it wasn't layin' for stray planes," Monk opined.

Doc flew over the lake of jade. Its placid surface was dotted with what seemed to be platters of jade of a slightly darker hue. None of the group could make out what these were, but they seemed to float stationery on the lake's unrippled surface.

"Snares?"' Ham wondered.

"Hard to say."

A second pass failed to produce any response from the Quon temple, which continued to brood in the center of the green lake.

"Maybe nobody's home," Monk muttered.

"We might have beat that devil Quon back, after all," Rex Pinks suggested. This optimistic notion was not met with any encouragement.

Doc, after a third pass, decided to set down. Preparations were made. The amphibian came around, heeling, and drew a line across the lake, breaking the eastern reflection into a thousand shimmering miniatures.

The strange-looking plates proved to have a commonplace origin. This came out as they wobbled, impelled by the wake ripples.

"Lily pads," Monk breathed. "I can see tiny green frogs jumpin' offa 'em. How 'bout that?"

Doc cut the three great engines and the air giant settled into a ponderous glide.

Since it was convenient, they made for the big square float. The eastern face of Quon regarded them with stony composure.

"Brrrr," Monk breathed. "He looks like he ain't afraid of nothin'."

The visage was chiseled from many blocks of some verdigrised stone—not jade, as Ho had claimed. The eyes were wise slits, the nose a broken snub of rock, and the mouth seemed to form a kind of long door, or portal.

Abruptly, this opened, shedding a fan of wan light.

Then, as if a giant were exhaling, gushing billows of green smoke rolled out of this, enveloped the finger of a jetty and its float, crawled ponderously across the water in their direction.

Doc Savage immediately reengaged the three big motors. He threw them into reverse. The amphibian began to back away from the looming cloud. Its forward edge recoiled and was beaten back momentarily, but the thing only spread wider, continuing its inexorable progress in their direction.

"That stuff looks to be the same color as the gas that almost got our Chink stowaway," Chick Alfred pointed out.

"No doubt it is," Doc bit out.

"It is the breath of Quon!" Ho shrilled. "We will catch Jade Fever!"

"We may not live that long," inserted Ham. "Look!"

His pointing cane indicated the wan portal, from which native men—some brown, some yellow—of the military type. A machine gun was set on a tripod mount. A brown man squatted behind it. The muzzle began spitting red fireflies. The weapon ingested twitching loops of cartridge belt, spewing brass empties every which way.

"Is this thing proof against machine guns?" Rex Pinks demanded.

"Yes," he was told.

"How about gas?" muttered Shad O'Shea.

"No," the bronze man said.

"Then, boys," clucked Chick Alfred, "we're finished."

Like a fog from the netherworld, the green poison gas swept around their helpless craft, seeking to envelop it completely.

XXIX

CUPID'S SKELETON

At the moment the nodular billows of green vapor rolled across the placid expanse of Jade Lake, Patricia Savage had her pretty nose jammed to a tiny grilled port set in the wall of her cell.

"Oh!" she gasped. "Doc!"

She turned her face away from the verdigris-encrusted grille. The honey coloring of her face paled visibly. Her eyes fluttered shut.

They snapped open when the bar of her cell door clattered under fumbling hands.

Pat, still attired in the fetching canary-yellow dress that showed off her sinewy, athletic curves to perfection, shook off her horror.

She moved to the door, prepared herself.

The door opened. An old brass lantern came in first, suspended by a lean brown hand.

It was the hand that Pat seized. She took hold of the wrist, lifted, whirled, and brought the arm across her shoulder.

The effort expended was small—the results spectacular.

The lean brown Cambodian dropped the lantern on his way to the floor.

The jujutsu throw Pat had inflicted upon the native would have upended a giant. The Cambodian landed on his back, made a very universal *whoof!* sound as air exploded out of his lungs, and writhed feebly.

Pat snatched up the lantern, turned toward the open door.

She discovered herself looking down the bore of her

own six-shooter. Behind it was another Cambodian. And beyond him, two more.

Pat quickly calculated her chances of wresting the antique weapon away, and discarded the opportunity.

"You allasame come," the Cambodian who had Pat's pistol cackled.

Pat's command of pidgin English was not good.

"Say again?"

"You come alongside Quon, chop-chop. Savvy?"

"Allasame to you," said Pat, "no thank you."

The Cambodian barked a low order. The others entered, seized Pat by her bare arms, and escorted her from the cell by force.

They left their insensate confederate where Pat had laid him low.

The cells—they were rather like monks' quarters in a monastery—occupied the crown of the hump of a ruin that was the temple of Quon.

One way led out of this. The cells were arrayed in a circle around a central area. There was a circular hole in the stone floor. A leaning ladder of lashed bamboo poked up from this.

Pat was invited to descend this ladder in an unmistakable way: The lead Cambodian prodded her back with the six-shooter's muzzle and grunted something coarse.

"Hold your horses," she said, maneuvering around the ladder.

A voice called out from one of the surrounding cells.

"Miss Savage!"

"I know that voice!" Pat said. Her tone was not friendly.

"It is I, Dr. Harper."

Pat stepped off the ladder. "So, you're here too. It serves you right!"

"Whatever do you mean?" asked Dr. Mawson Harper through the heavy ironwood door of his cell.

"I overheard that yarn you fed my cousin, Doc."

"Yarn?"

"The one about our sudden betrothal," Pat said, acid-voiced.

"I—I can explain, Miss Savage."

Whether or not Dr. Mawson Harper could satisfactorily explain himself, Pat Savage was destined never to learn.

Behind her an explosion of angry Cambodian, mixed with impatient pidgin English, erupted. She was given a hard shove.

"All right, I'm going," she snapped.

Pat made haste to descend the ladder. She jumped the last four feet. The Cambodians, not well organized, scrambled down after her.

Outside the crumbling walls, the crackle of machine-gun fire came again. It reminded the bronze-haired girl of the plight of Doc Savage.

"Doc needs me," she muttered under her breath.

A determined expression on her lovely face, she grabbed the bamboo poles that formed the ladder supports, gave a hard yank.

It was a stoutly built affair. It groaned under the combined weight of two Cambodians, but held its shape.

The weight of her captors kept Pat from upsetting the ladder, and the bullet that whistled past her head to whang off the stone floor and bury itself in a far wall discouraged further effort.

Pat stepped back from the ladder and two Cambodians leaped off and seized her by her bare arms.

The third took his time coming down. That was because he did not wish to discharge the six-shooter, whose hammer he was holding back with his thumb. The lack of a trigger evidently did not faze the man in the slightest.

Pat allowed herself to be escorted to an ornate door. This was opened for her.

Darkness lay within. She was urged to enter.

No sooner had she stepped within than a green light blazed into life at a point along the high ceiling. This shot a jade ray toward a spot on the far wall.

The green spotlight disclosed a raised dais of sandstone blocks. Another spotlight—this was yellow—came to life at another point.

A throne was illuminated. Unlike the dragon affair that had been discovered in the Hongkong warehouse, this was a rude affair of wood. It was more a great plate, like a second dais set perhaps two feet atop the one on the floor. It was considerably smaller, yet was quite wide.

Pat judged it to be no less than five feet in circumference.

There were silken cushions set in the center of the wood dais, but no one seated on it.

On either side squatted glaring brass lions, such as populate Chinese mythology. Between them, jade designs were set in the floor in a row. They gleamed like tiny neon letters under the weird light.

Another light added to the garish display. This one threw blue luminance on a curtain back of the raised dais. Dragons squirmed in and out along its folds.

Her eyes squinting against the harsh, unpleasant light, Pat braced herself for the figure she assumed was about to emerge from behind the dragon curtain.

A long moment passed, during which the only sound in the room was the shallow but rapid breathing of her captors. The machine-gun rattle had died. The lack of combat commotion made Pat shiver.

"Oh, Doc," she sobbed.

Then, another presence began to enter the chamber of a throne room.

The first sounds were a dry rattling, like small stones falling.

Pat tried to see into the rays of light, but they crossed weirdly, making patterns of blue and green and yellow. At one point the blue and yellow rays crossed, created a bright slice of green.

The lights were being manipulated. They converged on the spot where the silken cushions were piled in the center of the ironwood dais. Blue, green, and yellow fans were merging, becoming an ultra-green that hurt the optic nerves.

Pat looked away. Then the rattly sound came again.

All around her, her Cambodian captors sank to hands and knees and bumped their foreheads against the cold stone flags.

They began to chant: "Quon—Quon—Quon."

And from somewhere came a reverberant clangor of a gong.

Bong—bong—bong!

Pat would ordinarily have made a move then. In another second, she might well have.

But just then two slippered feet appeared within the jade confluence of light.

They did not appear where she expected. Nothing stepped through the curtain. But at the topmost point where the lights merged, there was a zone of black.

It was down from this blackness that the slippers came.

They were ornate, almost feminine. They seemed to dance in mid-air, as if the light were providing support.

Leggings came into view. The calves were lean. They worked spasmodically as they lowered themselves into view.

A fall of some shimmery fabric appeared, covering the jerking leggings with sudden modesty. It was green—or appeared green in the lambent jade light.

Straining to see above the cone of illumination, Pat made out the ceiling then. And the place from which the figure was issuing.

There was a small hole in the ceiling—too small to allow the passage of a grown human being, even of the diminutive Cambodian variety.

The thing that was oozing out of this aperture, however, appeared to be a full-sized human being. Still, it extruded down as if no bones supported its thin frame.

Pat watched in horror as the gaunt, silk-covered chest worked downward. A sleeve, empty and wrinkled, dropped free. Then another.

Then the entire being abruptly fell.

Pat recoiled then.

The thing plopped into the nest of cushions like a green squid that had been hauled up on the deck of a ship.

"Quon!" a voice breathed.

"*Yook Kweitzu!*" another said, addressing the maimed creature by its other name.

Pat had no choice but to look. Even though she had encountered the armless ogre of a thing before, she was not prepared for the sight of it.

It squatted, its legs tucked under it, amid the profusion of silken cushions. Its sleeves dangled like withered limbs, wide-mouthed cuffs lost in the cushions.

The face that stared at her was smooth and polished, a visage of jade with unwinking slit eyes. Atop the thing's head towered the brass crown not unlike some fantastic drill bit.

Midway up this impossibly ornate shaft, the tiny jade faces that stared out in four directions, mimicking the four-featured temple of Quon, gleamed in the light, a coloring so green it seemed impossible.

The slit eyes of both forward-facing countenances swiveled in Pat Savage's direction. Their gaze was stern, inhuman. The effect was that of a being who possessed the power to see in all directions.

"Greetings, *Chingtung Mao*," hissed the Jade Ogre. "In my language, *Chingtung Mao* means 'Bronze Hair.' "

Pat, perhaps because she had not got hold of her nerve, said nothing to this. Her small fists clenched at her side.

"I had thought that possessing you would deter the one called Doc Savage from following me to my temple."

Pat found her tongue then. "A lot you know about Doc, you—you human turtle!"

"Still your tongue!" the Jade Ogre shrilled. "I was old when your ancestors wore the skins of animals for warmth."

"So you say."

"It is true. In the Chinese tongue I am what is called *fei lu fei ma*. Neither horse nor donkey. Once I was an ordinary man. Like other men." The twisted creature shrugged its stumps, which were decorated by crescent moon epaulets. "Through misfortune, I have become what you see now. My true face is too terrible for human sight. But in my heart, I am a man. And the man that I was looks upon you with favor."

Pat made a face. The evident revulsion she felt at hearing those words said more than any sounds she might have made.

"What have you done with Maurine Baird, you—you stone-faced gargoyle?" she demanded.

"She lives. But she no more interests me. I look with favor upon you now."

Pat lifted her firm chin. "Then let her go."

The Jade Ogre did not reply to that demand. Instead, he said, "Previously, I had my servants take you from your cell and put you in a place of comfort. But you refused the hospitality of the Jade Ogre."

"I refused to wear that—that dancing-girl dress, if that's what you mean," Pat retorted.

"It would have become you. It belonged to a dancing girl whose beauty was unrivaled—even if her heart held treachery."

The tones of the Jade Ogre's voice mingled sadness and bitterness. His head bowed, as if in unhappy reflection. Some trick of the ultra-green light produced a downcast effect in the set jade features that looked out in all directions. Abruptly the head lifted, the tall brass crown coming level again.

"I like the dress I'm wearing, thank you," Pat bit out.

The stumps rolled again in resignation. "It is a lean dog that shames its master, but no matter. There will be time for you to discover the goodness that still resides in this crippled old form—now that the one you call Doc Savage is no more."

"Doc dead? I don't believe it! Not for a minute. Doc followed me this far. I don't know how, but he did. And bet your boots he has plans for you."

"He *is* dead. I have breathed on him and all who travel with him. Those who fill their lungs with the breath of Quon breathe no more afterward."

"Bunk!"

The Jade Ogre shook his unwieldy head. "Their bodies lie at the bottom of Jade Lake, along with the bones of a thousand before them—all who ever attempted to breach the temple of Quon, Ruler of Quon, Blessed of Siva, The One Destined to Exhale Death Upon the Universe."

There was a quality to the voice emanating from the jade face that was convincing. It made Pat Savage shrink inside her skin.

"I don't—I don't believe it!" she gasped, her breathing ragged.

"It is true."

Pat Savage had taken an involuntary step backward. This brought her to a position between two of the kowtowing servants of Quon, the Jade Ogre.

The backwash of light from the jade spotlights glinted off the six-shooter clenched in the hand of one of the Cambodians.

Pat saw it. She made her move then.

Diving for the weapon, she simultaneously thrust a knee into the jaw of the Cambodian who had possession of the pistol.

The crunch the jaw made was loud. The man upset. His hands flew out, and with them the six-shooter.

Pat snagged it, rocked back on the hammer, and came up firing.

To her astonishment, the Jade Ogre had found his feet. He stood before the upraised dais—tall, proud, unafraid, his empty silk sleeves swaying as if stirred by air currents.

"Fool! I am immortal! Unkillable!"

"I aim," Pat said fiercely, "to bark you good."

She let the hammer fall.

The report bounced off the high ceiling. It was the only sound for a long moment. There was no other. No thud of impact with flesh. No ricochet sound bouncing off stone wall.

Pat switched hands, began fanning the hammer. She had the muzzle leveled low, at a disabling spot—the creature's skirted knees.

The Cambodians found their wits at that point. But they were too late. While they were getting organized, Pat emptied all five remaining chambers into the unflinching figure of Quon.

And from the set lips of the polished jade face burst forth low-toned, mocking laughter.

XXX

CONTAGION

Out on the mirrorlike disk that was Jade Lake, the green monster of vapor flinched and roiled, spreading out questing tentacles of bilious hue as the tri-motor's props fought to dispel the deadly stuff.

Doc Savage, his aides Monk and Ham, as well as Chick Alfred, Shad O'Shea, Rex Pinks, and the stowaway, Ho, were crowded into the amphibian's control cabin.

They all saw that the cloudy green mass could not be held at bay forever. Not the way it was insinuating itself around the blast of prop-driven air.

"Gas masks!" Monk howled.

"Are there enough to go around?" Ham wondered.

"No," said Doc Savage. "Gas masks will not help."

"What do you mean?" Rex Pinks said, dumfounded. "It's a gas, isn't it? If we don't breathe it, it can't hurt us."

Doc said, "No." The bronze man gunned the ship around, endeavoring to position the great plane as far from the gaseous exhalation as he could.

"Break out boats," he rapped.

Monk leaped back into the cabin, popped a ceiling hatch that gave access to the high wing, and recklessly—given the presence of the three big propellers—scrambled to the nose hatch, where the collapsible boats were stowed.

The apish chemist got one of these out, unfolded it, set the locking struts, and threw it into the water. It made a splash—instantly drawing shots from the temple of Quon.

The vapor was opaque enough to inhibit careful shooting. Still, bullets *whupped* all about the amphibian. The engine noise was evidently being used as a marksman's guide, too.

Doc chopped power. He whipped from his seat. The

look in his eyes was like hardened gold. All gave back before him.

"Take weapons," Doc rapped.

The bronze man accosted Ho roughly. "Your life is at stake. Will you throw in with us?"

Ho bobbed his head in a very Oriental fashion.

"Y-yes."

"Here," said Shad O'Shea, producing a revolver. "Take this."

Ho accepted the weapon gratefully.

They went out a side hatch, dropping into the weirdly green water. Disturbed, the tiny emerald frogs scampered along lily pads in fright.

It was then they saw that the "frogs" were not frogs at all.

"What the hell?" Chick Alfred said, poised at the hatch. "Those things look like hands! Walkin' hands!"

"No time!" Doc said, and gave the storklike gunman a hard shove.

The others followed them into the water. Ham went last, first pausing to scoop up the frightened porker, Habeas Corpus.

"Dag-gonit!" Monk called from the nose. "Snap it up! That pea soup is almost here." Another boat splashed into the water, hurled by powerful, simian arms.

They struck out for the boats. Monk leaped from the amphibian's nose, making a gargantuan splash that startled "frogs" from lily pads all over Jade Lake. These did not enter the water, but scuttled from pad to pad for the dark shore.

Chug-chug-chug-chug!

The sound of lead hitting the lake surface was like an evil rain. Spray lanced high in the air.

With frenzied strokes, they reached the boats.

"What good will these do?" panted Shad O'Shea, his eyes growing wide at the boiling wall of green that was almost upon them. "We can't outrun that stuff."

Grimly, Doc Savage laid hands on the outboard motor of a boat. He gave the pull cord a hard yank. It produced a sputter, died. He whipped it out again. This time, it caught.

Then the bronze man did a strange thing: He gave the

boat a two-handed push, sending it into the green cloud, its screw idling.

"What'd you do that for?" Chick Alfred screamed.

Without answering, Doc upended the remaining boat.

"Under," he clipped.

Rex Pinks stared blankly. "Huh?"

"I get it," Monk exclaimed.

There was no time to explain the bronze man's stratagem. He, Monk, and Ham took control of the situation. They began shoving heads under water. They were not exactly cooperated with. Ho, in particular, fought back.

Doc simply dived in place, and got hold of the Chinese stowaway's ankles.

Ho's head vanished beneath the lake water.

When the sputtering Celestial could breathe again, he found himself treading water in darkness.

"We are," Doc explained to those who required explanation, "under the boat."

"What good will that do?" Rex Pinks howled.

"It is bullet-proof, in addition to water-tight. The vapor—which is fatal on contact with the skin—cannot reach us here."

There was silence while this morsel of information settled into their agitated brains.

A bullet, striking the metal shell, made a metallic snapping that induced the ears to ring. When the sound abated, Chick Alfred growled, "We ain't exactly long on oxygen, what with six of us under this cockleshell."

Doc explained, "Judging from past experience, the vapor neutralizes itself quite rapidly."

"What is it, anyway?" Rex Pinks demanded. "You said it isn't gas."

"It is Jade Fever," Ho said hollowly.

"You said that before," Doc stated. "What do you mean?"

"Yeah," Shad O'Shea rasped. "Spill it, guy."

"A disease," said Ho. "Quon controls it. For many weeks now, he has been terrorizing certain areas of Cambodia and China, infecting rich men with Jade Fever."

"Why would Quon do that?" Ham asked.

"The first to die were examples to others. Then, Quon inflicted Jade Fever on certain persons who had been secretly inoculated before. Quon do this by bribing servants of these rich men. They would turn green like others, but not die. Quon would tell these men that their lives were in his hands."

Doc said, "Ransom, eh?"

In the gloom, Ho nodded. "They would pay to receive cure. A second dose was needed. The first only slowed Jade Fever."

Ham demanded, "Where do you fit into this, fellow?"

There was a long pause. Ho cleared his throat noisily.

"I was one who Quon enslaved through Jade Fever. One day, I turn green. Quon appear before me and demand that I do certain things or I would die. I am ashamed to say that I did these things. One of them was to stow away on your plane, and place tube that contained death."

"You have been given the second cure?" Doc asked.

"No," Ho croaked. "And now that I have betrayed Quon, I have no hope. I will die soon. I do not wish to die. Not that way."

There was something in the man's tone toward the last, a despair that communicated itself to everyone under the upturned metal boat.

The click of the hammer being cocked was so loud that possibly only Doc Savage understood its significance.

The tiny space exploded with noise, violence, and the stink of cordite fumes.

"Doc!" This from Monk.

"What happened?" Ham shrilled.

It was doubtful that any of them heard the shouted questions. Their ears were stopped up by concussion.

Only Doc Savage reacted. And he was too late.

Reaching out in the darkness, he grasped Ho's shirt front. The Celestial was already sinking.

The bronze man felt the heavy wetness crawling down Ho's head onto his bare arms, knew that there was too much blood and other matter that was not blood for the unfortunate Chinese to be numbered among the living.

Reluctantly, Doc released the limp form. It sank without ceremony.

Another bullet struck the boat. It brought winces all around. There was surprisingly little bullet threat. Evidently, the empty motor boat Doc had sent in the direction of the snipers had drawn the lion's share of their wrath.

Doc produced his generator flash, thumbing it on. Chick Alfred cursed the sudden glare.

Doc waited until his ears cleared and addressed the others.

"Our air is running low," he said.

"We're sittin' ducks if we try swimmin' for it," Chick Alfred said.

"The firing has ceased," Doc told him. "No doubt the Jade Fever contagion is dissipating, as well."

"Can we count on that?" Rex Pinks muttered.

"No. We must reach shore before our air runs out."

"Which is any second now," Shad O'Shea grumbled.

The flash winked out. "Stay with the boat," Doc ordered, just before he submerged.

A moment later, Monk, who had the stern to himself, was bumped on the head.

"Hey! We're movin'!"

"You dope!" Ham said impatiently. "Doc grabbed the painter."

Treading water, they moved with the boat, which was being impelled by the bronze man.

It was tricky work, but they managed to stay with the up-ended turtle of metal.

"Hey, are we going toward the shore or the temple?" Rex Pinks asked suddenly.

Ham considered. "I judge toward the temple."

"Isn't that going from the frying pan to the fire?"

"Do not forget, our task is to rescue Pat, Jason Baird, and his sister Maurine, if she is here," the dapper lawyer—hardly dapper now—pointed out.

"Not me. I'm out to save my own skin."

At that, Rex Pinks submerged himself.

Monk, who was closest, made a wild grab for the colorless society reporter. He managed a prodigious amount of splashing, given the fact that one arm was encumbered by his pet pig, but was forced to give it up.

"He got away," Monk muttered.

"Good riddance, I say," said Chick Alfred.

"Yeah," added Shad O'Shea. "More air for us."

"Maybe we should drown that infernal pig next," Ham suggested.

The boat bumped something and every one held their breath.

"What was that?" Chick Alfred demanded.

"Float," ventured Ham.

Shad O'Shea muttered nervously, "Do we make a break for it, or what?"

"Wait for Doc," Monk admonished.

They waited. They did not wait long.

A light blossomed into a radiant flower under their kicking feet.

A bronze head, shedding water more quickly than seemed normal, popped into view. The light disclosed Doc Savage's grim features. He showed no strain from his long exertion. The bronze man was capable of holding his breath for extended periods of time—a skill he learned from the pearl divers of the South Seas.

"Where is Pinks?" he demanded.

"Lit out," Monk said.

A rare frown warped the bronze man's lips. "Follow me," he said.

They dived.

The lake bottom, very silty, was not many feet below. They wriggled through the greenish water—some species of alga seemed to impart a tint that moonlight made a quicksilvery green—after the bronze man.

They waded out of the water on the northern face of the temple of Quon—"face" having a double meaning, in this case.

The first thing they noticed were the bodies. Cambodians and other Oriental riffraff.

"You bump 'em?" Chick Alfred asked, low-voiced.

"Anæsthetic gas," Doc explained.

"Yeah," Alfred said harshly. "I see 'em breathin', now that you mention it." He yanked a long-barreled revolver from his trousers. "Watch me finish off these heathens."

Shad O'Shea raised a big paw, swatted the gun out of his chief's hand.

"What's eatin' you?" Alfred demanded hotly.

"He has the right idea," Doc said quietly.

Alfred grunted. "No killin'? Soft, I calls it."

"A shot would alert those inside," Doc pointed out.

They were hunkered at the edge of the lapping water. The temple was built on a kind of sandstone-block plate. The blocks appeared to be of as ancient workmanship as those that had composed the ruin that was Bankor. Weeds grew in cracks. The outermost stones were moist with lake water. Moss made soft squishing protestations under their weight.

Monk peered up at the great brooding face that loomed above them, paused, and squinted his piglike eyes. Simultaneously, Habeas Corpus squirmed in his arms, as if about to emit a piggy squeal.

The apish chemist grasped the shoat's snout, squeezing off any outcry. Then he emitted one of his own.

"Hey! I see things movin' over the brow of that face yonder."

" 'Things'?" Ham asked.

Monk gulped. "They—look—like—hands!"

This brought a widening of eyes all around. They scanned the crumbling green—the green was the result of drippings from moss shoved into the chinks and cracks to hold the blocks in place—for signs of animation.

They saw three of the things that had filled Monk with such frog-mouthed disbelief.

They indeed resembled hands—disembodied hands that managed a kind of nervous locomotion by frantic employment of their digital extremities. They scuttled up the face of Quon and sought cracks, where they retreated and hid.

"I don't believe it," Ham burst out.

"They were hands, I tell you!" Monk hissed. "Crawling, and with nothin' attached to 'em. Looked like they had a million fingers, too."

"Eight," Doc said.

"Huh?"

"You saw eight limbs."

At that point, Chick Alfred's nerve wore thin.

"I had enough of this!" he growled. "I'm for busting into this spooky joint."

Suiting action to words, he started forward.

Had Doc Savage been stationed closer to the storklike gunman, it was conceivable the bronze man might have saved Chick Alfred.

Alfred lifted off the moist stones, waded into the weeds that grew close to the lapping lake waters.

He had taken no more than four steps—possibly only three—when he threw out his arms, in the fashion of a man who realizes he is about to lose his footing.

Came a sizzlingly sound—the pungent odor of burning hair.

Chick Alfred flung himself across the weeds. He jumped and twitched on his stomach, as if endeavoring to get up.

"Chick!"

Doc blocked horse-faced Shad O'Shea.

"One side, guy," O'Shea growled. "Chick's my pard."

The big adventurer started to work around the bronze man. Doc shifted, getting in his way.

"Last time you caught me by surprise," Shad warned. "It won't be that way again."

Doc Savage showed that surprise had nothing to do with his earlier vanquishing of big Shad O'Shea by taking hold of the man's thick wrists. Bronze fingers squeezed inexorably.

Sweat popping up on his forehead, Shad O'Shea attempted to move his arms. To his astonishment, he could not. All he managed was to flap his elbows like a turkey. His wrists might have been sunk into stone—or concrete.

There was no trace of strain or exertion on the bronze giant's metallic features, etched by Cambodian moonlight.

After a moment, Shad O'Shea simply sat down in place. Doc allowed this.

By this time, Chick Alfred had stopped twitching.

"Wait," Doc said.

He melted away, then came back carrying a dry stick, which he used to prod the weeds. All eyes were on him.

In the moonlight, they saw the copper wire. It was set in a series of tiny posts of nonconducting ceramic material that presumably surrounded the tiny stone isle that supported the temple of Quon.

"Electrified wire," Monk breathed.

"Alfred didn't have a chance," Ham added. "Looks like Doc saved your life, O'Shea."

Shad O'Shea buried his long dray horse of a face in his paws. He said and did nothing for many moments—unless one counted the agitation that nerves brought to his limbs.

When his hands came away, his eyes were dry. He looked up at the bronze man, new-found respect in his mournful eyes.

"You saved my life, Savage. I ain't forgettin' that."

"It is time to move," Doc said firmly.

They stepped over the wire. It was low enough to be concealed from the unwary by the weeds, but sufficiently high to catch toes and ankles—the fate that had befallen Chick Alfred. Once its existence was known, it ceased to be a threat.

"Some temple," Monk muttered to no one in particular. "It's got electricity. Seaplanes. You name it."

Their gazes on the stone face of Quon for signs of the disembodied hands that haunted its crevices, they worked their way to a point under the stern-chiseled mouth from which the deadly green vapor bearing Jade Fever had been exhaled.

There were no windows apparent on the lower portion of the stone temple. Higher, the four sets of eyes stared out at the four quarters. They fancied that these shadowed orbs doubled as windows. It was not possible to be certain of this, however.

Doc Savage leading, they crept around to the eastern face, from which the Quon minions had poured forth. Their weapons lay about here and there. The big military machine gun sat on its splayed tripod, a snoring Cambodian prostrate behind the trips.

Shad O'Shea fell upon this. Hefted the weapon out of its mount, and turned, grinning.

"Brother, let me open the way for you," he said broadly.

"Leave it," Doc admonished.

Losing his grin, Shad O'Shea meekly eased the big weapon to the stonework.

"That lug learned who his betters are, looks like," Monk muttered.

The door that formed a mouth lay open. It also lay in shadow. It was not very inviting.

Doc started in. The others followed gingerly.

They crept along a kind of stone gullet, supermachine pistols sweeping before them. Doc's hands were empty. He did not believe in carrying firearms, feeling that too much reliance on such weapons made a man all the more helpless when relieved of them.

"I'm reminded of Jonah," Monk muttered, feeling the stonework with curious fingers.

At the other end of the narrow neck of stone, a stout door hung open. Something scuttled out of their way.

"Another of them walkin' hands," Monk breathed.

"It *did* look like a hand," an astonished Ham Brooks sputtered.

The hand—or whatever it was—had melted into a chink in a shattered floor brick.

They passed the crack warily, slipped up to the door.

An open area lay before them. Not much light spilled, so the gunshot report seemed all the louder in the confined murk.

"A shot!" Shad O'Shea exclaimed.

"Pat!" Doc rapped. "That sounds like her cannon."

The sound came again. Five times. And Doc Savage bolted into the murk of the temple of Quon, his bronze mask of a face like something that had been cast of cold, terrible metal.

XXXI

THRONE ROOM FIGHT

Doc Savage, mighty Man of Bronze, drove toward the echoes of the flurry of gunshots, a specter of metal.

There was a door—stout, of ironwood, unbelievably ornate. It was not barred. Nevertheless Doc plowed through it with a cabled shoulder, knocking it off its top hinge pin.

The *scrape-bang* of the door jumping open drew all eyes toward the fabulous figure of Doc Savage.

Pat Savage, poised amid a tangle of Cambodians, looked up. Her eyes were wide, her mouth open. She pointed toward the weird jade light which was bathing the wood dais on which the misshapen figure of Quon, the legendary Jade Ogre, stood, thin sleeves jittering.

"Doc!" she cried. "Bullets—bullets don't hurt it!"

The Cambodians fell upon the bronze-haired girl.

Still moving, Doc Savage veered toward the human entanglement. He began pulling half-naked brown natives off his cousin. Pat employed the empty six-shooter to brain a man who had leeched about her waist in an effort to drag her down. The Cambodian squawked, released his hold, collapsed.

The others charged in then. Their eyes went to the weird green figure before the dais.

"There he is!" Monk howled lustily. Monk loved to give vent to his leathery lungs when in action. "Get him!"

All at once, gunshots made a pandemonium of thunder in the green-lit throne room.

Supermachine pistols emitted their extended bullfiddle moan. A big revolver in Shad O'Shea's paw jumped and blew out saffron spikes of fire.

And standing in his jade lambency, as if protected by unholy light, stood the Jade Ogre. Unhurt. Unflinching. Taunting.

He was still standing there when their weapons ran empty.

Monk and Ham fell to unsnapping ammo drums and clipping new ones in place. O'Shea dug into pockets for fresh shells.

Then, one limp green sleeve began to stir. There was no hissing accompaniment, this time. No sound at all.

"Hop to it!" Monk yelled. "It's about to fling another of them dang witch claws!"

They got organized, raised their own weapons. A murderous racket ensued. Brass empties rained about their feet, threatening footing.

They saw the wide sleeve come up to shoulder level. Out poked bony, questing fingers, hideously green under the harsh jade light.

Monk yowled, "Forget the spook! Get the arm! We know they can be hurt."

They focused their fire on the emerging talon. Unbelievably, Quon withstood the withering storm without effect. Even his empty sleeves, which should have been twitching and snapping as lead gnashed them, hung unmoving.

"We ain't hurtin' it," Shad O'Shea moaned in distress.

Rolling up his sleeves, Monk announced, "Let's see what a bust in the snoot will produce."

Then the Jade Ogre stamped his foot once. They all saw it. No sound did his slippered foot make. It might have been a stamp of futile anger.

But the unholy jade cones of light winked out in obedience.

"Duck!" Ham shrilled. "That arm could be anywhere."

A grim voice lifted above the din—Doc Savage's voice. It rapped out inarticulate words.

Instantly, Monk and Ham hit the floor. Shad O'Shea found himself tripped to a prone position. Monk's voice was in his ear, saying, "Stay down, you!"

And in the darkness, Ham Brooks lifted, and pulled back on the lever of his mercy pistol. He spun in a tight circle. Mercy bullets splashed their colorless contents on the surrounding walls.

Bodies fell. There were moans, cries in Cambodian and related tongues.

Doc Savage thumbed on his generator flash. He was on his feet now. He gave the lense a twist, widening the fan and disclosing Pat Savage, shaken but game, levering herself into a standing position amid a group of prone Asiatics.

"What happened?" she was saying.

Doc said, "I instructed Ham in Mayan to spray the room with mercy bullets."

Nearly tripping over the fallen Cambodian native, Pat said, "Oh! Remind me, somebody, to take lessons. Say, that was a hard shove you gave me, Doc."

"It was necessary," Doc Savage told her. He was moving toward the throne on the dais.

"I don't see that hocus-pocus arm," Monk muttered, peering about. "Where the heck did it get to?"

"It cannot reach us on this side of the throne," Doc said.

He stopped before the glaring brass lions, reached up with metal-hard but sensitive fingers.

Monk, Ham, Pat, and Shad O'Shea crept carefully up on the bronze man, their faces puzzled.

"Gone!" Ham breathed. His sharp eyes were dull with shock.

For the light had shown that the Jade Ogre was no longer standing before his rude throne.

"Musta slipped through them ugly curtains," Monk ventured, indicating the dragon hangings.

"Not if he went out the way he dropped in," Pat said tightly.

"Dropped?" This from Doc Savage.

Pat pointed to the ceiling. "He came down through that square hole—like a rattlesnake out of a knot in a tree."

"That hole's too small for a normal person," Ham protested.

"The Jade Ogre is not exactly normal," Pat insisted. "Once, he squirmed out of a box that wouldn't hold a little boy—and I do mean squirmed."

She marched toward the throne and received a surprise.

Her pretty nose bent, and she made a startled sound as she bounced back, as if rebuffed by an invisible hand.

Doc, somehow prepared, caught her.

"What on earth!" Pat said, finding her feet.

"Bullet-proof shield," Doc explained.

They all came forward to prove this to themselves.

It was a sheet of glass, they found, so polished as to be invisible in the weird green light. Doc's flashlight, questing about, revealed it only because the transparent pane was moist with the chemical anæsthetic deposited by the rain of mercy bullets.

"Huh!" grunted Monk. "Just like the rig we got back in our reception room."

The reception room of their New York headquarters was protected by a similar contrivance—one which had innumerable times saved the lives of Doc Savage and his men from would-be assassins.

The bronze man was feeling along the sheet. There were no stars or spiderweb cracks, as are commonly created when lead strikes ordinary bulletproof glass. This was modern, high-quality sheeting.

It extended from wall to wall and had dropped from a narrow decorative lip that ran the width of the stone ceiling. The irregular stonework cleverly concealed the existence of the lip. There was a similar lip along the floor, no doubt lined with rubber to absorb the sound of the glass plate's fall.

"Won't budge," Monk said after pounding on it noisily for several moments with rusty knuckles.

"Controlled by one of those jade buttons," added Doc, pointing to the strip of designs on the floor opposite the glass.

Monk blinked. "Howja know that?"

"I encountered a similar arrangement in the dragon throne room in Hongkong," Doc said. "It is the logical method of control for a man who lacks arms. No doubt another button actuates the lights."

"Well, that human snake is gone now," Pat said huffily.

"Back, please," Doc ordered.

They retreated. Ham went to cover the door, the only apparent way in and out.

Doc Savage removed a button from his shirt, another from his sleeve. He pressed these together, faded back.

The buttons—one impregnated with aluminum powder, the other with iron oxide—combined as Thermit.

A hole was swiftly melted in the shield of glass.

It was large enough for Doc Savage, after wrapping his shirt around his bare arm for added protection against spitting droplets of molten glass, to put his hand through.

He stabbed at a jade design on the floor.

He got the weird greenish light first. He pressed the button beside that one.

Then, the invisible glass started up.

Doc extracted his arm with haste.

The shield lifted with complete soundlessness. With the green jade light again punishing their eyes, it was possible to track the upward progress of the glass only because of the melted opening.

The glass withdrew from sight. Doc Savage stepped over the threshold.

He found the weighty brass crown of Quon behind one lion, where it had fallen.

"Our jade pal musta been in a hurry, I betcha," Monk said happily.

Doc went to the dragon curtain. He swatted the folds, looking for a part. He found none. Monk bent, lifted the heavy fabric, searching for a hidden door.

If one existed, the heavy sandstone blocks did not give up its whereabouts.

Monk straightened, began worrying his bristly nubbin of a head in bafflement. "I don't get it. He *had* to go this way."

"A trick throne," Ham suggested.

They fell to pulling apart silken cushions.

The wood beneath was old, worn, blank.

"This disappearin' stuff is startin' to get me down again," Monk muttered. Snapping his anthropoidal fingers, the hairy chemist took up a pillow and placed it under Habeas Corpus's long snout.

"Here, Habeas. Find!"

Habeas, taking up the scent, backed away and started snuffling about like a deformed bloodhound. He circled the raised ironwood throne, reversed himself, and circled it again. Then, he jumped atop the throne and raised his hackles, as if not understanding the problem he faced.

"Blazes!" Monk squeaked. "Habeas never done that before."

"I always said that hog was overrated," Ham called from the door.

At this juncture, their eyes were irresistibly drawn upward, in the direction of the square ceiling aperture.

"That floppy-armed spook musta floated up through that ceiling hole just like he done back in that jungle city," Monk ventured. He did not sound as if he completely accepted his own explanation.

"I told you so," Pat said snappily. She grabbed Doc Savage by one cabled arm. "Say, Doc. I don't mean to sound ungrateful for the swell rescue and all, but don't you think we should liberate the others?"

Doc asked, "Where are they?"

"Come on. I'll show you."

Pat leading, they swept out into the central chamber. Pat pointed toward the lashed bamboo ladder that leaned against the hole in the stone ceiling above.

"They're all upstairs," Pat related. "Along with goodness knows what else. And if no one minds, I don't plan to go first."

"I'd like that privilege," Monk Mayfair said fiercely, literally leaping for the ladder. Like a monkey, he started climbing.

He changed his mind less than halfway up the groaning ladder.

The thing that changed the simian chemist's mind was green, and appeared at the lip of the flagged hole above his head. It scuttled to the edge and flopped down, trailing a tail of garish green silk that could only be a sleeve. It roosted on a crosspiece not less than a foot before Monk's pleasantly homely visage.

"*Yiii!*" Monk howled.

Ham yelled, "Jump back!"

For once in his life, Monk Mayfair appeared transfixed. His clutching knuckles were white with tension. His ludicrously-wide mouth gaped like a cloth sack.

The thing extended silent greenish talons toward him.

Shad O'Shea drew a bead on the phantasm, fired once. The bullet struck the end of the sleeve where the green fingerlike extensions were squirming.

The sleeve jumped up, fluttered downward. Where the bullet had struck, a bamboo crosspiece hung brokenly, each splintered end smeared with gore and other unidentifiable matter.

"It was real," Ham muttered. "And it bleeds."

"Come on," Doc rapped.

The bronze man got under the hairy chemist, boosted him up. Monk, shaking off his momentary paralysis, demonstrated simian agility in his climbing.

They quickly assembled on the second level of the fantastic temple.

Pat pointed a slim finger toward one of the circle of barred, hard-wood doors that surrounded them—the cloisterlike cells.

"Jason's in that one," she hissed.

They converged on the indicated door.

"Baird," Doc called.

The bulldog face of Jason Baird appeared in the grillwork. It took on a relieved cast.

"Savage! Thank God. I was down on the floor, figuring a bullet would come through the door at any moment."

Doc lifted the heavy iron bar out of its catches, set it down with no apparent effort.

Jason Baird emerged from his cell, his blondish hair dirty and his clothing decorated with rents and tears from past struggles.

"Has any one seen Maurine?" were his first words.

"No," Doc told him.

The bulldog facial lines grooved unhappily. Then Jason Baird squared his thick shoulders and said, "Anybody have a gun to spare?"

Shad O'Shea, who seemed to be a human arsenal, offered a snub-nosed revolver.

"It'll do," Baird said grimly.

"Do not forget me," a voice called out.

Monk grunted, "Hey! Ain't that—?"

"None other," Pat said tartly.

They surged to the door adjacent to Baird's former cell. This time Monk levered the bar free.

Out stumbled diminutive Dr. Mawson Harper, his neat black Van Dyke beard looking like the hindmost portion of a frightened skunk. His white hair was a fright, as if he had slept on straw.

"Thank you," he said shakily, wringing his hands.

"Don't mention it," Pat inserted dryly. "If it were up to me, I would leave you to rot, you—you goat-chinned prevaricator."

"If you will allow me to explain—" he spluttered.

Commotion from below cut off all conversation. The whisper and pad of naked feet on stone was the predominant sound.

Mixed in with it was the cackle of Asiatic tongues.

"You can't do this to me," complained a voice they all knew.

"Pinks!" Ham hissed.

"Another one who can rot, for all I care," Shad O'Shea muttered darkly.

"Stay," Doc said, quietly. He drifted up to the circular hole, winding a key on one end of an object like a miniature soup can. He pitched this down.

It had no sooner left his hand than the bronze man's voice lifted—sharp, attention-getting.

"Pinks! Up here!"

Something let go mushily, triggering a frantic gobble of fright and complaint, and Rex Pinks came up the ladder one step ahead of a boil of black smoke generated by Doc Savage's pitched smoke grenade.

"I almost got away," the colorless society reporter said

excitedly as he emerged from the pall. "But they captured me. The jungle seems too full of them, and they're converging on this place. I guess it made no difference what I—"

Doc took the man, yanked him along. The smoke, black as octopus ink, made an evil mushroom over the hole, sought the ceiling, spreading outward in rolling waves of soot.

Monk met them. "I checked all the other rooms. No way out, Doc."

Dr. Harper put in, "But there is a way. A secret door. I saw it in use when they moved me at one point. The devil Quon uses it because he obviously cannot negotiate the ladder."

"Why did they move you?" Ham asked sharply.

"Quon attempted to enlist me in his cause," Dr. Harper admitted. "He told me that my experience could be of use to his plans. He declined to explain further. Of course, I refused to have anything to do with his scheme—whatever it may be."

"Show us this secret door," Doc said.

"This way."

Dr. Mawson Harper led them to one of the empty cells. It was bare, except for a stone grille in the floor, evidently for drainage.

"Through there," he said, indicating a wall. "False wall. It pivots out."

"I don't trust this fibber," Pat put in.

"We have little time to waste," Doc said. "Reenforcements have come from the jungle."

They started for the wall, clustered in a tight knot. Ham had the rear, his superfirer prepared to unleash a withering storm on any ambusher.

It was an unusually large trapdoor, as those devices go, and it managed to catch them all by surprise when it let go.

They had the sensation of running on solid flooring, and then the floor dropped out from under their feet.

There was no warning, no time to react, no possibility of grabbing for the edge of the trap, not even for Doc Savage, whose reflexes were normally like chained lightning.

No one so much as emitted a cry of surprise or fright.

Thus, Doc Savage, Pat, Monk, Ham, Shad O'Shea, Jason Baird, Rex Pinks, Dr. Mawson Harper, and Habeas Corpus were deposited into a yawning abyss of unknown depth.

XXXII

ELECTRIC HELL

It was not a straight drop, although it was long.

They fell farther than expected, considering the height of the four-faced temple of Quon; easily past the lower floor level and into what had to be a cellar—if temples have cellars.

Such a fall should have broken numerous outthrust limbs. But they were precipitated along a slide. It was hewn of some rough wood so that before they began collecting in a human pile, their worst injuries were inflicted by nothing worse than long, dry splinters.

The first to hit, Doc Savage absorbed the shock of impact with his powerful leg muscles and rolled out of the way.

Ham was not so lucky. He had the air forced out of his lungs twice: once by the fall—he hit on his stomach—and the second time when Monk Mayfair landed atop him.

"You mistake of nature!" Ham howled.

Then, in succession, came Pat, Rex Pinks, Jason Baird, Shad O'Shea, and Dr. Mawson Harper.

Looking around, Monk wanted to know, "Where the heck are we?"

Doc answered, "Blind pit."

They picked themselves up. As a first order of business, they attacked the vicious splinters that had lanced arms and legs and other portions of their anatomies.

The room was illuminated. The lights, they were hardly surprised to find, were green. The place into which they had fallen was a long rectangle of dressed stone. The walls were very high, and the only way out was to scramble back up the slide.

This latter fact was unfortunate, because the trapdoor quickly spanked upward and the rough slide detached itself and fell with a clattering bang to the polished metal floor, almost knocking Rex Pinks flat.

This, in turn, disclosed a steel wall studded with vicious spikes at the opposite end.

"Uh-oh," Monk muttered, in the act of freeing a stubborn splinter from one meaty thumb. "I don't like the look of them spikes."

With a rumble, the wall of spikes began to advance in their direction, scraping the sides of the long rock chamber.

"For once," Ham Brooks said fervently, "I must agree with this ape."

Pat Savage, not exactly accustomed to situations as dire as this one, turned to her bronze cousin and said, "If you can't yank a mighty fancy miracle out of that trick vest of yours, Doc, we face a very thorny end."

"Not me," growled Shad O'Shea. "There's gotta be a way to stop that thing." He started forward.

Doc intercepted him.

"Look at your feet, O'Shea," he suggested.

The big gunman looked down. Between his monster brogans lay an insulated track running the length of the polished floor. Shad looked up. The wall of spikes was walking this.

"Insulated to prevent the steel of the wall from touching the metal floor," Doc explained. "No doubt the spikes are electrified."

Shad O'Shea lost his composure. His jaw came to rest on his chest. He wavered on his feet as if his knees had turned to water.

"That's another one I owe you—that is, if we get out of this fix," he gulped. "Which don't look likely."

The steel wall of spikes inched along. There was detritus on the floor—bits of stone and rock dust that no doubt had been chopped off the rock chamber's sides during the construction of the clever death trap. As the block rolled over these, it produced unpleasant grinding and scraping noises that made them think of their bones when the spikes got to them. Somehow, this was more unnerving to contemplate than the electrical shock that was certain to snuff out their lives long before they could be crushed.

Doc Savage herded them to the far end of the room. Not that any one required much urging. The advancing walls had already caught up the dropped chute like a menacing cowcatcher and was bumping it along the floor.

"Station yourselves on the rubber track," Doc directed.

"What for?" Dr. Mawson Harper demanded.

"Do as Doc asks," Ham said testily, placing his feet on the insulated track. It sat about two inches off the floor, and was wide enough to accommodate their feet if they planted them with care.

"Wait!" said Dr. Harper. "Look! Here is a vent of some kind."

The goateed medico straddled a grilled ventilator, not unlike a forced-air register in an apartment house. He got down on hands and knees and clawed at the edges, in an effort to lift the metal grille.

"It may be an escape tunnel," he said hopefully.

"Too small," Doc pointed out.

Dr. Harper looked up, haggard of feature. "Then what could be its purpose, if not escape?"

"Drainage," said Doc.

There was a moment in which every one present contemplated what would soon be draining down the vent if they could not find a way out of their predicament.

Hastily, they took places along the rubber-sheathed track.

Doc Savage turned to Ham Brooks, held out one hand.

"Your machine pistol."

One eye on the advancing monster of fanged steel, the dapper lawyer surrendered his intricate weapon.

Doc Savage removed the drum, and ejected a shell from the chamber. Then he advanced toward the moving wall, straddling the insulated track.

He bent low, like a man about to pitch horseshoes. The

bronze man was taking careful aim, perhaps showing more caution than any of his aids had ever before seen.

Once, he was forced to retreat. The chute was skittering toward him. Doc slid the superfirer into his belt, heaved the chute to one side, where it resumed its clattery progress.

Doc set himself once more, his feet on the insulated track. No expression was mirrored on his bronze mask of a face. But there was a forged quality about it that denoted intense concentration.

Then, with an underhand toss, he flung the supermachine pistol.

It struck, bounced, and Doc swept in to retrieve it. Backing away, he tried again. Fully a third of the chamber space had been eaten by the remorseless wall. Time was fast running out.

This time the bronze man did not hesitate. He drew back his hand, let go.

The supermachine pistol's trigger guard hooked one of the lowermost spikes, settled—a perfect ringer.

The superfirer muzzle clanked to the metal floor.

The next thing they saw was a tremendous flash of hissing blue flame. Then darkness, in which the blue flash lived on, a ghost of electrical discharge.

Monk said it first.

"Doc blew the fuse!"

It was true. They could no longer see. But neither was the spiked steel wall grinding remorselessly on. It was a trade-off for which they were more than happy to settle.

Ham Brooks snapped a jeweled lighter to flame. He did not smoke—none of Doc's men imbibed of tobacco—but the lighter had many other uses.

The wavering yellow flame threw fantastic shadows across their faces. It showed for a fact that the spike-mawed wall was inert, no longer a threat.

Stepping off the rubber track, Doc rejoined them. All looked to the bronze man for their next move, wondering what that would be.

None of them were prepared for Doc Savage's quiet but startling question.

"Where is Harper?" he asked.

"With me," Rex Pinks said, turning around.

Behind him there was nothing but naked stone.

Pinks gasped. "Holy smokes! He was right behind me— just before the short circuit happened."

Doc's flash came into play. Monk extracted one of his own. Soon, twin rays were scooting along floor and walls.

It was so unexpected, they could find no words.

Dr. Mawson Harper, facing death with them scant moments before, had evaporated like so much steam.

"This is goofy!" Shad O'Shea offered.

"Uncanny, I would call it," Ham murmured.

Pat Savage marched around the available area. Her canary-yellow dress was holding up remarkably well for all the bronze-haired girl had been through.

"This has me beat," she fumed at last, her eyes flinty.

Monk, his expression plaintive, eyed his bronze chief. "What about it, Doc?"

Doc Savage's reply was lost in a sound that was now familiar to those trapped in the blind pit.

Bong—bong—bong!

They looked up. It was a natural thing to do. The gonging sound seemed to reverberate over their heads from somewhere high in the gloomy ceiling.

"Know, interlopers," came a weird, hollow voice, "that the Jade Ogre has decreed that you will all die."

"Baloney!" Shad O'Shea said, taking a pot shot at the murk over their heads.

The bullet ricocheted twice, snapping a spark off one of the inert steel spikes, changing its shape.

"Nix!" Monk said. "You wanna wing us with a ricochet?"

Shad subsided.

The hollow voice of Quon came again.

"It is the will of Quon, Blessed of Siva, that the girl known as *Chingtung Mao*—Bronze Hair—be spared."

"Thanks just the same," Pat said bravely. "I'm staying with Doc."

"Then you will all die. For there is no escape. But I

offer life for one of you—if she will only accept this boon. This is your choice. Death for all or life for one."

This sunk in.

"If the bronze devil does not wish *Chingtung Mao* to accompany him to the afterworld," continued the voice of Quon, "he will make her step to the north corner, from which she will be transported to safety, just as was the doctor, whose will I intend to bend to my own."

"What's Harper to you, anyway?" Rex Pinks demanded.

"His skills are of use to me now that I am prepared to visit my Jade Fever upon the civilized world. For I am He Who Is Destined to Breathe Death Upon the Universe."

Jason Baird spoke up then. "Where is my sister, you devil?"

"Dead. You are too late. Jason Baird, had you heeded the words of Wan Sop, First Limb of the Jade Ogre, you could have saved yourself untold misery—not to mention your life."

"I don't believe it," Jason Baird said defiantly.

"Soon, you will join her." The hollow voice sank. "Now the girl must decide."

"Nothing doing," Pat said gamely.

Monk piped up. "Doc! We can't let Pat die."

"Observe the ceiling over our heads," the bronze man said, low-toned.

"Huh?" Monk looked up again, his flash ray darting about.

"Notice the construction? Blocks."

Monk grimaced. "Yeah. So?"

"They are larger and fitted differently than others we have seen through this edifice," Doc related. "The corner—where Quon wants Pat to stand—lacks this feature. It is smooth."

"I get it. Once Pat gets out of the way, that Quon bird plans to drop some of them blocks on us."

"Exactly."

The green light came on at that point. And the frozen wall jerked and started moving along the track, sending the wood chute rattling along.

Ham groaned. "Here we go again!"

Doc got the others together, herded them to the north corner, and went to collect the wood chute.

He brought this back, and set it down for the others to stand on. It was very dry and thus would not conduct electricity.

"Watch carefully," Doc instructed. "If a block begins to dislodge itself, call out."

The bronze man started to the oncoming forest of steel fangs, each carrying its brutal electrical charge. He carried Ham's supermachine pistol, which he had earlier recovered.

This time his task was doubly tricky. The bronze man had to aim with care, trusting to his aids to warn him of peril.

"Doc! Left! Go left!" It was Pat.

The bronze man rolled to one side.

The falling stone was no wider than a butcher's block, but it weighed in excess of an eighth of a ton.

It shot down like a plummet, cracking into three big sections and spitting brick splinters that broke the skin at points along the bronze man's face and arms.

It had missed him by less than four feet. Doc worked around it, looking for opportunity.

The sepulchral voice of Quon intoned, "You must think of the girl. No resistance can save her otherwise."

Doc set himself, crouched, and released the pistol.

It hung up on the same spike as before, rattled precariously. Even Doc Savage thought it would slide off.

The flare of blue hissed and spit and filled the chamber a split second before blackness clamped down upon him.

The ugly sound of falling stone came again, shaking the floor and bringing a scream of pure fright from Pat Savage.

"Doc Are you all right? Answer me!"

"Fine." Doc Savage's voice was calm as metal. "Stay at the safe end—and no lights."

The others listened eagerly. No sounds rewarded their efforts.

Half a minute dragged past. Then a full minute. After a while, Monk whispered.

"Doc?"

He received no reply.

Then it dawned on them.

"Doc's gone," Ham breathed. "Somehow."

A chill settled in their bones. This new development was as mystifying as the disappearance of Dr. Mawson Harper.

"Goodness," Pat said, horror squeezing her voice tight. "Which one of us is next?"

XXXIII

LEGERDEMAIN

Doc Savage's dramatic disappearance was easily explained.

The dropping blocks had created openings in the ceiling.

Unfolding his grappling hook with attached silken line, the bronze man had sent this snaking upward. He had some luck. The flukes snagged the first time.

Ligaments standing out on his cabled arms, Doc went up the thin line with all the silent ease of a spider.

There was no light to guide him, but the dank smell— markedly different from the musty odor of the death chamber—told him that an opening yawned above.

Doc gained this. His sensitive nostrils detected human perspiration odor when he lifted his head clear.

In the murk, a hand grabbed hold of his hair. Another hand brought a sharp-edged creese to his throat.

A jabber of Cambodian warned him that his next move could be his last.

Another voice, a bit removed, spat out a ripping command in singsong Cantonese.

"*Sha!* Kill!"

Doc did not wait for the caress of the keen blade.

His strong fingers had the silk line. There was no time

to release it in order to fend off the coming throat-cutting slice.

Doc Savage took the knife wielder's wrist and sank strong white teeth into the lean flesh.

The unexpected maneuver brought a bleat of pain. His hair was promptly released.

Doc topped the wall. Another dark form came up behind him. A fist was brought down on the bronze man's broad back. A dull gleam winked briefly, and something scraped—literally—along the bronze man's spine: a stabbing knife of some sort, its tip turned by the chain-mail lining of his vest.

Whirling, Doc knocked the steel thorn of a blade from the attacker's grasp with a blow to the stomach, turned his attention back to the first Cambodian. The man was hopping and spitting like a cat, trying to stem the flow of blood from his bitten wrist.

Doc settled him down by the simple expedient of kneading certain spinal nerves. The man was lowered to the flags, where he stared into the dark, helpless.

Something rustled in the near-dark. Padding footsteps retreated. Doc Savage moved toward the sounds. A door slammed. Doc found it in the dark. It was one of the cell doors. It was unbarred, yet it resisted the bronze man's efforts to open it. Plainly, it had been locked from the other side.

He gave it up, returned to the pit.

Cupping his hands over his mouth, he called, "Monk! Ham!"

Echoes bounced up from below. There was no reply. He tried again.

"*Monk! Ham!*"

Hastily, the bronze man took hold of the silken cord. He slid down this.

At the bottom, his grim metallic features jumped into view in the backwash of his flash ray.

The beam made an efficient circuit of the death chamber, showing without any shred of doubt the fact that the space was entirely unoccupied!

He went to the wall of steel fangs, noted a line of rock fragments that had been pushed ahead of the advancing wall. The wall seemed to have retreated in his absence. Not much. Less than an inch.

The faint trilling that signaled a discovery on the bronze man's part filled the chamber. It held a knowing note.

Doc Savage quit the chamber in great haste. He seemed to no sooner lay hands on the silken line than he was carried up to the second floor of the Quon temple.

There, he paused. Sound came to his alert ears. The creak of bamboo. Ragged breathing. The stealthy pad of naked, catlike feet.

The minions of the Jade Ogre were pouring up the bamboo ladder!

Doc Savage made a quick inventory of his equipment vest. The furious action of the last hour or so had depleted much of the store of gadgets with which he was armed.

If he were to rescue his friends, he realized grimly, he would have to conserve his stores.

The bronze man slipped out of the room—it was one of the many cells that ringed the upper story of the ugly Quon temple.

It was dark. The residue of the smoke bomb might account for that, but the fuse Doc Savage had twice short-circuited more probably explained the unrelieved darkness.

Doc sensed cautious approaching figures. He let them pass, then fell in with them, undetected.

They were executing a careful search of the upper floor, showing no light.

Doc halted. A trailing skulker caught up, bumped him.

"*Fan Tung!*" the other hissed. "Rice Bag! Watch where you go!"

"*Wamba Dan!*" Doc replied in guttural Cantonese—evidently the common language of the Jade Ogre's tools. "Turtle's Egg! I have found the bronze devil."

"Where?"

"Foolishly, he has returned to the pit of spikes," Doc said, not exactly lying. "And fell."

"*Ssu la!* Dead?"

"No," Doc replied. "*Hui tau chyla.* He has broken back."

"*Hao!*" said one. "Good! We will inform He Who Will Rule Eternity of this good fortune."

"*Tsoahh!*" Doc spat back. "Pig! I have found the body, and I claim the right to bring these good tidings to the Blessed of Siva."

There was grumbling about this, but after some consultation in darkness—no one seemed to have any light—it was agreed that Doc Savage would take this glad tiding to the Jade Ogre himself.

Doc started off to do just this.

He took hold of the ladder and started down.

Fate is a fickle wench at times. In another moment, Doc Savage would have disappeared down the shaft to the ground floor of the temple.

The lights were restored while his bronze hair was showing. It was unmistakable in the sudden blaze of illumination.

"*Aiiee!*" a Cambodian shrilled. "*Ha me yuda taw!* He is not killed yet!"

There was a general rush in the direction in which Doc had retreated.

Doc dropped to the ground floor, snatched the bamboo ladder away.

Angry, mean-eyed faces clustered in the hole above him.

A pistol was snaked down. It began discharging. Shouts were bringing others from outside.

Doc whipped to the handiest door. It was shut—locked, as it turned out. He tried the next one. It, too, was unmovable.

The bronze man was digging into his vest for a pocket grenade when Cambodians began dropping down from above. Others surged from opening doors.

A bullet dug into the wood over his shoulder. Another struck him square in the chest, driving him back. The vest turned it.

Doc had one smoke grenade. Monk called them "blackies," and Doc proceeded to demonstrate the appropriateness of the name.

He set it on the floor at his feet, where it began uncoiling a long worm of smoke.

Under its spreading cover, Doc dropped flat. Creeping on his stomach like an Indian, he crawled toward advancing feet.

As soon as his fingertips encountered bare feet, Doc began to yank squawling men off them. His hard bronze fist began to lash out, cracking jaws, stunning temples.

In the confusion, no one dared shoot. Knives waved in the air, bringing oaths from those who had been sliced by the enthusiasm of their fellows.

Doc, coming up, had hold of a man by wrist and ankle. He employed this insensate unfortunate as a battering ram. A path was cleared. Doc flung another for effect, drawing howls and directing attention elsewhere.

The bronze man found a wall, felt along it. Each door he came to, he tried. The fourth one opened.

Doc slipped in, shut the door quickly. There was a bolt affixed to the inner side. Doc threw this.

There was no light, but neither had the smoke insinuated itself into the room.

Popping his light on, he prowled the space.

It appeared to be a bedchamber, rather sumptuous in the Oriental fashion. The bed was a four-poster, an incongruous thing in the wilds of the Cambodian interior.

Doc ignored the appointments, searched the walls for an exit or secret panel. He found none. He next directed his attention to the floor.

It seemed to be of bare stone, smooth except for the aperture in the center of the room.

It was too narrow for human passage. Nevertheless, Doc Savage knelt before it. The edge consisted of laid flagstones. The mortar was not old, but had set.

Doc inserted a hand, found purchase.

The flag made a gritty sound of protest. Under the relentless pressure, it came loose in Doc's hand. He went to another. This gave more easily.

Soon, the hole was wide enough to drop through.

Doc used his flash to scrutinize the hole thus excavated. The light was wan. He cranked the generator and it brightened noticeably.

There was a pile of silken cushions at the bottom. Whether the bronze man intended to explore further was a decision made for him by the abrupt pounding on the locked door to the bedchamber.

Doc levered himself down, let go.

He landed amid the cushions. The light showed dripping walls, wet with lake seepage. The smell was not pleasant.

The space the bronze man found himself in was narrow—less than two feet wide. It was impossible to walk freely along it. He was forced to angle his broad shoulders and squeeze along the passage.

Something rustled.

Doc swept the light down.

Creeping toward him was a thing dragging a sleeve of green silk. The thing progressed with a crablike lifting and dropping of its limbs, like a hand using its fingers to walk along.

The narrowness of the passage prevented Doc from stooping to grab it.

He stepped over it, turned his head around.

The thing continued its creeping progress. Doc placed a heel on the trailing tail of silk.

The thing at the other end struggled, eventually worked free of the sleeve.

It continued creeping along. In the back-glow of Doc's flash it bore an unmistakable resemblance to a hand that had been severed from its wrist but, like a beheaded chicken, had not yet lost animation.

Doc moved on.

The other end of the passage was stoppered by a door. Doc made for this.

He was rarely caught as flat-footed in his career as he was now.

Something prodded the bare skin of his arm like a cold fang.

Doc froze. He did not have to look down. He was a physician. He knew the biting touch of a hypodermic needle when he felt one.

And a twisted voice said. "If you so much as move, I will discharge every drop of this vile stuff into your veins."

XXXIV

EXTORTION

Doc Savage did not wait for the question he knew would come.

"I am Doc Savage," he volunteered in a deliberately calm tone.

The other voice lost its brittle, fear-twisted quality, became unmistakably feminine. "Pat Savage's cousin?"

"Yes. I am here with my friends—and Jason Baird."

"Jason! Here?"

Doc nodded. "A prisoner of Quon."

"That devil!"

The bronze man stole a look. The hand holding the hypo projected from a narrow crack in the moist, irregular wall surface. It trembled.

"If they are to be rescued," Doc pointed out, "there is little time to waste. And if you are who I suspect, you will appreciate that fact."

The needle withdrew. "The door will be open," the voice said.

Doc finished his traversing of the too-narrow passage.

The door fell open, disclosing a fairly cramped cubicle that was crammed with chemical equipment of various sorts.

The girl who greeted the bronze man looked as if she had spent a great deal of time in this dimly lit space. Her hair was blond and she wore studious glasses that did not take away from her natural beauty.

She bore no resemblance to Jason Baird. Still, Doc ventured, "You are Maurine Baird, of course."

"How did you know?"

"Your picture was on the mantel of Jason Baird's San Francisco home," the bronze man related.

Suddenly, the blond girl sat down on a hard stool. Her thin frame was swathed in a laboratory smock that was much discolored by chemicals and grime.

"You have come just in time," she said wearily. "Quon is about to embark on his mad scheme to terrorize the world."

Interest flicked in the bronze man's active orbes. "Terrorize?"

Maurine Baird looked into the bronze man's eyes. Fatigue had etched her pallid features into tight lines.

"I am a disease specialist, Mr. Savage. My field is germs, as they relate to contagious diseases. While in China, I heard of a plant that I understood had germ-fighting properties. Searching for this, I was abducted by natives and brought here, a slave to this Quon. He is a horrible creature, hardly human—if he ever was. I have never seen his face."

Doc looked around the room. He saw petri dishes and other receptacles for growing germ cultures. He examined these.

The Jade Fever is manufactured here?" he asked.

Maurine Baird nodded. "Yes. Quon discovered the beastly stuff. But he could not devise a cure, without which Jade Fever cannot be controlled."

"But you did?"

Maurine Baird's shoulders shuddered and she took hold of her elbows to steady them.

"I had no choice," she sobbed, "you must believe me. Quon threatened to kill me if I did not assist him. I thought he was some local warlord bent on extorting natives, but recently he let slip his insane scheme."

"You mentioned terror," Doc prompted.

"Quon intends to release his Jade Fever on the city of New York," explained Maurine Baird. "I am unclear on the details, but it could be accomplished. The bacterium is able to survive in a liquid solution, and can also be borne through the air suspended in vapor droplets. Contact with either form is invariably fatal unless one is first inoculated against Jade Fever. The initial symptoms mimic an ordinary heart attack."

"How does Quon plan to profit from infecting New York City?" Doc asked.

"He will promise a cure, in return for tremendous sums of money."

Doc said, "Extortion."

"Yes. Quon boasted that he could force virtually every city in the world to pay him—or else suffer horrendous loss of life. He recently visited New York City to set up his scheme. I gather he has a network of followers in cities from Hongkong to Manhattan, all of whom are frightened to death of him. As am I."

A frantic scuttling came from a draped box of some kind on a workbench.

Doc lifted one corner of the concealing cloth. Something retreated from the weak light. It resembled a many-legged hand shrinking from the ax that had lopped it off.

Doc asked, "What have these creatures to do with your work?"

Maurine Baird said, "The germs exist as parasites on the skin of these horrid—things. The jungle is crawling with them."

"You have samples of the Jade Fever cure here?" Doc demanded.

"Yes."

Maurine Baird produced a rack of test tubes, in which a clear liquid sloshed. They were stoppered by tight-fitting corks.

"One swallow will enable a person to survive contact with the Jade Fever contagion," she explained. "He will turn green, but not die. A second dose is necessary to effect a permanent cure. This is how Quon will insure that he receives his ransom. The source of this antidote is the Chinese plant I mentioned to you."

Doc removed the tubes, stowing them about his person. He uncorked one, and imbibed half of its contents, then carefully restoppered it.

"You have swallowed some of this?" Doc asked Maurine Baird.

"Of course. Otherwise I could not have survived working with the Jade Fever germ."

"Are you game to rescue your brother?" Doc asked.

Maurine Baird stiffened. Her fingers made and unmade tiny fists. She took a deep breath, said, "Yes."

Distinctly, came a splintery crash. It floated along the narrow passage. It seemed to emanate from the bedchamber through which the bronze man had come to this weird laboratory.

He turned to Maurine Baird. "Is there another way to the ground floor of this place?"

Maurine Baird shook her blond head. "No. After I was brought here, the hole was repaved so that only Quon could enter and leave at will. This temple is honeycombed with tunnels and passages a normal being cannot negotiate. We are trapped here."

The sound of approaching skulkers grew more sinister.

"What—what can we do?" Maurine Baird said fearfully.

A grim expression overspread the bronze man's features.

Then a tall cabinet of chemicals began inching forward from its position against a far wall.

Maurine Baird whirled, one hand going to her shocked mouth.

The cabinet gave a final lurch, and out from behind it wriggled a Cambodian carrying a modern rifle. He brought this to his brown shoulder, took aim.

Maurine Baird screamed then. Doc Savage whipped into the line of fire.

Strangely, no shot came.

Instead, a sinister figure stepped out from behind the chemical cabinet.

It rustled as it emerged. The rustling was the sound of limp sleeves brushing silk.

For the crippled figure was the Jade Ogre!

The jade face lifted in the weak light. From set lips emerged a harsh command.

Behind him, the Cambodians who had been slipping along the passage entered the laboratory, brandishing an assortment of weapons.

"Trapped," Maurine Baird choked.

Then Quon spoke.

"It is time you joined your friends, bronze man," he hissed. He had recovered his brass crown, which sat atop his head like a minaret set with the faces of jade godlets.

Maurine Baird turned to the bronze man. Her eyes imploring, she whispered, "My work is done. We will be killed."

"We will do as he bids us," Doc said quietly.

The rifle toter motioned for Doc Savage to step aside. He did. Quickly the bronze giant was surrounded and made to surrender his outer clothes. His equipment vest and all its gadgets were taken.

When they were done, Doc stood in a pair of black silk bathing trunks.

His Herculean musculature caused the Cambodians to shrink from him in awe. Their eyes were impressed. Their lips fell apart in surprise.

Then, Quon issued orders.

Doc Savage and Maurine Baird were forced to step through the concealed passage behind the cabinet.

On the other side, there was a square chamber of rock. Light came from a single unshaded light bulb hanging from an electrical cord.

The room was dominated by a sphere of iron held together by thick rivets. Various pipes led in and out of this object. Pressure gauges and other simple controls studded its black skin. There was additional mechanism between the spherical portion and the stone wall. It suggested a pumping function.

Seated on the floor before the contraption, and bound to it with chain, were Monk Mayfair, Ham Brooks, Shad O'Shea, Rex Pinks, and Jason Baird. Habeas Corpus was not fettered, but the ungainly porker huddled close to hairy Monk.

Of Patricia Savage and Dr. Mawson Harper, there was no sign.

"Doc!" Monk cried. His voice mixed pleasure and disappointment. Clearly, the simian chemist had looked to the bronze man for rescue.

Jason Baird's eyes fell upon the wan figure of his sister, Maurine.

"Sis!"

"Jason!"

Maurine Baird struggled free of her captor, rushed to her brother, and threw her arms around his neck.

"I never believed for a minute you were dead," Jason Baird choked out.

Cambodians seized Maurine Baird and chained her to the iron sphere.

Doc Savage was forced to stick out his big hands. A Cambodian approached with a pair of manacles. One was clapped about a thick bronze wrist. Then Doc was led to the iron pressure tank—for that was plainly what it was—and the other manacle was clamped to a stout pipe.

Doc was made to sit with the others.

Ham whispered, "We don't know what happened to Pat."

A Cambodian hissed at them for silence.

The Jade Ogre spoke. "You have caused me much trouble, bronze one. But here you die."

"Says you," Shad O'Shea spat.

A brown hand slapped the gunman across the face.

"Do that again and I might take it personally," O'Shea growled.

"Behind you," went on Quon, "is the fruit of many months of toil. Within that iron caldron swims the germ culture I call Jade Fever. Soon, it will bring terror to the outer world, just as the merest squirt of it sent you all scurrying like rats out of your metal-winged bird from the land of mortals."

"You can cut the act," Doc interposed.

"What words are these—?"

"I said," bronze man repeated, "you can stop acting as if you are the Jade Ogre, a creature from legend. I know who you are."

"I am Quon."

"I've known it for some time," Doc continued. His flake-gold eyes were steady, unperturbed. The sound of his impassive voice brought calm to the other captors. Their attention was focused on the mighty bronze man.

The misshapen figure that was the Jade Ogre teetered on his slippered heels. His empty sleeves rustled with the movement.

Then, like a viper stirring, one sleeve began to lift.

They had seen it before. Still, it held them mesmerized.

The sleeve—it was the right—swelled as it lifted.

The Cambodians retreated from the immediate vicinity of their armless master's presence.

One, clutching Doc's clothes, backed toward the captives. The bronze man's foot got in his way. He tripped, fell. Picking himself up, the Asiatic gathered together what clothing he could, his eyes darting fearfully to that inexorable lifting sleeve.

The yellow fingers seemed like a skeletal talon emerging from a fresh grave.

"I have but to will it," intoned Quon, "and my Limb of Retribution will smite you dead."

"A trick," Doc said flatly.

"Those who are touched by Quon always die."

"Unless they know the trick," Doc countered.

His pronouncement seemed to give the macabre creature who called himself the Jade Ogre pause. He hesitated, his gaunt fingers pointing.

"If you are supernatural," Doc prodded, "then you can send that arm you are pretending to grow directly at us."

"What're you—tryin' to get us killed?" Shad O'Shea gulped.

The Jade Ogre stood immobile for a time.

"Such a quick death would be a mercy," Quon said at last. "I go now to the outer world. You will die the excruciating death of slow starvation."

Then, with a swirl of his empty sleeve, the Jade Ogre

turned around and disappeared the way he had come. His up-lifted arm stayed rigid. Oddly, he did not employ it in any way.

His Cambodian minions followed. The cabinet rasped back into place.

Once they were alone, every one began speaking at once.

"What do you mean—you know who he is?" Jason Baird demanded.

Monk inserted, "Yeah, Doc. What's goin' on?"

Doc Savage cut through their questions.

"Pinks!"

"Yeah?"

"Slide as close to me as you can."

"Why?"

"Just do it."

Shrugging, Rex Pinks pushed himself toward Doc Savage. Monk Mayfair scooted aside to allow this. The chains were short, movement restricted.

The bronze man was gifted with remarkably long toes that possessed the prehensile ability sometimes found in circus performers who tie knots with their feet and perform similar feats of dexterity.

Doc lifted bronze toes to the back of Rex Pinks's shirt. They plucked at the fabric. They were at this some moments.

When they came away, something white and curved rested between the first and second toes.

Ham, squinting, blurted, "Another tiger claw?"

Doc drew the claw to his lap.

"Did you plant that on him, Doc?" Monk asked.

"No," was the bronze man's only reply.

"Then how—"

Doc reached down and took the claw. He lifted it to his manacle and inserted the sharp point into the lock aperture.

"A lock pick!" Monk grunted.

"Will it work?" Ham worried.

"If it does not break," Doc Savage said.

They all held their breaths.

The claw made scraping sounds. It seemed a frail thing with which to attack a mechanism of iron. After a time, the manacles snapped free.

Doc shook off the chain, came to his feet.

Elation wreathed the faces of the others.

It died when a voice from somewhere—they realized it must be coming from a hidden loophole—screamed, "Fools! You have squandered your final hours of life!"

Then, accompanied by a frightful hissing, a valve in the great iron pressure cooker let go.

A jet of green vapor charged out—carrying the Jade Fever germ.

"Blazes!" Monk squawled. "We're goners!"

XXXV

COLLAPSE

Doc Savage made a dive away from the iron boiler of a pressure chamber.

Rex Pinks, misunderstanding, shrieked, "Don't leave us!"

The bronze man skidded, scooped up a fallen article of clothing, pitched back to the others.

He came back carrying his trousers—which had been dropped by the Cambodian he had earlier tripped.

Doc went through the pockets, extracted several stop-pered flasks. He uncorked these, distributed them.

"Every one drink half," he cautioned. "No more, no less. There is enough for all."

As the green vapor started to fill the room, the captives drank down the fluid. Doc forced a small quantity down Habeas Corpus's throat.

Quickly, the contents of three flasks were consumed.

The green germ-carrying vapor continued to fill the room.

Methodically, Doc Savage attacked their bindings. They

were not as stout as his own had been. He simply grasped link-age, and applied pressure. Weak links separated. Monk helped by stepping on his own chains, exerting himself, and popping his bonds free.

"I—I feel mighty queer," Rex Pinks said, getting up.

"No wonder," Shad O'Shea grunted. "You look kinda green around the gills."

It developed that all were turning green.

They stood about, not knowing quite how to react to the disconcerting phenomenon.

Some of them turned a kind of aquamarine. Others ran more to a jade hue. Monk Mayfair, for some reason, turned the exact color of an unripe apple. The pig, Habeas, took on the aspect of a movie-cartoon porker.

"Are we—are we going to die?" Jason Baird blurted out.

"No," explained Doc Savage, who resembled a bronze statue patinated by exposure to the elements.

"Jason," Maurine Baird said reassuringly. "Mr. Savage has given us the antidote to Jade Fever."

"Then why are we turnin' green?" Monk wanted to know.

"The antidote must be taken in two doses," Maurine replied. "If you do not get the second dose within two days, you will succumb to the disease germs. The first dose merely slows the death process."

Monk grunted. "Looks like we die unless we bust outta here mighty soon."

Doc Savage was at that problem. He began examining the closed exit door, still blocked by the back of the chemical cabinet, to which it was attached.

While the bronze man was about this, a click sounded.

Out of a loophole set in another wall, tumbled a thing of green, seeking fingers. It plopped to the floor, dragging a ragged trail of rustling green silk, moved uncertainly toward them.

"*Yeoow!*" squawled Monk, who had encountered one of the crawling things before.

Calmly, Doc Savage stepped up to the creature and planted a bare foot on the trailing silken rag.

The creature strained to continue its advance. Something popped, and the walking entity stepped clear of the sleeve mouth, dragging a tiny thread—which had obviously served to anchor the silk sleeve—behind it.

In the light, they saw the crawling creature clearly for the first time.

It marched on methodical legs, eight in number. They were a bilious green. An equal number of tiny eyes gleamed evilly in the light.

Shad O'Shea, eyes popping, exclaimed, "A spider! It's a spider!"

Monk, howling with rage, snatched up Doc's discarded manacles—the heaviest item he could lay hands on—and flew at the scuttling horror.

"Take that, you faker!" Monk howled.

He dashed the thing apart, much to relief of every one except Maurine Baird, who said, "The spiders are not harmful in and of themselves—although Quon uses them to keep his followers in line."

Doc called Monk to his side.

"This door might give under sufficient pressure," he said.

"Let's see if it does," Monk said boisterously. They put their shoulders to it. The cabinet had not looked very solid, but the door—it was actually a section of wall—was heavy sandstone. Even their combined efforts only made it shudder and bang in stubborn protest.

Shad O'Shea, hitching up his pants, said, "Count me in."

"And me," said Jason Baird.

They set themselves, piled on.

It took three attempts, but the solid panel gave a little with each lunge until it simply surrendered, falling inward, cabinet and all.

They pushed into the laboratory.

Sleeves jittering, the Jade Ogre ducked through the door opposite, slamming it after him.

"Man, oh man!" Monk howled. "Let's mop up this place."

"Wait!" Doc said.

The bronze man was gathering up racked flasks.

"These are the second dosages," he added.

"We drink them now?" Ham asked.

"Yes," replied Maurine Baird.

"Then we are safe from that green stuff?"

"Yes."

They drank down another dose, the bronze man included.

"Well," said Shad O'Shea, throwing his flask to the floor. "That's that!"

Doc pocketed one flask and said, "Let us find Pat."

Ham noticed they were short by one person. "Where did Monk go?"

A moment later, the hairy chemist—a vision in green—emerged from the other room. "Thought I'd turn off that goblin gas," he said amiably.

He was swinging the manacles with which he had dispatched the green spider. "Might bring me luck," he grinned.

"Let's go," Jason Baird said impatiently.

Doc Savage led the way. They squeezed along the narrow passage.

The green vapor followed them out. That, if anything, explained the absence of enemies blocking their escape route.

Where the silken cushions lay scattered—obviously for the comfort of the Jade Ogre—Doc and Monk formed a human pyramid.

The others climbed the pyramid. Habeas was handed up last.

Monk, on top, was lifted off Doc's shoulders, got down on his stomach, and reached down with a furry beam of an arm. Doc crouched, leaped, and took his aid's offered hand in his. Only Monk's long limbs could have accomplished this.

Straining, the apish chemist assisted Doc Savage to the ragged lip.

They joined the others.

The bedchamber door lay open. The room had been evacuated.

Doc, his muscles gleaming like piano wire that had

been lacquered with verdigrised bronze paint, crept toward the door.

"Coast clear," Ham hissed, peering out. His hands flexed nervously. He lacked his ever-present sword cane, which had been left behind in the plane.

Doc motioned for the others to follow him out.

They stepped out and a voice caught their attention.

"Doc! Be careful!"

"Pat!" Ham breathed.

Doc nodded. "Coming from upstairs."

"How we gonna get up there?" Jason Baird pointed out. "The ladder's gone."

"Betcha that Quon's upstairs, too," Monk growled.

Doc went to the hole leading to the upper level.

He flashed back. It was well that he did.

For a harridan, disembodied limb of yellow fingers and green silk darted down after him.

It bobbed, righted itself, seemed to hesitate in mid-air.

Eyes popping, Monk exploded, "Blazes!"

Then Doc Savage did something that made their hair stand up on end.

Moving cautiously, he began to circle the hesitating limb. Perhaps it was confused by the abundance of potential victims presented, but the discorporate arm wavered toward the others; when Doc moved, it yawed in his direction.

Doc was swifter, however. He came up behind the thing and, to the astonishment of all, clapped the gaunt apparition between two bronze hands.

The thing trembled, but did not resist the bronze man's sudden seizure.

Carefully Doc brought it over, slipping the ragged green sleeve off the thing's bony length.

"Is—is it real?" Rex Pinks gulped.

Near by, a door banged open. An Asiatic face peered out. A pistol showed. Death impended.

Doc turned, propelled the ghostly limb in the direction of the startled brown face.

The limb literally floated in a straight, unerring line.

The door clapped shut. The questing, bony fingers did not pause. They hit the door and blazed up yellow and hot.

There was no sign of the naked yellow arm when the hurt went out of every one's eyes.

"Hell's bells!" Shad O'Shea blurted, obviously dumfounded.

"Come on," Doc urged.

Every one followed the fast-moving bronze giant. To their surprise, he raced in the direction of the throne room. The door hung askew on its remaining hinge.

There was no one on the other side.

Doc motioned for silence.

He strode up to the dragon throne, mounted one of the goggle-eyed brass lions.

The thing was high enough that the bronze man was able to brush the aperture in the ceiling with the tips of his fingers.

Doc called up. "Pat."

A pretty face appeared in the aperture.

"Doc! You found me."

"Where is Quon?"

"On the other side of the glass shield that's up here," Pat reported. "The Cambodians are guarding the way into the cell. And do you know whose cell this is?"

"Reach down," Doc rapped.

Pat's athletic arm came down, and took from Doc Savage a flask containing Jade Fever antidote.

"Drink half," Doc instructed.

The hand went away. "How does it taste?" Pat called down. "I'm a particular kind of gal, you know."

"Never mind that," Doc said flatly.

Just then, the throne room entrance became a choke of shouting, spitting Asiatics.

"Doc!" Ham called wildly. "Trouble!"

The bronze man leaped from the brass lion.

He landed on his feet as the minions of Quon, cocking pistols and waving creeses, parangs, and other exotic blades, charged for the dais.

"And us without rods," Shad muttered.

"We can take 'em," Monk said fiercely, windmilling his rusty arms.

Doc Savage, seemingly oblivious to the threat, calmly stood where he had landed.

Spreading like a surging cataract, the charging Asiatics were almost upon them.

Then, unnoticed by any in the great room, the bronze man placed a metallic toe on the outermost of the row of jade buttons at his feet.

With a suddenness that was breathtaking, the sheet of bullet-turning glass dropped from the ceiling.

It slid into its rubber lip with almost no sound. Every one's hair was stirred by a breath of air. That was all.

In their headlong fury, the Cambodians did not see the glass, or notice the telltale hole Doc Savage had earlier created with Thermit.

They piled into the invisible barrier, bounced back. It was comical the way they picked themselves up and attempted to breach the barrier, only to encounter an invisible wall. It seemed they knew nothing of the true nature of the pane.

One found the circular hole. He pointed it out to his fellows, jabbering excitedly.

They tried to crawl through. Their wiry bodies were too thick around to manage that feat, so they settled for thrusting revolvers and blades into the gap.

Monk, Shad, and Doc were ready. They fell upon the waving brown arms. Twisting wrists, breaking fingers, they collected a handsome assortment of weapons.

Monk, getting down on one knee, took aim. Asiatics scrambled to get out of the way. Still, Monk managed to clip one in the knee. That worthy fell, was hauled away by his comrades.

No one dared approach the gap after that.

From upstairs, Pat Savage gave out a scream.

"Doc! That ogre! He's grown an arm—*and it's got me!*"

Below their feet, something rumbled. The rumble stretched out, became a grinding and tumbling of stone that was joined by other brittle sounds. A rushing of water followed.

The transparent sheet of glass acquired a silvery lightning bolt, groaned.

The dais split. The dragon hangings shook. The stone blocks at their feet seemed to knock together and writhe.

Ham looked at his feet with an incredulous expression. "Good grief! What now?"

"Explosion," Doc rapped.

Stone rained from above. Not whole, fortunately. Merely segments. But they were undeniably dangerous.

Up from the chinks in the floor hissed tendrils of green vapor—the Jade Fever.

"The boiler musta blew!" Shad O'Shea blurted.

"Impossible!" Maurine Baird wailed. "The pressure was carefully regulated."

Ham Brooks looked at Monk Mayfair, said, "Didn't Monk go back in that room after we had left?"

Monk, still holding the Cambodians at bay, swallowed, and said nothing.

Doc rapped, "Monk!"

"I thought I'd shut the thing off, but couldn't find the right valve," the hairy chemist mumbled. "So I threw them all. I guess I musta gummed up the works or somethin'."

Beyond the shattered bullet-proof shield, Jade Ogre minions saw green gases rising up around their feet. Evidently most had not partaken of the Jade Fever antidote, but they understood the significance of the terrible green exhalations, for they made a mad scramble for the exit.

Some of them made it. Others dropped, turning weird shades of blue, green, and aquamarine.

"Monk," Doc said again.

"Blazes!" Monk gulped. "Blazes!"

A block dropped then. They looked up. It had fallen from the aperture, widening it significantly.

Pat Savage, struggling in the grip of the Jade Ogre, became visible. The Jade Ogre was now possessed of a left hand. It was firmly on her wrist. The bronze-haired girl was using her free hand to fight back.

The Jade Ogre was getting the worst of it. His brass crown fell off, and Pat began pulling at his hair.

Doc leaped for the ceiling rim, levered himself up. He was quickly lost to sight.

Monk and Shad O'Shea horsed a brass lion atop the wood dais, creating a platform for climbing purposes.

The lion wobbled warningly, telling of the uncertainty of the floor beneath.

They all started up. Maurine Baird had to be assisted. Ham Brooks assumed this duty with a courtly—if brisk, given the circumstances—bow.

They found, up in the second-floor cell, a veritable pandemonium.

Pat Savage had the Jade Ogre backed into a corner. Both her hands were now unfettered free and made fists, which she was using freely. Quon was attempting to beat her back with his single arm. It seemed weak, as if unused to life.

"Good old Pat!" Ham said approvingly.

At the door, where danger was most immediate, Doc Savage had his hands full. He was laying out the bodyguards of Quon with expert, scientific blows. His hard fists landed, rocking back heads and changing jaw shapes. Asiatics fell like sickled corn, and others piled over the fallen. The bronze man seized two by the hair, brought his hands together.

Two heads colliding made a *bonk!* of a noise and two more brown bodies joined the fallen.

"Save some for me," Monk howled, pitching in.

"Me, too," Jason Baird gritted.

Coming to the bronze man's side, they swiftly beat back the minions, forced them out of the cell.

Ham rushed to Pat's assistance. He was not needed.

The bronze-haired girl maneuvered herself behind her foe, taking his oddly-ineffective arm with her. She twisted it up behind his back painfully, simultaneously tripping the jade-faced being to the floor.

Whetting her hands together, she crowed, "His mistake was growing that handy arm. I couldn't use my jujutsu before."

The room settled down.

Doc shouldered the door closed. There was a latch. It held when engaged.

The bronze man strode over to the corner, where Pat Savage stood over the prostrate form of the Jade Ogre.

The others surrounded the weirdly incomplete creature.

"Who wants to do the honors?"' Pat said jauntily, tapping the creature's jade face with a toe. Quon recoiled like a wounded serpent that had been kicked in the snout.

"He's mine," Jason Baird said fiercely.

"Nothin' doin'," Shad O'Shea insisted. "I owe him for what he done to my pards."

"And I have a score to settle over my sister's abduction," Baird retorted hotly.

The question went unsettled, as it turned out.

The rumble returned, lower, throatier than before. Water sounds came from below, a Gargantuan sloshing.

"What on earth was that!" Ham bleated.

"The lake is pouring into the temple cellar," the bronze man said with unsettling calmness.

Pouring in was the least of it, as it turned out.

The entire temple of Quon was ancient, despite its modern electrification. The rush of water they had been hearing doubtless came from a hole in the cellar walls excavated by the boiler explosion. Action of incoming water was undermining the foundation walls.

They saw proof of this in the walls of the cell in which they had barricaded themselves. Chinks of red light—dawn was breaking outside—glared at them as the walls sagged and buckled.

Out of nooks emerged scuttling green spiders that had so uncannily resembled animated hands.

"Ugh," said Pat.

Doc Savage warned, "We must clear out! This place is about to collapse!"

Doc moved to an outside wall, where a carved disk of wood was set like a bizarre shutter. He yanked this open, uncovering a grille of woven bamboo strips. It was not old. Doc made short work of it by driving a bronze fist through the center, then yanking back. The grille came loose.

"Not big enough," Jason Baird pointed out.

"Another of this devil's secret escapes," Monk gritted, giving the prostrate Quon a kick in the ribs.

The walls were groaning now. Doc went to work on the stone rim. The mortar—moss and crumbling cement—offered relatively little resistance.

Monk joined in.

They quickly had an opening that would accommodate the largest of their party.

Doc organized every one. A rope was improvised out of blankets found on a bed of straw. This was let out the ragged hole. Maurine and Patricia Savage were sent down first. Rex Pinks and Jason Baird went next.

"We're runnin' outta time," Monk warned. It was an unnecessary comment. The rush of water was abating somewhat, but the damage had been done. Outside, they could actually see turmoil on the lake created by the sudden inrush of greenish water.

When the first to leave had reached the ground, Ham started down, carrying the ludicrously-green pig, Habeas Corpus.

"I'll go next," Shad offered.

Monk jerked a thumb in the direction of the beaten figure of Quon, looking pitiable and helpless where he had fallen.

"What about him?" the homely chemist asked.

"I will carry him down," Doc said.

The improvised rope ceased to tremble with weight. Monk took hold of the line, swung himself out. He started down.

Doc went to gather up the misshapen Jade Ogre.

He reached down to touch the figure, and it exploded.

Actually, it only seemed that way. The report was loud, and some green silk tatters flew about.

The bronze man, moving swiftly, had avoided the bullet that had emerged from the breast of Quon, leaving a smoking hole.

It struck the ceiling, actually knocked a loose stone free.

Madly, the weird figure of the Jade Ogre flung himself for the broken hole in the center of the cell floor.

The walls started going then.

Some freak of destruction caused the bullet-proof pane of glass to toil upward. Evidently, the generator that furnished power to the temple remained above the water line.

The glass, cracked and under stress, broke into jagged fangs as it lifted into view.

Doc, seeing escape about to be cut off, vaulted the rising row of transparent teeth, gained the other side.

He paused at the opening.

The Jade Ogre, in attempting to reach the floor escape route, had become tangled up in the rising glass pane. One sharp tooth of it had snagged his long silk robe. It was lifting him off his feet.

A voice called from below, "Doc! What's keepin' you?"

It was Monk, his voice twisted, fearful, frantic.

His face a mask of concern, the bronze giant called over to the one-armed ogre.

"You must come with me if you are to survive," he warned. "You will not be able to climb down on your own."

Struggling one-handedly, the Jade Ogre croaked out a single word: "Never."

Doc started back.

Another hole jumped from Quon's green chest, spewing tatters. This time, the bullet went wide.

The bronze man wavered. He knew the jade-masked one was a being of evil, that the blood of many lay upon his hands—such as they were. Still, he was averse to leaving the man to his doom.

It was clear that Doc Savage would have swept in to gather up the Jade Ogre, despite the danger to himself.

But the opportunity became lost forever. The temple began to shake itself to pieces. The glass wall lost sections. One was the portion that had snagged the Jade Ogre.

Instead of releasing him, this caused Quon to fall across a valley of sharp glass, onto his back.

A clear shard streaked with crimson emerged from the silken folds over his stomach. The jade-faced fiend threw back his head, and from his set lips came a torrent of crimson. There was quite a lot of this.

His face grim, Doc Savage whipped out, took the tail of bedding, rode it down to the ground.

His last sight of the being called Quon was of a squirming emerald figure, one arm flopping helplessly as it attempted to worm itself free, being lifted to the trembling ceiling on a shard of impaling glass.

The ripping scream that came when the jagged teeth met the crumbling temple roof was one that none who heard it would ever forget.

Mercifully, it was very short.

XXXVI

THE DISEMBODIED

Doc Savage released the rope before he was halfway to the ground. He flung himself off and away. The others were already retreating from the imminent peril of collapsing stonework.

Together, they reached the edge of the stone jetty that jutted tonguelike from the temple of Quon, and plunged into the warm waters of Jade Lake.

They waded in, got chest-deep, looked back.

An incredible sight met their eyes.

The eastern face of the temple of Quon, fashioned to resemble the Jade Ogre's countenance, caved in, as if a mighty fist had dealt it a great blow.

The nose fell in first, taking with it the eyes—one of which was the circular window that had provided them with escape.

Water poured into the mouth, as if in its death throes, the four-faced stone head was greedily drinking the lake that had nurtured it.

Out of cracks all along the crumbling stone face crawled the green spiders, seeking frantic escape.

The crown, lacking support, caved in. That was the

coup de grace. The weight of falling stone smashed through floors and supports, creating a terrific uproar.

A long rumble followed, like nearby thunder. Up came an exhalation of brick dust and smoke. The green vapor that was the Jade Fever showed as weak tendrils. Clearly, the great crush of stone had sealed the largest part of it in air-tight pockets.

Silence followed. It had been quick, the destruction of the ancient, sinister temple.

Their eyes were fixed on the destruction wrought. Jaws hung slack. Maurine Baird buried her face into the thick shoulder of her brother, Jason.

"The nightmare is over—at last!" she sobbed.

No one had anything to add to that particular statement.

It was hours before they felt up to searching the broken thing that was the symbol of the Jade Ogre's ability to see to the four quarters and send out his preternatural vengeance.

Doc, Monk, and Ham picked at the rubble. They were grimly silent—especially Monk, who would have normally rejoiced in the bloody punishment visited upon Quon and his servants.

They found many Asiatic bodies. Most were a very livid green. Some were merely crushed. All were dead.

Doc Savage was speaking.

"The man who pretended to be Quon, the legendary Jade Ogre, was as clever a fiend as we have come up against."

No one disputed that assertion.

"But," Doc continued, "he gave himself away at certain points. He was with us on the *Mandarin*, mingling with the passengers. It was he who signaled Wan Sop to murder Fuzzy Wool and Kitten Borzoi, to prevent them from revealing that the body in the ship's morgue was not the true Jason Baird."

Ham, who had recovered his sword cane from the amphibian, was thrusting the blade into breaks in the tumbled stone. Sometimes, the blade came out red—much to the fastidious barrister's visible distaste.

"It was this mastermind who caused the death of the pilot on the San Francisco-bound flight," Doc went on. "I was the target then. Obviously, he had finished scouting New York in preparation for his extortion scheme. The pilot died in my place, his killer taking poison to save face."

Sadness underlay the bronze man's quiet tones.

"I did not begin to suspect him until we were at sea, however. He lied at several points—once, when he claimed to have seen Pat attacked by one of the phantom limbs. I had been keeping a close eye on Pat, and he was not present on deck when the attack came—unless it was he who had set the limb on her."

Monk Mayfair, looking ludicrous in green, was digging at a spot he thought promising. He made a methodical pile of sandstone.

In time, he uncovered fragments of thick glass. He redoubled his efforts.

Ham pitched in. Together, they uncovered a head. It stared upward, the eyes fixed slits, the jade of the face layered with rock dust and streaked with scarlet. The mask had not changed. Yet now it looked somehow dead and devoid of spirit, even though it had never been anything other than mere lifeless stone.

Monk reached down, found an exposed arm. It felt solid enough, so he pulled on it.

The upper body of the Jade Ogre was thus brought to light. The green silk gown tailed off in the vicinity of the body's waist. There was no more to it than that.

They all gathered around the body. Out of respect for the dead, they were quiet for a time. No one cared to excavate further in search of the severed lower portion.

Doc Savage resumed speaking.

"This man gave himself away again when he lied and claimed that Pat had accepted his proposal. And again in the Hongkong dragon throne trap from which I rescued him. He deliberately pressed a jade button that caused a trapdoor to open under my feet. That attempt on my life was particularly ingenious. It might have succeeded, had I not already had cause to suspect him."

Doc Savage fell to one knee. Carefully, he removed the jade face of Quon, which came away dragging a coarse wig of glossy black hair.

Exposed to the rays of the climbing sun were the twisted features of Dr. Mawson Harper. His black-streaked white hair was discolored by gore. His ebony Van Dyke was a frightened dab on his chin. His features, like every one else's, were a livid green.

No one expressed any surprise at this revelation. They had come to the realization of the Jade Ogre's identity in the aftermath of all that had happened.

Doc closed the eyes, which even now mirrored the horror of the man's going.

Maurine Baird offered in an unsteady voice, "I—I knew him. That is, I had encountered him in my Chinese travels. He—he showed great interest in my work."

"It does explain how Quon came to learn of you and your research," Doc said. "Obviously, his own work enabled him to exploit the legend of the Jade Ogre, to bring the natives under his control and build up his organization, which is now smashed forever."

"What I would like to know," inserted Ham Brooks, twirling his cane, "is how this creature was able to accomplish some of his feats of spookery."

By way of answer, the bronze man took hold of the silken robes of Quon, tore them open.

Exposed was a perfectly normal left arm. The right, however, was folded close to the man's chest like a broken bird wing. It was held in place with a thin leather harness, very tightly bound. Another, identical, harness hung slack beside it.

The bound hand clutched a small, flat automatic—the hidden weapon that twice had discharged when Doc Savage had attempted to seize the Jade Ogre only minutes before.

"Dr. Mawson Harper was a clever contortionist," Doc explained. "He was double-jointed, and had the ability to compress his body into extremely small confines. Further, he had mastered the escape artist's trick of unhinging the collar bone, which provides structure to the shoulder, and folding the shoulders inward."

Doc indicated Dr. Harper's right shoulder, which was weirdly deformed. He unbound the arm, freed it, reset the shoulder. There was an audible pop that made every one queasy.

"With both arms bound under his concealing gown," Doc added, "and his shoulders hunched forward, Harper was able to squeeze through places where a normal person would not. Through a porthole of his stateroom on the *Mandarin*. Again in the Bankor ruins. And all through his tunnel-honeycombed temple stronghold."

"Sounds thin," Rex Pinks sniffed.

"Do not forget that he was a small-boned individual and the widest part of him was his shoulder breadth."

"That doesn't explain how he escaped the death chamber when the wall of spikes was coming at us," Jason Baird put in. "We got out only because after the lights went out, the Cambodians hauled back the steel wall by hand, exposing a niche in one side of the chamber, through which we were marched at gunpoint. Harper could not have escaped that way. We would have seen it."

"You have forgotten the drainage vent in the floor," Doc pointed out. "He lifted this up, unhinged his collar bone, squeezed down, and replaced the vent. Houdini is reputed to have employed the same trick, under just such difficult time constraints."

"Do you mean," Ham asked, "that Harper deliberately led us into that death trap?"

Doc nodded. "He was as determined to preserve his secret as he was to eliminate any obstacle to his mad scheme."

"I figured it out when they separated me from the others and threw me in that cell," Pat interposed. "I saw the bulletproof shield, and recalled that that was the cell where Dr. Harper had been held prisoner. It was directly over the throne room, so he could come and go unsuspected, just by wriggling through the floor drain."

"Obviously, Dr. Harper wished you to believe he was an innocent," Doc said. "His infatuation was another item that gave him away. It explained Quon's determination that you not perish with the rest of us."

"Bally strange," Ham remarked.

"But, Doc," Monk squeaked. "There's still a lot I don't

figure. I know them walkin' hands were spiders. But the ghost arms. What were they?"

"The answer to that," stated the bronze man, "is not very complicated."

Doc maneuvered the half-corpse until he found what he had sought—a tiny cannister affixed to some mechanism concealed in one of the empty sleeves. It was at the shoulder seam, where a folded hand could reach it. Doc touched a tiny knurled knob.

Instantly, a hissing was heard. And from one side of the body of the late Dr. Mawson Harper, a yellow, bony protuberance began to swell and unfold. It gained shape, length, until it became a Quon arm—gaunt and sinister to behold.

Frowning, Ham poked it with his cane.

The thing popped, collapsed.

"An inflatable arm," Doc said. "Helium in the cylinder gave it shape and lift so that it would appear that the Jade Ogre could grow arms at will. A tug on a valve could collapse it at will."

"That was no phony hand that grabbed me, let me tell you," Pat said grimly.

Doc said, "He was forced to unlimber his left arm when things got tough. Lack of circulation made it less than effective."

"That don't explain the ones that chased us everywhere," Monk pointed out.

"They were another matter entirely," the bronze man related. "Recall that the Jade Ogre never released the so-called Limbs of Retribution in our presence. He invariably retreated from sight, and the truly dangerous arms were released unseen."

"So what were they?" Monk exploded, impatience stamped on his pleasantly homely features.

"Balloons," stated Doc. "Filled with flammable hydrogen, coated with radium paint to create a ghostly glowing effect, and the fingers tipped with Jade Fever. They were counterweighted at either end to create neutral buoyancy, so they would float at a constant height. No doubt there was an igniter device—probably a flint and tiny mousetraplike arrangement set in one finger so that upon contact with a solid object, whether a wall or victim, the hydrogen would ignite, destroying all traces of their true construction. The covering sleeves with their ragged tails added a chattering effect that further concealed the artificial nature of the things."

"That doesn't explain the arm that chased me," Pat said. "Balloons just don't up and chase folks."

Doc stood up. His flake-gold eyes were unusually quiescent, as if he were looking into the past.

"In several instances," he said quietly, "in Jason Baird's office, on the liner, and elsewhere, the arms were hooked to the clothing of their victims, unsuspected, so that when they became aware of the things, they would naturally flee, pulling the contrivance after them. The illusion of being pursued by a disembodied supernatural limb was convincing."

"That tiger claw I found in my outfit!" Pat said brightly. "That explains it. It was dark in that companionway when I saw the glowing arm. Harper could have been lurking there, all right, and hooked me."

"And that explains the claw you pulled from my clothes," Rex Pinks chimed in.

Doc nodded. "It was the only physical manifestation that did not burn up when the arms destroyed themselves. Yet when discovered, they were as unnerving as the arms themselves."

"Quon—I mean Harper—musta used a thin silk thread that couldn't be seen and was coated with black powder so that it would burn up, too," muttered Monk Mayfair.

"And the bonging sound we heard was easily produced," Ham offered. "Merely a portable gong."

"It does explain a lot," Shad O'Shea admitted.

"The illusion of life was given when the things floated," the bronze man continued. "Air current created by passing bodies would disturb them enough to make it seem they were selecting victims. In reality, they were simply reacting to quite ordinary drafts and eddies."

"When you explain it like that," Monk said, "I feel kinda foolish gettin' so worked up about them spook arms."

"Make no mistake, they were death-dealing devices," Doc said gravely. "Although they were early on planted to intimidate rather than kill. No doubt the one that chased Ho's taxi cab was tied to the machine's bumper by Ho himself, at the instruction of Dr. Harper. Others were affixed to closed doors so that when opened, they would be propelled outward."

"It's ironic," Pat inserted. "Had Harper not bound one of his hands, he might have escaped a grisly end."

Doc Savage studied Monk Mayfair, and remarked, "A number of mistakes were made to-day."

Monk stuffed his hands into his pockets and looked at his feet. Doc was not given to lecturing. This was the bronze man's way of scolding his aid. For it was Doc Savage's inflexible rule to avoid bloodshed at all costs—even that of deserving-of-death malefactors such as Dr. Mawson Harper. And the hairy chemist had broken that rule. It was not the first time, either.

They set about readying themselves to depart.

The Quon seaplane had survived the cataclysm. They set about draining its tanks of gasoline, transferring the fuel to the Doc Savage amphibian, which was low.

It was decided to return the visible remains of Dr. Mawson Harper to the tomb the temple of Quon had become. This was accomplished in somber silence. No words were spoken; at the end, Doc Savage simply placed the Jade Ogre mask atop the cairn they had built.

Some time later, as they were finishing preparations for the long homeward trek, Monk ambled up to Doc Savage and muttered, "Doc. I want to say—What I mean—Aw, heck!"

Doc nodded. "We will speak no more of it."

Monk brightened. "I been talkin' to that Shad O'Shea."

"Yes?"

"He's all broke up over this. His friends bein' killed and all. I was tellin' him about our place up-State."

"Shad would like to start a new life?"

"He says he ain't lived a bad life, especially, but he was no angel, either."

"Then we will send Shad to college," Doc said.

Monk grinned. The idea seemed to lift a burden from his

apish shoulders, as if the good deed might atone for his earlier mistake.

For the "college" was a mysterious institution hidden in the mountains of up-State New York. There, Shad O'Shea, as had many criminals who had come alive into the bronze man's toils, would undergo treatment which would turn him into an honest, upright citizen.

This treatment would begin with a delicate brain operation which wiped out all knowledge of the subject's past. Then the man would be taught honesty, good citizenship, and a trade. Returned to society, he would a assume new identity and forever hate crookedness.

So effective was this treatment that no graduate of Doc's "college" ever returned to a life of crime.

They finished transferring gasoline from the seaplane. Rex Pinks was grinning, despite the labor involved.

"What's with the grins?" Monk demanded suspiciously.

"Oh, I was just thinking of the swell story I'm going to write when I hit Frisco again."

"Oh, yeah? Well, Doc don't like publicity."

"He'll like what I write," the society reporter said confidently.

"You may write whatever you wish," Doc Savage informed Rex Pinks some minutes later, "but your editor will refuse to print it."

"Why's that?"

"Because," Doc explained, "I own a controlling interest in his newspaper."

Rex Pinks lost his grin and his enthusiasm for work at the same time. He sat down on the temple rubble, set his elbows on his knees, his chin on his fists, and took on a look of dejection.

As a final act, Pat Savage dosed herself with the remaining Jade Fever antidote. Habeas also was forced to partake.

"How long until this green tint fades?" Pat asked Maurine Baird.

"A day, now that you've had the complete treatment."

"That's a relief," Ham Brooks said, examining his once-white outfit, now a soiled and torn ruin. "For I have nothing that goes with this hideous shade of aquamarine."

The laughter that greeted the dapper lawyer's disconsolate remark caused him to blush a deep royal blue.

The amphibian was idling when the last of the tiny band began clambering aboard.

Jason Baird made a speech.

"I can't thank you all enough for what you have done for my sister and me," he said simply. "Without you, Maurine would still be a—a—"

There was a trace of moisture in the gruff jewelry proprietor's flinty eyes.

Maurine Baird put in mildly, "What my brother means to say is that we are forever in your debt."

"Shucks, it was nothing," Pat said cheerfully. "Look at all the hair-raising excitement we got out of it."

"I had rather hoped," Doc put in dryly, "that this particular outing would have cured you of your excitement-chasing mania Pat."

"Not I," the bronze-haired girl said enthusiastically. "All this tearing around only gives me a hankering for more."

"I was afraid of that," Doc said.

Jason Baird cleared his throat.

"What I said earlier about the twenty thousand dollars in diamonds still goes," he added. "Half to the charity Doc Savage names, the other half to Shad O'Shea, who is the only survivor of Fuzzy Wool's old crowd."

Big Shad O'Shea grimaced, growled, "You can ship my share wherever Savage says to. Where I'm goin', I won't be needin' it."

Doc Savage said, "A portion will be set aside so that Shad, when he embarks upon his new life, will have a good start."

That seemed to satisfy every one. They took seats.

The big bronze amphibian roared to life. It went skimming across the troubled expanse of Jade Lake, sending the green spiders of Quon leaping along their lily pad nests in fright.

Once in the air, they settled down to watch the steaming

jungle unroll under their wings. Now that their long ordeal was over, fatigue began to settle over the cabin.

"I cannot recall," opined Ham Brooks, "when we last experienced such a bloody adventure. I guess this could only happen in the Orient, where life is cheap."

"This?" Monk snorted. "It was nothin'. Last time I was in China, I saw a woman bein' hanged from a tree."

Ham looked startled. "Shanghai?"

Monk grinned broadly. "Oh, about six feet."

60th Anniversary Preview

Continue the all-new series written by Will Murray, writing as Kenneth Robeson, with a grim Cold War exploit based on a complete novel written by Lester Dent and resurrected in celebration of the 60th anniversary of Doc Savage's birth!

Doc Savage has been sentenced to death by the Kremlin for past espionage activities. He knows the name of his would-be assassin—Anna Gryahznyi, the infamous Red Widow, whose bite means death. But no one knows what face she wears.

Stalked by the perfect killer, defenseless because he has sworn never to kill, Doc Savage takes on a new identity as The Face and undertakes a supersecret State Department mission into the last place on earth the Commissars would expect to find him—the Russian heartland itself! His assignment: Make the Man in the Moon wink and safeguard America's beleaguered shores forever.

Sequeling *The Red Spider*, here is the exciting first-chapter preview for FLIGHT INTO FEAR.

By a piece of luck he found a tool for the ambush. His toe kicked against it in the gloomy street. Instinctively knowing it would do, he stopped and picked it up. It was a perfect thing for dealing with the trouble-making possibilities of an armed woman. An iron scrap two feet long and an inch through. Heavy. An iron rod pitted with rust, foul with soil.

Perhaps it had just fallen off a truck; off a junk truck or off one of the endless truckloads of debris from the tenements they were still demolishing to make room for more of the great, simple buildings they were perpetually constructing for the U.N. The tall, pure-looking buildings of pale stone and bluish glass for the United Nations, which he feared might be only premature containers for dreams—although he sincerely hoped they wouldn't be.

He put himself in ambush for her at once. There was a fork in the path, a Y of tunnel in thick shrubbery, darkness. It was very dark now. There was no moon, a fact whose irony was not lost on him. All they had told him when he had set out on the long trail that had brought him to this point was that it was very important and it involved some person or thing they called Moonwinx.

The right-hand fork would be altogether the more inviting to a woman, he decided. It had a flower border. It was drenched with the odor of fall-blooming asters and mums.

Everything in his experience told him that women invariably choose the inviting things, so he took his ambush on the right-hand fork. Not that his experience with women was great. To the contrary.

Women never fail to surprise me, he thought ruefully. *Never.*

Cold air touched his face. He had a handsome, regular face. But he was not wearing it now. The face he wore was wide and brutal, and as unlike his own as could be imagined. It was a devil face. Huge, almost repulsive. The air seemed clammy from the breath of all the people in the great city and faintly rancid from the odors of dinners cooked hours before.

The air had a chill, dead-animal quality remindful of the atmosphere hanging over a corpse.

He grimaced and buried his chin against the turned-up collar of his neat lightweight topcoat. He smelled deeply of the crisp new store-bought aroma of the dark cloth. He drew this newness into his lungs, savoring it. There were no new things in the terrible places he had spent the recent past. It was not as tasteful a style as he would have preferred. His mission did not permit him to indulge in good taste, and attract the wrong kind of attention. Hence the plain style of dress.

The topcoat helped him to look like a dressed-up laborer sauntering in Central Park. A youngish laborer with a stupid face and an overabundance of muscular strength. Not a spectacular type and not worth remembering. A dim-witted and brutal sort of fellow out for a night stroll. That was all.

He listened to the woman's shoes tapping the path, approaching.

He waited for her to turn into the right-hand path.

She turned left.

Left!

For a moment, he did not believe it. The *tap-tapping* of the woman's shoes went down the left-hand path. He had the impression of suddenly standing there in a world that was incomprehensible. The club hung useless in his hands; abruptly, it seemed to weigh as much as another man. It was of no use at all, the bludgeon was.

He lay the iron bludgeon on the grass. One did not hurry about New York City carrying such an object. Especially this close to midnight.

The loose feeling in his hands told him they were trembling slightly. He was surprised at the severity of his case of nerves. But this entire affair had been in the pipeline for too long. To have it exposed at this late hour could be fatal.

He began to run. He could hear her *tap-tapping* walk

carrying her along at a surprising rate. He must get ahead of her again.

He found a place ridiculously soon. It was almost as good as the first ambush spot. He crouched in the leaves and waited, regretting the loss of the cast-aside bludgeon. He never carried weapons. It was a personal fetish not to do so. He sometimes had cause to regret this choice. If she carried a knife, or worse, a pistol, a length of iron pipe could be a handy thing, possibly a lifesaver—if his aim was true.

Presently, he had to make his stomach butterflies calm. *Am I this afraid of her?* he wondered.

Why not? She is a goblin, a devil in skirts. She is a virtueless, depraved, heartless, poisonous, unprincipled vampire. She destroys live bodies and spits into living souls.

His mud-colored eyes, like the comparison microscopes the ballistics people use, caught her approaching figure and checked it to be sure she was the one. No mistake there. She was the blonde who had been following him for almost two hours. He could tell by her walk. He had yet to see her face. She had become his shadow. She must be very efficient, to be given a job like this one. If she failed to find him again, it would go hard on her. They would not forgive her readily. They never do.

He watched her cross a place where a streetlamp made the moon-lost night a bit lighter. He could see now that she wore gloves; this pleased him. The gloves covered her fingernails. Women had a disconcerting way with fingernails in a man's eyes. He could see some sort of beads flash at her throat.

There was a lot of bounce in her figure. She had dyed her hair. She dangled a hat, a turban thing, in her hand as she walked. He could see that her hair was a garish reddish-blond mess, like a shepherd dog astride her shoulders. The real color of her hair was a raven black. He could take oath to that. If only he could see her face clearly.

He was appalled by the confident lack of haste with

which she walked. She had trailed him into the park. She had lost him. But she was not excited about it, obviously.

Her self-sureness was horrifying. It was as if he was sure to be the victim, not she. He fought the feeling, drove it back, as she came to him.

She called, "Banner!"

He almost laughed. She had called him by the name she should have. It meant danger. Yet, had she used his right name, it would have meant that the months of preparation had been for naught. That his carefully crafted imposture had been penetrated. And death. It would certainly have meant his death. But if she did not know who he truly was, she might not be intent upon harming him. As Banner, his reputation was fierce. But the whole world knew who Doc Savage was.

Steeling himself, he let her approach.

As soon as she was within range, he got her throat in his strong hands.

She gave vent to a thick scream that sought volume and achieved only a kind of tangled ugliness.

It raked his nerves. He was not in the habit of man-handling women. He was not, in fact, accustomed to their nearness in any way, shape, or form. His life's work precluded such entanglements. He changed his hold, his fingers questing along the shiny beads banding her neck, seeking a certain cluster of nerves, intent upon squeezing the consciousness out of her wildly animated form.

His brain experienced a sudden explosion. Angry red sparks danced before his retina. Her infernal handbag! She had whipped it around on the end of its strap and whacked him on the head. There must be a gun inside to make it so skull-jarring. It would be a gun, he knew. Never overlook a women's handbag in a struggle, he reflected grimly.

His head bellowed at him. He had lost his place among the beads.

She brought a hand to her throat and clawed. A lot of good that would do her, he thought. She couldn't tear loose;

there was no judo expert good enough to rip free of his expert hold. He had learned it many, many years ago, while pursuing his medical studies. All he had to do was locate the lobe of her left ear, and work his fingers toward the nerve center. . . .

The trouble was, he could not find it. In the absolute darkness, this frightened him almost as much as not being able to discern her features in the murk.

He was puzzled and surprised to realize she was crushing her beads. The shiny baubles that had looked so cheap; squeezing them until they burst. He thought he heard glass crush.

And now his nostrils filled with the reek of marrubium that came—violently minty—from the crushed beads.

The sudden odor of marrubium shocked him. It was like a nail driven with one blow into his skull between the eyes. For this perfume, this marrubium, was a sensory password. It was used as the sign of a friend. It was a membership token. It was one of the ways by which a member of the Moonwinx team identified a fellow worker.

His thinking screamed: *She can't be one of us! She's a she-spider born with the name Anna Gryahznyi. I can't be mistaken. I've spent too many hours listening to the recordings of her fiendish interrogation sessions, and her shrieking, devillike questions. And I've heard her sentence me to death.*

Yet the odor of marrubium was supposed to be the sign of a friend.

He thought: *But I just heard her voice. It was Anna Gryahznyi's voice. I know Anna Gryahznyi's voice as well as I know my cousin's. Just as I know that Anna Gryahznyi is as deadly as a black widow spider.*

He hesitated, uncertain whether or not to release her throat and hear her out.

While he hesitated, she gripped his wrists and jerked his large hands off her throat. Uncertainty made him momentarily unresisting, despite his great strength.

She said, "You stupid devil-faced oaf!"

He was shocked terribly—her voice sounded completely American.

She fell back a step from him. Her hands fluttered, settled in front of her throat. The helpless-damsel posture was bizarre under the circumstances.

"Don't curse, Anna," he admonished.

"You brutal, murdering son of a—"

"Anna Gryahznyi," he cut in, irony twisting his tone. "Imagine Anna Gryahznyi cussing with that accent."

"What accent?" she asked, momentarily startled out of her rage.

"Walnut Street, in Kansas City, I believe," he said. And instantly regretted it. Banner would not have such encyclopedic recall of accents. Banner was an oaf.

"I'm not Anna Gryahznyi," she said sharply, the slip going past. "My accent is my own damn business."

Now he thought: *She may not be Anna, after all. Really, I can't tell. I might have imagined the sound of her voice when she called Banner's name.*

But it was hardly conceivable that he would fail to know her, know the one enemy who he had so intensively studied because she had been personally selected as his executioner.

She asked, "Who is Anna Gryahznyi?"

"You are," he said quickly. He tried to sound convincing. It was an effort. He could feel his heart climbing his throat with every beat. The ground under his feet felt rubbery. He realized the feeling was in his knees.

"You're crazy," she snapped. "You're a damn crazier crazy man than they said you would be. The hell with you."

"Don't curse," he said wearily.

"Why not?" she said blankly.

"Anna Gryahznyi never curses. It does not become you," he stated.

"Oh, hell!" she said. "You're really nuts, aren't you?"

He sucked in his wind. It was like kicks in the belly, this

elemental fury coming out of her. Thunder from the lips of Anna Gryahznyi, that precise female fiend.

But she had used the right name, which happened not to be his. Or was that imagination too?

"What name did you call me?" he asked abruptly.

"You want to hear it again, you ugly brute?" she said. "Well, I'll be goddamned glad to—"

He leaned down for her purse, which had gotten loose from her in the scuffle. She stopped swearing, jumped for it too. But he got to it first. The purse was heavy in his hands.

She swore at him again, too hoarsely to be intelligible. It might had been in Russian, not English. He could speak the former as well as the latter, but the muttered imprecation was simply too unintelligible for comprehension.

He opened her purse. The thing that made it so heavy was a gun, all right. It lay in his hand in the murk. He did not look down at it. He felt his mouth drying. He could tell it was an Oostahf model such as *they* would give an agent to carry, unimaginative as they were.

He thought: *She doesn't know I'm Doc Savage. She thinks I'm Banner. Banner would not hesitate to shoot her, and whoever she is, she has to know that. If she suspects I'm Doc Savage, this bluff won't work.*

His hands jacked back the gun-slide. A cartridge flew out of the ejector; another went into the chamber as the slide snapped shut, making a noise like a steel beast closing its jaws.

"No! No! Oh, please don't!" she wailed, her eyes going wide with seemingly genuine terror.

He pointed the muzzle of the Soviet-made pistol in her direction, his finger barely grazing the cold steel of the trigger. He did not want a mishap. He put enough coldness in his stare to communicate otherwise. He hoped it would show through the tinted contact lenses that masked his flake-gold eyes.

"My name?" he said tightly.

"Banner! You're Banner!" she bleated, seeming to

shrink in her own skin, much like a trussed prisoner before a firing squad. He hated to subject her to this mental torture. Or any woman, for that matter. Even Anna Gryahznyi, who, it was said, broke the souls of her victims to extract the information she needed and then shattered their bodies for the sheer enjoyment of it.

"And your name?" he prompted.

"It won't mean anything to you," she gasped. "Baker. It's Eva Baker. You never heard of me."

Her voice had terror on it like hairs of frost.

Into him came a hideous playfulness of a sort he had never felt before.

"So, I'm Banner, a crazy man," he said carefully. "And you are a stranger. What was that name? Baker? Eva Baker?"

She was wordless. She stood there grotesquely, hands shielding her face, as if she feared a bullet that would disfigure more than one that would kill.

"Well?" he said patiently.

As if sensing he would not fire, she lowered quivering hands. Her eyes had a wet, glassy hugeness. In the gloom, their color was impossible to read.

"You were full enough of hard words a minute ago," he prompted.

He watched her pale face struggle and still remain absolutely immobile. It was a shape, and nothing more. He wished he had a flashlight.

Presently, she began to break words off the cold mass inside her, a few at a time, and push them out. They were stiff, lifeless sounds. He had to bend forward to catch them.

"I carry it as a gag," she said breathlessly.

"Carry what?" he asked.

"That gun." She pointed toward the Oostahf. "You decided to kill me when you recognized its make, didn't you? Isn't that right?"

"Yes," he lied, "I suppose that is true."

"Listen to me, Banner." Her words were rushing out now, fright hushing and garbling them. "The gun is a gag. A conversation piece. A New York City cop gave it to me. The cops took it away from one of their diplomats because he had no permit to carry it. That's the same gun. You remember reading about it in the newspapers, don't you?…Oh, damn! That's right—where you've been, you don't see the newspapers, do you?"

He straightened. He gave up straining to catch her voice. And he was thinking: *If she is Anna Gryahznyi, she would want me to hear as little of her voice as possible, to keep me from being sure.*

"I can't hear you very clearly," he said. "It doesn't make much difference anyway. Anna Gryahznyi could explain anything. She's a very good explainer, is Anna Gryahznyi."

"I don't know any Anna Gryahznyi," she said, stubbornness creeping into her voice and giving it clarity.

"All right," he said, letting the hammer down slowly with a thumb. He had taken the bluff as far as he cared to.

"Don't you believe anything I say?"

"No."

"Look, you've got to listen, Banner. I was just doing my job. They told me to follow you. I was to make sure nothing happened to you. If anyone else was following you, I was to call Dryden. And Dryden would rush agents to protect you. Those were the only instructions Dryden gave me and—"

His astonishment must have come out of him as a grunt. At least, some sound from him stopped her. He prayed it wasn't that old trilling habit of his, which he had long ago suppressed. He was often oblivious to it, on those increasingly rare occasions when surprise dragged it from his vocal cords like a lost fragment of his strange childhood.

"Who did you say you work for?" he demanded.

"Dryden," she said. "But you don't know Dryden, either, do you?"

He got the surprise quelled in his voice and said, "Why didn't you tell me that before?"

It was her turn to express surprise. "You mean you know Dryden?" she asked.

"Yes."

"Whew!" Life came back into her voice. "Whew! Thank goodness. I don't know when I was so scared. Point that gun somewhere else, will you?"

"You're not out of the woods yet," he warned.

"I'm not dead, anyway." Her nerve was coming back. "What are you going to do with me, besides stand there like we're both posing for the cover of one of those cheap true-crime magazines?"

"I'm gong to show you to Dryden," he said flatly, thinking that if he could steer her toward a streetlamp, he would finally get to see her face.

"Fine. If you don't mind, I'm going behind that bush and repair my makeup. I'll bet you've ruined it with those big uncouth paws of yours." She held out her hand for the purse. He shook his head and kept it. She shrugged and said, "Okay . . . but I assume you are gentleman enough to allow me to repair my hose." She pointed toward her right leg. The nylon was a dim serpent of sags and folds, having become undone from its anchorage.

Doc Savage did not want her out of his sight, but he knew he could not pilot her very far through the streets of the city in such a state without attracting undue and potentially harmful attention.

Reluctantly, he nodded agreement.

She started into the bushes, paused, and called back, "You know something, Banner? These goshawful stories I've been hearing about you—I think I'll believe a little of it the next time."

He did not say anything and did not interfere with her as she disappeared into a spreading lilac bush.

He stood, attentive to the rustling, trying to keep an eye on the bushes while not prying on her personal business, and simultaneously staying alert for passerby. As a result, he performed all three chores poorly.

* * *

In about three minutes, he realized what he would find when he looked for her behind the now-still lilac bush. He looked anyway. She was gone.

He plunged into the bushes, shoving aside dimly fragrant clumps of branches. He could not find her anywhere in the shrubbery.

He tried to make himself leave at a decorous but brisk pace. But he could not keep it down to a walk. Soon he was hurrying along in a wild, devil-ridden way, as if on a carpet of sticky spider-silk.